Accolades for Pamela Fagan Hutchins

The Emily Series

"Breath-taking roller coaster ride to a surprising and satisfying conclusion." — Ken Oder, author of *Old Wounds to the Heart*

"Laughed out loud and cried a bit, too. Pamela, you did it again. Thank you. (And please keep doing it!)" — Kimberly Black, author of *Lydia, Woman of Purple*

"Wild ride full of crazy twists and turns." — Terry Sykes-Bradshaw, author of *Sibling Revelry*

"Gets your pulse racing between scenes that make you cry." Mel Algood, author of *Clear*

"Full of heart, humor, vivid characters, and suspense. Hutchins has done it again!" — Gay Yellen, author of *The Body Business*

"Hutchins is a master of tension." — R.L. Nolen, author of *Deadly Thyme*

"Intriguing mystery . . . captivating romance." — Patricia Flaherty Pagan, author of *Trail Ways Pilgrims*

The Michele Series

"Immediately hooked." — Terry Sykes-Bradshaw, author of *Sibling Revelry*

"Spellbinding." — Jo Bryan, Dry Creek Book Club

"Fast-paced mystery." ——Deb Krenzer, Book Reviewer

"Can't put it down." — Cathy Bader, Reader

"Full of real characters and powerful emotions." — Rhonda Erb, Editor

The Katie & Annalise Series

"An exciting tale . . . twisting investigative and legal subplots . . . a character seeking redemption . . . an exhilarating mystery with a touch of voodoo." — Midwest Book Review Bookwatch

"A lively romantic mystery." — Kirkus Reviews

"A riveting drama . . . exciting read, highly recommended." — Small Press Bookwatch

"Katie is the first character I have absolutely fallen in love with since Stephanie Plum!" — Stephanie Swindell, Bookstore Owner

"Engaging storyline . . . taut suspense." — MBR Bookwatch

My best.
JF Hutchins

Earth to Emily

The Emily Series #2

By Pamela Fagan Hutchins

SkipJack Publishing books may be purchased for educational, business, or sales promotional use. For information, please write: Sales, SkipJack Publishing, P.O.B. 219, Burton, TX 77835.

First U.S. Edition
Pamela Fagan Hutchins

Earth to Emily/Pamela Fagan Hutchins
ISBN-13 978-1-939889-31-7 (SkipJack Publishing)

Dedication

Thanks to Eric for claiming with me our own piece of Earth in Nowheresville, and for so much more.

Foreword

Earth to Emily is a work of fiction. Period. Any resemblance to actual persons, places, things, or events is just a lucky coincidence.

Table of Contents

Chapter One

Multicolored strands of lights twinkled from every surface around the dining room of the Big Texan Steak Ranch, even from the antlers of mounted deer heads and the ears of one embarrassed-looking coyote. Only the buffalo head maintained its dignity. Well, he and the giant fiberglass Santa guarding the exit door. I'd wanted to come here ever since my rodeo-cowboy father ran off before my promised seventeenth-birthday dinner, but, in light of the news I'd just received, all of the decorations were suddenly a little too much. I cradled my iPhone between my ear and shoulder, one hand clutching the neck of my poncho and the other slinging my purse straps over my other shoulder.

"Come on," I whispered to Jack, my boss—a man who can't figure out if he's a southern New Mexico rancher or a West Texas criminal defense attorney. Throw in the fact that he is mysterious, wounded, and part Apache, and you can probably see why half the women and nearly that many men in both locales had him starring in their own dreamland versions of *Fifty Shades of Grey*. Not me, though. In my dreams, he starred with me in *The Notebook*.

One eyebrow shot toward his hairline, and he answered at a normal decibel. "But we're celebrating, and our food hasn't come yet." The celebration was for my graduation from the foster-parenting classes I'd been taking for the last two months. "And I really need to talk to you about something."

In my ear, Child Protective Services investigator Wallace Gray answered. "Hello, Emily. I'd almost given up on you."

"I just saw your texts."

They'd come in a flurry, so by the time I'd read them, the whole story scrolled before my eyes. Two teens living in a CPS group home, Greg and Farrah, had run away and were reported as soliciting rides at Love's Travel Stop, not ten minutes from where I now stood glaring at Jack. Love's was a cross-country trucker mecca, situated right off I-40 outside Amarillo. The kids were likely to get more than the kind of ride they intended from the type of person who'd pick up runaways.

"I thought you'd want to know," he said. Wallace and I had taken a special interest in the pair recently when we accidentally rousted them from an abandoned house while looking for a missing girl. They'd run away from us then, too.

"Definitely. Thanks."

"Their caseworker is picking me up in ten minutes."

"Who is it?"

"Byron Philly. I don't think you've met him."

"Uh-uh."

"I need help. We can't get there for half an hour. Any chance you can get there sooner, see if you could find them?"

I didn't like the thought of Greg and Farrah out there in the cold. "We can be there in ten."

"We?"

"I'm with Jack."

"I hope you mean *with* Jack, and not just with him, if you know what I mean."

I knew, but after one incredible-if-tipsy make-out session that seemed to be going somewhere, I had blown it with Jack, who didn't seem big on second chances. As for me, my oops-I-prefer-men-who-dress-as-women husband, Rich, wasn't officially an ex yet. Any day now, though.

A waitress sashayed up to our table. From her diminutive size, she couldn't possibly eat here much, at least not the famous 72-ounce steak dinner. She popped a tray stand into place with her hip in a strangely provocative way, then balanced a load of food on it. Jack pretended to be staring at his phone instead of her tush. Her hands now free, she tossed a long braid behind her shoulder and turned to us with an electric smile, flashing a mouthful of metal.

"Who's rare and who's"—she glanced back at the tray again and frowned, as if still in disbelief—"grilled beefsteak tomatoes?"

Being a vegetarian in the cattle capital of the universe isn't easy. I put my hand over the mouthpiece of my iPhone. "To go. Check, please." Then, into the phone: "See you soon." I hung up.

Her brown eyes made **O**s, but she pulled out a handheld waiter pad and tapped a few keystrokes. "Your bill will be here in a moment." She smiled again. "Y'all come back, now, when you've got more time to enjoy your dinner."

Jack sighed, long and vibrato, and pulled out his wallet.

***

The trip in the dark along the I-40 access road to Love's only took us five minutes because I had stuck out my hand for Jack's keys when we got to his Jeep Wrangler—a monstrosity of patchworked panels in colors neither nature nor the automobile industry had designed to be used together—and Jack had obliged. I turned the Jeep into the yellow, red, and orange rainbow of the Love's compound, and it jounced and splashed in brown melted snow from earlier in the day. New flakes were beginning to fall, though, and it would soon be a blanket of white once again. I eased the Jeep across the apron of concrete past the noncommercial pumps and store, and onward toward the big-rig pumps and acres of overnight truck parking.

I glided to a stop. "Where do you think we should look?" I asked.

"I wasn't aware you cared what I thought. You know, since you basically kidnapped me from my dinner."

I threw him a side-eye look, but I smiled. "Can you please help me find the kids?"

"It takes a little longer than a quarter of an hour for a prisoner to develop Stockholm syndrome." From my peripheral vision, I saw his one dimple indent for a nanosecond.

The man had a quick wit, I'd give him that, even if he rarely answered a question head on. "Thank you for the psychology lesson, Patty Hearst." I let off the brake and we crept forward, salt crunching under the Jeep's slow-rolling tires. "Okay, they're trying to hitch a ride out of town, so they'll be watching the truckers, but they won't want to be seen." I scanned the three sides I could see of the store. Nada. Not even Christmas decorations. Maybe Love's didn't celebrate the season.

"A lot of activity here for a Wednesday night." Jack was referring to the fact that Amarillo basically shut down on Wednesday nights for midweek church services.

"I doubt that long-haul truckers go to Wednesday night church on the road."

Big rigs were lined up at the pumps and covered all of the lot I could see. Engines rumbled, and dark gray diesel exhaust escaped the dual chrome pipes on each side of one truck's cab, like puffs of smoke rings from the end of a cigarette. The sooty heaviness of it made me feel dirty.

Searching for the two teenagers catapulted me back to my own childhood for a moment. When I was young, my father had encouraged my obsessive love of all things Native American by teaching me to scout like an Indian. "A real scout gets close to the land," he would say, as we'd get out of the car. "He tests for scents." We'd sniff together. "He touches the earth." Together, we'd lean down and run our fingers across dirt or grass. "That's it, my little Sacajawea," he'd say, and throw me up onto his shoulders for a ride.

Twenty-plus years later, I rolled my window down, and my hand itched to open the door, to get close to the earth, sniff it, and touch it, but I didn't do it. Cold air bit my exposed skin. I pinched my poncho together high on my neck as a tight popping noise resounded from somewhere in the truck lot. Jack and I met eyes during a long silence, then three more pops blasted through the air in rapid succession.

"Backfiring truck?" I asked, even though I didn't think it was.

"Possibly yes, but probably gunshots."

And Greg and Farrah were out there somewhere. "We'd better check it out."

I accelerated past the truck pumps and into the relative darkness of the parking area. I skirted the outside edge, and we peered down the rows. One after another revealed nothing but cabs with blackout curtains and hulking trailers with personality mud flaps—Dallas

Cowboys, Yosemite Sam, the ubiquitous posing nude woman. I turned down the side of the lot farthest from I-40. Shadowy figures darted from between two rows halfway across the lot and into the field on the other side. One looked taller than the other, and they appeared to be holding hands.

"There they are!" I floored the Jeep, and we rocketed over the lot, gaining speed rapidly.

A tire hit a pothole and jarred us so hard I worried we'd broken an axle, but the Jeep kept charging forward. When we reached the spot where the two people had disappeared, I turned sharply to the left. Lighted asphalt gave way to dark field, and we bounced over clumps of prairie grass and God knew what else. Jack braced himself with one hand on the ceiling and one on his door's armrest. The snow hadn't melted out here, but it wasn't deep, and the Jeep smashed through its half-icy crust.

"I can't see anything. Can you pan the headlights?" Jack said.

I slowed and turned first to the left for twenty yards, then drove in a huge circle. When I judged that we'd completed a loop back roughly to where we'd started, I turned to the right to continue across the field.

Wham—crunch! The Jeep slammed into something immoveable. My head bounced off the steering wheel, and I bit my tongue, hard. Warm, coppery fluid oozed into my mouth.

"Mother Goose!" I yelled. "Are you okay?"

An enormous deflating airbag muffled Jack's response.

"What?"

The bag fell away. "I said, 'Other than I can't breathe.'"

"Oh." I pounded the steering wheel with one fist. "We lost them, and I wrecked your Jeep." I turned to him. "I'm so sorry."

He pushed the limp airbag off his legs. "I'm sorry your airbag didn't deploy." He turned to me and covered up what sounded suspiciously like a laugh with a cough. "You look like Count Chocula."

I turned the rearview mirror to me and saw the blood trickles out of each corner of my mouth. I almost laughed, too. He reached over and wiped the blood from beside my lip, and the heat from his thumb seared my skin. I gasped, and he jumped back.

The inside of the Jeep sizzled and popped with electricity as we stared at each other. Then he broke eye contact and fumbled for a flashlight from the glove box and opened his door. I put my fingers to my throat. They bore witness to the slowing of my jackrabbit heartbeat.

"I'll go assess the damage." Jack jumped out, leaving his door ajar.

I shivered, cold from more than his sudden absence. It was snowing harder now, and—this being the coldest and snowiest winter in one hundred years in Amarillo—of course the wind was blowing it straight sideways at what felt like a bajillion miles per hour, right through Jack's open door. Flakes dappled his empty seat, closer and closer together. People had died of hypothermia in warmer conditions than this. The heater was already on high. I leaned over and shut his door, or slammed it, rather, then put my cheek on the steering wheel and looked out the side window into the night, shivering.

A white face under a black knit cap appeared like a specter outside the window. I screamed before I could stop myself. It was the young man we'd been chasing. Greg. I rolled down my window.

"Hey," he said. "I know you."

"Yes, you do, Greg. I'm Emily. We met when you were squatting in that deserted house by Llano Cemetery. Where's Farrah?"

A female face with one brown and one green eye framed by pixie-short black hair materialized from the darkness behind him, her body blending with the night. "Are you hurt?" The girl pointed at my bloody face.

I used the back of my hand to wipe some of it away. I glanced at my hand. Now I had smears of blood across it. "No, I'm fine. My friend is seeing if our Jeep is, though."

"It's not," she said.

"Your front end is, like, wasted," he said.

Ugh. And here I was trying to scrounge up enough money to get a place of my own—as in, not with my mother. "You guys have created a bit of excitement tonight."

Greg harrumphed. "Maybe."

"How would you describe it, then?"

"I'm not going to let the same thing happen to Farrah twice."

"What do you mean?"

Farrah put her hand on Greg's upper arm. "It's okay."

He shook his head. "It's not. No one believes us about what that, that"—he threw up his hands—"monster did to you." He glared at me. "He should be in jail. Why do they take his word against hers?"

I knew that Farrah claimed she'd been sexually abused, that CPS was investigating the father—although it didn't feel right to think of him that way—in their last foster home, but that they hadn't reached a conclusion yet. "I'm sorry—"

Farrah stepped between Greg and me. "There's an older boy in the group home. It was about to happen again. I'm not stupid. So Greg said we had to go."

I heard clanging from the front end of the car. "I can understand that." Better than she knew, thanks to a drunken lout from the Tarleton rodeo team. He got a feel of my breasts and a knee to the balls. I was maybe thirty pounds heavier than her, though, and seven inches taller. Suddenly, I understood her vulnerability in a way that I hadn't when I'd heard her story third person from Wallace. "But where will you go?"

Greg moved forward, too. Both of them were so close I could have touched their cheeks. "We'll be fine. I can take care of her."

A sharpness rent my chest. "Let me help you."

"You can't. No one can."

"I can try."

Farrah smiled with her mouth only. "Thank you. Really. It's . . ." She trailed off.

I gestured toward the backseat. "Hop in, where it's warm."

Both kids took a step back, then another, as the boy shook his head. "We wanted to see if you were okay. We have to get out of here."

"Wait! At least take my card. It has my office number and my cell number. Call me if you need anything, *please.*"

I pulled a card from the outer side pocket of my handbag, where I'd learned to stash them for easy access. People in need of a criminal attorney were often in a hurry to get someplace else, it seemed. The card had the addresses for both the Amarillo and New Mexico offices for Jack's firm. I stuck it out the window. Snow fell and melted on my bare hand. The wind flapped the edge of my wrap, and I held on to the flimsy cardstock with a tight grip between thumb and forefinger.

Greg leapt forward and snatched the card, then retreated just as quickly. The two kids took another step back and the snow and the night swallowed them whole.

Jack hopped back in the car, letting in a gust of icy air and swath of falling snow with him. "You hit some kind of concrete stanchion."

"I'm so sorry. I'll pay for the repairs."

"No need." His lip twitched. "It didn't even dent the bumper."

For a moment, his words didn't make sense. Greg said the front end was "wasted" and I'd heard a clanging. Then a warm glow spread from my chest outward as I realized that Jack was pretending I hadn't caused any damage, and I could only guess it was to keep me from paying for repairs. A truly kind gesture, given the state of my finances, which he knew all about. I played along. "Really? Wow. We hit the concrete so hard."

He stomped his boots on the floorboard. "Lucky break."

The glow spread further, grew hotter. "Did you see the kids?"

"No, sorry."

"No, I mean, they were right here, at my window. Didn't you hear me scream?"

"I didn't hear a thing except the wind." He craned to see out my side. "I don't see anyone now."

As hard as I stared into the darkness and swirling snow after them, I didn't either.

Chapter Two

I parked the Jeep at the edge of the truck lot near where a crowd had gathered. Blue and red lights flashed in all directions. Curiosity clawed at me, and I took a few steps closer to the throng. It parted for two EMTs and a gurney, and through the gap I saw someone big and black on the ground, his head in a pool of blood. He wasn't moving, and the people around him had the hushed mien I'd come to associate with tragedy. I shuddered. Behind his body, a woman peered between the curtains of what looked like the sleeping compartment above a tractor cab whose license plate read TUCK69.

"Crime scene, ma'am, you need to step back," a female officer said. She was bundled to her eyeballs with a thick scarf, and she shouted through it to be heard. A roll of yellow tape hung in her hand.

"What happened?"

"A man's been shot."

So the noises we heard had been gunshots. "Is he dead?"

"Afraid so. Now, move along. Give us room to do our jobs."

I backed away, still mesmerized by the blood on the new layer of snow in the parking lot.

"Isn't that Wallace?" Jack asked, reclaiming my attention.

I turned, and he pointed back toward the Love's store. Another crowd had formed there under the shelter of the big-rig gas bay. A tall, lean man with sandy-blond hair stood out among them.

"It is."

Wallace lifted a hand to us as we started walking toward him, then put it on one hip and shook his head, his highlighted hair swinging perfectly over his eyelid. How could he always look so put together, even in the cold and blowing snow, when I looked like the Abominable Snowwoman? I fluffed my bangs, hoping for presentable, and snow fell from them to my face.

Wallace said, "What took you so long?"

"We were following the kids," I told him.

"You found them?"

"We did. And lost them again. They're gone."

Something about my words tore at me. I'd lost a baby of my own in October. A miscarriage, and I'd lost my one Fallopian tube, or most of it anyway, at the same time, meaning I was probably barren. Babies. Children. Loss. Thinking about it made time slow down, and as I watched the snow fall I could see every individual flake in the sky around me, suspended almost to the point of not moving. I had to shake it off; I was nearly over it, and I couldn't let everyone see it still leveled me. I huffed a deep breath, and let it out slowly through my mouth.

Jack had been standing beside me like a wooden drugstore Indian, but he ended his silence. "She wrecked my Jeep."

Wallace turned to him now. "She's hell on wheels, but I hear she's much better on horseback."

Jack made some kind of noise halfway between a snort and a laugh.

Wallace introduced a chunky guy with acne and lank hair who had materialized beside him. "This is Byron Philly, you guys. Despite the fact that he looks like a bad episode of *21 Jump Street*, he's actually a married father of three and a responsible adult."

"Nice to meet you, Byron. I'm Emily Bernal, paralegal at Williams and Associates. I work for him." I hooked my thumb at my boss.

"Jack Holden." Jack shook Byron's hand.

"Byron Philly. Sorry." He shook his head, like he was trying to clear it. "We have a newborn at our house and no one is getting to shower or sleep. Nice to meet y'all. Now, which direction did my kids go?"

I gestured behind us. "Way out across the field." The snow fell faster, and I could feel the flakes landing on my nose.

"Could you tell if they were dressed for the weather?"

I thought back, eyes closed. I'd gotten a good look at Greg. Black watch cap. Faux leather lined aviator jacket. Gloves? I wasn't sure. As for Farrah, I couldn't say. She'd blended against the darkness, and by the time she'd appeared, it was her words I had focused on, not her clothes. But even hats, coats, and gloves wouldn't do much good on a night like this. "Coats and hats. Other than that, I couldn't say. The weather looks like it's getting pretty bad."

He grimaced. "I'll update the cops." Byron walked toward the Love's entrance and a congregation of men and one woman in blue uniforms.

I turned to Wallace, who was admiring Jack while Jack picked at a fingernail, which of course he made look smolderingly hot. Wallace waggled his eyebrows in Jack's direction for my benefit. Bless his heart. Wallace never quit trying to promote a match between us, and I had to admit I hoped he'd succeed. I rolled my eyes at him anyway, though.

Wallace said, "Well, you guys missed some excitement. One of the truckers was shot and killed out in the lot."

"Yeah, I saw the scene. Gruesome."

Jack dipped his chin once. "Yep. I think we heard the shots, too."

To Wallace I said, "I'd guess we almost drove up on it, but then the kids came sprinting by, and we forgot about the shots."

A tiny woman approached from the direction of the truck lot. She strolled slowly, almost casually, but her eyes darted left-right, left-right, left-right as she picked her way across the snowy ground cover in sky-high wedge-heeled boots. Fake leather extended all the way up to her thighs where it almost met a zebra-print tube skirt. The one inch of exposed leg was covered by nothing except fishnet. On her upper half she wore a waist-length jacket with black strands of something that wasn't fur. Her eyeliner, fingernails, and long, straight hair were as black as the coat.

She zeroed in on Wallace, calling to him. "Hey, I know you, right?"

As she got closer, I saw that her makeup didn't hide the testaments to hard living that time had etched around her eyes and mouth. Thirty-five or more years of time, if I had to guess.

Wallace evaluated her for a few seconds. "Yeah, I think so, but I can't remember where."

"Well, I'm a dancer. Do you ever go to any clubs?"

"Do you by any chance dance at the Polo Club?"

"I do."

"That must be it. I was in there not too long ago on an investigation."

Her eyes opened so wide I was afraid they'd get stuck that way. "Are you a cop?"

"Not that kind of investigation. I work for Child Protective Services."

She exhaled. "Whew! Well, thank God." She whispered in his ear and his eyes widened. Goose pimples rose on the back of my neck. I didn't like secrets unless they included me.

After a good thirty seconds of furtive back-and-forth whispers, Wallace reincluded Jack and me in the conversation. "I'm going to walk Ms.—"

"You can call me Ivanka."

An eastern European name with that drawl? I didn't think so.

"—Ivanka over to my car, and give her a ride home."

"Good night, then," I said.

"Ivanka" shot a last furtive glance over her shoulder at the Love's then took his arm, pulling him along. It was hard to say which of them had the better swing to their walk, but I gave Wallace the edge.

I looked at Jack and he arched his left brow.

I frowned. "I wonder what that's all about."

Byron walked in our direction with a uniformed officer. As they neared us, though, Byron peeled off after Wallace and the woman. The policeman kept coming. He had on an Amarillo Police Department coat, and it looked warm, as did his blue knit cap with a white owl's head on it, the Rice University mascot logo. I envied him that coat and hat. I was freezing to death. My toes had started losing feeling. I'd worn thin socks under my boots, not expecting to spend the evening out in the weather. I stamped my feet one after another to warm them.

The officer stopped in front of us. "Emily Bernal and Jack Holden?"

The guy looked familiar. Jack caught my eye and raised the same eyebrow he had a moment before. He recognized him, too?

"I'm Emily. Have we met?"

The officer got out a small spiral flip notebook and a pen without looking at me. "Possibly. I'm Officer Samson, and I need to ask you a few questions about Greg Easley and Farrah Farud."

"Okay." I stared at him, my mind flipping through a card catalogue of faces.

White male. Puffy, dark-circled eyes. Uni-brow. Dishwater hair shot through with gray. He was Jack's height, maybe six foot one, not lean like Jack, though. But the guy I pictured in my mind's eye had a good six inches of Wonder Bread protruding over his belt and skinny legs. Right now this one looked thin under his jacket. Still, I knew it was the same guy.

So I recognized him, but from where? I cross-referenced places, looking for a match, and got one. He'd questioned Wallace and me at a witness's apartment when the little girl we were searching for had been abducted. Not just any little girl. Betsy, the one I would adopt as soon as the great state of Texas approved me, if all went as planned. Jack—who I could tell definitely knew the officer, too—didn't say anything about it, so I didn't say any more either.

"I hear the two of you saw Greg and Farrah tonight, the runaway teenagers?" Officer Samson stood with pen poised.

Jack gestured at me. "I saw two figures running from the truck lot. She saw more than me."

I nodded and pointed toward the field we'd plowed up with the Jeep. "I talked to them, about ten minutes ago, out in the middle of that field. They took off from there."

Samson squinted at me. "What did you talk about?"

"I ran our vehicle into some concrete thing, and they came up and asked if we were all right. I said yes, and then they took off."

"To where?"

"I have no idea."

"Which direction?"

"I'm sorry, it was so dark and snowy that I couldn't tell."

He frowned and wrote something. "Where did you first see them, when they ran from the lot?"

"On the back side, about halfway down."

"And you were where?"

"Also on the back side, but we were pretty far away. We'd made the turn to the back."

Two women hurried past us, dressed not unlike Ivanka, but one was bonier than Ivanka and the other had horrible teeth. They cut their eyes down and veered away from Samson.

He scowled after them. "Damn lot lizards. They're half the problem out here."

I hadn't heard that expression. I looked at Jack, and he mouthed, "Hookers." Oh. *Oh.*

Samson was talking again. "Did you hear any gunshots here tonight?"

I nodded. "Yes, several. Right before the kids came running out."

He looked up quickly. "Did they have any weapons on them?"

"No, not that I saw. They just looked scared and young and cold when I talked to them in the field."

"Did you see anyone else when they ran from the parking lot?"

"No."

He turned to Jack. "And you?"

"No."

"Did you happen to see the shooting"—he pointed toward the murder scene—"or anyone with a weapon?"

We answered almost at the same time. "No."

Officer Samson chewed the end of his pen. "All right. Call me if you think of anything else." He handed each of us a card.

We agreed, and Samson walked back toward the Love's. There was nothing left for us to do there, and Jack and I walked toward the rear of the Jeep. I was frozen through and through by that time, and Ivanka, Wallace, and Byron had disappeared, and I still didn't know what my best guy friend had learned from the dancer.

My stomach growled. "You know, I'm really cold, but even more, I'm strangely hungry."

Jack snorted. "No one to blame but yourself for that."

"Yeah, well, I'm eating my dinner the second I close the door to the Jeep." Then I leaned toward him, my voice low in case the friendly Officer Samson could still hear me. "Say, had you met that police officer before? I met him once, at Victoria's apartment, when we were searching for Betsy."

"He was one of the cops at the scene when they charged our client with assault, one of the state's witnesses against Alan Freeman."

Alan Freeman was our client. I'd first met Alan a few months ago, when he was retiling our office floor to pay his bill. I didn't know which I loved more, the fact that Jack let his clients pay in whatever form they could swing, or that Freeman was the kind of guy who lived up to his responsibilities.

"I thought it was a former cop, Jason somebody or other, who Freeman supposedly assaulted?"

Jack walked me to the passenger side and opened the door. I climbed in, and he leaned in a little after me. My pulse accelerated and my brain function decelerated in response. "Wu, yes."

"Woo what?" As I spoke, I realized he meant "Wu," as in Jason's last name, and not "woo," as in seek the affection, love, or support of another. My cheeks started heating.

He raised his left eyebrow, and it was all I could do not to bridge the last few inches of gap between our lips. The dimple puckered. Flames climbed my face. "Woo-hoo." He slammed the door, and I caught a glimpse of his lopsided smile.

I exhaled. "Whew," I said, and put my cold hands to my flaming hot cheeks.

Chapter Three

On a self-declared break from Freeman trial prep the next morning, I parked my aging green Mustang on Wentworth alongside the almost treeless playground at Windsor Elementary. Someone had hung red and green tinsel garlands around the one scraggly evergreen near the school building. The previous night's snow still clung to the ground around the tree and across the playground, but the precipitation had stopped. Not a great day to pretend to power walk through the neighborhood. Usually I parked farther away—it made me less conspicuous—but today the temperature hovered below freezing, and with the wind-chill factor it felt like fifteen degrees. No way was I walking any farther than I had to, even to see Betsy.

If I could see Betsy, that is. I glanced at the time on my phone. It was still two minutes until recess time.

When I found the orphaned girl and Jack and I brought her back from New Mexico, I'd handed her over to CPS via Wallace. She had become the most important person in my life by then, and I was desperate to make her my forever daughter. Wallace showed me how to work within the bureaucracy of the state system, and urged me to trust it. I'd signed up on the foster-care and adoption lists. I'd taken the classes. I was saving up to move out of my mother's and into my own place, at which time I could schedule a home study. I scrolled back to an email I'd sent myself with the link to a listing for a duplex off Soncy Road that sounded perfect. I needed to book a time to see it. Meanwhile, CPS had placed Betsy with a large foster family with a good record. The Hodges. Trevon and Mary Alice.

The Hodges had fostered, all told, twenty-three kids, per Wallace. They specialized in noninfant and nonwhite kids, and kids with disabilities; in other words, they took the kids who were hard to place. Wallace said they had a history of keeping them long-term, until someone else adopted them or they graduated from the foster system, whichever came first. I initially found this admirable—astounding even. How difficult it must be to raise so many children, some of whom required extra care.

Then jealousy crept in. They had Betsy. I didn't. I'd stalked them a little. On Facebook. While grocery shopping. At their church. Okay, I admit it, the Hodges were an impressive sight with their line of multicolored ducklings in all shapes and sizes following behind them. I'd finally decided maybe Betsy had drawn a lucky card from the deck with them. All those siblings. A family with values, with morals.

But the Hodges wouldn't allow me to visit Betsy. It was their right, but I didn't like it, and it made me even more determined to maintain a relationship with her, not less. I checked the playground again. Still no kids. It was time for them to be outside.

I'd begun these clandestine visits to her school as soon as she'd started the first grade, which was the first time she'd attended a school of any kind. Betsy and her parents had entered the U.S. courtesy of a scurrilous human trafficker named Paul Johnson. When other kids her age were discovering the joys of recess and snack time in kindergarten, she was captive in southern New Mexico on Johnson's Ranch where her undocumented parents were enslaved in a silver mine. When other kids her age started first grade, Betsy was hiding under her mother's housekeeping cart at the Wyndham/Ambassador Hotel, coloring pictures and singing to her doll, after her mother had escaped from the ranch. So, she hadn't had a chance to go to school before now. The girl was smart, though, and I knew she would catch up with her classmates fast.

A text came in on my phone from Wallace: *No word from Greg and Farrah. Getting really worried.*

I shot a quick text back: *Me, too.* Then I remembered the thing that was still bugging me from the night before. *Why'd you leave so fast with "Ivanka"?*

Wallace: *She was looking for a sympathetic person to help her make an escape before she got busted.*

Me: *For what?* I could make a good guess since I'd heard Samson call the two skanky women lot lizards.

Wallace: *She's a lady of the night, honey.*

Me: *Oh. Okay.* She'd picked the right person for empathy. *You're such a nice guy.*

Wallace: *Outcasts are my kind.*

We ended our text conversation, and my mind flashed on Sunday school past, of stories of Jesus washing dirty feet and hanging out with prostitutes. Wallace could try to pretend it was just solidarity, but the man had the biggest heart I'd ever seen.

The bright voices of children floated across one hundred yards of open playground to my ears as they charged out a side door. *Bravo, Windsor Elementary,* I thought, *for not letting a little inclement weather throw you off your game plan.* The kids were wrapped like mummies, and I realized that they were probably running late because of the extra time needed to get them all bundled up.

Knuckles rapped on the window by my left ear, and I jumped, spilling my Roasters large breve with sugar-free hazelnut—my favorite coffee drink—on the black Red Raiders sweatshirt I was wearing over a long-john top.

"Spit in a well bucket!" I shouted. It was an expression I'd picked up from my father, before he'd split.

Mother hated cursing, but she didn't mind the work-around expressions favored by Dad and me. So spit, heck, darn, and Mother Goose made the cut. Any variants of damn, shit, crap, hell, ass, and—gasp—the f-word did not. Nor expressions she considered vulgar, like douche or vagina. I tried not to even think them, even in the direst of circumstances, let alone say them.

I glanced out the window and recognized the woman standing there in a gray wool dress that cascaded from the bottom of a white jacket. A white wool cap covered her head, and she'd crammed long, curly brown hair under it, given away by the messy strands that had escaped. She'd knocked with bare knuckles, and I watched as she pulled an insulated ski-type mitten back onto her hand.

"She" was Mary Alice Hodges, with a runny-nosed, snowsuited toddler of indeterminate gender on one hip. We hadn't met, but I'd seen her, of course, when gathering information on her and her family. Not that I was going to disclose that I recognized her, or how. I hit the down button on my window with one hand and scrounged with the other in my purse for something to sop up the spilled coffee. Jackpot: a fistful of napkins from Taco Villa. I pressed them to the spill site like it was a bullet wound as cold air violated my warm, cozy space.

"May I help you?"

"Ms. Bernal?" She pronounced my Colombian (married) surname Burr-NAL, like most every other non-Hispanic person north of the Mexican border. But I had to wonder how she even know who I was.

"I'm Emily Bernal." I stressed the correct pronunciation: Bare-NAHL. "What can I do for you?"

"I'm Mary Alice Hodges, Betsy's mother, and—"

The word *mother* tore at my gut, and I couldn't let that slide. "*Foster* mother, isn't it? I've been trying to reach you through CPS about bringing a Christmas present over for her. You may recall hearing my name. I'm the person who rescued her when she was kidnapped."

I knew Betsy would love my gift, too. She had lost her treasured pink backpack when she'd been held captive, and I'd bought her a new one like the one she described—since I hadn't found the one she'd lost, despite repeated calls to the task force of federal, state, and Alamogordo officers and the trustee for Johnson's Ranch.

"I'm sorry, but that won't be possible. We don't allow Christmas presents in our home. That's our special time to praise God for the birth of the Christ child."

I could feel my jaw drop, and I stared at her. I had no response to that. Poor Betsy. Presents rocked. I'd considered the Hodges top tier because of siblings and morality, but I also hoped for fun and happiness. Maybe they were a loving family who made up for it in other ways, though. I knew how much worse it could be—neglect or abuse was a whole 'nother level of Hell from unhappy—but it wasn't what I wanted for this sweet little girl who had stolen my heart.

Mary Alice switched the child to the other hip. "Betsy said she's seen you here."

I didn't doubt that she had. Betsy and I had talked on one of my many visits, until a teacher put the kibosh on it. After that, I would wave to her as I walked laps around the school block, soaking in the sight of her and her nearness.

My pulse sped up, throbbing in my ears. "Yes, and . . . ?"

"I thought my husband made it clear that we don't welcome outside interference with the young people we bring into our home."

The child in her arms suddenly threw its head back and wailed, flailing and kicking. I stared at the toddler, distracted. The hood came off its head, revealing short locks of wavy cotton-candy hair. The haircut looked very male, even though still babyish, and I decided to run with that gender classification. The little boy lifted his face again, still squalling, and I took a closer look. He didn't look like your normal everyday kid. Something about the eyes. Down syndrome, I realized.

"Ms. Burr-NAL?"

"Um, yes, well, I've never spoken to your husband, but Wallace Gray with CPS did let me know you've turned down my requests to see Betsy. I wasn't given a reason."

She bounced the boy up and down and made shushing noises for a few seconds, then turned her attention back to me as she continued to bounce him. "We keep tight control over the type of people our children associate with."

My face grew hot. "All righty then. You have a nice day." I reached for the button to raise my window.

She put her free hand out as if to stop me. "You need to stop bothering her here."

I recoiled and released pressure on the button. "Bothering her? I'm in a parked car a football field away."

"You know what I mean."

A roaring started in my head. "I'm not really sure that I do."

Her eyes narrowed and I saw her arms tighten around the child. He squealed. "Don't make me take this further, Ms. Burr-NAL."

The roaring intensified. "Further? Should I be scared of some-thing?"

She leaned away from the child, toward me. "The wrath of God," she whispered. "You should always be fearful of the wrath of God."

I laughed aloud. "Okay, gotcha. Thanks for stopping by." I rolled up my window.

She took three steps backward, then whirled, almost falling on the packed snow along the gutter. I watched in my rearview mirror as she strapped the boy into a car seat in her oversized army-green van, then went around and climbed in on the driver's side. She started the engine, but she didn't leave. Instead, she looked at me—or the back of my head, at least—then lifted a phone and spoke, waving a fist in what looked like punctuation to her words. Her eyes fell. She nodded. She set the phone down and stared toward me again, a half smile on her lips. Finally, she grabbed something at the height of a steering wheel gearshift and her vehicle engaged. She accelerated away from the curb, her van fishtailing for a moment as she passed me, snow spitting up behind her tires as they caught.

"Well." I said it aloud, even though I was by myself. "She's a whackjob." I chuckled, but it wasn't a laugh of mirth. If that woman had been holding up a cross instead of a baby, I would have sworn she was attempting to exorcise demons from my soul in her last moments at my window. I wouldn't have been completely surprised if the archangel Saint Michael had swooped from the sky to assist. But now I was the one thinking crazy. I breathed out through my pursed lips, very slowly and deliberately.

Clearly, the Hodges were ultrareligious, in a way that made my church-lady mother look like a trifler. Still, I didn't understand Mary Alice's behavior. Wallace said he had informed the Hodges that I intended to seek adoption of Betsy as soon as I could gain state approval. They'd known that when they first got Betsy, just like they'd known that I'd saved the girl's life and forged a strong bond with her. So why forbid me to see her in the first place, and why the fuss now? Maybe they considered me to be an unsuitable kind of person. Yes, I'd been the talk of Amarillo for a few months after I moved back from Dallas, pregnant and humiliated by my cheating husband's sexuality and paramour. But that was him, not me. Surely I was not such a threat to a child that I had to be warned off.

I peered through my passenger-side window, looking for Betsy in the playground full of shouting kids. My eyes sorted through them. Too tall. Hair too light. Hair too short. Skin too dark. Skin too white. When I'd narrowed them down to short brown girls with long dark hair peeking out from under their winter caps, I found her. Tiny and adorable. She saw me looking at her, and she waved at me, using her whole body.

I raised my hand, waving back. She looked around and I saw her eyes lock on the back of a teacher, and then she took off, a tiny pink dynamo hurtling in my direction. I jerked open my car door without hesitation, cutting the engine and pulling the keys out as I did, and ran toward her, coatless. Betsy made it twenty-five yards and I covered the other seventy-five. She slammed into me and I lifted her into a huge swinging-around hug.

"Hi, Emily!" Her high-pitched voice sang out, as she pressed her cold face against mine. It felt wonderful.

"Hi, sweetie-pie! How are you?" I set her down. Her long hair hung in braids fastened with pink scrunchies on each side of her head. She had lost a front tooth.

She frowned, very serious and adult suddenly. "I'm good, but I miss you and Thunder." Thunder was the horse we'd escaped on together.

I laughed. "I miss you, and I'm sure Thunder does, too."

Her face lit up. "Have you found my backpack? Mama would be so mad I lost it."

I stuck out my bottom lip. Per Mary Alice Hodges, I couldn't give her the new one, so I didn't mention it. "No, no one has seen it. I'll ask them to keep looking, okay?"

A whistle blew.

Betsy looked back toward her teacher, who was walking toward us, fast, head shaking back and forth, whistle in hand near her lips. "Uh-oh."

"Yeah, uh-oh." I hugged her one last time, and she ran back to the teacher.

I walked toward my car. At the last second, I turned. Betsy was walking backwards, waving to me, and I pulled out my phone and quickly snapped a picture. I got in the Mustang, restarted it, and blew on my cold hands as I watched her.

She rejoined her friends in what looked like a game of tag, a good way to stay warm out there. Watching her kept my face stretched in an ear-to-ear smile. Even though she'd lost both parents and now lived with the killjoy Hodges, I hoped she took some comfort in knowing she had me, and that I truly wanted her. I thought of my parents. Until I was sixteen, I'd felt wanted and loved by them both. After my dad left, especially after he cut off contact when I was a senior at Texas Tech, I still had my mother. It's not that losing my father's love didn't hurt me, because it did, but I knew I wasn't alone. Of course, it was possible the Hodges were loving people and made Betsy feel wanted, too. It just seemed highly unlikely to me after meeting Mary Alice.

My phone rang. I answered it without looking, my eyes still on Betsy. "This is Emily."

"This Ava," a lilting, cheery voice said. "You know, Katie's Ava in St. Marcos."

My best girlfriend and former boss at Hailey & Hart in Dallas, Katie Kovacs, had left the practice of law to live in the Caribbean, where she had reinvented herself as a singer and keyboardist with her new friend Ava Butler. I'd gotten to see Katie and Ava perform several times. They were the real deal. They'd almost landed a New York recording contract but Katie got cold feet when she became a mother. I remembered that Katie said Ava had a little girl now, too.

"Hi! Wow, what a nice surprise to hear from you."

I watched Betsy, half-listening to Ava. Betsy got tagged and was "it." Her friends dispersed, and she began to chase them.

"I got a manager book me a bunch a stateside gigs. I gonna be up your way soon."

"That's great. You realize it's winter here, right?" Ava was an island girl. I couldn't imagine her here in the waterless, palm-treeless Panhandle anytime on purpose, much less in this freezing cold weather. And if Ava was coming all the way to Texas for gigs, motherhood must not be slowing her down as much as it did Katie.

She laughed. "Yah, mon. I asking for double rates."

Another rap on my window. This one sounded like it was shattering it. I gasped and wheeled, dropping my phone and ducking toward the center of the car as I did so. No glass fell in on me, and I regained my composure quickly, ready to shout at Mary Alice, only it wasn't her.

Chapter Four

From the console where my phone had fallen, I heard, "Emily? You okay, Emily?"

An officer waited outside my car, one hand clutching a baton that he had tucked under his elbow. He was young. And short. Red haired. Full faced and thick bodied. Behind him stood Officer Samson. I rolled my window down again.

Before I could speak, the new officer said, "I'm Officer Burrows. Step out of the car, please, ma'am."

"Certainly, Officer Burrows." I held up one finger. He shook his head, so I made it fast before he could object further. I grabbed my phone and said to Ava, "Sorry, gotta go—police."

Ava's voice sounded concerned, but I was already hanging up the phone. "Oh, bad news. Okay, I call you."

I set my phone on the passenger seat. "Do you need my license and registration, sir?"

The officer's voice grew louder. "Step out of the car, ma'am. Don't make me say it again."

Officer Samson echoed, in a more gentle voice, "Ms. Bernal, if you could please do what Officer Burrows asks you to do."

My throat constricted. I unbuckled my seat belt and grabbed my winter coat. I opened the door and got out, then started to put it on.

Burrows snatched it away from me. "Hands on the hood of the car, feet shoulder width apart."

My mouth went dry and it took a second for his words to register. He gave me a shove on the shoulder, spinning me around. It jarred me out of my confusion, and I did as he said. Behind my car I saw not one but two squad cars parked at an angle, blocking me in like a dangerous criminal.

I moistened my lips. "What's the problem, sir?"

He didn't answer, just patted me down everywhere, and I do mean everywhere. It was the first time anyone other than my OB/GYN had touched me *there* in four months, and this wasn't exactly the way to break that unwelcome streak.

"You're going to wait in the back of my car while we search your vehicle."

"Why do you need to search it?"

He took me by the upper arm—his fingers biting into it even through fleecy sweatshirt material and long johns—and led me to the cruiser, my coat still in his other hand.

"Officer Burrows, am I under arrest?"

He said nothing.

Thinking back to the advice I'd heard Jack give clients, I said, "I do *not* consent to a search of my car. Nor do I consent to being locked in your vehicle, unless I am under arrest."

Burrows opened the back door to the cruiser and dropped my coat to the ground. Without warning, I felt a cuff snap around my right wrist and my arm pulled behind me. My first reaction was to struggle, but I stopped myself. My father had always told me to respect authority, even when it didn't deserve it. Might made right, in the moment, because dead couldn't be undone. Jack could help me sort this out later.

I looked up at Officer Samson, but his eyes were hidden behind aviator sunglasses. Burrows grabbed my left arm and jerked it behind my back to join the other. The second cuff snapped closed. I wanted to shrink into invisibility. Betsy's recess bell hadn't rung yet. She was still outside. If she was looking, she could see all of this, with no one to explain it to her, to tell her I would be fine. Her mother had died in prison, and her father had died escaping Johnson's Ranch. Watching me, powerless, could be incredibly traumatic for her, and I prayed she was playing with friends and didn't see what was happening one hundred yards away.

Burrows put a hand on top of my head and shoved me down enough to topple me into the backseat of the car. The whole scene was surreal for me. My only brush with the law had been a few traffic tickets. A vision flashed through my mind of a tie-down roper's lariat sailing over the head of a calf. The rope jerked tight as the quarter horse stopped and threw its weight in reverse. The calf thrown on its side by the cowboy, who then wrapped three of its ankles with a piggin' string and threw his own arms into the air to signal he was done. Now I knew how the calf felt.

"We're searching your car because a citizen called in a pervert taking pictures of kids. We were given a license plate number and vehicle description same as yours, and you match the description of the photographer." Burrows leaned over and picked my coat off the ground and threw it in after me, then slammed the door.

Mary Alice Hodges and her wrath of God. It had to be. My heart beat like a hummingbird's wings against the inside of my chest, and I struggled to think of what Burrows and Samson would find in my car that could get me into trouble, or give them reason to give me trouble. My purse was there with my "baby" Glock 26 inside, and my license to carry in the wallet inside the same purse. I had nothing else in the Mustang except my dry cleaning and the half-spilled cup of coffee.

Well, nothing except for my iPhone on the front passenger seat. I had never taken a dirty picture in my straitlaced life, certainly not of any children. My mind raced through its contents. There was a photo of my husband's girlfriend—a man named Stormy who lived as a woman, although he kept his junk, if you know what I mean—wearing my red negligee. The tramp had texted it to me, and I'd saved it for the divorce, just in case. That one was embarrassing and inappropriate. But did I have any pictures of kids?

I had saved one on there of Betsy with her mother, which I'd used for identification purposes when I was searching for her. Then there were a few I'd snapped of her on the playground, innocent stuff, because it made me feel better to be able to look at them, like the one I'd taken today. Pictures any mother would take, and while I wasn't her mother, I was going through the process of trying to *become* her mother, after all. But I'd password protected my phone with the ultra-secure "1111." I figured it was so obvious no one would ever guess it.

Hopefully that included the police, so they wouldn't be able to look at my photos. Then all of this would be moot, and it would get straightened out quickly enough. It had to. I hadn't done anything wrong.

I strained to see what the officers were doing, my view obscured in part by the metal barrier between the front and back seats of the police vehicle. I could see that they had popped open my trunk. Geez. I knew it was empty except for my spare tire, but months of working with Jack kicked in and my brain moved past what they might find to whether they even had a right to search my trunk in the first place. Burrows was treating this like I was Public Enemy Number One, and I was pretty sure Jack would tell me it was an illegal search.

I heard the trunk slam. Footsteps crunched on the snow, coming closer to where I sat trapped in the backseat cage. The driver's side door opened in front and a body landed on the seat. Air whooshed out in protest. The door slammed. In the confined space, I smelled garlic and cheap aftershave. My nose and forehead wrinkled. Burrows put my purse and phone on the seat. He spoke into the radio, holding it with his left hand while he continued to mess with something I couldn't see in the front seat with his right.

"I need a tow into impound on a Ford Mustang, green, on Wentworth Drive across from Windsor Elementary." He read off my license plate number. "I've arrested a suspected child molester, an Emily P. Burr-NAL—B-E-R-N-A-L. I'll be bringing her in. Also, she was in possession of a handgun."

"I have a license to carry! It's in my wallet."

I wanted to scream. How did we jump from the bogus improper photos to the inflammatory and even more screwed-up child-molester accusation? And then the bit added on about my gun to make it sound like some kind of huge deal, like I was a dangerous felon, when it wasn't and I wasn't either. I knew it wouldn't do me any good to argue with him about the semantics, no matter how damaging, but I couldn't believe his gall.

Burrows holstered the radio and turned to me, unloading my Glock as he did. When he had it empty, he inspected it. I saw him read the words engraved around the mouth of the barrel. "So, you think I'm messing with the 'Wrong Girl'?"

"My dad thought so, at least." The gun, and the words, were a fifteenth-birthday gift from my Wild West-throwback father. "I only know *I* didn't do anything wrong, and I don't understand what's going on."

Burrows lowered the gun and shoved it into something I couldn't see from the backseat. Still facing the center of the front seat, he said, "Emily Bernal, we take sex crimes very seriously in this town, and you're under arrest for taking improper photos of a child."

A klaxon horn sounded in my head, and white-hot panic seared me from the inside. Burrows turned his head forward in the driver's seat, and all I could see was his red hair and fuzzy neck that needed a shave.

"Arrested? Improper photos? That's ridiculous. I didn't do any such thing."

He switched on the ignition. "If you haven't done anything wrong, Ms. Bernal, then I'm sure we'll get it all straightened out at the station."

He spoke by rote. "You have the right to remain silent. Anything you say can and will be held against you in a court of law. You have the right to the presence of an attorney before and during any questioning. If you cannot afford an attorney, one will be appointed for you free of charge before any questioning. Do you understand these rights as I've explained them to you?"

He turned back to me again. This couldn't be real. I shook my head.

"You don't understand them?"

"I understand them." I shook my head again. "When do I get my phone call?"

Burrows snorted, and we accelerated into the street with a jerk that snapped my head back against the seat.

Chapter Five

Utilitarian gunmetal-gray steel and dirty industrial-white paint filled my view of the storage area before me. Odds and ends of paraphernalia littered the inside of evidence cages. Phones. Wallets. Jackets. Belts. Caps and hats. A motorcycle helmet covered in Arizona Cardinals bumper stickers.

Jack stood behind me while I signed for return of the personal items that I had been required to check in earlier. The officer behind the desk—young, freckled, and open-mouthed, with a nameplate on her chest that read TINSLEY—couldn't tear her eyes away from Jack. *Get in line, sister,* I thought.

I pawed through the tray of my belongings. My purse was there, with my wallet, gun license, and gun (unloaded), as was my coat, but there was something missing. "My phone?"

Without looking away from Jack, she said, "Huh?"

"Officer Burrows took my phone. I need my phone back." I looked at the voucher, which listed my personal property. The phone wasn't on the list. "This voucher's wrong, too."

"Is that your signature on it?"

"It looks like it, but the one I signed listed my phone."

"Well, now, isn't that strange." She smiled at Jack. "Let me check with the officers." She picked up a desk phone and punched a few numbers. "We're missing the inappropriate-photo suspect's phone. Burrows brought her in; Samson was with him. Yeah, Rin Tin Tin." She put her hand over the mouthpiece and whispered, "They call Burrows the drug-sniffing dog because he's so good at busting kids smoking pot." She winked at Jack and spoke into the phone again. "Burr-NAL—B-E-R-N-A-L. Okay. Thanks." She hung up. "Someone's gonna ask him. You can wait over there." She nodded her head at a bench against the wall.

Jack and I looked at each other. He shrugged and we sat. From our side of the room we had a view of the balding strings of silver tinsel strands tucked above the window to the evidence room. Above it, cut-out red letters that hooked together and hung crookedly spelled MERRY CHRISTMA. I wondered if anyone would replace the S.

Jack's phone beeped, but he didn't look at it. "You're sure they checked your phone in earlier?"

"Positive. Why do you think Burrows would keep it? He knows I didn't take any dirty pictures. This whole arrest was just harassment."

Jack pulled his bottom lip. "Is your phone password protected?"

"Yes."

"Did you give the password to them?"

"No. Why?"

"Do you get work email on your phone?"

"Yeah, but—"

"It's the thin blue line."

The Dallas Area Rapid Transit Light Rail Blue Line went from downtown out past White Rock Lake. I had ridden it occasionally when I worked for the Hailey & Hart law firm in Dallas. "I'm confused. How did we get on the subject of trains in Dallas?"

His left eyebrow drew toward his hairline. "I'm talking about how police officers stick together. They call it the thin blue line."

"Oh." I picked some imaginary lint off my sleeve.

His dimple sunk in and out like it was in spasm, and his eyes twinkled. "We have a case against Wu. The police stick together. Maybe someone is trying to see if you have anything on your phone about the Freeman case."

I considered it. Could Jack be right? "Really? Would they even know I work for you?"

Jack said. "'Hmm. Dunno. Probably. It's a small town."

Jack and I had been together the night before when we talked to Samson at Love's, but we weren't working a case. We could have been two people out on a normal date, albeit a really lame one at Love's Travel Stop. I thought back through the last two months. Had my name appeared on anything related to Freeman's case? Paralegals didn't sign pleadings. I hadn't been with Jack when he deposed the officers, either. That was before I came to work at Williams & Associates.

But it hadn't been the first time I'd met Samson. Honestly, I couldn't remember my conversation with Samson two months before when Betsy had been kidnapped. Oh well, like Jack said, it was a small town.

"That'd be too convenient, right after Mary Alice rousted me. I saw her make a phone call, then, bam, ten minutes later, Burrows shows up. He's harassing me for her."

"Maybe."

"That woman terrifies me."

"Hodges? Why?"

"I told you. She *threatened* me with the wrath of God. It was creepy. And then this." I gestured around the room. "What did she do that could make them do this to me?"

"If she did." Jack's phone beeped. He ignored it.

"She did." I snorted. "How'd you get me out, anyway?"

"After a discussion with your attorney, the assistant district attorney decided not to book you."

My voice came out at a higher pitch than I would have liked. "Thank you, but how—"

He pretended to pop his knuckles. "You have the best criminal law attorney in two states."

"No, seriously."

"I'd at least put me in the top five."

"Jack."

"The charges were BS. Plus this was a new ADA, and I told him you worked for me."

Which was good. If it had been my archnemesis, ADA Melinda Stafford, my butt would still be planted on a bench behind bars.

"That was smart."

"I promised him you wouldn't go anywhere near Betsy again without supervision."

"But that's impossible."

He looked at me slant-eyed. "Emily, I'm not sure if you understand the seriousness of your situation. This is a felony involving a child. You can't afford to be charged in the first place, even if I get you off five minutes later. Period."

"I know." The implication of the type of charge I was facing wasn't lost on me. "Even the suggestion of this could ruin my chance of adopting Betsy."

"We won't let that happen."

Ugly truth smacked me in the forehead, a few hours too late. "She knew. Mary Alice Hodges knew what this would do to my adoption chances, and she did it on purpose."

Jack's phone beeped again, and he didn't even glance at it.

"Check your darn phone already," I snapped.

His left eyebrow lifted, pulling the dimple in and mouth up. "It's going to be okay, Emily." He typed a few keystrokes on his phone and swished through text messages. "Wallace. The Hodges called him, and so did Burrows. You're not answering your texts. He's a tad concerned."

"Do you think I need to call him?"

He held his left hand up in the "stop" gesture and a scar caught my attention. I'd seen Jack's hands plenty of times, even felt them on me in ways that made my cheeks flame to remember, but I'd never noticed the scar on his left palm before. And it wasn't insignificant. It was round, like a cigarette burn, but bigger. And puckered. I stared at it as he spoke.

"Let's focus on what's on your plate here, for now."

"Where'd you get that scar on your hand?" I pointed at his left hand, which was now on his leg.

Jack's yellow-brown eyes flicked to mine and then down, and butterflies went crazy in my tummy. How could he irritate me so much, then calm me, intrigue me, and excite me all in less than a minute?

Officer Tinsley called my name from behind the counter. "Ms. Bernal?"

I jumped up and hurried over, Jack moving in long, lazy strides beside me. "Yes?"

"The officers didn't see a phone in your car. They're real sorry and hope you find it."

"But I saw Burrows put it in the front seat of the cruiser, and Samson was right there."

"I'm sorry, ma'am, but that's not how he remembers it."

"He?"

"Burrows."

"Don't all cops have those body camera thingies after Ferguson? Those would prove I'm telling the truth."

"Um, no, sorry, ma'am, our department doesn't have body cams. We do have the dash cams, but they're only triggered in certain situations, or when an officer turns them on."

"So was the camera on when I was arrested?"

She stared at me, slack-jawed.

Jack put his hand on my shoulder. I looked up into his eyes. They were warm, and he nodded at me. I took a small step back and he moved into the gap I'd left.

"Officer Tinsley, thank you for checking for us. Could you let Burrows and the other officer—Samson, was it?—know to expect me to file an official complaint of misconduct with the department, on behalf of Ms. Bernal, for excessive force, falsifying paperwork, and refusing to return her phone? We'll be seeking the dash cam footage then."

"Um—"

"Thank you. Now, let's talk about getting Ms. Bernal's vehicle back."

Chapter Six

After Jack took me to pick up my Mustang from impound, we had enough time left in the day to squeeze in one more productive task. We headed toward the office, and I drove behind Jack, caressing the leather by my thigh in a soothing way. My Mustang was closing in on nine years old, but she was still beautiful, and she'd suffered a violation at Burrows's hands every bit as much as I had. At eight, though, she was still only half the age of Jack's vehicle.

The Jeep still bore the ignominy of the previous night's crunch into concrete. Jack had tucked the deployed airbag back into the dash and duct-taped it up. As he backed the Jeep into his parking space in the garage, I saw that the front bumper hung askew with a big fat crease where the chrome had flaked away in the center. The grille had also caved in partway and the left front quarter panel had buckled.

He ducked into the passenger side of the Mustang as I turned on the radio to a country station.

I tightened my lips so I wouldn't smile. "I thought you said there was no damage to your Jeep last night?"

Jack didn't look at me. "There wasn't."

"But the bumper is all messed up, Jack. However did *that* happen?"

"It was already like that."

I shook my head. "I don't remember it looking like that before."

"I did it last week."

"You didn't mention a fender bender." I let my smile out, and he realized I was onto him and grinned with a sheepish look on his face. "Hey, is your Jeep even street legal now without the airbags?"

He nodded. "But the whole system has to be replaced and reset. On both sides."

"Yeah. Since one side tried to kill me, I think that's a good idea." A song I loved came on, and I turned it up. "As long as I'm rockin' with you, girl, you know I'm Cool Whip—"

"Cool with," Jack interrupted.

I turned the radio down. "What?"

"The song. 'As long as I'm rockin' with you, girl, you know I'm cool *with*.' You said 'Cool *Whip*.'"

My cheeks heated just a little. "That's what I said." I put my hand on my signal switch. "Which way?"

Jack had only told me we needed to run an errand, not where or for what reason.

"ABC Half-Price Resale."

I turned my trusty steed north. ABC Half-Price Resale—which was as much a discount clearing house as a resale store—belonged to our client Alan Freeman. "Why for?"

"Continuance until mid-January."

Alan's trial had been set in two weeks, right after New Year's.

 "Since this morning?"

The Second Baptist Church flashed by on our left. In temporary letters, an announcement blazed across a white sign out front: LOW SELF-ESTEEM SUPPORT GROUP WILL MEET THURSDAY AT 7:00 PM. PLEASE USE THE BACK DOOR. It made me smile.

Jack said, "Got a call while you were, um, detained."

I pumped my fist in the air. "Woo-hoo!"

A continuance wasn't a surprise. In fact, the real surprise would have been if it hadn't been continued. But we'd prepped only enough to stave off emergency, and we would have had some serious scrambling to do these next two weeks if the post-New Year's schedule had stayed firm.

The case wasn't a shoo-in, but we expected to win it. It was Freeman's word against Wu's. Wu claimed he'd caught Alan soliciting sex from an unidentified woman who had run off in the alley behind the resale store. Wu said when he approached Alan's vehicle, Alan leapt from his car to make a run for it. Wu claimed he gave chase, and that when he caught him, Alan assaulted him with a beer bottle.

Alan's version was completely different. He said he'd gotten out of the car at Wu's request, there was no prostitute, and that Wu had tackled him, and both men fell to the ground. Wu had hit his head on a broken bottle when he landed.

And that was it, as far as evidence would go. No dash cam. No *real* witnesses. Wu had been a rookie in training, and Samson was riding with him, but Samson said he'd run after the supposed prostitute. Alan wasn't charged for solicitation, and he didn't have a history of priors. Wu had since left the force. It looked and smelled like something from the back end of a cow. The recent high-profile cases of police violence and false statements against black men didn't hurt us at all.

I cruised down historic Route 66, now known as Amarillo Boulevard, heading east from downtown toward Alan's shop. Alan worked two jobs: one laying tile for his own little one-man tile company—he did that nights and Sundays and holidays—the other running the resale shop his parents had left to him early that year. The shop was in the part of town you'd expect for resale: stubby strip malls, barred windows, homemade signage, and shallow parking lots. Cars with snazzy rims riding low to the ground. Small storage units. Fast food restaurants on every corner. Everyone talking on brand new mobile phones.

Which made me think of something. "I have an idea."

I glanced at Jack, and he raised the eyebrow on my side. He wasn't the world's most verbose human, so I took that as, "Please, Emily, do continue."

"There's some app that is supposed to find your lost iPhone. Maybe we can see who has my phone that way, since the police are insisting I lost it."

"Doesn't it have to be turned on for that to work?"

"Maybe. Why?"

"Whoever has it has long since copied all the data, removed the SIM card, and deactivated it."

"But they're cops!"

"Cops know every bad-guy trick in the book."

"Bastards."

"Some of them."

I turned into the cramped parking lot for ABC Half-Price Resale, Joe's Barber Shop, Broughton's Shoe Repair, and Cisneros Automotive. Despite Jack's pessimism, I was still planning to try the app. Maybe the cops had misplaced my phone. Or been sidetracked. Or were stupid. I pulled the Mustang into the one tiny parking space available, and we walked toward the storefront.

A man had just left Alan's store, and I nearly ran into him on the sidewalk. He smiled down on me with a weathered face, then tipped his gray felt cowboy hat. "Emily Phelps. Merry Christmas to you."

It only took a second and it all came back to me. Heavy equipment whirring near my head. A mouth filled with plaster of Paris. Giant needles. Saliva running down my chin. Numb cheeks. My childhood orthodontist, Dr. Parks.

I was able to smile, barely. "Hello, sir, and Merry Christmas to you."

His face drooped. "Oh no." He leaned closer. "Smile again." I obeyed without thinking. He shook his head. "You haven't been wearing your retainer, have you?"

Jack snorted, and I shot him a look.

"Um, well, I did sometimes, for a while"—by which I meant for two to three weeks and never again—"and then I moved, and I couldn't find it."

Dr. Parks opened his wool overcoat and reached into a shirt pocket. He handed me his card. "Make an appointment, please. You'll regret it for the rest of your life if you don't. Headaches. Painful chewing. Mouth breathing. Alteration in the shape of your face. Speech problems."

I gaped at him. "Are you serious?"

He nodded, gravely. "Come see me."

"Thank you." I felt dazed for a moment, then regained my manners. "Nice seeing you."

He waved and walked into the parking lot.

I touched a fingertip to the gap between my two top front teeth.

Jack pulled the door open, and the bell jangled. "After you, Snag-gletooth."

I kept my eyes to the front, trying to pretend I hadn't heard him. We walked into the scent of a Christmasy cinnamon-apple pie that had to be coming from a room deodorizer, as I knew there was no kitchen onsite. Alan saw us and waved. His shaved head wasn't covered by his usual LSU Tigers cap. At six foot two, he towered over the woman peering into the glass-counter display of jewelry in front of him. He was one of those muscular guys you knew just from looking at him could outwrestle a grizzly bear. I'd first met him when he was tiling the office lobby—which doubled as *my* office—and he'd been kind and respectful of my space on a particularly bad day for me. I had warmed to him instantly, and I didn't believe for a second he had tried to pick up a prostitute. Or assaulted a cop.

"Be with you in a few minutes," he called.

I smiled at him. To Jack, I said, "You can do your Christmas shopping while we wait."

My boss made a sound like *Great idea* or *Bah humbug*. It was hard to tell which. Actually, I knew Jack never left this place empty-handed, and I didn't either.

Alan worked the shop alone, mostly, while his wife cared for their children, and he had an eye for display. The tile artist in him, I supposed. He'd used for-sale items to create a cozy Christmas scene: a tall, skinny wooden Santa attended by a legion of "elves"—garden gnomes in Santa hats—and surrounded by beribboned "gifts" like books and jewelry. I picked one up. *Owl Babies.* I thumbed the pages, but it was too young for Betsy. I returned it to its spot in the display. I surveyed the music section, looking for something small and piano related for my friend Katie. Most of the items here were too big to ship to her in the Virgin Islands, though, so I moved on. Electronics, then electrical equipment. I hefted a well-cleaned chainsaw. Not much call for it in country as thin on trees as the Texas Panhandle.

In the household items, I came upon an exquisite toy horse, a black stallion with a silky tail and mane, posed mid-prance. I'd had one very similar to it when I was a girl, and it reminded me somewhat of Thunder. If I were buying a present for Betsy to go in her new pink backpack, this would be the one. I knew I shouldn't let myself think about her, but I couldn't help it. The price tag read seventy-five dollars. It seemed steep, but the item was probably vintage, and it was in pristine condition. I could always give it to her later, when the Hodges didn't have her anymore. When I adopted her. A lump formed in my throat. If that ever happened, after today. I tucked the horse under my arm. I was buying it, darn it.

"Son of a bitch." Jack's voice wasn't exactly a shout, but it carried enough that Alan and his customer looked away from their discussion toward him.

I looked at him. "What's up?"

"Goddammit."

It wasn't like him to use the Lord's name in vain. He cussed, but rarely in a profane or vulgar way. I hurried over to him. He didn't look like he'd thrown a shoe.

"Jack?"

"Take a look at this."

He was standing in front of a sawhorse on which was mounted a gorgeous men's Western saddle. The leather gleamed and the black suede seat begged to be stroked. The same black material adorned the silver corner plates, which were accented with inset turquoise. I'd never ridden on anything so beautiful, in all my years of rodeos and pageants.

I set the toy horse down on a shelf, then ran my finger over the seat. "Wow. What is that gorgeous material?"

"Ostrich. And it's mine."

"You're buying it?"

"No. I already did, in a manner of speaking. Fifteen years ago."

I scrutinized my boss. He didn't look crazy, unless you counted crazy mad. His lips were pressed and his pupils dilated. I knew if he had a pen in his hand he would whack a desk with it right now, something he did whenever he was royally pissed. The bell jingled and Alan's customer left carrying a small bag.

He walked over to us. "Hey, guys. Jack, is something wrong?"

Jack stuck out his hand and Alan shook it. "This saddle. Tell me about it."

Alan rubbed his chin between thumb and forefinger. "I got it in last week. I'm told it's by Harris, a fancy saddlemaker out of Carolina."

"It is."

Alan's eyebrows rose. "You know your saddles."

"You could say that."

"So anyway, again, from what I'm told, the seat is made of ostrich hide and the accents are sterling silver and turquoise. New, a saddle like this goes for about thirteen thousand on their website."

"That's only a little more than my wife paid for it."

In the months I'd known Jack, he had never once mentioned that he had previously been married, that he had a wife and two children until a car bomb meant for him took their lives in Alamogordo, New Mexico. I only knew about them from other people. Hearing him mention his wife now froze the blood in my veins. This was big.

Alan squinted at Jack. "What?"

"When she had it made for me, as a wedding present."

"You're telling me this used to be yours? What are the odds?" He grinned.

"No, I'm telling you it's still mine. It was stolen two weeks ago."

Chapter Seven

I've always found it difficult to tell when the blood drains from a black person's face. It's not like they go pale. I lose all color; literally, I look like bleached flour. Alan looked ill now.

"Seriously?" he asked.

"I'm afraid so. But don't take my word for it." Jack pointed at the saddle. "Underneath the left stirrup, way up high, you'll find my initials, JPH, and a date. June 7, 1996. Then hers: LTH."

LTH. Lena Talbert Holden. I knew this because I had resorted to Google to fill in the blanks about Jack's past.

Alan lifted the stirrup, turning it for us to see as well. JPH 6-7-96 LTH. "I don't know what to say."

"Tell me about the person who brought it in."

Alan's eyes closed. "Oh man." He walked to the shop door and turned the OPEN sign to CLOSED.

I whispered to Jack, "I didn't know there'd been a robbery at the ranch."

"Greg and Farrah interrupted us."

My brain whirled trying to understand what he meant. Jack was often unclear to the point of obtuse. I hadn't been able to decide if it was his greatest skill or greatest curse. Greg and Farrah had come up to the Jeep when I crashed it into the concrete, but they hadn't interrupted anything. Then I realized he meant that the issue with Greg and Farrah had interrupted our conversation at dinner the night before, when he'd told me we needed to talk. Probably. That, or he was speaking in tongues.

Alan's voice and shoulders sagged. "We need to talk." He trudged back from the front door to us, instantly twenty years older. "Follow me."

He took us behind the U-shaped display counter of guns, jewelry, and coins and on through a heavy closed door in the center of the back wall. Alan flipped on light switches as we walked down a short hall. There were three doors at the end of it. One stood open, to a bathroom on the left. Another closed door on the same side had a plaque that read OFFICE. The last one, on the right, was closed as well. Alan opened the door on the right, again switching on a light. We entered a room filled with cardboard boxes, office supplies, and merchandise.

Alan stopped but didn't turn around. "I keep most everything sellable out front, but if things aren't moving, or if a customer puts something on layaway, I put 'em here. Also, stuff I haven't gotten around to pricing and preparing for display is back here, and a few other things. Things that don't feel right, sometimes."

He crouched down and reached for a box under a table and dragged it out. He opened the flaps. Inside was a cigar box.

He lifted it out and flipped the lid, handing it to Jack. "Does any of this look familiar?"

Jack sucked in a breath. He lifted a currycomb from the box, sterling silver with inset turquoise and something engraved on it. I peered over his shoulder. Jarhead. The date. All American Futurity. Second Place. I put my hand on Jack's shoulder. He sifted his hands through the box and his eyes glazed and drifted far, far away.

I turned to Alan. "Jarhead, the name that's engraved there, is Jack's horse. A very famous racehorse. These are keepsakes, or really more like treasures."

Alan sank into a crouch, his head in his hands. "Shit. It's bad."

"What? What is it?"

He stood back up and began to pace. "When Mama and Daddy died, it messed me up. A gas leak. Who has gas leaks anymore? At least they didn't know what was happening to them; they didn't suffer." He wiped his eyes. "I didn't want this place. I was real happy doing tile. Man, it's like therapy to me. I get in a zone, and when I'm done it's the most satisfying thing in the world."

"You're very good at it."

He smiled, but it was a sad smile. "Thank you. There's so much more to this place than I'd realized. The first week I was here, an eighteen-wheeler pulls up out back. The guy unloads boxes and wheels them in on hand trucks like he owns the place. 'Where do you want your merchandise?' he asks me. 'What's going on?' I say. 'You Edward Freeman?' 'Hell no, that's my daddy and he's dead.' 'Well, I was told to drop this off for him and let you know that payment will be collected in the usual manner.' I'm like, 'What is this shit?' And all he tells me is, 'Special merchandise. Hot sellers, if you know what I mean.'"

Alan stopped and mopped his brow, and I squeezed his arm. It looked like he was about to have a heart attack. Jack had put the box down and was listening, arms crossed.

"I tell him to get that stolen shit out of my store. He does, but not before he warns me that this isn't going to go well for me or him. He practically begs me to take it. Says he'll pay for it, only don't make him put it back on the truck. It was some good shit, too. Jewelry, high class. Phones. Laptops. The kinda stuff that sells, I've learned, and sells for top dollar." He took a deep breath. "They sent an enforcer to see me three weeks later."

"Oh no," I breathed.

"The guy says I owe him some money, that my father had paid him once a month, that it is the price of doing business. Man, I didn't know what to do. By then I'd dug into the books, and our income had been down in the last few weeks. Now I understand why, even though I didn't then. Daddy was getting hot inventory at a reduced price, and that's how he was making enough money to share it with the likes of this guy. He was burying the payments back in Cost of Goods Sold for the merchandise. But I hadn't figured any of that out then. So I told him to get stuffed."

"What did he do?"

"Nothing then. But he comes back the next month. Asks if I'd gotten any smarter. I hadn't. He beat the shit out of me right then and there and said next time it's gonna be my family." Alan and his wife had three daughters, five, eight, and twelve.

"Jesus," I said. "That's scary."

He nodded. "Yeah, and I still didn't get any smarter the next month. I figured he was bluffing. Somebody burned a cross in my yard the next night. My girls still cry when they talk about it."

"I'm so sorry." And I was. Alan was breaking the law. He was hurting other people by his involvement in this scheme. But I wasn't sure what I would have done in his place.

"I'd been mad at my pops until then, but suddenly I felt sad for him. Sick, even. A month later the guy came back. I paid him. A truck showed up the next week and dropped off merchandise, and they've been coming like clockwork ever since. The trucks, and the collections."

Finally, Jack chimed in. "How's that going for you so far?"

"Not so good."

"Are you ready to take it to the cops?"

Alan closed his eyes and licked his lips. The silence in the room was shattered by a loud noise from right behind the back wall, the distinctive almost-train-like sound of the horn of a big rig.

"I'm too damn scared of 'em to cross 'em. Plus, I'm on trial for beating up a cop. You think the police are gonna believe my black ass if I take this story to them? No. No way. And at the end of the day, I can't let anything happen to my wife and girls." Alan shuddered, then opened his eyes. "That's probably a delivery outside. I gotta go see."

Jack nodded but said, "If it's them, don't let them know we're onto you guys."

Alan snorted. "No way in hell." He reached up with both hands and rubbed his cheeks, hard. "I can't take a chance you'll be seen, but you can listen from the hallway if you want."

Jack nodded and motioned to the doorway at me with his head. We went inside, one of us on either side of the door.

"We should get his license plate number," I whispered.

Jack shook his head no.

"I could walk out the front door and around the back."

"In an alley in a bad part of town. No one has a good reason to be back there, certainly no former Miss Rodeo Texas."

I growled. *First runner-up.* "You're letting this go? Chances like this are about as rare as . . . as . . . as . . . as wings on a cat." As soon as I said it, my cheeks heated. Whatever I'd meant to say, that wasn't it. Well, surely Jack would get the point.

His left eyebrow shot sky-high.

I lifted my chin to match it. "In my experience, anyway."

He grinned and put a finger over his mouth. "Shhhh."

The horn honked again. I heard a roll-up door ascending, and then Alan's voice. "You're early."

"So sue me."

"I have customers. If I'm not expecting you, I haven't cleared my schedule. Chill, man. You're drawing attention back here blasting your horn."

"Fuck you."

"Where's Chuck?"

"How the hell should I know? Are you going to help me unload or not?"

Alan didn't answer, but moments later we heard the two men grunt and something heavy land with a thump. A squeaking that sounded like wheels turning came closer, then more grunting, louder, and another thump. More squeaking. Clanking. A resounding clang followed by lesser similar noises.

"I won't be here next week. Christmas."

Alan answered, "Good."

"Yeah? Well, fuck you, too."

The rolling door descended noisily and a scraping sound and click followed. The thud of rubberized footsteps approached.

Alan came around the corner. "He's gone."

Jack nodded. "That's a pickle you've got yourself in."

"Man, you have no idea."

"You gonna let this continue?"

My eyes swung to Alan. He said, "I don't know what else to do. My family . . ."

"We could offer this information in return for the DA dropping the assault and resistance charges."

Alan backed up, his foot hitting the wall behind him. "No way, man. No damn way. I'd rather do time than mess with these people."

Jack held his hand in the air. "Okay. I don't want to see you end up in worse trouble later."

Using my least nosey and most winning voice, I asked, "You don't happen to have that driver's name or license plate number, do you?"

Jack took a giant step over to me and stepped on my foot.

"Ow," I said.

Alan shook his head. "What? No." He walked quickly into the storage room again and came out with the cigar box. "Take these, and your saddle. Please. I'm sorry as hell about 'em. And if you can send me a list of what else you have missing, I can see whether it ended up here."

"Thank you." Jack took the box. "Oh, before all of this, we had come by to tell you that your trial is continued until mid-January."

Alan's shoulders slumped farther. "I don't know which is worse. The trial sooner, or worrying about it longer and having it later."

Jack smiled, but it didn't reach his dimple, or his eyes. "I'll send you that list." He stuck out his hand and Alan shook it. "We'll talk to you the first week in January for sure, if not earlier."

"Jack, um—" I wanted to buy the toy horse for Betsy, but as soon as I started to speak I thought better of it. Now wasn't the time.

Jack cocked his head as he waited for me to continue.

"Never mind. Merry Christmas, Alan."

Jack went and got his saddle. I followed him back out into the store and to the front door. The door was locked by a keyed deadbolt. Alan had come with us, and he pulled keys on a metal hoop from his jeans pocket and let us out.

"Merry Christmas to you both." Alan locked the door behind us.

I glanced back and saw that he'd left the sign as CLOSED. I pulled my own key ring out and walked to my Mustang.

As I clicked to unlock its doors, Jack looked at me and shook his head. "He's not telling us something. Something big."

Chapter Eight

Jack still had the *Amarillo Globe News* delivered to Williams & Associates every morning, and I grabbed the paper from the floor outside the door as I walked into the office. Snowflake spun in circles as she waited to see what I'd brought her. The four-pound Pomeranian ruled the place. Not that Jack told me this himself, but she'd belonged to Jack's young daughter. I'd seen the picture of her holding the dog as a pup with a red bow around her little white neck out at Jack's family's place, a racehorse breeding facility in southern New Mexico called Wrong Turn Ranch.

"Hi, girl." I offered the dog one of the buttery toast crusts I brought her from my own breakfast each day, and she gobbled it up.

Setting my purse down on the desk in my lobby office, I shook the paper open and laid it beside my keyboard. Standing, I read the highlights. The murder at Love's grabbed the headline below the fold. "No Leads on Truck Stop Murder." I scanned it. Charlie Tucker—that had been the guy's name—from Oklahoma. No mention of a suspect, or even witnesses. The article mentioned that this was the first murder at that Love's Travel Stop, but that the police had been called out on multiple occasions before for "public indecency." My nose wrinkled. Public indecency could be a whole lot of different things—child sex crimes, pimping, prostitution, obscenity—none of them something I wanted to think about this early in the morning. Officer Samson's lot lizard remark sprang to mind.

The right-hand article below the fold caught my eye, too. "Phil Samson Named APD Officer of the Quarter." A picture of Samson accompanied the article.

"Speak of the devil," I said aloud.

I sat down in my chair. I scanned the article while my computer booted up. Apparently Samson crawled in through the sunroof of a car that had been hit by a drunk driver. He discovered a boy who had stopped breathing. The story described how he'd dragged the child out and saved him with CPR, amongst other acts of heroism.

Someone shoved the door open, rattling the walls.

Wallace's voice shredded the silence. "What the hell, Emily?"

Snowflake sprinted over to dance around Wallace's size-twelve feet, the tags on her collar jingling and her toenails clicking on the beige and rust-colored tile floor.

"In a minute, Princess," he said to her, as he balanced a tray holding two coffees.

A tall woman in biker clothes with jet-black hair, sleeve tattoos on her pale arms, and a nose ring followed closely behind him, holding a coffee of her own. Our mutual friend Nadine, a Thai waitress by day and a drink slinger by night at the Polo Club, one of Amarillo's finest stripping establishments.

"Good morning, Nadine."

"Morning," she mumbled. Her bloodshot eyes suggested she'd worked the late shift.

I addressed Wallace. "I'm fine, thank you, Mr. Gray, and how are you?" I tilted my head. "Oh, is that coffee for me?"

He handed me a tall Roasters cup and pulled the other out and set it on the corner of my desk. Then he leaned over and ruffled Snowflake's hair.

"Breve?" I asked.

"Do bears relieve themselves in the woods?"

Wallace had memorized how I took my coffee even though I secretly kept my Roasters order on a page in my iPhone's note app. Some things just didn't stick in my gray matter. Coffee orders, phone numbers, whether or not it was okay to wear white shoes before Memorial Day.

"Ah, you're so sweet. Thank you."

Wallace air-kissed at me, then put his grim-lipped face back on. "You're making my life difficult, you know that? This situation with Betsy is tres tricky. You can't go around stalking the kid behind my back when I'm trying to help you adopt her."

Nadine took a seat on the tweed couch underneath a Remington knock-off of a cattle drive, but Wallace remained standing in front of me with his hands on his hips. Wallace was over six feet tall, but today his hair poof gave him an extra inch of height.

"Hardly stalking. I've tried to be patient, but those people are impossible." I sat down and jarred my desk with my knee, almost knocking over the framed picture of Geronimo that Jack had given me, along with one of his most famous quotes: *There is one God looking down on us all. We are all the children of one God.*

I continued my rant: "They won't even let me take her a Christmas present. I don't think they're allowing Christmas presents at all, for that matter."

Wallace frowned and pondered the Christmas tree Jack had let me buy for the corner of my office area. Instead of putting a star on top, I'd crowned it with a berobed Lady Justice with her blindfold, sword, and scales, who I'd glued to a Popsicle stick before attaching it to the tree with pipe cleaners. Christmas rocked. What was wrong with those people?

Nadine swallowed her coffee too fast and coughed, then said, "That's nucking futs."

"I know! Please, Wallace, can you get permission for me to take Betsy a gift? Please?"

He looked back at me from the tree. "I'll do my best, but I can't make you any promises."

"Or at least deliver it to her." I pulled the new pink backpack from where I'd stashed it a few days ago under my desk.

Nadine pointed at it. "I could get that to her, tell them it's from the Rainbow Room." In addition to her two part-time jobs and raising two kids as a single mom, Nadine volunteered a few hours a month at the Rainbow Room, helping outfit less fortunate kids and families with the bare necessities. They worked hand in hand with CPS, which is how she and Wallace had come to be friends.

Wallace nodded. "That could work."

"Thank you, Nadine." I handed the empty backpack to her. "I'm not exaggerating, Wallace. They're freaky—and scary."

"What do you mean by 'scary'?" He pulled a blue upholstered armchair from beside my desk that had been displaced by the Christmas tree. He plopped down into it.

"Babbling about the wrath of God, siccing the cops on me. She gave me nightmares. If she can do that to me, how must those kids she fosters feel around her?"

"They have nothing but nice things to say about her."

"Because she'd threaten them with the wrath of God if they didn't, I'll bet."

"You're serious, aren't you?"

"I am."

Nadine chimed in. "I think there's such a thing as too religious."

He laughed. "Coming from an agnostic, that isn't surprising."

I said, "History is full of horrible things done by zealots in the name of religion."

"As are current events. I'm not sure the Hodges are zealots, though. They are definitely very religious, and they're strict. But the kids do well under their watch, so far. And it's a blessing to me to have someone eager to take the special needs kids."

I frowned. "But Betsy isn't special needs."

"She is in the foster system. It's different than in the medical and educational worlds, where special needs means autism spectrum or learning disabilities or cystic fibrosis or something like that. Foster-care special needs includes all that, but it also means kids that are older, and thus hard to place, or part of a sibling group, and thus hard to place, or a minority over the age of two, and you get the picture." He'd described the line of ducklings I'd seen with Hodges to a T.

"And Betsy falls in the last category."

"Six-year-old Mexican girl? Definitely."

"But she wouldn't be hard to place. I want her."

"I know you do. And I know you're getting set up to foster and adopt as fast as you can. I am so proud of you, honey, really, I am, but where are you on the house hunting?"

"I'm going to look at a duplex today." I held up three fingers in the Scout's honor gesture.

"Okay, keep me posted. Meanwhile, a stable family has taken her in. Try to think of that as a good thing."

I shuddered. "Stable except that they keep expanding. Exponentially, practically. How many do they have right now?"

"Including their own? Twelve."

Nadine's eyes popped wide. "No way. Twelve?"

I shook my head. "Holy guacamole. How can they take care of that many?"

"How have people ever? My best friend at SMU was a Mormon. Ninth of twelve. The older ones help by taking care of the younger ones."

I hadn't known he'd gone to SMU, but somehow I wasn't surprised, even though he was from Houston. "I was one of one. And my mother barely held it together."

Wallace smacked his palm to his forehead. "'Things not to say in your foster and adoption home study interviews,' by Emily Bernal. Closely followed by 'I was arrested for taking improper photographs of children.'"

"Noted." I sipped coffee. Wallace pointed at me then pantomimed wiping his lip. I ignored him and took another sip. "I guess the bigger question is why anyone would want twelve or however many temporary kids. Besides being a do-gooder, I mean."

His eyebrows shot up. "Really?"

"What, is that a dumb question?"

"Not from a former beauty queen, I suppose." He changed his voice to a southern drawl. "Some people out there in our nation don't have maps."

"Huh?" Nadine said.

You'd either caught the famously clueless answer to a pageant question by Miss South Carolina in the Miss Teen USA pageant back in 2007 or you hadn't. Or maybe I watched too many beauty pageants.

"Very funny, wise guy." To Nadine I said, "Beauty pageant joke."

Wallace flipped his hand over, dismissing me. "They're Christians. They believe it's their duty, plus they get to save all those souls."

Nadine shook her head. "They want the kids because of money. They get seven hundred dollars apiece, monthly. Do that math."

"In my head? I wasn't a math major." I punched it into the calculator on my computer.

"It was sort of a rhetorical question."

"Except that it wasn't a question." I looked up. "Eight thousand four hundred smackers a month. One hundred thousand and change a year. Wow."

"And if you're frugal, you can live on that, even with twelve kids. No outside income required."

"So it's Mary Alice's job."

Nadine snorted. "Proving I'm in the wrong line of work."

Wallace said, "And her husband's job, too, what's-his-name."

He hadn't asked, but I filled in the blank anyway. "Trevon." I had their dossier memorized.

"Yep. Well, enough of that." Wallace jumped to his feet and grabbed a bronze bell with a black handle off my desk. Jack kept it there so I could let him know when I was coming down the hall, since his office doubled as his condo, complete with a Murphy bed cleverly hidden in some built-ins. Wallace rang it vigorously. "I have to see Jack."

I winked at Nadine. "He's still straight, Wallace."

"Details." He kept ringing. "I need an update on Betsy's petition."

Wallace was referring to a Special Immigrant Juvenile status petition that Jack was putting together, pro bono, for Betsy. On top of that, Jack was preparing to file a survivor action on her behalf for the wrongful death of her mother, Sofia, who was murdered while incarcerated in the Potter County Detention Center. First we had to exhaust the completely unhelpful grievance process with PCDC, though, however long that took.

"Don't mind us," Nadine said.

Wallace kept ringing.

"He's probably on the phone and gonna come down the hall and kick your butt for making that racket." I pointed at the still-ringing bell.

Wallace set it down. In a thick accent and girly voice he said, "You think Jack's gonna 'kick my butt'? Well, spit."

"Mock my ladylike manners if you must, but we'll see who gets to move to the front of the line at the Pearly Gates."

Heavy footsteps stomped down the hall toward us before we saw Jack.

"What in hell is so important?" He stalked into the lobby, the hem of his jeans halfway in his boot tops, his shirttail untucked. His hair was mussed and pupils wide. A spider web of creases marred his cheek, and he had a little wet smudge by the corner of his lips.

I tried not to laugh but felt my lips compress.

Wallace put a hand on one hip. "I thought this office could use a little more cowbell."

Jack rubbed his eyes and looked blank, but Wallace, Nadine, and I laughed.

"Hi, Jack," Nadine said.

"Morning, Nadine."

Wallace reached his hand out, and Jack shook it. "Seriously, I want an update on Betsy."

The office phone rang, which only happened during business hours when Jack's secretary, Judith, transferred calls directly to us from his office in Tularosa, New Mexico. Otherwise, she handled it, or it went to voice mail. I looked down at the phone. A red light by my extension indicated the call was for me, not Jack.

I picked it up. "Williams and Associates, Emily Bernal speaking."

I heard deep breathing on the other end. Jack and Wallace continued talking without me.

"May I help you?"

Click.

Weird. I hung up and tried to rejoin the conversation, but it didn't take long to get lost when the subject was immigration. I was a litigation paralegal—board certified in civil litigation, in fact—recently converted to criminal law, where I had far to go before I achieved mastery, as it was. Now I was tackling immigration, and I'd learned a lot about this foreign-to-me (no pun intended) area of the law in the past two months, more than I'd ever aspired to. My head swam with acronyms: DACA, DAPA, DHS, USCIS, ICE. Family law, too. Fewer acronyms there, but lots of new concepts around guardianship, foster care, and adoption. And I'd even picked up some estate/probate where it crossed over with family law. Throw the immigration, family, and estate laws in on top of the criminal, and I had one overfull cranium.

One thing I did understand clearly: Betsy needed permanent legal resident status, and the only way she could get that was if the Department of Homeland Security, the aforementioned DHS, granted her Special Immigrant Juvenile status and issued her a J visa. Which they might do if we could produce her birth certificate, prove that she was a ward of the state of Texas, and show that it was in her best interests to remain in the U.S.

We had jumped through some of those hoops already. CPS was administering her temporary living arrangements and issuing checks to the Hodges for her care. The probate court that handled Sofia Perez's estate—which included virtually nothing except guardianship of Betsy—had signed an order making Betsy a state ward. Jack had received it the day before.

"This is my first J-visa case," Wallace was saying.

Jack leaned against the wall and crossed his arms over his chest. "Mine, too."

"The CPS attorney—Ralph Hanson, do you know him?"

"Of him. Haven't met him."

"Ralph gave me some forms to fill out for the application." Wallace pulled some documents from a black leather briefcase. He handed them to Jack.

Jack scanned them quickly. "Looks like the two we need. Filling them out should be easy enough. The tough part is that we need a copy of her birth certificate."

"Yeah, and I've been trying to find hers practically since the day we found her. It's like looking for a needle in a field of haystacks. She doesn't know where she was born, and we don't know if Perez is really her last name."

"Can't you get a birth certificate at the Mexican consulate offices now?"

"Yeah, but you have to be from an area that isn't so rural that their records aren't computerized, and appear in person with an ID. Betsy is six. She has no ID."

My throat tightened, and I felt my pulse in its hollow. The phone rang again. I snatched it up. "Williams and Associates, Emily Bernal speaking."

Breathing again.

"May I help you?" My tone was curt, I knew, but the prank caller was interrupting me at a seriously bad time.

More breathing, then a throat clearing. Nadine looked up at me from playing with her phone.

"Listen, whoever you are, either speak up, or don't call again." I hung up the phone, and winced at the sharp sound it made as it hit the cradle.

Jack and Wallace both turned to me. Jack's left brow lifted.

"Prank caller," I said.

Jack's forehead creased in a frown that didn't reach his lips. "Okay." His face relaxed, and he turned back to Wallace. "So until you find it, we're dead in the water."

"Find what?" I asked.

"We're still talking about Betsy's birth certificate," Wallace said, then, "If ICE shows up and takes her before we find it and file, they can deport her." He was referring to Immigration Customs and Enforcement, better known as ICE.

My hand flew to my throat over my drumming heartbeat. "They wouldn't do that to an innocent little girl, though, would they?"

The phone rang again. I yelled, "Spit!"

Wallace and Jack shared a look. Nadine laughed.

I tried to sound pleasant. "Williams and Associates. This is—"

"Um, Emily, I think you know me and my friend, and we're in trouble. You offered to help and we think you're the only one that maybe can. But we can't talk to you unless we know you'll keep it between us."

I recognized Greg Easley, even though we'd only met twice. I didn't know many boys his age, for starters, and his voice had a raspy quality to it that was unforgettable. My eyes flicked up to Jack, then Wallace, then Nadine. All three watched me, the conversation about Betsy at a standstill.

I smiled at them and used my brightest voice. "Hi, Katie, great to hear your voice. Sorry, I thought you were a prank caller. I'm in a meeting right now with my boss and my friends Wallace and Nadine. Can we talk later, like in fifteen minutes?" My friend Katie and I talked a lot, and my watchers all knew her by name. They relaxed and looked away; Jack and Wallace resumed their conversation about Betsy. I strained to hear them in one ear and Greg in the other.

"That CPS guy is there? You can't tell him it's us. Please."

"I won't."

He exhaled loudly, like a horse almost. "You want us to call back in half an hour?"

"Yes. We should be done by then."

"This number?"

"Yes, please."

"Okay, yeah, that's fine."

"Great. Talk to you then."

"Yeah, um, thanks. Bye-bye."

"Bye."

Six eyes settled on me again, and I prayed they couldn't read my emotional state from my face, because inside my stomach was doing flip-flops about Greg and Farrah.

I picked up a stack of papers on my desk and tapped their bottom edges against my blotter, straightening them. "So, where were we?"

Chapter Nine

Jack walked Nadine and Wallace to the door ten minutes later, and the phone rang as it shut. I prayed it wasn't Greg again and lifted the receiver to my ear.

"Williams and Associates, Emily Bernal speaking. May I help you?" I needed my greeting on a recorder at the rate I was using it today.

"Hello, Emily. This is Mickey. May I speak to Jack?" Jack's cousin Mickey Begay worked as the ranch manager at Wrong Turn Ranch. His wife, Laura, raced their quarter horses as a jockey. A good one.

"Of course, Mickey." I pressed hold. "Mickey for you, Jack."

Jack dropped his lanky frame into the chair in front of my desk. My skin tingled at his nearness. "Can you put it on speaker?"

I pursed my lips in a questioning way, but he didn't react. I pressed speakerphone and nodded toward him.

"Hey, Mickey. What's up?" he said.

"Hey, Jack. You still coming out tomorrow?"

"Weather permitting."

"I need to bring you in on something."

"Shoot."

"Laura's had a miscarriage. Another girl."

My eyes shot to Jack's. I hadn't known they were trying to have kids.

Jack's voice softened. "I'm sorry, man."

"Yeah, me, too." Mickey sighed. "She's taking it even harder this time. You know her doctor told her the reason she's having so much trouble getting pregnant is her body weight?" Laura kept her weight way, way down as a jockey.

"I remember."

"There's also like a seventy percent higher risk of miscarriage for women who are underweight. After the first miscarriage, he said she has to be serious about iron and folate and fresh fruits and vegetables when she *does* get pregnant."

My mind went back to my own miscarriage and surgery. I closed my eyes, sad for Laura. I knew obesity was a risk factor for miscarriage, but I hadn't known that being underweight was, too.

"I'm sorry," Jack said again.

"Yeah, she didn't even know she was pregnant this time, so she didn't realize it was time to supplement and change her diet." Mickey cleared his throat. "She's decided to retire so she can gain some weight."

"Wow, that's big."

I nodded, agreeing with Jack even if I couldn't speak and let Mickey know I was on the phone, too.

"Yeah. So I wanted to give you a heads up that she's having a tough time right now."

In the background, I heard Laura's voice. "I'm home." Then, "Who are you talking to?"

Mickey said, "Jack."

"Okay."

"You all right?"

"I'm going to lie down."

"I'll be in there in a minute, hon."

Silence for a few seconds. Mickey whispered, "Okay, I think she's gone."

Jack had rested his forehead in one hand, elbow on my desk, but he lifted it now. "Let me know if there's anything I can do."

"I will."

"For you, too."

"Thanks, Jack."

They said good-bye and hung up. Jack and I stared at each other. His eyes were soft and warm and golden and kind, and I rested there in them for a moment.

"You okay?" he finally asked.

I nodded, still looking into his beautiful eyes. He reached a hand across my desk, palm up, and I placed mine in his. Electricity shot up my arm as his fingers closed around mine.

A loud, long whine interrupted us. Jack looked down. We both knew who it was.

"Need to go, Snowflake?" The tags jingled madly, and he reached down to pet her. "I've got to take her out," he said to me.

"Do you need me to do it?"

"No. Some cold air will do me good."

I pulled my hand away from his, grabbing the leash from my desk drawer and handing it to him. He snapped it on and they walked to the door.

"Don't you need a coat?" I asked.

He turned to me one last time and grinned big, all on the left. "Coats are for sissies." Man and tiny dog exited, and I caught one last glimpse of them through the sidelight window before they disappeared down the hallway.

The phone rang again immediately. I snatched it up, repeating my standard greeting by rote at twice its normal speed.

Greg's voice said, "Emily? I called earlier. Can you talk?"

"Hi, Greg. Yes, I can."

"Are you alone?"

"Yes, but only for a few minutes."

"Okay." I heard whispering in the background.

"What is it?"

"Remember how last night we said we didn't need help?"

"Yes."

"Well, we've changed our minds. We, um, saw something. Last night."

I reached for my Roasters cup. Cold, half-full. "What was it?" I took a sip. Still delicious.

"We saw someone shoot a man."

A chill settled over my face. The gunshots. The black trucker's red blood against white snow. "At Love's?" I put the cup down.

"Yeah. And now today we saw on TV the person that got shot died."

"Yes, he did. But I don't see how that changes things. Not that I don't think you need help. I do. But what's the problem?"

"We didn't just see it. We were really close, and the person saw us, too."

That did change things. They were witnesses to a murder, to a murderer. "Oh my gosh, that is scary. But it was dark. I'm sure you weren't recognizable. Please try not to worry." Like my words would stop them from it. Poor kids. *I* would worry in their shoes. But then I had an idea—they could help the police bring the killer to justice. I stood up, wireless receiver to my ear, and walked to the door. "I know it would be upsetting, but do you think you would be able to look at suspect photos or work with a police sketch artist, maybe? To help them ID the person? The paper said they don't have any leads." I leaned until I got a look down the hallway in the glass. No Jack and Snowflake. I walked back to my desk and sat.

His voice was firm. "No. We're not safe. Before, we only had to find a place to stay, find jobs. Now, no matter where we go or what we do, they'll always be out there."

I jiggled my mouse and my background picture of Betsy popped up, one I had taken outside the school a month before. She had pigtails high on either side of her head, and she was laughing so hard her face had scrunched. I touched an index finger to the screen on her button nose. A pang of longing shot through me.

I turned my full attention back to Greg. "I understand. But CPS and the police can protect you. Why don't you let me come get you, and I can take you in to talk to Byron and—"

"No. We can't. We won't. It has to stay a secret, or you'll never hear from us again."

I felt the wrinkles between my eyebrows furrow. "I don't get it, Greg."

"You don't have to." His voice grew shrill. "But Farrah is never going back where someone can hurt her, never. I won't let her. If you won't help us, fine. Just say so."

I used my most gentle tone. "That's not what I'm saying. But there are things I'm scared of, too." I touched Betsy's nose on the screen again. "I'm trying to adopt a little girl right now. I can get in big trouble if I help you guys and don't report it to CPS." I ran through what little family law I knew from my years as a paralegal and from my CPS training. I was pretty sure harboring a runaway was a criminal offense. "I could even go to jail or be fined a lot of money."

"Not if no one finds out."

"But people *do* find out things."

"We won't let them."

Ah, to be invincible and in control, or at least to be young and convinced you are. "What exactly is it you guys are asking me to do?"

"Help us find a way out of Amarillo so we can be safe."

My gut clenched. Even though I'd told him the consequences, he didn't know how much they were asking of me. Of course they didn't. They couldn't. They were young, and in trouble. "Where are you now?"

"Are you going to help us?"

"I'm going to think about it." And pray about it.

"We'll decide whether to tell you where we are *when* you decide."

The door opened. Jack and Snowflake had returned. Jack's nose looked red and runny. Well, it was colder than a witch's you-know-what out there. His eyes looked bright, though, and he had a bounce to his step. Snowflake ran to greet me and I leaned down and petted her.

I pointed at the phone and mouthed, "I'm on a call," to Jack.

He unclipped Snowflake and mouthed, "I kind of guessed that," smiled, and walked toward his office.

"Are you still there?" Greg asked, and his voice had lost its strident edge. It sounded scared, desperate. It hurt my heart.

"I am. But I have to go now. I'm sorry."

"When will you decide?"

"Call me at five. I'll let you know then what I'm able to do. And you can let me know whether you guys have changed your minds."

"Okay, but we won't." He hung up.

Betsy. I had dodged one bullet with the bogus arrest. I couldn't let anything jeopardize an adoption. Could I? I sat with the phone in my hands, paralyzed with uncertainty and a growing dread.

Chapter Ten

At lunchtime, Nadine and I dined on green veggie curry at My Thai courtesy of her employee discount. Our food came, Nadine chatted, yet all I could think about was the predicament Greg's call had put me in. My mind flitted from Betsy's smiling face to horrible images of Greg and Farrah in a succession of dire circumstances: running from a barreling eighteen-wheeler with TUCK69 plates, crouched inside a closet while an enormous man pounded on the door, shivering and hungry under a snow-covered overpass. I had barely said "boo" to Nadine the entire meal, and I smiled and nodded when she talked, without really hearing her.

I had to do better.

I shook myself mentally and forced words out of my mouth. "What're you doing this afternoon?" I scooped up a bite from my dwindling plate of curry.

She swallowed and wiped her mouth with a paper napkin. "I'm putting in a few hours at the Rainbow Room."

I held the fork poised in front of me. "I don't know how you do it. I really don't. Two jobs, single mom, and you volunteer, too? You're my hero."

A petite Asian waiter stopped at our table and filled our water glasses. She looked at us with a thumbs up, and we nodded. She reached into her apron and pulled out a faux leather bill holder and set it in the center of our table. She stepped back, cocked her head, then scooted it with one finger an imperceptible distance to the left and moved away behind a sparse plastic fichus tree to another table.

Nadine said, "People have always helped me out. I owe it back."

"Still." I shoveled a bite in and chewed. The tastes and textures registered, a little. Sweet coconut milk, spicy curry, an al dente bell pepper.

She lifted her eyebrows and lowered her fork to the mauve plastic placemat. "When I was sixteen, my mother's bad-news boyfriend Bill moved in. He started visiting me in the middle of the night, and Mama didn't want to hear it. Things got pretty wild from there. Drugs. Staying out all night. Older guys, just not as old as Bill. Anything to keep away from him and forget. You know?"

"Yes. I'm so sorry," I said, nodding. Not that I had personal experience with any of what she'd gone through—my high school days were Sandra Dee compared to hers—but I knew what she meant, and I couldn't imagine how hard it must have been for her. I set my fork down, too. She had my full attention now.

"I ran away a few times, and the police threatened to refer me to a CPS group home or put me in a detention center. Then Mama discovered crack cocaine."

"Nadine, that's so awful." My words felt like dust on my tongue. Dry, insubstantial, useless.

"Yeah. It was. So I showed up on the doorstep of one of my teachers from Fannin Middle School—Ms. Davidson; she was retired—and she said I could move in with her if it was our secret. I stayed with her and her longtime girlfriend for months."

"You're kidding!" I wanted to squirm in my seat. Well, Ms. Davidson wasn't trying to adopt a sweet little girl. There was no comparison between our situations.

Nadine smiled, her eyes soft and sad. "I would have stayed forever, but she died suddenly, and Bill had left, so I went home."

"Oh no!"

"I still miss her every day. But Ms. Davidson wasn't the only one to take a chance helping me. A few years ago my first son's dad left me. My mother was in the gutter, literally. Homeless, showing up at my doorstep. Stealing from me. Buying drugs right outside my house. Screaming so loud the neighbors could hear." She wiped a tear away with a rough backhand motion. "Someone called CPS. And instead of taking my son away, the Rainbow Room ladies helped me. They gave me a car seat and diapers and formula and some clothes, which was great. But they went way beyond that." Her voice grew thicker. "Referred me to a state-funded rehab facility for Mom. Helped me get on a list for a subsidized daycare place. Encouraged me. Followed up with me. Never judged me."

My throat tightened and my eyes stung. I'd never imagined Nadine had had it so bad. "Nadine." I tried to say more, but I couldn't find the words. I reached out and grabbed her hand and squeezed it tight, then held on.

"So, that's why I make time to work in the Rainbow Room, and to take flowers to Ms. Davidson's grave. Because without either of them, I wouldn't be here today."

The enormity of what Ms. Davidson had done, of what she had risked to prevent harm to Nadine, came crashing down on me.

I spoke, but my words came out broken and raspy. "I understand." I cleared my throat.

Why, why, why was I being tested like this, with Greg and Farrah and their problems? Betsy needed me, too. But as soon as I thought it, I was hit with a deep sadness. That wasn't really true, was it? She was clean, fed, in school, with new siblings, and had a safe place to sleep at night. I'd seen her. She was playful, confident, and happy. A far cry from Greg and Farrah. My resistance wasn't because Betsy *truly* needed me, not like the teens did. It was because I truly *wanted* Betsy. Ouch. Forced to choose between the teens' needs and my desires, I felt cornered, like the feral dog that I'd found sleeping in our barn one winter morning long ago, snappy and snarly and untrusting.

I took a deep breath. I was surely more rational than a wild dog. What did Greg and Farrah really need me to do, after all, that was so huge? Come get them, let them stay for the night, then take them somewhere safe and far away? Those weren't big things, not really, and no one had to know. I would just have to put the fear of God in them about never, ever, ever telling a living soul I was the one who had helped them. And if worse came to worst, I could turn them over to Wallace. I didn't want to, but I could. Whichever way it went, I would be careful, and I could still adopt Betsy.

"Cat got your tongue?" Nadine asked.

I smiled at her, not really feeling it yet, but closer. "Sorry. Got lost in my thoughts there for a moment. Your story is powerful."

She nodded. "But all that is in the past. Are you ready to go?" she asked, yanking me the rest of the way out of my head.

"Sure." I fished a twenty and ten from my wallet and stuck them in with the bill, then slid it to overhang two inches past the edge of the table, but centered precisely.

"Wait, you can't get that." Nadine grabbed her purse.

The waiter appeared out of nowhere and took the folder like a trout taking a fly.

"I already did." I smiled and stood up. "Want to come with me to see the duplex I'm hoping to lease?"

She got to her feet, towering over me in high-heeled boots. "My kids are in school, and I've got nowhere to be for a few hours. Why not?"

Nadine drove her Harley, following me south on Soncy Road toward a new neighborhood on the outskirts of town. After a mile or two of stoplights, I veered left onto Hollywood, through former prairie on both sides of the road. Other than a few real estate signs, there were no marked improvements to the land I'd known since childhood, until we came to a cluster of houses on the left. Even once we'd turned into that neighborhood, I couldn't see much change to the land's former condition, other than houses plopped down onto square plots of snow-speckled brown grass. The houses themselves were nondescript: brick flanked on each side by mirror-image driveways and entrances. The vehicles out front were mostly midrange hybrids and electrics, a far cry from what you'd find in old Amarillo. I pulled in behind a Ford Focus and got out. Nadine rumbled to a stop behind me and parked at an angle to the curb.

A pregnant woman stood in the doorway on the right side of the house in a flannel empire-waist maxi dress and a heavy gray shawl.

"Hello," she called out and waved.

I raised a hand in greeting, waiting for Nadine to dismount and join me. We walked up the sidewalk together.

"I'm Emily," I said, holding out a hand, which the woman took. "This is Nadine."

"Nadine, Emily, I'm Sara Edwards, one of the homeowners. Nice to meet you."

"You, too." Nadine shook Sara's hand.

Sara tucked her chin-length brown curls behind one ear. "Shall we go inside?"

"Absolutely," I replied.

The three of us walked to the far side of a tiny entryway with earth-toned ceramic tile floors. The tile ended at each edge of the entrance and gave way to neutral tan carpet. We stood on the edge of the large space that held the living room, dining area, and kitchen, with windows all across it to a barren backyard.

As I admired the maple kitchen cabinets in a natural finish, the light granite countertops, and the stainless steel appliances, I thought I saw something out of the corner of my eye. A little girl flew high in a swing, kicking her feet, being pushed by a teenage boy. Another girl about his age sat in another swing, twisting side to side with her toes on the ground. They looked familiar but were too far away to recognize for sure out of my peripheral vision. I glanced away from the kitchen and looked for them, and they were no longer in the yard—if they were ever there. I sidestepped and put my hand out, suddenly feeling dizzy.

Movement in the kitchen caught my peripheral attention again. Three dark heads in stairstep height, six hands busy washing and drying dishes. I switched my gaze quickly from the backyard to the kitchen. No kids.

What was wrong with me? A psychotic break? Normal people didn't see imaginary kids in strangers' houses. I put my fingers to my cheek to refocus myself and studied the interior décor.

The walls in the kitchen and the other two rooms were a tasteful-if-nondescript almond with crisp white trim. My Dallas condo had been white, black, and silver to suit Rich's taste, so this would be a refreshing change for me. I lowered my hand and swiveled to look in either direction off the foyer. Hallways jutted toward doorways beyond.

The faint laughter of children bounced toward me down one hall. I wanted to clap my hands over my ears; that, or see if Sara had any Valium.

Sara's voice pulled me back into the real world. "My husband and I are moving into a bigger house." She put her hand on her enormous belly. "Number four. We need more space. But he's always wanted to own rental properties, so here we go, right?" She beamed, revealing perfect white teeth.

"Congratulations," I said, as I tried to peer down the hallway without drawing attention to myself. Maybe there really were people down there. Sara's kids, perhaps? But why did I think it had sounded like Betsy's laugh?

"Thank you," Sara said.

Nadine shot me a "gag me" look with her index finger jabbing into her mouth behind Sara's head, but I barely noticed, my mind on the tricks my imagination was playing on me. Seeing people that weren't there? Hearing sounds that weren't real? Maybe it wasn't a psychotic break; maybe the curry was spoiled, and this was food poisoning.

Sara put her hand on my arm. "Is it just the two of you that would plan on living here? Not that we have anything against lesbians, of course."

Nadine set down the framed picture she had lifted from a low table in the entryway. "Good to know." She took a deep breath, raising her shoulders an inch.

I hurried to prevent Nadine from going any further. "Us either. But, it's only me. Nadine's providing me with moral support today."

"Ah. Well, it's a lot of house for one person."

The sound of Betsy's voice broke through for a moment, and I fought not startling and widening my eyes in reaction. "Can I have the bedroom with the purple butterflies?" her little voice asked. "Farrah can share with me until she moves away."

Just like that I was certain, as certain as I ever could be. I would get this house and adopt Betsy and help Greg and Farrah and have it all, dang it, because I could pull this off and everybody would be the better for it.

"No," I said to Sara. "It's the perfect amount of space. I'll take it."

Nadine raised her eyebrows, and I flashed her a weak smile.

Chapter Eleven

Hours later—per Greg's instructions—I pulled my Mustang flush alongside an unremarkable apartment complex in the center of town. I eased forward until I was as near as I could get to the stairs on its north side. Twilight had fallen, and the meager lighting cast an eerie glow on the hulking brick building and asphalt lot around it. Red, green, yellow, blue, and orange lights blinked from a lone window on the upper floor. Somewhere behind me, an engine revved. Glasspacks, loud enough to wake the neighborhood.

Greg and Farrah had taken refuge here with a young man who had aged out of the foster system, a guy Greg had lived with in a previous foster family. It was a decent enough solution to their desperate situation the night before, but obviously their problems had morphed from those of mere runaways in the dead of winter into those of a much more dangerous kind.

The passenger-side back door opened suddenly, and I squeaked. I whipped my head around in time to see Farrah's tiny figure scoot across the backseat and Greg's bigger but still-too-thin body follow her. Each teenager wore black, head to toe. Greg shut the door softly, and Farrah laid her head on Greg's legs. He lowered his to her back, which put them well below the bottom of the windows. They were hidden, unless someone walked right up to my car.

"You scared me to death. I never even saw you guys out there," I said.

"Sorry," Greg said.

"Thank you," Farrah added.

"You're welcome." I hadn't even put my car in park yet, so I eased off the brake and made a wide left back to the parking lot exit. "Do you need anything in town before we drive out to Heaven?"

"Heaven?" Farrah's voice rose in pitch.

"Sorry. Bushland. Where I live. Heaven is my boss's nickname for it."

"Why?"

"It's west of town, and he says that makes it halfway to the Heaven that is New Mexico."

"Is New Mexico Heaven?"

I laughed, turning left on Paramount toward I-40. "Parts of it are quite lovely."

"We need to get where we're going, quick, before someone sees us," she said.

Her words made my skin prickle. I checked my rearview mirror, getting a fix on the cars behind me. Black Ford F-150. White minivan of some type. Silver Camry. "Greg said the shooter saw you guys. Do you think he knows who you are? Or followed you?"

"Yes."

"How do you know—did he call you by name?"

Neither kid answered. I let the silence linger as I merged onto I-40 going west. "Have you seen him before?" I scanned the rearview for cars again. The minivan was still behind me. I cut my eyes back to the road, then stretched upward to catch the kids in the rearview. It didn't work, so I adjusted the mirror until I could see their faces. They were both staring back at me. "Well?"

Farrah answered. "We can't talk about it."

"Why?" Silence met my question again, like a brick wall. Then it hit me. "You guys don't trust me."

"Nothing personal."

"Then why'd you call me?"

"We trust you more than anyone else."

"How come?"

"Remember that time when we met you?"

"Yeah. What about it?"

"We could hear you out there, you know, talking to that CPS guy. Walter or whatever."

"Wallace."

"Yeah. Anyway, he didn't want to come in the house, because he wouldn't break the rules, even though you guys were looking for a lost little girl, and she could have been in there."

"Right, so?"

"So, you were. You were brave enough to go in by yourself, too. So, we trust you, mostly."

I laughed. "Most people would reach the opposite conclusion from that story."

Greg's deeper voice— not by much—said, "Not us. And it's not just about trust. If we tell you, then you could be in trouble."

I met his eyes in the rearview mirror. "Greg, if you're being watched, whoever it is assumed you've already told me, as soon as he saw you get in this car. Don't kid yourself."

I looked away to check the road and then back at him again. He stared at me and nodded, his head sideways over Farrah's shoulders, but he didn't say anything else. They looked so young and vulnerable. Remembering that they'd been seeking a ride out of town at the Love's the night before, I recalled that the newspaper article I'd read that morning mentioned public indecency issues at the truck stop. I cringed. They'd probably come closer than they'd known to a lot more than witnessing a murder.

I watched the road again. "So, at my house, there's one other person. My mother. But it's cool. You guys can stay in my room, and she'll never know you're there."

"No one else can know about us," Greg reminded me.

I chose my words carefully, not wanting to overcommit. "I understand."

As we exited Amarillo proper, we passed the iconic Cadillac Ranch on our left, or at least we passed where I knew it to be. It was too dark to see the ten angled Cadillacs planted in the dirt, every square inch of each covered in a rainbow of spray-painted graffiti that would be partially obscured by snow right now. I saw them every day, sometimes more than once, and I knew them by heart.

I checked behind us again. No white minivan. No nothing, no no-body, as far as I could see. If the murderer had been watching them, he or she didn't seem to be following us now. And if CPS or the police had been onto their whereabouts, they would have been doing more than watching. Maybe the kids were being paranoid that they'd been recognized, that the murderer was searching for them, even following them. Or maybe they weren't.

Acid churned in my gut. I was out on a limb here, transporting known runaways from the same state system I was trying to get permission from to foster and adopt, on the heels of getting myself arrested on charges of inappropriate behavior with a child, however bogus. Going behind Wallace's back, too, and smack dab in the commission of a crime, maybe even a felony if harboring underage runaways was as illegal as it felt. Risking Betsy's adoption. Putting myself squarely in the sights of the same killer that was after Greg and Farrah. Yeah, I was way out on this limb, to its very tip with the bough bending toward the ground as far as it would go, and the loud crack of it snapping in two only a heartbeat away.

But my heart told me I had no choice, and I would have to have faith that it wouldn't break.

***

I parked a few minutes later in front of the little white house on fifteen acres where I lived with the maternal half of my gene pool. Once again, I checked the side-view mirror. No headlights. I scanned the street ahead of me. No chatty neighbors out braving the cold temperatures. Our porch light had burned out the week before, and I meant to replace it, but kept forgetting. Now I was glad I'd procrasti-nated. Under cover of darkness, we ran to the house. I put a finger to my lips, and two heads nodded.

"Mother?" I leaned my head in the front door and listened for a reply. I knew she'd made it home before me. Her Civic was out front, and I smelled pot roast cooking.

"In the kitchen." Her perky voice ended on two descending sing-song high notes.

I motioned Greg and Farrah in ahead of me. I whispered to the two young people. "Down this hall, first door on the right." I used a half shout for my mother. "I'll be in there in a second. Gotta run to the bathroom first."

"Okey dokey," she sang.

I scurried ahead of the kids to my room, the kitchen noise and hall carpeting muffling what little sound we made. My feet were like raindrops; theirs were as silent as dew. I may have trained to be Sacajawea, but they'd had a lot more real-world experience at becoming invisible and soundless. We entered my Western-themed room and I pulled the door shut behind us, turning the knob so that the latch wouldn't click as I eased it closed. I flipped on the bedside table lamp, and low light bathed my childhood bedroom. Green and brown-clad cowgirls rode horseback across every fabric surface—the wall included—twirling their lassos against a red background.

Greg made a prune face, like he'd gotten a snoot of vinegar. "Holy shit, this room is—"

"Really cool." Farrah smiled for the first time since I'd known her.

My mother kept the house a sweltering eighty degrees in the winter, yet neither Greg nor Farrah removed their black knit caps. The ends of her pixie hair curled around the edges of hers. Her smile sparkled from her eyes like onyx.

Greg shook his head. "That wasn't what I was going to say." The boy's hair, lighter than Farrah's, showed below the edges of his cap, and it was longer and stringier, like a young Kurt Cobain. So was his body. I'd have to feed him while he was here—a lot.

Farrah turned to me. "I love horses."

"Me, too. As you probably guessed, this was my room when I was a lot younger." And now, for the time being, anyway. My divorce had left me essentially destitute. I planned to move out when I had enough cash, which I hoped would be soon. "We can make spots for you to sleep on the floor in here with me for tonight, and figure out a better plan for tomorrow."

"Thank you." Pink spotted Farrah's cheeks, the only color besides her lips on her entire body. "We know you could get in a lot of trouble for this. We won't let it happen."

"Yeah, thanks." Greg lowered his voice. He couldn't be more than fifteen, and Farrah younger than that, and the affectation made him sound even younger.

"Yep. We just have to keep you guys a secret from everyone." Especially Wallace. He would be fired or even arrested if he didn't report the runaways back to the authorities. "Okay, I'm going to see my mother so she doesn't come looking for me. There are blankets and pillows in the closets, the password's taped to the monitor for the desktop, and there are books down there." I pointed to the bottom shelf on my nightstand. "Lock the doorknob, and I'll be back soon, with food."

They nodded, and I slipped out the door, shutting it quietly behind me. On the other side, I leaned against it and drew in a huge breath and held it, counting to five-one-thousand, then let it out. I pasted a smile on my face. It felt wrong, and I tried again. Better. I walked to the kitchen.

The kitchen décor made my bedroom seem blah. Red cedar paneling competed with gold Formica countertops and wallpaper of blue and purple flowers and twirling green vines. The chrome-legged table had a Formica top, too, but green. It could drive a woman to drink, which sounded like a good idea about now. I opened the refrigerator and pulled out the box wine.

"How was your day, Mother?"

"You'll never believe it, but Pastor Robb announced today that he's leaving. Only this must have been in the works for a while, because we'll have a new pastor by Sunday. And it's a woman! I've never worked for a woman before."

Mother doubled as the secretary and most fervent worshipper at the Panhandle Believers Church, with a belief system older than she was by several decades. She wiped her hands on a frilly white-skirted apron longer than her skirt. Even with the homespun apron, she looked like an aging Vegas showgirl. Mother had a penchant for stilettos, and she didn't like to cover too much of her long legs if she could help it. She never went in public without a full face of Mary Kay and half a bottle of Aqua Net—White Rain would do in a pinch—holding her baby-fine blonde hair perfectly in place.

I pulled a glass tumbler from the red cedar cabinet. "Want one?"

"A smidge." She indicated about a sixteenth of an inch with her finger and thumb.

"So, that's pretty big news. How are the Believers taking it?" I grabbed a second glass and poured her smidge and my own full up.

"People were quite devoted to Pastor Robb, and I'm not sure everyone accepts that God intended women to lead the church." My eyes fluttered up into their sockets, but she didn't seem to notice. "I'll be surprised if we don't lose members over this. That big church outside of town, Mighty is the Word or whatever they call it, is recruiting new members, and I do mean recruiting." She shrugged, a hopeless gesture. "They have a male pastor."

Ah, Mother and the Believers. I love the woman and I look like her, but I don't think like her. And Mother didn't know everything about her soon-to-be-former boss and worship leader. My friend Nadine counted Pastor Robb as one of her top customers at the Polo Club, quick with a fat tip and always paying in cash. Was it a coincidence that most people left cash in the collection plate each Sunday? I didn't think so. Anyway, Nadine would hate to see him go. I handed Mother her glass, then clinked mine to hers. "Well, I'm sure you'll grow to love the new pastor, too."

Mother harrumphed. "How was your day, dear?"

I took a tiny swallow of the white zinfandel. I shuddered. The first sip was always the worst. "Same old."

This was my standard answer. Mother had an insatiable urge to feed the gossip gristmill of her Sunday school class at Believers, and they'd ground up my personal life a few too many times, talking to the Lord and whoever else would listen. I'd learned to keep the interesting things to myself. For instance, I had neglected to tell Mother about

88

wrecking Jack's Jeep two nights before or the murder we'd almost stumbled upon at Love's, and I sure hadn't told her I'd spent half the day cooling my heels in lockup yesterday.

"Anything new with Ja-ack?" Her voice trilled his name.

For someone upset that her boss and worship leader was leaving her, she sure sounded happy. Actually, she'd sounded downright perky for a week or two now. Could she have met someone? I looked closer at her. I'd never seen the snug skirt she was wearing or the soft pink sweater. Hmmm, something to keep an eye on.

"We're working on Betsy's case and a few others." I pretended not to understand her meaning about Jack. She had finally given up on reuniting Rich and me, although I wasn't sure she'd accepted that he couldn't be re-established as a red-blooded heterosexual. She now pinned her hopes for my happily-ever-after and her grandbabies on Jack. Which brought up another subject I'd neglected to update her on: my very iffy reproductive potential. It could *definitely* wait.

"I got her something little for Christmas. To go in the backpack you got her."

"About that." I slugged down half my wine in one swallow, skipping most of the too-sweet taste experience. "Her foster parents aren't allowing her to accept gifts. Or visitors."

"What? Whyever would they not?"

"On account of it's Jesus's birthday." The rest of the white zin slid down my hatch.

Mother set her unsipped-from glass down on the counter. "Well, I never. I daresay I'm as well-versed as almost anyone, and I don't see anything in the Bible that *prohibits* exchanging gifts, at Christmas or any time." She picked her glass back up to salute with it. "Tasteful ones, and not in excess. All things to the glory of God."

I refilled my wine.

"Do you have plans for your Friday night, dear?"

"I'm going to take some roast and vegetables back to my room for now. I'm really tired," I ladled an enormous bowl.

"You don't want to watch *Murder, She Wrote* with me?"

We'd seen every episode at least three times. I smiled at her. "You tell me whodunit at breakfast tomorrow." I kissed her on the cheek. "Thanks for making dinner." What I left out telling her was that I needed to get in touch with Jack. He didn't know it yet, but he was going to have passengers on the way to New Mexico tomorrow.

Chapter Twelve

Early the next morning outside the Maxor Building, Jack dropped his bag and Snowflake's collapsible kennel into the trunk of my Mustang, then opened the passenger door. Snowflake hopped in and he followed her. She adjusted herself into his lap.

Jack swiveled in his seat. "Morning."

I'd texted Jack late the night before, asking to hitch a ride to his ranch for me and two, which he'd agreed to if I'd pick him up on my way to the airport, since his Jeep was still in the shop. The kids accepted that he would believe our cover story that they were two family friends who I was dropping in Alamogordo. I knew the chances of him buying it were slim to none, but a) I trusted him with the secret and b) I was still going to give it my best shot.

"Jack, these are the two family friends of mine I was telling you about, George and Frannie." I used the cover names we'd picked together. "Guys, this is my boss, Jack." I paused, then added the nickname I occasionally used for him on a whim. "Short for Jack Ass."

Greg and Farrah stared at me for a split second.

Greg—who I had to remember to start thinking of and calling George—laughed first. "Nice to meet you, Mr. Ass."

"Jack, please." Jack rolled his eyes. "She doesn't show me a lot of respect."

"Who, me?" I winked toward the teens.

We drove out of downtown, passing several of the older, more established churches on the way. At the First Baptist Church's sign, I read POTLUCK SUPPER SUNDAY AT 5:00 PM—PRAYER AND MEDICATION TO FOLLOW. I laughed.

"What's so funny?" Jack asked.

I pointed at the sign and he chuckled. "I can just picture some little blue-haired lady carefully writing that in her shaky handwriting for one of the youth group members to put up." Remembering the one from the night before, I decided that I really needed to start writing them down. I could write a hilarious little book, and surely authors made more money than paralegals.

Jack's left dimple appeared. "Church bulletin typos made Sundays worth it for me as a kid."

I merged onto I-40, keeping a sharp eye on the rearview mirror, as I had the entire way from Heaven in to pick up Jack. No followers that I could tell. Jack chatted with the kids as I exited and made a few quick turns to get us to the nearby Tradewind Airport. I parked as close as I could to the edge of the surface lot nearest Jack's hangar—on the opposite side of the facility from the airport's small terminal building—and checked the mirrors one last time. Still no suspicious vehicles.

Jack grabbed Snowflake's kennel and his suitcase, and she walked beside him on a leash. I followed with my one rolling bag, and the kids fell in beside me, each of them carrying mostly empty plastic grocery bags. We passed a pole crowded with painted arrows pointing in different directions and denoting mileage to a multitude of destinations. It looked like an old-school Rolodex in mid twirl. Jack unlocked the door and we entered his pitch-dark shared private hangar. He flicked a switch. Fluorescents crackled, hummed, and then flooded the interior, revealing eight small planes. It was barely warmer inside than outside.

"Wow," Greg/George said. His voice echoed in the cavernous space. "Cool!"

"Do you like to fly?" Jack asked him.

"I think so, but I never have."

"I did when I was a baby," Farrah/Frannie said, but her voice was less enthusiastic.

"If either of you want to learn more, you can help me get ready."

"I do!" Greg said.

"I'll stay with Emily," Farrah said, moving so close to me that her side pressed against mine.

Jack spent the next ten minutes prepping the plane, under a watchful teenage eye. We girls visited the hangar bathrooms, then we all loaded up. Five minutes later, we were under way to Wrong Turn Ranch.

Cabin conditions in the Cessna 172 were not ideal. For starters, I still hadn't fallen in love with small planes and the concept of amateur pilots. I trusted Jack, and his Skyhawk seemed airworthy, but I'm of the belief that humans are creatures of the earth rather than the sky. I'm not overly fond of big planes and professional pilots, either. Not only that, but before today I had my own spot in the backseat. Today, Greg and Farrah had bumped me into shotgun, where I held Snowflake's kennel, with Snowflake in it. Even a tiny dog in a tiny kennel gets old fast when it's on your lap for three-plus hours, buckled in the seatbelt with you. It reminded me of the times Dad had me ride in the stock trailer with the horses as a kid, something probably akin to forcing your unhelmeted, unbelted children into the back of a pickup truck these days. I'd always considered it a badge of honor to shepherd the animals back then. Now? Not so much.

Other than Snowflake in my lap, though, the front seat was better than the back. Up here, I could wear headphones that allowed me to talk to Jack during the flight. It was much too noisy without them to hear each other even from less than two feet away. In general, I'd found that, in the two months I'd known him, Jack didn't talk much. Today was a different story. His voice crackled in my headphones, surprisingly loud and clear. He looked straight ahead as he spoke, although I noticed that he couldn't see much of anything but his instrument panel in front of him while in flight. That was something I would have to try not to think about.

"I'm an officer of the court. You realize I could get disbarred for this, right?"

I knew he was talking about the kids, and I did know how much trouble this could bring down on him. It bothered me. A lot. "If, hypothetically speaking, you knew you were doing something wrong, then, yes, you could get disbarred. You've got plausible deniability, though, and I'd like to keep it that way." My heart clenched like a fist as

I said it. I would never forgive myself if I got Jack in trouble, so I would have to make sure I didn't.

"So that confirms my pretty good guess about who those two are." Now he glanced at me, and I saw his chest rise and fall. "You do keep it interesting, Emily." His lips pulled tight as he looked away, and my heart did its normal little flip-flop when I had earned one of his lopsided smiles.

I nodded. "Friends of the family, like I said."

"Ha. The same ones that called you at the office yesterday, I suppose."

I licked my lips. "That was Katie."

"She never calls you on the office phone."

I guess I hadn't fooled him after all. I turned to check on the teenagers, shooting them an okay sign with my thumb and forefinger in question. Greg's arm was slung around Farrah, and her head was tucked in the **V** his underarm made with his chest and shoulder. Her face looked pale, but they both gave me thumbs skyward.

"Hypothetically, my two friends tell me they may have seen a murder take place at a certain truck stop Wednesday night."

Jack's head whipped toward me for a second. "No shit?"

"None." He shook his head, eyes wide, and I continued. "I gave them my card when I saw them in the field the other night. They said I'm the only one they can trust, but they haven't trusted me enough to tell me who it is. They're plenty scared though, and they're convinced the shooter saw them and is coming after them."

Jack's thumbs danced on the yoke. "That's why they were running away from Love's."

I nodded. "Yep. They've had such a rough time. Losing their families. Sexual abuse at the foster home where they met, at least Farrah. On the run from the group home CPS put them in after that. Honestly, it doesn't sound like the group home was all that bad, but they've lost faith in the system and are just young enough to believe they're invincible together."

"Young and stupid."

"Young and, sadly, experienced. And idealistic."

"Did you tell Wallace?"

"No, no one else. I can't put him or the kids in that position."

His lips twitched. "But you can put me in it."

I decided it was best to pretend I hadn't heard his last remark, even though my gut tightened with guilt. I looked out the side window at the ground far below us, like the surface of a Life game board without its color. Treeless, wrinkled, brown dotted with white. Ribbons of black asphalt wound through the landscape, vehicles crawling along them at the pace of snails compared to us. Here and there, small clusters of roofs gave evidence of community. We'd long since crossed the border into New Mexico and I tried to identify the towns. Clovis? Portales? Or were they even on our route?

Jack's voice crackled in my ear again. "So, what now?"

I stuck a finger in Snowflake's kennel and was rewarded with a tiny, rough tongue. Snowflake didn't hold back her affection, or her constant search for a crumb or tiny dried remnant of whatever I'd last eaten.

"I was hoping we could let them lay low in Tularosa for a while. At least for the weekend with me. Maybe longer if I figure something out." Jack's family ranch was between the tiny towns of Bent and Tularosa, New Mexico, but closer to Tularosa.

"Such as?"

Snowflake's tongue bath over, I used my fingertip to scratch behind her fluffy white ears. I couldn't hear her, but I knew from the many times I'd scratched there that she was humming her special happy noise.

"Maybe someone at the ranch could take them in for a while. It'd be good for them." I braced myself for Jack's response, expecting a verbal wallop.

Instead, he nodded again. "That might work. We can ask Mickey and Laura what they think." Jack turned and met my eyes, looking deep into them. "No promises."

"Of course not."

"You sure do seem to have a knack for finding the lost souls." He reached over and chucked his knuckles gently against my cheek.

My heart jackhammered in response to his touch.

***

Jack taxied to the barnlike hangar from the rough dirt runway at Wrong Turn Ranch. He pivoted the plane, and turned off the propeller. Two minutes later, Greg and Farrah hopped out of the plane, jaws hanging open.

"That was the coolest thing ever," Greg said, his voice almost a shout.

"You're a better flier than me," I told him.

I patted Farrah. She still looked a little green around the gills, but she hadn't used the barf bag, which was more than I could say for myself on my first trip out here. The kids loitered and watched as I helped Jack. He opened the hangar and I got in the awaiting old blue Suburban. The keys stayed in the ignition, so I pulled it out and around the side of the building. Jack retrieved a tow bar and hooked it to the plane's front strut, and together we started to push it over to a spindly-legged silver fuel tank—with Greg scrambling to help on my side when he saw what we were doing—then the boys maneuvered it backwards into the hangar when Jack had finished fueling it up. Greg shut the hangar for Jack, then we all piled in the land vehicle with the dog and the bags.

Jack drove us down a dirt road away from the private airport, through high-desert pastureland and toward the foothills of white-topped mountains beyond. A light layer of snow covered the ground and bushes around us, enough to look like icing on an Italian cream cake, but not enough to make driving—or landing a plane—difficult. I could still see the outline of yucca stalks and blades, but the snow rendered most of the other flora unrecognizable.

"Where are we?" Farrah asked.

Jack put one hand on my seat back as he turned himself toward Farrah. Even with him facing away, the Suburban stayed on course, practically steering itself through the rutted dirt track. With his hand almost touching me, I could feel his nearness in every cell of my body, and I wished it didn't make me tingle all over. Or that he'd lower that hand to my shoulder. Or my leg.

"We're a little more than a hundred miles from the southern border of New Mexico. Of the United States, for that matter. Less than two hours that way"—he pointed to his right—"is Mexico."

"How far are we from Amarillo?"

"About five hundred miles."

I turned toward her in my seat, my mouth now close enough to Jack's hand to kiss it, if I'd wanted to, which I did. I lowered my voice. "Far enough away that no one will follow."

Greg said to Jack, "Is this all yours?"

Jack lifted and dropped his shoulders. He moved his hand away from my seat and back to the steering wheel, causing a twinge in my chest. "Most of it, although it belongs to my parents, not me."

"Will it be yours someday?"

"I guess so. Unless I go before them."

"You must be really rich."

Jack laughed. "You'd be surprised. It costs a lot of money to run this ranch. But we do okay. Plus, I have a job."

"You're Emily's boss, right? A lawyer?"

"Yep."

I smiled and looked from one kid to the other. "The house is really nice here, and they have lots and lots of horses. Racehorses."

Farrah leaned forward, eyes round. "Can we see them?"

Jack turned the Suburban to the left at a **T** intersection in the dirt road. "Absolutely. In fact, if you'd like, we could take a ride this afternoon."

"That would be awesome." Farrah bounced in the seat, regressing a few years in her excitement, then stopped. "But I've never ridden a horse."

"Me either." Greg's voice sounded tight and worried.

"Nothing to it. We'll put you on some gentle ones that will do whatever mine and Emily's do. It will be as easy as riding in this old Suburban." Jack patted the dashboard.

The two kids looked at me, Greg clearly still uneasy with the arrangements, Farrah as clearly thrilled.

Jack continued. "Did you know Emily was a rodeo star in college?"

Farrah's brows rose and scrunched together. "Really?"

I smiled. "I went to college on a rodeo scholarship, and my dad was a professional rodeo cowboy. I rode horses before I could walk. And Jack's right. This will be a piece of cake."

Chapter Thirteen

Greg and Farrah were riding along with us through the snow-dusted coniferous trees of the foothills only two hours after Jack had landed the plane. Every now and then, a branch would dump its snow in a cascading plop surrounded by a shower of powder. The scent of pine and sap tickled my nose and I wanted to throw my arms in the air and shout with joy. Even though it was snowy, Tularosa air was even drier than Amarillo, so the cold didn't feel as painful, and the trees shielded us somewhat from the wind that whistled through their highest branches. The kids didn't have clothes for this type of weather and activity, but Jack had loaned Greg a long leather duster. It hung on him and flapped around his legs. Farrah had on one of Laura's puffy down jackets and it fit just right.

Farrah had gotten the hang of the rudimentaries of horseback riding in five minutes, and she was keeping up a steady stream of chatter to her mount, Lilac, a fifteen-year-old brood mare with a white star in the middle of her red forehead. I had clipped the lead line from Lilac to my saddle on Jarhead, the former racer whose special treasures had ended up at ABC Half-Price Resale in Amarillo.

Pink splotches brightened Farrah's cheeks, and she was far more talkative than she'd been since I'd known her. "I like your—" She pointed toward her teeth, lips bared.

I knew what she meant: my gap. I had a love-hate relationship with it. "Thanks. It's because I didn't wear my retainer after I got my braces off, but it's not bad."

"I think it's cute." She lowered her voice, and motioned her head toward Jack ahead of us. "Does he like it?"

"Jack?" I laughed, remembering my orthodontist's lecture and Jack calling me Snaggletooth. "I don't know."

Jack didn't react, so maybe he hadn't heard the question. I wondered what he thought about it. I hadn't had much of a gap when I met

my soon-to-be-ex-husband, Rich, but over the years it had widened
back to the size it had been pre-braces. Rich hadn't liked it.

Louder, she asked, "Are you guys married?"

My mouth worked a little, searching for words, and Jack's head
turned back toward Farrah. Then his eyes locked on mine, and I could
feel the heat rushing to my cheeks.

He said, "Huh. No, we're not."

Greg didn't give any sign that he was keeping up with our conversation. He had a two-handed death grip on the saddle horn in front of
him, his knuckles strained and white. His tall horse, Buzz, had a rolling
gait that seemed to be giving Greg the willies. Jack had clipped Buzz to
the saddle on Jumper, the tall black thoroughbred who was Jack's
normal ride.

Farrah nodded. "Is that why she calls you Jack Ass?"

I broke in quickly. "It's a term of endearment."

She cocked her head. "What's a term of endearment?"

I stuttered a little. "I-i-it's a nickname for someone you like."

"You call people you like Jack Ass?"

Jack said, "The girl has a point, Emily."

I couldn't think of an answer before Farrah thought of her next
question. "Are you married to anyone else?"

"No," Jack and I said, almost at the same time.

"Have you ever been married to anyone before?"

"Yes," we said, again in tandem.

"Do you have kids?"

I shook my head.

Jack cleared his throat. "A boy and a girl."

I drew in a breath as quietly as I could and held it for several seconds. Jack had never mentioned his kids in front of me.

"Do they live here?"

Jack drummed the fingers of his left hand on his saddle horn. "Follow me."

He clucked to Jumper, who moved off, tugging Buzz behind him. I worried about Greg for a moment, but he didn't panic. His eyes were the size of silver dollars, and not the Susan B. Anthony kind.

I squeezed my ankles against Jarhead and he broke into a slow lope before I pulled him up beside Jumper, Lilac following suit, and Farrah giggling like a kid on a carousel.

I leaned into Jack and whispered. "Where are we going?"

Jack didn't answer.

Silence fell over us, save for the soft plop of the horses' hooves on the snowy ground. The tall trees muffled even that noise, creating a cathedral-like atmosphere. The air grew colder as the horses climbed. Heat and the smell of sweat and leather clung to the animals. I marveled at the moment, these kids—orphans, runaways, witnesses to a murder, victims of abuse—here, in these pristine conditions. It was like the forest was giving them back their innocence. I could feel the tension easing in them, *and* me.

After ten minutes, we reached a partially cleared hilltop. The ground fell away over a pond on its far side. A large coyote was drinking and his head shot up at our approach. He sniffed with his nose in the air. His enormous ears twitched our way and he lifted one front paw, preparing to bolt. He froze, statue-still, for long seconds, then bounded into the forest. I wondered what he was doing out in broad daylight, but guessed he was hungry. The ranchers hated the coyotes. The clever animals preyed on livestock when their natural food sources dwindled, especially in the dead of winter, like now. Their reputation had been tarnished of late, too, by the poorly named coyotes that crossed the border with contraband of various kinds, usually drugs. But I admired the animals. They were survivors, often relying on their wits and bravery to stay alive when other animals perished in dwindling habitat and harsh conditions.

I shivered, remembering the mask of the Clown, the Apache Mountain Spirit Dancer that I had seen on my last visit to New Mexico, as Betsy and I ducked into Jack's plane and her kidnappers bore down on us with guns. The Clown had worn the snout of an animal on his face, and the ears of an animal in his headdress. I had thought it was a wolf, then, but maybe it was a coyote. This creature today reminded me of the Clown, and brought some of the magic of New Mexico back to my conscious thought.

Jack stopped his horse. I felt his eyes on me, and I looked over at him. We held each other's gaze for a moment. I barely breathed.

Then, with his eyes still locked on mine, Jack pointed to his left, to the edge of the clearing, at a collection of about a dozen headstones of varying ages, sizes, and angles. A low, rusted iron fence surrounded the plot. A cemetery.

"A few years ago, I had a case against a very bad person, a man who made teenage runaways work for him as prostitutes."

I snuck a glance at the kids, wondering if they saw the parallel to their precarious situation. They didn't react.

Jack was still telling his story. "I started getting death threats, but I ignored them. One day after my wife picked our kids up from school, she came to my building to borrow my car. She called me, but I didn't pick up. She parked and loaded the kids and my son's yellow Lab puppy into my car. When she turned it on, a bomb exploded. I heard it—everyone for miles around heard it. I realized when I got outside that it was my car, but I hadn't checked my messages. I didn't know my family had come, and I didn't know they were in it. I stood there watching it, not knowing. I couldn't have saved them, but still, I didn't know."

A warm wetness worked its way down my cheeks. I'd known what had happened to Jack's family from his secretary, Judith, but the version she'd told me was from her perspective. It had been sad, but nothing like his. My mouth fell open but no words came out. Still, Jack's eyes held mine.

"Someone was trying to kill you?" Greg asked.

"Yes. And got my family instead." Jack swallowed and his Adam's apple worked hard to get it down.

"Did he go to jail?"

"Not for that."

My hand covered my mouth. "Oh God. I'm so sorry, Jack."

He inclined his head to me, acknowledging my words. "There wasn't much left when the firefighters were done. But there was enough to give them a place here, to be remembered, at the family cemetery"—he pointed—"facing the sacred White Mountain."

His words drew my eyes upward, and I realized that the cemetery had a perfect view of Sierra Blanca Peak to the north, the jewel of the Sierra Blanca range. I swiveled my head around, searching, but the clouds blocked my other views. Thanks to Jack's cousin Mickey, I knew that to the southwest was the Three Sisters Mountains, to the northwest the Oscura Peak, and to the southeast the Guadalupe Mountains. The mountains provided a frame of reference for directions within the Mescalero Apache territory and were embodied in their sacred Mountain Spirits. I understood the placement of the cemetery now, and I was glad his family had found a resting place there.

"See the dark spot against that hillside?" I looked up and saw Jack was staring in the same direction as me, and that he was talking to me.

I peered again at the next hillside up the range. I did see a dark spot. "Yes."

"That's the old Sacramento Silver Mine. My family's occupation before my grandfather got us into horses."

"Like the photograph in your office?" He kept a black and white of an entrance to an old mine on his wall of fame back in Amarillo.

"Yep."

"That your wife took."

He turned to me, nodding. "The summer before she was killed."

"She was very talented."

He smiled with sad eyes. "Yes, she was."

Jack dismounted, stepping over to help Greg off of Buzz while still holding on to Jumper's reins. I hit the ground ready to give Farrah a hand, but she'd already slipped off Lilac's back on her own.

"What do I say to Jack?" she asked me, quietly.

I wiped my pooled tears and squeezed her arm. "Nothing." I shook my head. "There's nothing you can say, except you're sorry."

She walked toward the cemetery, as did Greg, but she paused to whisper something to Jack, who nodded and hugged her around the shoulders with one arm before she moved on. I watched as hers and Greg's paths converged. Greg opened the creaky little gate and they stopped in front of a headstone. Farrah knelt and rubbed snow from its face.

Jack turned, meeting me as I moved toward him, Jarhead following me. My arms wound around Jack of their own accord. He looped his around my waist, and I laid my head against his chest. "I am so sorry about your family."

He squeezed hard.

"I was wondering if you were ever going to tell me about them."

I felt his head nod. "I'm a little slow, but I get where I'm headed, eventually."

Jarhead's muzzle pressed into the back of my head.

"The horse is getting jealous," Jack said.

I laughed, softly, and rubbed my tears off on Jack's coat then held perfectly still, afraid of breaking the spell, of Jack's arms pulling away from me. I watched the two teenagers in the graveyard and listened to his heartbeat.

Greg called out, "There's an Indian name on this one."

Against my ear, Jack's voice rumbled in his chest. "My family is part Apache."

"Was your wife Apache?"

"No."

Farrah wiped another headstone. "Some people think I'm Indian, but not like your Indians here. Like from the country of India. I'm not, though. My family is mostly Syrian. Sometimes I think it would be easier if I *were* from India."

Greg's fists balled. "People blame her when they do bad things to her. They tell her it's because she's a Muslim, and that she and her family should go home."

Jack squeezed me tight again.

"Only I have no family. Not anymore. They were Muslim, but I've never even been to a mosque. Not that I remember, anyway. I've always been in 'Christian' foster care." She made quotes in the air around her head. "I want to learn more about the Koran someday. I think it would help me understand my family."

"So you don't have any family here in the U.S.?" I asked.

"No. My mother died in a car crash in Amarillo when I was little. My dad and brothers disappeared back home before I was born."

"I'm so sorry."

Jack turned toward the kids, one arm still around me. "Family makes us who we are, even after they're gone. If it were easy, we would be less."

My mind flitted to the father I took after, the one who had run away, and the mother I loved but was nothing like, the one who had stayed. To the family Jack had lost that still shaped him. To the fact that all of us here had lost the people closest to us.

Farrah nodded. "It's hard sometimes, but I wouldn't want to be someone else."

She stood up and walked through the plot, her hands trailing on the tops of the stones, her champion beside her.

Jack turned to me again, and this time he leaned down and pressed his lips against mine. They were warmer than I'd have expected out there, and so, so soft. Mine clung to his for long seconds. When the kiss ended, he pulled me to him again. I tried to swallow, but I couldn't get past the lump in my throat as I hung on to him for as long as I could.

***

Mickey and Laura leaned against the gold, rusty brown, blue-gray, and tan granite island countertop in Jack's kitchen. Or his parents' kitchen, rather, although they now traveled the states in an RV and only came home every year or three. Mickey had one arm around his dark wife's tiny waist, and he was nodding as Jack spoke. Snowflake gobbled down kibble from her silver bowl to their left, by the hallway to the garage. The kids were upstairs getting cleaned up, Farrah in my room, and Greg in Jack's.

"Emily took in some more lost children. These two are teenagers. A boy, George, who's fifteen, and a girl, Frannie, who's fourteen." It felt odd to hear their cover names from Jack's mouth. "They're runaways, and they're witnesses to a murder. We shouldn't have them, but we didn't know what else to do."

"Shouldn't have them like 'could go to jail for it,'" I said.

Jack nodded. "We'll have them here for the weekend, until we can figure out a plan for them."

Laura looked from Jack to me and back to Jack. "What about their families?"

I answered, stirring boiling pasta as I did. "Both of them said their parents are dead. No other family in the picture. They've had a terrible time of it."

She sucked her lips in and spoke in a softer voice. "Have they been in any trouble with the law?"

"Only for running away from abusive living situations." I lowered my voice, too. "Don't get me wrong. They're tough and savvy. There's probably not much Gr—George wouldn't do to protect Frannie."

My timer started ringing. I turned it and the gas off and grabbed a strainer.

Mickey and Laura looked at each other, and she nodded at him, shaking her sleek, brown bobbed hair.

He spoke. "Are they . . . intimate?"

I poured the pasta into the strainer over the sink, then turned on the cold water to rinse the noodles. "I don't know. They don't act like it, but then again, all they have is each other, and they're human."

Jack had on an apron with a cowboy Santa on it, and he slipped on a matching oven mitt. "I wondered if you guys wanted to shepherd them for a week or two, before I asked anyone else, because, well—" He stood there, his mouth open but no more words coming out.

"It's okay to say it, Jack." Mickey put his other arm around Laura, and he squeezed her to him. "Because you know we want kids but haven't been able to have any of our own."

"Yet," Laura said in a fierce voice from inside his bear hug. "I'm retiring, and the doctor is hopeful that when I gain weight I'll have better luck." Sinewy muscle defined Laura's body, and there wasn't an ounce of fat on her anywhere.

"And because I couldn't think of anyone I'd trust more with kids we aren't supposed to have that need protection." Jack opened the oven door and peeked in. "The garlic bread needs a few more minutes." He shut the door. "Plus you've already had the foster training, haven't you?"

"No." Laura extricated herself from her bear.

Mickey looked down. "I jumped the gun on that. We weren't ready."

Laura's stiff body language and crossed arms left little doubt as to who wasn't ready of the two of them, then or now.

Jack didn't seem to notice the dissonance in the room. Back when I was an active horsewoman, I'd known this vibe well. It was the feeling I'd get when saddle breaking a young horse, like once when I was forcing a filly to accept a saddle cinch. She was scared, and her eyes were wide and white rimmed. It was a sign to step back, to let things progress at a speed she was more comfortable with, so that she learned to give in instead of fight. I'd praised her and given her time to think about the saddle cinch loose around her belly, and an hour later, she'd let me tighten it without a fuss while she chewed the apple treats she'd taken out of my hand.

"No need to make any decisions now," I said, as I poured the pasta back into the pot and dumped half a jar of pesto into it. I stirred it briskly with a wooden spoon, shaking a blend of Romano and Parmesan cheese in as I did, trying not to look like I was desperate to hear them say they'd host the kids. Snowflake showed up at my ankles, hopeful that I would spill a little cheese near her mouth. I pinched some and dropped it to the floor. She scarfed it up.

I saw Laura's chest heave, and she moved an inch back toward Mickey. "It's really bad timing for us."

I could hear the wind outside and icy individual snowflakes pelting the window, the heater cycling on, and the dishwasher running with the load of lunch dishes. I'd forgotten to turn it on until we started cooking dinner. Jack and Mickey didn't make a sound.

"I understand." I did, even if I didn't like it and prayed she'd change her mind.

Footsteps thumped down the stairs. Greg appeared, looking both ways at the bottom. To his right was the great room.

I hailed him from his left. "In here."

He grinned and ducked his head. Water glistened in his hair, and I realized he didn't have on his grimy cap. He shuffled into the kitchen, hands deep in the pockets of Jack's too-large maroon New Mexico State University sweat pants. Snowflake pranced to meet him, and he bent down to ruffle her ears. "Where's Far—"

I hurried to cover his slip. "Frannie's still upstairs. George, this is Jack's cousin Mickey and his wife, Laura."

Greg stood up. "Whoa, now I can see what you meant about part of your family is Apache."

We laughed. Mickey had long black hair that he wore tied back low in a leather thong accented with silver and turquoise. He couldn't have looked more Native American if he'd had on a full-feathered headdress.

Greg blushed. "Nice to meet you, sir." He held out his hand, and Mickey shook it. He nodded his head at Laura. "And you, too, ma'am."

"Nice to meet you," Mickey replied.

Laura smiled weakly at Greg.

I walked the pot of pasta to the table and set it down. "We're having pasta, garlic bread, and a salad. I put some plates and silverware here on the table. Could you set them out in six places?"

"Okay. I mean, yes, ma'am." Greg's sudden company manners were endearing.

"Thanks. There are napkins out for each place setting, too."

Jack pulled two bottles of salad dressing out of the refrigerator. As he walked toward the table with them he said, "Well, there she is."

We all looked up to see the diminutive Farrah in the kitchen entry, nearest Laura. The girl could have been her twin, twenty years before.

Farrah lifted her hand in a wave. "Hi."

Laura whipped her head toward Mickey, her eyes welling with tears.

Chapter Fourteen

The six of us shared cleanup duties after dinner. Afterwards, Jack showed the teens how to operate the electronics in the living room, and soon the sounds of a horror movie's overly dramatic soundtrack echoed off the walls and ceiling. Amused, I walked to the staircase to take a look into the great room. Jack's mother had plastered family photographs over the entire far wall. In the corner nearest the floor-to-ceiling windows looking out on the Sierra Blanca and Sacramento Mountains stood an enormous Christmas tree. I'd gotten a close-up of it earlier, and someone had strung it with popcorn and barbed wire, burlap ribbons, apples, and metal ornaments in the shape of the Wrong Turn Ranch "WTR" brand. Gold twinkled from it, the only illumination in the high-ceilinged room now, other than ambient light from the kitchen and the TV screen. Shadows loomed off the ceiling beams, and darkness hugged the corners like a blanket around the shoulders of the room. From the reflected glow of the screen, I saw one dark head, a small dark body, and one slightly lighter head and slightly larger white body, plus a white blob where Snowflake had opted to hold the couch down between the two of them.

I couldn't help but compare it to my own childhood Christmases, and it made me miss my dad. I remembered the year I found a bridle under the tree with instructions to go look in the little barn in the pasture behind our house. My first pony awaited me there. He was feisty, white, and just right. Dad had given me a leg up to his bare back, and I'd thrown my arms around his neck, my face buried in his scratchy mane.

"Well, what are you going to name him?" Dad had asked.

I had known his name from the moment I'd laid eyes on him. "Cotton," I said reverently.

More than twenty years later, my eyes teared up at the memory. I had outgrown Cotton, and the pony had moved on to another home and another child long before my father left. I shook myself and wiped my eyes. It wouldn't do to sully the present with memories of a past I couldn't change.

Jack walked up to me.

"They look contented," I said.

"Yep." He put his hand on my shoulder, which made me want to kiss him again, but Jack gave me a slight tug, then released my shoulder. We returned to the kitchen together. He went behind the breakfast bar and I stayed on its near side.

"Coffee, anyone?" Jack asked.

Mickey, Laura, and I raised our hands.

He laughed. "I'll leave the Tylenol PM out on the counter."

He added water to the coffee maker and opened the bag of cinnamon roasted beans that I loved. He filled the well of his coffee grinder and pulsed the on button. The machine whirred and grred and whined. He turned it over and tapped the side until the soft ground coffee fell into the removable clear lid, which he in turn dumped into the gold filter in the swing arm of the coffee maker. He popped the arm shut and hit the start button. Seconds later the gurgling and drizzling started, and the wonderful toasty aroma filled the kitchen.

I sat down at one of the cowhide-covered stools at the breakfast bar, feeling only a little bit guilty as Jack retrieved four tan WTR-branded porcelain mugs from the cabinet. "Do you need help?"

"Nope. I'm about done."

I watched, transfixed as he grabbed a carton of Half & Half from the refrigerator and set it beside the antiqued wooden tray that remained permanently on the granite counter. It held a tub of sugar cubes in white and golden brown, honey, cinnamon, a crock of stirring sticks, and a bowl with yellow and pink fake sugar packets in it.

He caught the direction of my gaze. "My mother's setup."

"It's great."

Mickey came around for two mugs. "Yeah, good ole Aunt Nell has never done coffee halfway, Standing Hair." He winked at me, teasing me with the "Apache name" he'd christened me with on my last visit, in reference to my bangs.

Mickey poured two coffees and added cream, brown sugar cubes, and cinnamon, then stirred them. He walked one mug over to Laura and kept the other for himself.

"Thanks, hon," Laura said.

I filled the spot Mickey had vacated by the pot and prepared my cup. A generous splash of cream went in first, then a shake of cinnamon and two packets of pink stuff. I topped it with coffee, not bothering to stir. I sunk my face in the mouth of the mug and inhaled. Deep, dark, wonderful scents flooded my olfactory system and I sighed. Better than red wine. Or at least as good as.

As if he'd read my mind, Jack said, "I'm getting old—or rude. Beer or wine?"

Mickey and Laura looked at each other and shook their heads. He said, "None for us tonight."

I remembered the last time I'd been here, how much we'd all had to drink, how the company had cheered me up, and how well the night had gone—despite the fact that I was recovering from surgery post-miscarriage and tube rupture—until my friend Collin got too drunk and made a pass at me and a donkey's fanny out of himself. And then? After a wonderful night with Jack, how poorly the next day went. Jack had gotten the wrong idea about Collin and me. Mickey and Laura had barely spoken to me that day, and it had marked the beginning and the end of Jack's and my fledgling relationship, until the flickers of the last few days. I sure as shootin' wasn't messing things up with him again.

I shook my head, holding in a sigh. "I'll pass, too."

"Mickey, do you mind looking at a few things with me in the office?" Jack sounded casual, but my radar went up. I'd seen the office on the far side of the great room—with its shelves of books and big desk and high-backed leather chair—on my last visit, but no one had used it in my previous two visits.

Mickey kissed Laura on the lips. "No problem. Let me top off my cup, first."

The men left and my ears followed them. I didn't want to be left alone in the kitchen with Laura, with this awkwardness. We hadn't seen each other in the two months since that very bad day. Our last conversation hadn't gone well, and she was partly responsible for the bad information Jack got about Collin. I didn't blame her, though. Most of the fault was mine—well, Collin's, really—and Jack was her family. I had just been some new employee of his that no one really knew. She was at the table behind me, and I stayed facing the kitchen, sipping my coffee, trying to decide how to handle our sudden pairing.

"Hey, what are you guys watching?" I heard Mickey saying, in the living room.

Farrah answered. "*The Fourth Kind.*"

"Well, I gotta warn you, that's some seriously bad medicine."

"What is?" Her voice sounded worried.

"That owl there, with his head rotating all the way around." I knew what he was talking about. I hated horror movies, but I'd watched *The Fourth Kind* with Rich, and that scene with the owl's head rotating around freaked me out. "You're in Mescalero Apache country, and around here, owls are like ogres. They carry off little children. I wouldn't be watching a movie about owls if I were you."

Farrah laughed, sounding relieved. "It's not about an owl. It's about alien abductions in Alaska. You should talk to Gr—George, though, because he used to play this game called Owlman." She made an ooooooo-ooooooooo sound.

"Shut up," Greg said. I smiled into my coffee cup.

"Well, all I know is that in our legends, the Coyote is the only one ever to defeat the Owl."

Farrah laughed. "Yeah, George never won when he played Owlman either."

Sounds of scuffling in the great room broke out.

Laura spoke, tearing my attention away from their shenanigans. "You'll never guess who I ran into in Alamogordo last week."

The universe of southern New Mexico residents we both knew was small. I could count the ones I was acquainted with on one hand, and most of them were present tonight. But I rotated my barstool to face her and pretended to be stumped. "Who?"

"Tamara." Collin's fiancée, or ex-fiancée, rather. An army pilot. She'd dumped him after he cornered and kissed me, right upstairs.

"How is she?"

"She's great. She said she's been dating a UFC fighter."

"Not Collin?" Collin had vowed to win her back last time I'd talked to him.

"Nope. She said she doesn't believe he'll ever change, and she doesn't want to be the woman he resented for trying to make him into someone he isn't. I would have thought you'd have known." She looked down at her hands around her mug.

"No, I haven't talked to either of them since—well, since the last time I talked to you."

She ran her bottom teeth over her upper lip. "You and Collin didn't date?"

"Heavens no. Never. We've been close family friends for years, but after that weekend, I haven't even talked to him. He knows I am none too happy with him."

Laura frowned, her black eyes dark and deep. "I'm sorry about what happened with you and Jack, and any part I had in it. Mickey and I are a bit protective when it comes to him."

I nodded once. "A bit" was an understatement, but I couldn't pretend I didn't long for family bonds like theirs. "What matters is that I found Betsy and got her back safely that weekend. I try to forget the rest."

Laura smiled. "How is Betsy?"

"Good, I think. I don't get to see her. She lives with an ultrareligious foster family who has weird rules. But when I talk to her, she always mentions how she misses that horse we rode in our getaway. Thunder."

"He's here, you know."

"What? Where?"

"In the stable, actually. No one ever asked for him, and we couldn't stomach the idea of sending him back over there to Paul's place. The police had arrested everything that moved over there, and the future of the animals was so uncertain. We think of it as a rescue."

"I'm so glad. What happened to Paul's daughter?" His teenager had facilitated our rescue by breaking us out and giving us Thunder. She hated her father, and it turned out she was right to feel as she did about him. He was a monster, trafficking, enslaving, and selling off Mexicans desperate to live in the U.S.

"She went to live with her grandmother in Alamogordo, I hear. Her mother's mother." Laura nodded. "If I thought that it would have helped her in any way, I would have given Thunder back, but the girl was in the same fix the animals were."

I wrapped my fingers around my mug. It was still warm. "Betsy's going to be happy to hear Thunder was rescued. It was amazing how she fell in love with him that night. She was scared of him at first, of course, but within minutes he had this mesmerizing effect on her. She was calmer and more confident."

Laura finished a sip of coffee, then smiled. "That happens. We've sold some of our older horses to an equitherapy group."

"Equitherapy?"

"Equine therapy, for humans. It's basically pairing damaged souls with gentle horses, and letting the magic you're describing happen."

"Lilac had a similar impact on . . . Frannie. The girl's been physically and mentally abused, really suffered from the bad things people have done."

Laura peered closely at me. "Sexual abuse?"

"Apparently so."

"Geez. Poor thing."

"Yeah.

Laura closed her eyes for several seconds, then sighed as she reopened them. "Well, enough of that serious stuff." She stood. "Little girl's room. Back in a flash."

I was alone in the kitchen, and I felt it. I wandered into the great room. Greg and Farrah were asleep in front of the movie, her head on his shoulder, his head on her head, and the sleeping Snowflake evenly distributed between their laps. I grabbed an afghan from the arm of a giant club chair and draped it across their legs, then moved on toward the office. I'd never entered it before, and I stood to the side of the door now. I could hear Jack talking inside.

"Besides the saddle, there was a box of our stuff. I'm not sure I got it all. If I can get an inventory, I'll go back and see."

I inched closer and heard Mickey.

"No problem. Any ideas where he got it?"

"Not yet."

"So, have you told Emily about—"

I stepped in. "Hi, guys. Has Jack told me what?"

Both men stared at me like I was Medusa. Jack stood beside a desk whose top appeared to be made of reclaimed lumber. He rubbed at something on its bare surface with his thumb, eyes downcast. "Uh, I was telling Mickey about what we found at Alan's shop."

Jack's cheeks puckered, and his eyes shifted around the room, landing everywhere but on my face. To the grandfather clock by the French doors, to the black iron stove by the window, to the plaid wing chairs facing the desk.

"Why do you look like that?" I said, and then realized how loud my voice was. Like yelling loud. Whoops.

"Like what? I don't look like anything."

But he did.

Mickey said, "Jack told me that your client ended up with our Wrong Turn Ranch things, and that, um, he's basically being forced to sell stolen merchandise."

I slitted my eyes back and forth between them. They looked and sounded skittish, like two colts before a thunderstorm. I leaned against the built-in bookshelves and crossed my arms over my chest.

"So Mickey and I were discussing the robbery here, and how we'd thought it was an inside job. And we still think it probably was. But now it seems maybe it's connected to something bigger."

"Hey, guys, what's going on?" Greg walked in, rubbing his eyes, with Farrah stumbling along behind him. She was holding a yawning Snowflake in her arms.

"I heard loud voices. Did the party move down the hall?" Laura slipped in behind them and walked across to Mickey, who was standing by the stove. She moved slightly in front of him, facing me, and it registered on me how wan she looked. Mickey pulled her closer against his chest.

I recapped quickly. "Mickey and Jack were talking about how our client, who is being forced to sell stolen goods, was coincidentally selling stuff that was stolen from here."

"Whoa," Greg said.

To Jack, I said, "So, someone that works here is involved, you think?"

"Possibly."

"Do you know who it is?"

Mickey said, "We think so, but he bolted."

"What do the police think?"

"We didn't report it." Mickey released Laura and shoved his hands in his back pockets, swaying from foot to foot.

"Why not?"

He huffed out a tense breath. "It's possible we're wrong, and we don't want to get a good guy in trouble if we are." He shook his head, opened his mouth, then shook his head again.

Jack stepped over to me and put a hand on my upper arm. "It's complicated. You're going to have to trust me on this. Okay?"

I looked around me. Usually I loved it when Jack touched me, but every eye was on me, and I felt conspicuous. Why should I trust Jack, I wondered, when it seemed he and Mickey—and probably Laura—all knew something I didn't? But it was his ranch, and his law firm, and, honestly, while he wasn't very open with me about his personal life, he wasn't untrustworthy, per se. His family trusted him. His secretary, Judith, trusted him. In fact, everyone in his life seemed almost fanatically loyal to him. I sighed, and as I did, I felt a little vertigo, like I was on the back of a horse that had spooked out from under me.

"Okay," I said. "I'll trust you." I turned and walked out.

Chapter Fifteen

The next morning, the kids were still wearing the same clothes we'd found for them the evening before. They sat side by side at the big plank table in the kitchen. Greg's eyes drooped and Farrah's were closed completely. Snowflake snuggled in Farrah's lap. Jack was in the kitchen, leaning toward them across the breakfast bar. I grabbed a mug of coffee and joined the kids. Even though they were right in front of them, neither appeared to have noticed the names carved into the table: JACKSON. JULIA. The names of Jack's children. I could hardly look at the etching without getting emotional, myself, especially after Jack's story yesterday.

I cleared my throat, and four eyes opened, a little, and looked in my direction. "Jack and I are joining Mickey and Laura for church this morning. We'd love for you to come, too, if you're willing."

Neither kid reacted, and I took one sip, then two. "After our talk yesterday, I didn't want to force it on you, um, Frannie."

She blinked. "No one has ever asked me if it was okay before."

I smiled at her.

"Yeah, it's cool. I figure there's one God and he probably would rather me do something instead of nothing."

I laughed. "Me, too. I've been trying to find the right place for myself to do something back home."

"How long have you been looking?"

Since I was twenty-one. I did the math. "Nine years."

Jack's voice came from behind me. "Where all have you tried in Amarillo?" I heard a pop from the toaster.

"Well, Believers, of course, because of my mother. I've given it several tries actually, but I'm too different. Then Unitarian with Wallace, but there, I don't think I'm different enough."

Greg snorted. "You want different? Our last foster family made us go with them to Mighty is His Word. That new place halfway to Oklahoma. Weird as shit."

"I think I can pass on 'weird as shit.'" I laughed. "What do you mean by weird, though, like what kind of stuff?"

"They hate everybody. They make you sign pledges to go to war—that's what they call it—against other religions, anyone they think are sinners, people from other countries, which sucks, because Far—"

"Frannie?" I interrupted.

"Yeah, because Frannie was right there."

"That does suck. And suddenly my mother's Believers sound pretty normal after all."

Jack brought a plate stacked with cinnamon-raisin bread in one hand and a tub of butter with a knife in the other. Two young hands snagged toast almost before the plate hit the table. I grabbed a piece, too.

"I can promise you the church we're going to today is nothing like that." Jack returned to the kitchen. "Orange juice in a pitcher and some glasses on the counter. We leave in half an hour."

No one answered him. We were already chewing. Jack brought a mug of coffee and glass of orange juice to the table and joined us. I had so hoped that Laura and Mickey would change their minds about the kids, but the time had come to address the fact that the plane was heading back to Amarillo after church, and that the kids needed to be on it.

"Listen, guys, Jack and I are flying back to Amarillo after church," I said.

I heard a door open and close in the front of the house. Footsteps approached.

"Morning," Jack shouted.

Laura turned toward us down the hall from the entryway. "Morning." She had a little color in her cheeks.

"Good morning," the kids and I chorused.

Farrah immediately redirected us to the topic we'd been discussing. "What are we going to do when you go back to Amarillo?" She held her toast poised in the air, but she didn't take a bite.

Laura took a seat at a barstool behind us. I turned to look at Jack beside me at the table, but he kept his eyes on the plated toast in front of him. I kicked his ankle and he jerked upward. When he looked at me, though, his eyes were so soft and helpless that I let him off the hook.

I chose my words carefully. "Well, I think the best thing to do is keep you with me, so you can ride back with us."

In a rush, Greg said, "Wait, what about—"

Laura spoke over him, to Jack, and Greg yielded to her. "Aren't you coming back here for Christmas?"

Ever verbose, Jack said, "Yep."

She nodded. "If it's okay with Emily, the kids could stay here and help us a little around the ranch. We don't pay a lot, but it's a good Winter Break job." She got up and walked around to the coffee setup. "Probably best if they stay at Mickey's and my house, though."

A moment of stunned silence followed her words. I had given up on her too soon. Not that Laura was a filly, but I couldn't help but think she'd taken to the cinch after all.

"Emily, please?" Farrah said. Her dark eyes bored into me.

"It would be so awesome," Greg added.

I wrinkled my face, pretending to think about it, and their wide eyes stayed on me like I was Santa Claus deciding if they'd been naughty or nice. "Well, I suppose so."

Happy noises erupted in the kitchen. Young arms grabbed me and hugged me, and my heart took flight.

***

Snowy fields flashed by on either side of the highway as we crossed onto the reservation. Jack, the kids, and I were following in the Suburban behind Mickey and Laura's Silverado. A steepled stone building about half a mile away rose out of the blanket of white, a hill tufted with snow-topped desert bushes behind it. ST. JOSEPH'S

APACHE MISSION PARISH, the sign read. An announcement bulletin with crooked letters spelled out DON'T LET WORRY KILL YOU OFF—LET THE CHURCH HELP. I wanted to giggle, but worried that it would be rude. I giggled anyway.

Farrah touched my shoulder. "What's so funny?" She was so pretty in a red dress Laura had loaned her.

I pointed to the announcement. She laughed, too, and her normally evasive eyes looked clear and happy. We pulled into the parking lot.

"You Catholic?" I asked Jack.

"I come here when I'm in town." He turned off the ignition.

Which didn't exactly answer my question. "Where do you go in Amarillo? St. Mary's?"

"No."

He opened his door and got out. So did I. Four doors slammed. Jack started walking toward the building with Greg beside him in jeans and a button-down shirt that would fit him in about ten years. Maybe. Laura and Mickey had parked closer in than we had, and we caught up with them.

"Good morning, Mickey," I said.

Mickey smiled. "Hey, everyone. We're only going to be five minutes late. That's good for us."

Laura's olive cheeks had a rosy glow at the cheekbone, the kind from fresh air and improving spirits. Mickey had his hand on her shoulder.

A new voice interrupted us, from my left. "Begays. Holden. Good to see you this morning."

All heads swiveled toward the voice. It was from a man, Apache, best I could tell, and tall. Maybe six foot two? He had a large, bony frame with broad shoulders and huge hands. Pits covered his cheeks. Teenage acne, it looked like. The pits were so big they made me think of smallpox, but I didn't think that was a possibility in the states anymore.

Mickey stuck out a hand. "Here for work or worship, Brown?"

They shook.

"Worship, although you never know." He pecked Laura's cheek and shook Jack's hand next. "Who are your friends?"

Mickey nodded his head at me. "Emily." Then at Greg and Farrah. "George and Frannie." He then nodded at the man. "Edward Brown, Alamogordo Police."

Out of the corner of my eye, I saw Farrah slip her hand into Greg's.

I smiled to hide the nerves that shot through me. A cop, when I was smack in the middle of the commission of felony runaway harboring. "Nice to meet you."

"Likewise."

The kids didn't speak. I rubbed my hands against the cold. I hadn't worn gloves, since we would be going straight from the vehicle to church, just my heaviest shawl over a sweater and pants. The wind was picking up, tossing the hair I had worn down. Luckily the skies were clear for our flight.

Jack started walking again, so we all did. "Let's get inside before it's over," he said.

Brown fell in beside him and kept his eyes on Jack's profile. "Haven't found any more dead Mexicans on your place lately, have you?"

I bristled. If I wasn't mistaken, so did Mickey, Jack, and Laura. I assumed Brown was referring, however rudely, to Betsy's father, who died a few months ago on Jack's land, after he was beaten and escaped from Johnson's place.

"All's quiet." If Brown's comment had bothered him, Jack's voice didn't give any feelings away, but, then, it rarely did.

"Hadn't seen you in, what, fifteen years before that?"

"Something like that."

Brown turned to Mickey. "I'll never forget it. Got a call about shots fired in a residence in town from a concerned neighbor. When we showed up, we found one dead, one injured." He grinned at Laura and me. "The refrigerator dead, ADA Holden injured."

"It was an accident," Jack said, his voice tight.

Brown laughed out loud. "People still tell that story. Drunken Assistant District Attorney, a local boy who should know better, shoots himself through the hand and takes out his wife's brand new refrigerator."

The scar, I realized. This was what caused the scar on his palm that I'd noticed a few days ago at the police station. Jack's tension was now palpable. None of us laughed. I itched to shake my finger at Brown for humiliating Jack, and my right fist clenched and unclenched.

"My gun had jammed. I was cleaning it."

"Shoulda charged you for shooting an unarmed refrigerator." Brown winked, and I cringed. "Let you see how your defendants felt."

Jack's anger was like a blast of heat from a furnace. I wanted to do something, anything, but I didn't want to make it worse. Before I could decide on a course of action, Mickey dropped back, letting Brown, Jack, and Laura lead on.

He lowered his voice, speaking to the kids, although I could hear as well. "You guys ready to learn how to do a little work on a horse ranch?"

I smiled at how naturally he had solved half the problem, distracting the teenagers from the unfriendly interaction ahead of them. My eyes followed Jack, hoping Laura managed to change the subject.

Farrah's eyes lit up like someone had struck a match inside them. "I can't wait."

Greg swallowed. "Yeah, sure."

Watching Jack the whole time, I said, "George will probably like the horses a lot better with both his own feet on the ground for a while."

Mickey clapped him on the back. "That can be arranged."

Farrah fell in step beside me as we climbed the front steps to the church door. "When will you be back?"

"Within a week. You'll be so tired and busy you probably won't even notice I'm gone." I dropped my voice to a whisper. "And hopefully the police will catch the shooter by then, and we can bring you guys back to Amarillo."

Greg caught the door from Jack. He and Farrah shared a look as she walked past him. They didn't have to say a word for me to realize they'd agreed "not over our dead bodies."

Chapter Sixteen

I got to Williams & Associates the next morning a little later than usual. An enormous fruit basket sat on my desk. Oranges, grapefruits, and apples surrounded a pineapple in a nest of crinkly paper shavings. There wasn't just fruit, though. I touched a wedge of cheddar in red wax and Monterey Jack in green. Walnuts and pecans in-the-shell filled the empty spaces between the pieces of fruit and cheese. A huge red and green bow graced the handle of the basket and a card in an envelope protruded from the display on a plastic stick. I pulled it out and read quickly.

Merry Christmas. Present under the fruit. Your ex, Rich.

I raised an eyebrow. I hadn't gotten him anything, but what was the appropriate gift for the husband who had spent all the money in your joint accounts on his new love? Coal? Still, this was nice. I lined the contents of the basket up on my desk piece by piece then shoveled out paper shavings into the garbage until I came to a flat manila envelope at the bottom. I shook a few last nuts off, then extracted the stapled papers from inside.

Our divorce papers. I flipped to the end. He had signed. So had the judge. A yellow sticky beside his name read: *Congratulations. You have managed to get rid of me. RB.* More like he was rid of me, although he had tried to halt the divorce when he'd learned I was pregnant. After I'd lost the baby and cut off contact with him, he hadn't bothered me again, until now. And I didn't mind this kind of bothering at all.

"Merry Christmas, me," I said aloud.

Belatedly, Snowflake appeared, trotting over to the desk. She put her front paws up on its sides, attempting to get a look at the bounty on top.

"So, girl, you're falling down on the job, not even meeting me at the door today." I ruffled her fur and she sniffed the air, searching for foods dogs like to eat. "Don't bother. Dogs aren't into fruits and nuts."

I'd have to hide the cheese from her. Dogs were way into cheese. I pulled her crusts from a napkin in my purse. "Sit." Her bottom hovered a millimeter above the ground, wiggling. I tossed her the toast.

Jack came down the hall, whistling "Jingle Bells."

"Morning," I said, before I saw him.

"More like good afternoon." He walked barefooted to the couch in his worn jeans and untucked red and blue flannel snap-front shirt, holding his briefcase. He sunk to the couch, put down his case, and pulled on his ancient boots, which I hadn't noticed sitting there before. Then he stepped over to my desk with his briefcase, set it down, and whisked an apple into one of his loose shirttails. He polished the fruit, flashing a little olive-toned ab as he did.

My throat closed. I fought to swallow. "I must not be too late since you're still half-naked." It sounded like I was talking through a wad of cotton. I cleared my throat. "That came out wrong. What I meant was ten percent naked." I shook my head, heat flaring into my face. "Not that I mind." I groaned.

He laughed and took a bite of apple. Juice dripped onto his chin. My throat closed up again.

I shook my head. "I need coffee."

He waved the apple at the basket. "What'd'ya get?"

"Signed divorce papers."

He nodded, his lower lip pushed out in a contemplative expression. "Cause for celebration."

I picked up a Redrope accordion file and straightened the papers inside. "It *is* a time for me to celebrate."

He didn't seem to get my drift. "Have you heard from your 'family friends' in New Mexico?"

I kept myself from pouting by sheer force of will. "No. I'll text Laura later and see how they're doing." And then I remembered. "Well, I can email her I guess, since I have no phone."

Jack frowned at me, creasing his forehead tight. "You haven't taken care of your phone yet?"

"Um, no, I was going to do it Friday, and then with Greg and Farrah—"

"You mean George and Frannie?"

"Yes, right, George and Frannie." I put my hands out to my sides, palms up. "I forgot about the phone."

"If the cops still have your phone, they can read anything new you get."

"I thought you said a police officer would have known to take out the SIM card and deactivate it?"

"I don't *know* what they did with it. They *could* have deactivated it. Or they *could* be turning it on occasionally to check your new messages."

He was right, and I'd missed it. "Ugh. I'll take care of it."

"Okay. On that topic, I'm heading out to file the complaint against Burrows and Samson. You need anything?"

I licked my lips. Um, yeah, a kiss would be nice. But I wasn't going to tell him about it if he couldn't figure it out himself. "I think I'm good."

"We'll talk when I get back."

"About?"

He looked at the ground. "A few things." With one hand, he tucked his shirt in. "I shouldn't be long." He took a few steps backwards toward the front door. "Oh, and thanks for getting yourself arrested. This is the highlight of my week."

I raised my eyes to the ceiling, shaking my head. "Glad to provide the entertainment."

He nodded. "You do that." He waved and was gone.

I fanned myself with my hand. The electricity between Jack and me had recharged considerably in the last week, and I was beginning to think he believed in second chances after all. We'd made progress in New Mexico. Now I had to figure out how to nudge him along further, especially since I was a free woman.

I had made a to-do list over toast and coffee with Mother that morning, while she read the paper. It read:

1) Work on discovery requests for Betsy's survivor action

2) Call orthodontist

3) Continue work on Freeman trial notebook

4) Work on discovery responses for Escalante

Escalante was a client with an armed-robbery trial coming up in a few months. In fact, I was expecting him to drop by and help me with his responses sometime today. I jotted a number five:

5) Report phone missing and get new one

The door swept open, and Nadine waltzed in. The first thing I noticed was she'd ditched her nose ring. Her black hair was tied back in a brilliant red scarf, its long ends hanging, but most of it had come loose. The baby pieces around her head were electrified. Static electricity in the cold, dry Panhandle winters was not a thing to trifle with.

I pulled a can of Static Guard out of my desk drawer and held it out. "Look what blew in."

She grabbed it. "Literally. Have you been out there in the last hour? It's practically a tornado." She sprayed liberally and handed it back to me.

"Two words: Aqua Net." I put the can back in the drawer.

She snorted and plopped down on the couch. Nadine stood about five foot ten—six feet in the black biker boots she had on with her jeans today—and most people would describe her as voluptuous. Very voluptuous. On top of that, she could probably kick my butt with one hand tied behind her back. I loved that about her, that and every one of her thirteen tattoos.

She tilted her head and stared at me. "Hey, you're blushing."

More heat suffused my cheeks. "Too heavy-handed with the makeup this morning, I guess."

She patted her chest. "No, I'm pretty sure it's all the way down to your rack."

My hand grabbed the V-neck of my lavender pullover sweater.

She laughed. "Where's your hot boss?"

"He just left."

"Ah, well, there you go."

I shrugged, noncommittal, but her smirk told me I wasn't fooling her.

The door opened slowly. Counting the fruit delivery this morning, this was our third visitor today. That tripled our daily average, and it was only nine a.m. An ancient man struggled to create an opening wide enough for his skeletal frame.

"Clyde!" I jumped to my feet and rushed over. "How are you?"

The name partner of Williams & Associates righted himself, stretching to reach his full five foot two inches. He raised a tremulous hand. "Merry Christmas, my dear."

"Merry Christmas." I let the door shut behind him then followed him across the lobby/office. "Clyde, have you met my friend Nadine? She's here about one of our clients." I crossed my fingers behind my back, although in truth she might be. I just didn't know yet.

Nadine jumped to her feet, all her best parts jostling each other as they rearranged themselves.

Clyde stopped, his rheumy eyes wide as he studied her. "Well, aren't you a fine-looking woman." He inclined his head at her, his version of a courtly bow—I knew from experience.

"Nadine, Clyde is the founder of Williams and Associates."

She smiled wide. Nadine had an incredible smile, with sparkly teeth from here to Dallas and back. "Thank you. So pleased to meet you, sir."

Clyde waved at her to sit, and she did, which he took the time to watch and appreciate before he resumed his walk. All told, he made it from the door to the chair in front of my desk in three minutes flat, a record for him. I suspected he was trying to impress Nadine. He put his hand on the back of the chair.

"What can I do for you, Clyde?"

"Jack called me for a consult. Is he around?"

"No, but he won't be long. Do you want to wait? If so, I'll let him know you're here."

"If you don't mind, dear." He hung his cane on the arm of the chair and positioned himself in front of it in tiny sidesteps. He put both hands behind him to catch the arms and began to lower himself, slowly, slowly. I couldn't breathe during this process. Jack wouldn't let me help Clyde, but that didn't mean I didn't worry and wish I could. I'd hate for him to break a hip on my watch. Clyde's hands gripped the chair's arms on his descent, arresting his fall. He settled in, and I resumed normal respiration.

Clyde turned to Nadine to flirt and I returned to my desk and typed an email to my boss:

Clyde here!!! Says you called for consult. He's waiting for you in front of my desk. Hurry? ☺

The front door to the office whooshed open for visitor number four. If this kept up, I'd have to start charging admission. Or lock the door and hide in Jack's office, so I could get something done. I hit send and looked up. Phil Escalante, one of our clients, was taking off his jacket by the doorway.

"Phil! Come on in. We're having a pre-Christmas get-together."

Phil grinned. "I forgot my fruitcake. You sure I'm welcome?" Phil wasn't a tall guy, but he made up for size in big personality and a lot of muscle. Not that there wasn't a goodly layer of insulation to his bulk, too, thanks to the fact that he approached everything in his life with gusto. Food, laughter, women, and booze. In fact, his trouble with the law related back to his enthusiasms. He ran a private swingers' club. It had attracted the ire of a militant religious group who'd started harassing them outside their events. Phil had broken into the home of the group's leader, looking for information to help fend them off, but he'd been caught, and charged with B&E and attempted burglary.

I gestured at my fruit basket. "I've got you covered."

Nadine stood again, and something about the way she moved caught my eye. She rubbed her lips together, then they fell apart slightly. She rolled her shoulders back, which did something magical to her chest, apparently, because Clyde nearly fell out of his chair, and Phil's attention moved from me to her in a flash of lightning. He froze for a full five seconds without breathing.

I broke the spell. "Phil, this is Nadine. Nadine, our client, Phil."

Phil moved to Nadine. She towered over him, although he was a good half a foot taller than Clyde. "So that's your name. Nadine." He took her hand, not like a handshake, like a caress. His hand dwarfed hers. My mouth fell open, and I gawked.

She smiled, but didn't. Like Mona Lisa. "Hello, Phil."

Clyde gaped at the pair, too, eyes narrowed. I got the sense he was a little jealous. I felt a little dirty, like a voyeur.

"Um, Phil, if I could make one more introduction?"

Phil didn't relinquish Nadine's hand or gaze. "Yes?"

"This is Clyde Williams. He founded our law firm. So he's like Jack's boss. A very important figure in Texas civil rights and criminal defense."

Clyde straightened in his chair.

Phil got the hint. He swung fully toward the old man, and stuck out his hand. "So it's you I have to thank, sir. Jack is representing me, and I know I'm in the best of hands. Thank you, thank you so much."

Clyde shook. "It's our honor. To facilitate you exercising your right to due process and a speedy trial by a jury of your peers. We couldn't ask for anything more noble."

Clyde had a way of making me want to salute the flag. Only there wasn't one in there. I settled for beaming with pride at him.

"So, Phil, are you here to work on the discovery responses with me?" I asked.

"I am." He shot a suggestive glance at Nadine. "Then I have a lunch date."

She tittered, and if I'd have been holding a drink, it would have hit the floor.

Glancing back and forth between the two of them, I said to Phil, "Well, if you can give me a few minutes, there seems to be a line forming at my desk."

He moved over to the couch and stood by Nadine. "I think I could bear the wait if you could spare a seat on this couch beside you, Nadine?"

The two looked at each other in a way that made me really, really hungry for chocolate.

I waved at him. "Have a seat, Phil."

Phil bowed to Nadine, and she sat first, and he followed suit, very, very close beside her.

Time to get control of the room. "So, Nadine, you want to go first?"

She rubbed her lips together to moisten them, a coquettish move if I'd ever seen one. "I wanted to tell you how it went with Betsy this weekend."

To Clyde, I explained, "Betsy is the daughter of our deceased client Sofia Perez, who was murdered while incarcerated at Potter County Detention Center. We're filing a survivor action against the county on Betsy's behalf."

Clyde nodded. "Sofia. Betsy. Yes, good, good." He turned toward Nadine again, holding on to the armrest to keep himself facing her. "We're all ears, Nadine." More like all eyeballs—eyeballs to Nadine's cleavage. Nadine was holding her girls up high, so I was guessing she didn't mind all the male admiration.

"I made the Rainbow Room visit to her at the Hodges' place this weekend, like we'd discussed. I told them we were clearing out some items that we had to have off the books in 2014. Never mind that it didn't make any sense. They bought it." She smoothed one side of her wispy flyaways behind an ear. "I gave Betsy the backpack, but it didn't go all that well."

My stomach clenched. "No? What happened?"

"She started crying. She said she already had a backpack, that she lost it in "Mexico," and that her mama made her promise she'd never lose it, so her friend Emily was going to find it for her."

"Oh no."

"Oh yeah."

"I haven't the slightest clue where to find that backpack."

"Sounds like you'd better start looking anyway."

"For real."

"It got worse."

"Oh?"

"The Hodges. They are some weird-ass people. Their place is like the Stepford wives, Branch Davidian version."

Phil lunged forward in his seat. "Trevon and Mary Alice Hodges?"

Nadine turned to him. "Yes."

"They go to that Mighty is His Word church, the ones where the assholes that harassed me go."

My fists clenched in my lap. "We've got to figure out a reason to get her away from them."

Clyde shook his head. "Freedom of religion is an important right, too."

I lifted my shoulders and dropped them. "I wouldn't disagree with you, Clyde, but in this case, it's more like they're inflicting their religion on others. Which can have the effect of depriving others of *their* right to freedom of religion."

"Not to mention freedom of association," Phil added. "And freedom to make a legal buck."

I was impressed. Not all of our clients became so knowledgeable about the law, but Phil seemed to have it down. That, and a healthy capitalist spirit.

Clyde opened his mouth, but at that moment Jack burst in. I glanced at my computer screen. I'd missed his email reply, but it was there: *Tell him I'm on my way.*

"Hello, all. Clyde, good of you to drop by," Jack said.

The notion that Clyde could spontaneously drop by tickled me. Clyde had a home nurse, a housekeeper, and a driver, all of whom worked full time to keep him moving at all. He thrived on the law, though, and I knew that his continued involvement with the practice he loved kept him one foot out of the grave.

"How'd it go?" I let my eyes drink in the beautiful sight of Jack Holden as he answered.

"Crooked cop complaint filed. Red flag waved at bull. Or bulls, as the case may be." He held up a plastic bag. "And one missing mobile phone returned."

"What? They found my phone?"

He tossed it to me. "Surprise, surprise."

"I'm so glad I hadn't replaced it yet." I pulled it out of the bag and turned it on.

Nadine snorted. "What is it about the cops in this town? We've got one Asian cop that practically lives up at the Polo Club, and he's not there working security. He's a lousy tipper, too. And one of our dancers is so freaked out about a bad cop she won't even come to work."

I had certainly had my fill of bad cops this week, but the others I'd encountered here were fine. "The one I met when I got conked over the head last fall was good enough." The conking had occurred when I'd stumbled across a murder in progress, while I was trying to find Betsy. That cop—Wilson, maybe?—had a horrible mustache, but other than that he seemed nice. "Hopefully it's a minority of them."

"I'm not the one to vouch for that." Phil shook his head. "I can't get any help with those fanatics harassing me."

Clyde raised a fist in the air at least six inches above his lap. "There's a thin line between police and police state, and it's our job to guard that line." And with that, he collapsed in a heap in front of his chair.

Chapter Seventeen

"How're you doing, Clyde?" I lifted the gnome-like hand from the bed and squeezed it.

We were at the Southwest Hospital Emergency Room, three hours after he'd bit the dust at our offices. I glanced around the curtained space and shuddered. I'd logged more time here than I'd cared to last fall, and I didn't love being back.

Clyde waved his other hand at me. "A bunch of fuss about nothing. I've told these quacks I have to be home before dinner."

Jack and I shared a smile, and Clyde's regular home nurse, Betty, clucked. "Slow down, Mr. Williams. We're gonna see what the quacks have to say before we go making any plans."

If Betty ever left nursing, the beefy woman had a future in sumo wrestling. She certainly threw her weight around when it came to Clyde. She'd met us here minutes after we'd arrived and immediately taken charge. Clyde's driver was out in the waiting room. The two doted on Clyde. We all did, really.

"Low blood sugar. That's all it was. Low blood sugar."

"Maybe. Maybe not. Whatever it was, you can't go running off by yourself like that anymore, you hear me? You're lucky you didn't break a hip in that fall."

As Clyde started to wind up, Jack stepped between the two of them. "See you later, Clyde. Merry Christmas."

I saluted him. "Merry Christmas, sir."

Clyde's face softened. "Merry Christmas, you two." He motioned me over to him and I leaned close. "Tell Nadine I'm fine."

I nodded gravely.

Jack held the door to the room open and I exited. As soon as it shut, Clyde's voice resumed, arguing with Betty. I felt bad for the old guy, but I sided with her on this one. Thank God I'd had help around when Clyde fell. Getting old sucked, although it did beat the alternative.

Jack and I walked down the hall without speaking. I was hyper-aware of his nearness, in a good way. When we reached the door to the parking lot, I slipped on my jacket, and he took my arm. We exited together, walking to my car. The cold hadn't eased up, and the wind whipped against my face. I pulled the collar of my coat closed higher on my neck.

"The shop called. My Jeep is ready. Can you drop me by to get it?" he asked.

"Sure."

"After that, can you hold down the fort by yourself for a few hours?"

"Don't I always?"

He squeezed my arm. "You're taking Wednesday off, right?"

"It's Christmas Eve. I had planned to. Do you need something?" We approached my car and I pulled my keys from my pocket and clicked to unlock the doors.

"No, no. It's just, well, in case we don't get around to it before then, I thought maybe we could talk Wednesday night."

"Christmas Eve night?"

"Well, if you don't have plans."

"Other than it being Christmas Eve, you mean?"

"Maybe you could come to services at my church with me. And then we could talk."

I stood at the driver's side, hand on the door handle, Jack beside me. My heart stopped beating in my chest. After a slow count of three it exploded into a chaotic rhythm. Was Jack asking me out?

Jack shuffled his feet. "If you aren't already committed—"

"No, no. I'm not. I mean, yes, I'll go with you."

"Good. I'll pick you up at five thirty." He opened the door to my car.

I stood there beside him, smiling, floating, not sure if it was real yet. "Sounds perfect."

***

I sat in an examination chair in Dr. Parks's orthodontic office half an hour after dropping Jack at the mechanic. Large mauve flowers floating in a sea of green ivy assaulted me from walls in three directions. Apparently, Dr. Parks had consulted my mother for decorating tips.

The orthodontist probed inside my mouth and shook his head. "Well, can't say I didn't warn you. Oh, your poor mother. All that money, wasted." He removed his hands from my mouth, then pulled off his gloves finger by finger, snapping the rubber as he did so. "I can have a treatment plan together for you after Christmas. Martha will take all your X-rays now."

"Treatment plan? Can't I get another retainer?"

He shuddered. "Goodness no. What's there to retain? Your teeth are nowhere near alignment. But these days we can do wonders with products like Invisalign that work as well as traditional braces and are less obvious, in less time, too. No one will even notice you're wearing them."

"How long would I have to have them?"

"Well I haven't seen your films, but maybe six months."

"And the cost?"

"A few thousand. My office would get you the exact figures." He pushed his stool away and rolled across the floor.

I nearly gasped. I wanted to ask him why I needed to do this, but before I could he said, "Martha will be here shortly," and was gone.

"Thank you," I whispered to the empty room.

My head reeled. My bank account couldn't take that kind of hit. Every cent I had was accounted for in the adoption process and with the duplex. Even after Dr. Parks's dire predictions—and presumptions—a few days ago, I wasn't sure whether I wanted to do this. So what was I doing here? The X-rays would have to wait. I ripped the bib from my neck and got to my feet. I retrieved my purse and headed for the reception and billing area. I stopped at the window for checkout.

"Hello. My name is Emily Bernal. What is the charge for my exam today?"

The woman behind the counter had gray curls that lay flat against her skull like they'd been painted on. She peered up at me through half-glasses perched at the end of her nose. "Emily Phelps? It's me, Mrs. Parks. How are you?"

Of course. The orthodontist's wife had always worked with him. "Hello, I'm good. And you?"

"Dealing with the insurance companies gets harder every year, but, other than that, fairly well, thank you." Her eyes swept the desk in front of her. "I'm afraid I don't have your file."

"Well, Dr. Parks examined me, and Martha was going to do X-rays, but my office called, so I'm going to have to run." I held up my cell phone. "An emergency."

"We'll take care of the billing by mail then. Are you still at the same address?"

"Yes," I said through gritted teeth. That question was almost as bad as when the host at a restaurant said, "Just one, ma'am?"

"Would you like to reschedule your X-rays?"

"I'll call. Thank you and good-bye."

She waggled her fingers at me.

I turned to go, and as I did, I almost ran headlong into a man coming in through the exit door. "Excuse me," I said.

"Pardon me." Police uniform. Red hair. Full face. He kept walking.

I called after him, "Officer Burrows?"

He looked back at me, eyes narrowed. "Yes?"

Steam built up in my ears. "You don't even remember me, after what you did?"

"Hmmmm." He pulled a small flip notepad and pen from his pocket.

Hissssssssss went the steam. "You arrested me and took my phone?"

"I guess." Burrows scribbled something in his notepad.

"Officer Burrows?"

He looked up and snapped the notepad shut. "Take care, now." He walked briskly down the hall, away from me.

What the H-E-double-hockey-sticks was up with him?

Chapter Eighteen

After I left the orthodontist, I returned to the office. I unlocked the door and let myself in. Snowflake didn't run out to greet me, which was odd.

"Snowflake?"

No jingle of bells and dog tags. I was still a lot unsettled by my encounter with Burrows, and my heart pounded in my ears. I pulled the baby Glock from my purse. I knew Jack had said he wouldn't be here, but he hadn't said a word about the dog. I tiptoed down the hallway, moving cautiously up to and around the kitchen door, checking for intruders within. Nothing but the normal white refrigerator, white cabinets, and wooden-topped table and white chairs. I did the same at the door to Jack's office, dropping into a shooting stance on the far side of the doorway as I peered in. No one. I bent over and checked for feet under his massive desk.

Clear.

I put my gun away. I felt a little silly wielding it, but better safe than sorry. This is why I practiced at the gun range, every month since my father gave me the gun. If the situation called for it, I knew how to handle my weapon. "You got no business owning a gun if you can't use it properly," he'd said. I'd just never needed to use it, and I hoped I never did.

I made a mental note to remind Jack to tell me anytime Snowflake wouldn't be here, so I could skip the whole heart failure thing. I walked normally down the hall to my work area as the booming in my ears subsided to a thumping and then to nothing. When I got to my desk, my cell phone rang, its harsh sound making me jump. It wasn't my normal ringtone.

"Geez!" I fumbled in my purse for it. Another note to self: change the annoying ringtone. As I answered I saw the caller was UNKNOWN. "Hello?"

Someone cleared his throat, at least I thought it was a he from the sound of it, but honestly, I didn't have much to go on.

"Hello??"

The call dropped. Greg again? Surely not. The kids were safe on the Wrong Turn Ranch with Mickey and Laura. To be sure, I texted Laura: *How are things going?*

Her reply was almost instantaneous: *We're having fun! Been out riding with them, and now they're exploring on their own.*

Okay, so probably not the kids. My phone made another unfamiliar noise. I fumbled with it and saw that I had four voice mails. Scratch "change ringtone." I needed to reset all my notifications and sounds. I hadn't known I had messages. I played them, one by one. Two calls last week from an 806 number. That was probably the kids. Two calls today from an unknown number, one of which I had just experienced. Weird.

I put my purse away under the desk and booted up my computer. The background screen loaded Betsy's sweet face and a pang shot through my heart. It was time to tell Mother I was moving out. That wasn't a conversation I looked forward to having, although she'd understand why. I pulled up the network and clicked on the folder for Elizabet "Betsy" Perez and opened the draft complaint.

The office phone rang.

"Williams and Associates, Emily speaking."

"Emily, give me Jack."

I recognized the voice, but no way was I giving this woman the satisfaction of admitting it. In my slowest Amarillo accent, I said, "May I ask who's calling?"

A withering sigh rattled the phone line. "Assistant District Attorney Melinda Stafford. You may remember me. Now give me Jack."

I hadn't talked to my childhood nemesis Melinda since I socked her in the jaw for telling me my miscarriage of Rich's baby was "for the best." She had threatened to sue me, but Jack had paid her off, and had a little too much fun doing it. Melinda was one of the ADAs, so I had to play nice, though. At least a little bit.

"I'm sorry, Jack isn't available at the moment. May I take a message or assist you in any way?" The words and saccharin-sweet tone puckered my mouth.

"You can tell him to get control of his client, for one thing."

"I'm sorry, I don't know what you're talking about. Perhaps if you give me a client name and a brief description of the incident I can relay it to him?"

"Cut the crap, Emily. Alan Freeman was up here demanding to meet with me so he could make a plea bargain." She huffed. "He chose to work with your firm, so I'm not about to meet with him without Jack present. I had the receptionist send him packing."

I paused, long enough that I could have written a message, if I were so inclined. I wasn't. "Got it. Anything else?"

"Yeah. Tell him if he wants to get a plea bargain done, I'm off for the Christmas holidays as of six p.m. sharp today. Otherwise, he's gonna get his ass kicked in court after the New Year." She hung up.

"Merry frickin' Christmas to you, too, Melinda." I slammed the phone down in the cradle, and enjoyed it.

Jack was going to want to know this, stat. I picked the phone back up and pushed speed dial for his mobile. It went to voice mail. I ended the call and sent him a text message instead: *Call me ASAP. Alan went to Stafford asking for a plea bargain?? She's off for holidays after 6 today.*

What in God's name had gotten into Alan? When we'd talked to him the week before, he seemed antsy about having his fate still up in the air. He hadn't mentioned second thoughts, though. His case wasn't rock solid, but neither was the city's, and they had the burden of proving his guilt beyond a reasonable doubt. Assaulting Wu and resisting arrest were serious charges, and we trusted a jury of Freeman's peers to treat them as such, especially in the wake of Ferguson: Freeman was black, Wu was a half-white Asian, and they told two completely different stories, with no witnesses to the alleged assault. Freeman had no priors, and he was no thug. I had faith the jury wouldn't swallow Wu's version of events. Freeman had faith, too, as far as I'd known up until five minutes ago.

With difficulty, I wrenched my attention back to the complaint for Betsy. The beginning of a case really didn't reveal anything shocking or sexy. We were alleging wrongful death, that PCDC had caused Sofia's by not providing adequate supervision to prevent her murder by other inmates, and that their violent actions were foreseeable. The upfront process was formulaic and had to do with establishing the county's responsibility. Honestly, I'd never worked on one of these cases before and neither had Jack, so I spent a lot of time researching forms online. I had to keep reminding myself how important this lawsuit was to Betsy's future to keep myself awake long enough to finish the draft.

I worked steadily for all of two minutes when the door whispered open. Without Snowflake to alert me to company and because I was concentrating on what I was doing, the visitor didn't even register in my consciousness until Alan Freeman was standing right in front of my desk.

"Emily, is Jack here?"

"Oh!" Alan had dressed to the nines today. He wore a black suit and shiny cobalt blue tie over a white shirt. His scalp shined. I'd never seen him like this, and it took me a moment to answer. "Alan, wow, you look sharp. Jack's not here, but the ADA called and spoke to me."

He looked up and then down furtively, but he said nothing.

"Let's go sit in Jack's office. I'll get you something to drink. Water? Soft drink? Coffee or tea?"

"Water. Thank you."

I grabbed my cell phone, a pen, and a yellow pad, and Alan followed me down the long wainscoted hall with its Western paintings, past the kitchen on the right, and down to Jack's office on the left. Really, it was Clyde's office first, but Jack had inherited it with the practice and it was magnificent. Richly stained built-ins dominated the farthest wall. His desk consumed most of the central space, and a conference table and leather chairs on rollers sat nearest the door. Behind it was a *real* Remington painting, a huge splurge by Clyde back in the day. I put Alan at the near side of the table. He could enjoy the long wall of windows or the facing wall of photographs, art, and diplomas from there.

"I'll be right back with your water."

"Thanks."

As I walked to the kitchen, I typed Jack another frantic message: *Alan here. Looking for you. Help.* Jack hadn't answered my earlier message, but it had only been twenty minutes since I sent it. I wouldn't panic yet.

I grabbed two glass tumblers from the cabinet and filled them with ice cubes and filtered water from the door of the refrigerator. I would have to talk to Alan, see what I could do to steady him, and stall like crazy until I heard from Jack. I walked back into the office.

Alan was standing at Jack's wall of fame, looking at an arresting black-and-white photograph of an old, abandoned mine. Above its entrance hung a lopsided sign: SACRAMENTO SILVER MINE. The photo even had a name: *Old Dreams at the Wrong Turn Ranch.* I knew it by heart. It was the one Jack had mentioned when we visited the cemetery with the kids on Saturday. It was a beautiful piece, but I preferred the charcoal drawing beside it of a little girl and a spotted pony. The artist? Jack. The subject? His daughter.

Alan heard me and returned to his seat. He had placed coasters from the holder in the center of the table in front of his chair and one across from him where I'd left my pen and yellow pad. I set the glasses on the coasters, and sunk into buttery leather.

"The ADA said you tried to meet with her about a plea deal," I said.

"Yeah." He looked down.

"So, tell me what's going on."

He shook his head. "I can't do this."

"Can't do what?"

"The trial."

"I don't understand. You didn't seem to have reservations before. Have you and Jack talked about you taking a deal?"

"No. Well, at the beginning."

"So, has something changed?"

He looked up at me. A single tear glistened in the corner of one of his eyes.

I put my hand over his. "What is it?"

His voice broke. "I can't do this to my wife and daughters."

"I know you're worried about them. But if you plead guilty, you'll be a convicted felon. That will impact them forever."

"I know. But if I don't it will be much worse."

I licked my lips. I wished Jack would hurry up and get here. "What was the plea offer before, do you remember?"

"If I'd plead guilty to assault, they'd drop the aggravated part, and I'd do two years and be eligible for parole in six months."

"So you want to be in prison for six months—or more? You think that will be better for your family?"

I heard the sound of the front door. Jack. I jumped to my feet.

A deep voice bellowed down the hall. "Anybody in here?"

Not Jack. But a voice that sounded familiar. Across from me, Alan's face had frozen in a look of terror. I walked over to Alan and put my hands on his shoulders.

I whispered, "What is it?"

He didn't answer, and I gave him a little shake.

He croaked out, "I need to go," and jumped to his feet.

***

Samson's uniformed bulk filled the doorway to Jack's office, and, worse, Burrows appeared behind him.

I took a step toward them, between the two officers and our rattled client. "If you gentlemen can take a seat in the lobby, someone will be with you in a moment."

Burrows ignored my words and pushed around Samson and inside, taking a visual inventory as he did. "I thought I heard voices. Where's Mr. Holden?"

Alan sunk back into his chair.

I didn't back up. "Sir, we're in the middle of a private meeting. I will see you in the lobby in a moment."

He lowered his voice. "I asked you where Jack Holden is."

He frightened me, but I was determined not to show it. "He's not here right now. I'm going to—"

From the doorway, Samson said, "Well, hello, Freeman."

Alan was looking down again. "Officer Samson."

I ignored the pleasantries. "Unless the two of you have an official reason to be in Jack's office, like a warrant to serve, I am telling you in front of a witness that you are not invited to be in here and need to go to our lobby."

"Not a problem. We'll wait out there." Samson held his hands up and gestured with his head for Burrows to follow him. To Alan, he said, "See you around, Freeman."

Burrows joined him and the two men walked out.

"I'll be right back, Alan." I hurried after them. "Jack may be awhile. May I help you with something, Officers?"

Samson entered the lobby and Burrows walked over to my desk. Between the two of them, they blocked access to both my desk and the exit. Burrows blatantly read my computer screen, shuffled my papers, then grabbed one of my business cards from their holder.

I jabbed at the off button on my monitor. "If you don't need something, then I need to ask you to leave, for the privacy of our clients and their information."

Burrows slapped my card against the thumb of his left hand several times then made a show of reading it.

Samson said, "We came by to see if you or your boss have heard from those two teenage runaways."

"What?"

Samson crossed his arms. "I spoke to you last Wednesday night about the two teenagers that had run away from their group home, Greg Easley and the Arab girl. I'm following up. Have they called you or come by? It sounded like you developed a rapport with them. And I hear you have a thing for strays."

"No." My head spun. Could he know they had, somehow? Surely not.

"And you'd tell me if they had?"

"Actually I'd call Byron first. They aren't accused of any crime that I've been made aware of. He's their caseworker. But I haven't had my phone, so if they contacted me on it, I wouldn't have known."

Burrows pocketed my card and cut in. "So sorry to hear that. But you've got it back now, right?" He didn't wait for me to answer. "I don't know what kind of magic you're expecting to happen by filing a complaint against Samson and me, though." He pantomimed magic hands in front of his chest, his fingers doing a poof and his hands moving away from each other, down, and around back to his waist.

Samson laughed, a short bark.

"I think filing a complaint against you will do a lot of things. It already made my phone reappear."

Burrows stepped closer to me. "Maybe other things will start reappearing now, too."

Burrows turned and the two men took their sweet time walking out.

***

Five minutes later Jack crashed in through the office door. "Sorry. I was Christmas shopping. Left my phone in the car."

"Please tell me you have Snowflake."

He mumbled something.

"What?"

"She's fine."

"Does that mean you have her?"

He mumbled again.

"Jack, where's the dog?"

"At a doggie daycare and spa, okay? It was her Christmas present."

Laughter burbled from deep inside me. "That's . . . unexpected."

He growled. "How'd it go with Alan?"

"Not great at first, then Burrows and Samson showed up, and it got much worse."

"What?"

"Yeah, they asked for you, but never really said what they wanted with you. They asked me questions about Greg and Farrah and left."

"Hmm."

"Alan seems adamant on that plea deal. Says he can't do this to his wife and kids."

"Huh."

"Are you even listening to me?"

"Thinking."

My leg started to bounce. "Okayyyyy." When he still didn't speak, I sighed and started working on my complaint document again.

"How'd you leave it with Alan?"

"I didn't. He's in your office, waiting for you."

He glanced at the wall clock. "It's already four o'clock. You said Melinda leaves at six?" I nodded and he continued. "We have to do something."

"Yet only one of us has a license to practice law."

"Come with me?"

I sighed and followed him down the long hall.

Jack and Alan shook hands. Within moments of joining him at the conference table in Jack's office, we picked up the conversation pretty much where I'd left it with Alan, with his insistence that a plea bargain was the right thing to do for his family.

"There has to be a better reason than that for me to participate in putting you in jail before Christmas." Jack leaned back in his chair, his arms crossed.

Alan hung his head. "There's no better reason than a man's family."

"If you're dead set on it, take the holiday with them, and we'll do it after."

He shook his head without looking up. "My mind is made up, but I understand if you can't do this for me. I can fire you, if you need me to, so I can work directly with the DA's office."

"I still don't understand," I blurted. "How does this make things better for your family?"

Alan looked up at me with the saddest eyes I'd ever seen. "You don't have to understand. I need y'all's help is all."

Jack leaned toward him, elbows and forearms on the table. "You understand, if we make this deal, you could be put in jail tomorrow?"

"I expected as much."

"Two days before Christmas."

"So my calendar tells me."

Jack frowned, but he picked up his phone. Fifteen minutes later, he had convinced ADA Stafford to honor the original plea offer. He looked pale when he hung up. "She'll meet us in court tomorrow morning."

"But her vacation—" I said.

"She said her flight doesn't leave until noon."

Alan shook our hands and thanked us profusely as he left. He seemed relieved, like an enormous weight had been taken off him. Not me, though. I was shaken and confused. Today had just about leveled me. I went back to my desk to try to work, but my brain was fried and my heart too heavy. I checked the time. Nearly five.

I hit intercom on the office phone. "Jack, do you mind if I leave a little early? I'm wiped."

"Okay."

Objection! I wanted to shout. *Nonresponsive!* But I wasn't up for it. I grabbed my handbag and slipped out.

Chapter Nineteen

The jingling bell on the door announced my arrival at ABC Half-Price Resale. A tall, slim black woman stood behind the counter ringing up a customer, a short woman with graying pin curls and French-roast skin tone, decked out in red and green sweats with flashing lights on the Christmas tree across her chest.

The customer turned and called out to a skeletal old man sitting in a folding chair near where I stood by the front door. "Herbert? I told you we'd find it cheaper here. Twenty-two ninety-five."

The man beside me grunted. His skin was so loose it looked like wrinkled fabric.

I went straight to the toys, looking for Betsy's horse, figuring someone had probably snapped it up by then. It was a fine toy. But no, it was there, still perfect. I grabbed the box and pulled it to my chest. To hell with the Hodges and their rules. I'd find a way to give it to her.

I kept browsing, looking for gifts for Greg and Farrah. I hardly knew them, but I would be with them over Christmas. They had so little, I hoped I could find something they'd like. I ended up with a multi-item hair-dryer set with brushes to straighten, curl, or diffuse, for Farrah, and a Swiss Army knife for Greg. I picked several ornaments from the tree display for Laura, Mickey, and Jack's secretary, Judith.

Jack would be harder. Or so I thought, until I ran across a collector's set of hardback, signed Tony Hillerman books. I stacked the small knife package on top of the books, which went on top of the hair-dryer box, which was itself stacked on top of the horse box. I gripped the ornaments in one hand and lifted the tower of boxes. I walked behind it, my head craned around to see where I was going, and set it on the glass display case beside the register, dropping the ornaments there as well. I prayed fervently as I did: *Dear Heavenly Father, please don't let me inadvertently purchase stolen goods. Or at least not regift to anyone things stolen from their own place. Amen.*

The tall woman rang me up, which gave me time to study her. She was attractive, her shoulder-length hair worn in natural-looking curls. She wore a small diamond ring and gold band on her left hand. She didn't smile, though, and she seemed distracted. She had to enter several of my items into the register more than once.

Her hands shook, and when she spoke, her voice was tight. "One ninety-nine thirty-two. Will that be cash or check, ma'am?"

"Check, please."

"I'll need to see some ID."

"Of course." I handed her my driver's license and started writing a check. "Is Alan here?"

"He's in back."

"I'm a friend of his, would it be okay if I ran back and said hello to him? Let him know I did my shopping here?" I gave her my most winning smile.

"That wouldn't be a good idea."

I looked up at her. Enormous tears threatened to spill. I pulled my eyes down quickly and finished filling in my check. In the memo line, I wrote *If you need help, call me*, and added my phone number. I handed it to her. "Thank you, ma'am, and Merry Christmas."

"Thank you, Merry Christmas to you, too, and God bless you."

I exited, and the bell jingled again behind me. I moved fast, depositing the presents and my purse in the trunk of my Mustang. I dropped my keys and phone into my deep skirt pocket and slammed the trunk. "Not a good idea," the woman had said when I asked to visit Alan. Which made it sound like a really good idea to go see if he was in trouble. Like maybe the delivery guy was here with stolen merchandise again. If he was, I could get a picture of the license plate this time, which would make a great photo to stick in Jack's Christmas present.

Dusk had fallen over Amarillo, as had lower temperatures, even while I was in the store. I walked quickly along the front sidewalk. I hadn't exactly dressed for running around outside. I didn't have anything but a light jacket that ended at the waist, over a thin black blouse and tank top. I pulled my jacket tighter around me. My high-heeled black boots and black maxi skirt looked great for impressing my boss, but now the wind whipped my skirt around my thighs as it distributed a dumpster's worth of trash around the parking lot. At least in the all-black clothes I had on the bad guys wouldn't see me as easily, I thought. I rounded the corner to the side of the strip mall, and the sidewalk ended. My heels teetered as I stepped off the concrete. Gravel, glass, and bottle caps littered the pavement. I kept a close eye on the ground, squinting in the near-dark.

I came to the back edge of the building. The alley extended to my left behind another strip center and to the right behind Alan's. Dumpsters lined the alley behind each business. An eighteen-wheeler was parked halfway down to my right. I was pretty sure it was behind Alan's store. Its headlights were on and pointed in my direction, limiting my vision, but it didn't look like there were any humans out between it and me. I decided to move fast from dumpster to dumpster until I was close enough to get a good shot of the truck's plates.

Keeping tight to the backs of the buildings, I hurried down the alley. My boots crunched glass and squished foreign substances I didn't want to identify. Nausea rolled over me in a wave, but I couldn't let myself think about it. I came to the first dumpster, panting, and I took a moment to catch my breath and peer around the trash can. Still no humans in my path.

Three dumpsters to go. I dashed around the next one and back to the building, tripping over something when I was a foot away from the wall. My toe smashed into a hard object, with nothing between it and the obstacle but soft, supple leather. I bit my lip to keep from screaming in pain. I caught myself with one hand on the wall and held still. Stars danced before my eyes. When the fireworks and shooting pain subsided, I hobbled along, using one hand on the building to steady myself.

I reached another dumpster. Tears in the corners of my eyes made it hard to see, and I began to wonder if this was a really bad idea. I put weight on my foot and winced, taking it back off again immediately. A

door flew open beside me. A huge black woman in a tent-like red wool
dress stepped out, holding a stuffed black trash bag.

She studied me for a moment. "Child, you look a fright. You be
needing a hand?"

I shook my head, half-smiling. "No, I was just walking down to
visit with Alan, you know, at ABC Half-Price Resale, and I stubbed my
toe."

She clucked. "It's dark as Satan's heart out already. Here, I'll turn
my light on so you can see where you're going, hon."

She leaned in and messed with something I couldn't see and the
light was on before I could scream, "No."

"You're so sweet." I pasted on a big smile. "Well, I'll be heading
toward Alan's now."

I shot a glance down the last ten well-lit yards. So well lit that I
could have taken a picture of the license plate on the truck, if it weren't
for the fact that the woman was watching me.

"You be careful now." She tossed her garbage in the bin. "I'll wait
here until you make it safe and sound 'fore I turn out the light."

There was no way I was walking out into the alley when it was lit
up like an operating room. I wracked my brain for a way to get the light
out and the woman inside. Inspired, I pulled out my phone and turned
on its flashlight.

"Silly me, I forgot about this. I'll be fine. I don't want to keep you
out in this cold."

"You sure?"

"Oh yes, this is great." I shined the flashlight all about to demon-
strate how great it was, like an epileptic radio operator sending Morse
code.

"All right."

"Merry Christmas, and thank you."

"God bless you and yours."

I waved, and she shut the door behind her. The light went off. I
heaved a relieved breath. Last dumpster to reach, then I could lean out
and get my shot. I turned off the flashlight, tested my wonky foot—it

was better—and ran, in what passed for a sprint in my current footwear and injured state, along the building. It was almost anticlimactic to have made it. I crouched at the edge of the trash bin and leaned around. I snapped the picture, checked the focus, and took another for good measure.

I smiled. Jack would be so surprised. And then I heard the voices.

***

"What have we here, Freeman?" a man asked.

I couldn't hear well enough to recognize it, but the tone wasn't a nice one.

Alan's voice replied, "You're getting what you want."

"I never thought I wouldn't."

"Then, please, can't you leave me alone?"

A third man spoke. "Hey. How ya doing?"

The sound of skin slapping against skin was unmistakable.

"I can't complain. And you?" first man said.

"I could use less hours and more money, but it could be worse," third man said.

"*Feliz Navidad.*" First.

"Yeah, Merry Christmas to you, too." Third.

A short, skinny silhouette sauntered around the rear delivery door and toward me. I slunk back around the dumpster, out of sight. I had barely seen the guy, but I was sure I hadn't recognized him. My heart hammered so loudly I wanted to clap my hands over my ears, but I knew it wouldn't do any good. The tractor-trailer roared to life, and I crouched and ran back to the building. I managed to wedge myself between the dumpster and the wall before the big rig rolled by.

Holy cow, that was close. With the noise of the eighteen-wheeler gone, I could hear Alan and the first man talking again. I moved out to peek around the dumpster. I couldn't see Alan or anyone else. I decided that they must be standing inside the delivery bay.

"Are you here to rub it in?" Alan said.

A car engine revved somewhere nearby and drowned out the other man's answer.

What the fudge were they talking about? Alan spoke again, but I couldn't understand him either. The engine noise stopped but Alan's voice moved away from me. I needed to get closer, but I had to find a better place to hide. There looked to be a door well on the building, about fifteen feet away from me. I wasn't sure if it would provide enough cover. I leaned out to get a better view, but saw nothing. The men had disappeared, and so had their voices. I crouched down behind the dumpster again. I'd just send Jack a text with the picture. I pulled it up and putzed with the lighting and contrast for a few minutes until the license plate was clearly visible.

A hand clamped over my mouth, and an arm wound around my body. The arm jerked me into an unyielding chest. My heart seized and felt like it would explode.

A man's voice said, "Not a sound, understand?"

I nodded, the movement of my head restricted by the hand pressing into my mouth.

"We need to talk. I'm going to remove my hand, but if you scream, things will get worse before they get better."

I nodded again.

The hand slipped away, and the arm loosened around me. I whirled to find myself in the grasp of Officer John Burrows.

***

Burrows hustled me out of the alley and to the front of the strip center by my car. He let go of my arm. I bent over, hands on knees, trying to catch my breath. He wasn't even winded. His eyes roamed the parking lot and street. For the first time, I noticed he was in plain clothes, dressed for stealth. Dark jeans. Black hoodie. Black baseball cap. His exposed white face glowed in the low light like a beacon, though.

"What"—pant, pant—"was"—pant, pant—"that"—pant, pant—"all about?"

"Trying to keep you from interfering in police business and getting your damn self killed. Now, get out of here."

"I thought you"—pant—"wanted to talk to me?"

"Not here."

"Where?"

"Later. Right now, we both need to leave before someone sees us together. Or at all."

Before I could respond, Burrows disappeared into the parking lot. I heard an engine rev, but with the interference from Amarillo Boulevard traffic noise in the background, I couldn't fix on the location. I stood up, searching for interested faces. No one was looking at me. I pulled out my keys and got in the Mustang.

I put my head on the steering wheel, still breathing hard. The car beside me started and pulled out of its parking space, but I didn't even glance up. What had just happened? Clearly, Burrows was keeping tabs on someone. It could be Alan. Or it could be me. He had shown up at my orthodontist's office that morning, after all, and he didn't wear braces. The thought of a police officer tailing me all over town made me sick to my stomach.

I reviewed what I'd seen and heard before Burrows interrupted me. The conversation made no sense. And what about the driver? Was he the one who delivered the hot goods? Or was he only a normal old delivery driver making his rounds? If normal, I'd peeved off a cop for nothing more than a hard working driver's license plate. The circuits in my brain shorted. I put the Mustang in reverse, then noticed Burrows had pulled into the emptied spot beside me in a silver sedan, passenger-side window down. I lowered mine, too. A woman sat beside him in the passenger seat, a skanky-looking woman not wearing enough clothing for the weather. She chewed rhythmically, like she had a big wad of gum in her mouth. She didn't look at me. Burrows didn't either.

He said, "You got a place we could meet where no one would see us?"

Last week this man had arrested me when Mary Alice Hodges had called on the wrath of God, just because I was watching Betsy. He wasn't any too nice about it, either. Then my phone had disappeared for days. I'd filed a complaint against him. He'd shown up at my orthodontist's and my office, then grabbed me behind Alan's store.

Burrows scared me, and now he wanted me to meet him somewhere private? *Whoa, big fellow.*

"I don't think that's a good idea."

"Would you rather I take you in to the station again?"

"For what?"

"Criminal trespass for starters. I could think of a few more things if I needed to."

He looked away from me, holding up one hand and inspecting the back of it. The woman blew a bubble and it popped. She reached up and peeled it away from her face, put it in her mouth, and resumed chewing.

My ears and cheeks burned. "Fine," I snapped.

I didn't like the idea of meeting him somewhere secluded, but I sure didn't want to be arrested again. I ran through the best possibilities I could think of. Jack was at the office. My gossipy mother would be home by now on a Monday evening. Then I had an idea.

"What about the parking garage for the Maxor Building? Most everyone's left for the day by now. The Downtown Athletic Club's there, but people park on the first floor for it. I could meet you on the third."

Jack frequented the DAC daily, for the workout and the shower facilities. So far, I hadn't caught the workout bug.

"Wait. Isn't there a restaurant in the building, too?"

"It's only open at lunch."

He nodded. "Okay. Pull in nose first by an empty space. Stay in your car. I'll find you."

He threw his car in reverse and backed out quickly.

"You're welcome," I called after him.

I cruised down Amarillo Boulevard slowly, getting honked at twice by impatient drivers. The worsening weather seemed to have everyone on edge. I pulled off the Boulevard back into downtown on Polk and came upon the Maxor courtyard seconds later. White Christmas lights sparkled from the iron fencing and trees. Someone had decorated the Center City's buckskin horse sculpture with a wreath around its neck. I turned on Fourth Avenue, then into the garage, winding my way up the darkened ramp.

The third story was empty, and I picked a space far from the lighted elevator. When I'd parked, nose in, a car rolled behind me. Too late, it occurred to me that I should have told someone where I was and with whom before meeting a scary man I barely knew alone in a deserted parking garage. Well, it wasn't like I didn't know how to protect myself. I pulled out my Glock for the second time that day.

The rear end of the silver sedan eased to the wall, its white backing lights illuminating the space for a moment. The engine noise ceased. A door slammed with an echoey sound. A tap sounded on the passenger-side glass, sharp and sudden. I jumped, instinctively half-raising my gun hand.

"Put that thing away." The window muffled Burrows's voice, but I could hear him well enough to know he was irritated.

I lowered the gun.

"Not down. Away."

I tucked the gun back into my handbag, but I left the purse in my lap. I hit the unlock button, and Burrows got in.

"You know how many people are killed each year with their own guns?"

I didn't answer him. He didn't know me and had no way of knowing the hours I logged in gun-safety courses and at the shooting range, or that my best memories with my father involved either horses or guns. Sometimes both.

So I changed the subject. "Who's the woman in your car?"

"Doesn't matter."

It did to me. His evasive answer worried me even more. While Burrows wasn't a large man, the interior walls of my car still seemed too close with him in it. I could feel the weight of the filed complaint against him in the air. I wanted this over with as fast as I could make it happen.

"This"—I waved my hand around the front seat in the air between us—"feels wrong." I breathed through my nose slowly. One one thousand. Two one thousand. Deep breath in. Deep breath out. "Am I under arrest?"

Burrows readjusted in his seat to face me. "Not yet."

I turned and looked him dead in the eye. "So I have no legal obligation to talk to you?"

"None." He held my gaze without blinking. "But you need to keep your damn nose out of police business."

"I don't have my nose in police business."

"Then what do you call tonight?"

If that was police business, were they onto Alan's part in the smuggling ring? If so, Alan needed help, and I had some of the evidence to help him here on my phone camera, possibly. Alan didn't belong behind bars like a criminal, not for the assault charge, and not for getting bullied and intimidated into this. I held my breath and prayed for our client and his family.

Finally, I answered Burrows. "Looking out for a client. I do work for a law firm, you know."

He shook his head and his voice dripped acid. "Don't give me that crap. You were spying, and we both know it."

Louder than I'd intended, I said, "You have no idea what you're talking about," and smacked the steering wheel with the palm of one hand.

The silence after my mini-explosion was oppressive. A car drove up the ramps behind us. I heard the thrump-thrump of its wheels and felt the slight vibration of the structure. The tires squealed as it turned and moments later the thrumps moved back in our direction. The car slowed as it came to us, and Burrows turned to watch it. I did, too. The driver rubbernecked at us then drove on.

Burrows looked around the garage, like he expected someone to be there, and lowered his voice. "I hope we don't have to have this conversation again."

A sharp knock on my window nearly sent me through the roof. Someone shined a spotlight-strength flashlight in at us.

A man's voice, high-pitched, asked, "Ma'am, are you okay?"

Burrows said, "Roll down your window. It's a security guard."

I turned my key to power the car and hit the down button. "Good evening, sir." Good, now someone besides Burrows and the mystery woman knew I was here.

Burrows leaned over and held a badge in front of me. "Is there a problem?"

The security guard, peg toothed and skinny, lowered his light from our eyes. "Just doing my job." He nodded at us and backed away. He put his free hand on his hip, where I saw a can of mace. I hoped he didn't run into real problems. He didn't look like he was strong enough to wrest the can from its holster.

Burrows tracked the security guard with his eyes.

I powered the window back up. "Were you following me, earlier?"

Burrows grinned, showing teeth so perfect they were like white-washed pickets in a fence. "I needed a new retainer."

He opened the door and got out, then leaned back down. "Quit making trouble with cops. Especially when you go around waving a fucking gun. It's a good way to get shot, yourself."

He disappeared into his car.

Chapter Twenty

Jack and I met Alan and his wife in one of the tiny attorney-client conference rooms off the foyer to the 499th District Court in the Potter County Courts Building at eight a.m. the next morning. As I had guessed, Alan's wife, Janelle, was the stressed-out woman who had rung up my purchases the night before at their resale shop. She recognized me, too, and we had a nice enough exchange, but really, how friendly can a woman be when she's in court to say good-bye to her husband two days before Christmas as he heads to jail for a crime she doesn't believe he committed? I didn't want to be overly familiar with her, but I patted her arm, trying to transfer a little positive energy. Jack went over the morning's schedule and strategy, and Alan didn't say much, mostly just looked at the tabletop. When we were done, we exited into the foyer.

"Do we have to go through another?" Janelle asked, pointing at an oddly placed metal detector against the wall.

"Nope." Jack held open the courtroom door. "This way."

He led us to the front row of the gallery behind the wooden bar that separated the public seating from the courtroom proper. We squeezed down the row and took seats. The hard plastic fold-up seats barely held my tush, and across the aisle sat a woman three times my size. Hers spilled over the metal seat arms on either side of her. It looked incredibly painful. Under my feet was scrubby carpet in a color I'd have to call government neutral. It blended with the walls and the leather counsel and jury chairs. The room itself was an odd shape, like a quarter of a circle. The jury box was tucked into the curved section of the wall. The judge, court reporter, and witness box faced it at an angle that also encompassed the counsel tables and public seating.

The double doors behind us burst open. I turned in time to see Melinda Stafford breeze in. Her navy pencil skirt was as tight as usual, and she'd slung her matching jacket over her shoulder so that she could give us all a better view of her tailored white blouse. I hadn't seen her since I'd punched her in the jaw, and, to my great disappointment, it didn't appear I'd done any lasting damage. She took a seat on the front row, opposite from us.

"All rise for the Honorable R. Charleston Herring," the bailiff commanded, moments later. She snapped the words out like a drill sergeant. "All rise, all rise."

Everyone stood. In my peripheral vision I saw that the heavy woman had a lot of trouble extricating herself from the seat. What had the courtroom designers been thinking? One third of America was her size or more.

Judge Herring pulled my attention away from her predicament as he swept into the courtroom from his private entrance. The man cut an imposing figure. Well over six feet before he donned his boots and ascended to the bench, he wore his head shaved and his gray mustache neat. He was a legend in the District Attorney's office before he became a judge, and most defense attorneys didn't relish appearing in his court.

"Be seated." He lowered himself to his chair. "Pretty big crowd for the day before Christmas Eve."

I looked around. Half the gallery was filled.

He donned some half-glasses and then slid them down his nose while drawing a piece of paper toward himself. He adjusted it in the air a few times, then nodded. "Anyone here to pitch a plea agreement?"

Judge Herring entertained plea agreements before starting court each day, either by advance appointment, or because, like us, you came early and got in line.

Jack and Melinda stood at the same time. Jack inclined his head and waited for her to speak first.

A squatty man with jet-black hair sped through the batwing gate in the bar and to the defense table on the right. "Your Honor," he said, in a voice with a New England accent, which sounded like Yowuh Ahnuh, "if I may, just a quick matter to discuss with you first."

The judge didn't look happy. "Counsel, return to the gallery until you have been called."

In a strident voice, the man said, "But Your Honor, I drove in from Lubbock this morning and I have an appearance in the 457th at eleven and the roads are—"

Judge Herring rapped his gavel. "Out of order." He pointed the gavel at the door. "You get one more chance to return to the gallery, and if you blow that one, you get no more chances."

"But—"

"Bailiff, can you please encourage our unnamed counselor to remove himself."

The man raised two thick hands. "I'm going, I'm going." He walked to the gate, and flung it open. There was a resounding crack as the split doors hit the front row seats. He kept going, doing roughly the same thing with the double door exit. The courtroom grew deathly quiet.

Judge Herring raised an eyebrow at the bailiff. "Bring that one back."

"Yes, Your Honor." The bailiff scurried after the attorney, and the doors, opened and closed more softly this time, were the only sound.

Seconds later, the two returned through the bar doors.

"Your name?" the judge said.

"Stanley Perkins," the attorney said, his voice belligerent.

"Ah yes, I recognize your name, Mr. Perkins. Since this is your first time in my courtroom, I'm going to give you a chance to avoid time in a holding cell for contempt of court. Do you have anything you'd like to say?"

Perkins shot a glance back at the gallery, his eyes searching for a clue as to his next move. Beside me, Jack kept his eyes down.

I whispered to him. "What's going on?"

Without moving his lips, Jack spoke so softly I could barely hear him. "Herring wants an apology."

Judge Herring's voice boomed. "Mr. Perkins?"

"What?" the man barked.

Judge Herring smiled. "You're not from around here, are you, Mr. Perkins? Boston, if I recall correctly."

"No, sir. Yes, Boston."

"Well, welcome to Amarillo, then. Bailiff, escort Mr. Perkins to the holding area. He will be allowed a phone call to reschedule his time in the 457th."

Sputtering, Perkins backed up a step.

"Oh, I wouldn't do that if I were you," Judge Herring said, and he smiled.

Perkins froze, then submitted and walked through the large metal door to the right of the defense table with the bailiff. Jack looked at me with one brow raised. Apparently, the rumors about Judge Herring's toughness weren't exaggerated.

"Now, where were we?" The judge looked at his watch then down at something on his desk. "Ah yes." He looked up again. "Does anyone have a plea agreement to pitch?"

"Yes, Judge Herring," Melinda said as she and Jack stood. "Melinda Stafford for the DA's office."

"Yes, Your Honor," Jack said. "Jack Holden for defendant Alan Freeman."

"Is the defendant present?"

Jack turned to Alan and nodded at him.

Alan stood, in the same suit he'd worn the previous day. "Present, Your Honor."

Judge Herring beckoned them with four fingers, palm up. "Come forward, please."

Jack, Alan, and Melinda went through the batwing gates in the bar, single file. Melinda moved to stand behind the table to the left, Jack and Alan to the right, next to the metal door through which Perkins had just disappeared.

The Judge waited for them to get situated then said, "ADA Stafford, you may begin." He frowned down at her.

Melinda beamed. "Thank you, Your Honor. We have aggravated assault against a police officer, and resisting arrest. We've reached an agreement, subject to your approval, of course, sir, to plead down to ordinary assault for a two-year sentence, with eligibility for parole at six months."

"Counselor Holden?" The judge smiled at Jack.

"Yes, sir. Judge Herring, this is Alan Freeman. Mr. Freeman is a tradesman by experience—does fine tile work, I highly recommend him—and recently came to inherit his parents' business upon their deaths. ABC Half-Price Resale. Mr. Freeman is married to Janelle Freeman"—Jack gestured back toward Mrs. Freeman, and she stood and half-curtsied—"and they have three young daughters. Mr. Freeman wishes to plead guilty, Your Honor, to expedite the resolution of his case and ensure his speedy return to his position in the community and, most especially, in his home, so that he can care for his family."

Judge Herring peered over his glasses at Alan. "Mr. Freeman, you understand that by pleading guilty you will wear the mantle of a convicted felon for the rest of your days?"

Alan cleared his throat. "Yes, sir."

"You understand that it is two days before your wife and children celebrate Christmas—that you are showing up here less than one month before your trial, but before the holiday, and while you are still legally out on bail, when you could have, if nothing else, waited until after Christmas to come in—and that all of this is *highly* irregular?"

Judge Herring took his glasses off as much by turning his head away from them as by pulling them away from his face.

Alan's mouth opened and shut.

The Judge continued, his voice deepening. "And, yes, I know who you are, Mr. Freeman. I know who all of my defendants are."

Sweat trickled between my breasts. I wished that Janelle and I were sitting with Alan.

Alan glanced back at his wife, then back at the judge. "Yes, sir," he said, but his voice was softer than before.

"This is all so irregular, in fact, that I have to ask myself what could possibly motivate you to do such an irregular thing. You understand?"

"Yes, sir," Alan whispered.

Beside me, Mrs. Freeman made an anguished noise and put her hand to her chest.

The judge's delivery sped up. "So, Mr. Freeman, are you here of your own free will?"

"Yes, sir."

"Has anyone threatened you, explicitly or implicitly, to obtain your agreement?"

Melinda jumped to her feet. "Your Honor, may we approach the bench?"

He glared at her. "No."

"But—"

"Did I not make myself clear?"

"Yes, sir, I'd—"

"Enough."

She sat.

The Judge grumbled to himself for a moment, then said, "Mr. Freeman, let me ask you again. Has anyone threatened you, explicitly or implicitly, to obtain your agreement?"

"Yes, sir."

Melinda leapt up again, but Judge Herring held his hand high in warning. She stood with her mouth hanging open.

"What, Mr. Freeman?" he asked.

"I mean no, sir."

Again, Melinda sat.

"Are you receiving anything in addition to this reduced sentence in return for your agreement today?"

"I don't understand what you mean, sir."

The Judge shot new daggers, first at Melinda and then at something in the back of the room. I turned to see who it was, and saw a pasty, redheaded man and a tall Asian guy. I did a double take. I'd seen the Asian guy in pictures: Jason Wu, the former cop who said Alan assaulted him, and Burrows. At Burrows's side was a woman who looked much like the one I'd caught a glimpse of in his car the night before. Maybe she was even the same one.

"I mean, has anyone paid you or offered you anything of value to enter this agreement?"

"Oh. No, sir."

"You understand that you will be sentenced to two years, to commence immediately upon my approval of this agreement, if I choose to do so, at the Potter County Detention Center—which, by the way, is a highly disagreeable place, if I do say so myself—and that you will serve a minimum of six months of that sentence, away from the pleasures of hearth and home, with people I trust you will find to be of a most unsavory nature?"

"Yes, sir."

The judge shook his head. "Mr. Holden, is there anything else I should be asking your client that could help us get to the bottom of this?"

"I wish I could think of something, sir, but I cannot. As far as I can tell, this is what he wants, and he understands what he's doing, even if I don't like it."

"Nor do I," Judge Herring intoned. He put his glasses back on. "With the greatest of reluctance, this plea is approved. Bailiff, remand Mr. Freeman into custody, please, sir."

Alan looked back at his wife and mouthed, "I love you. I'm sorry." A choked cry escaped from Janelle Freeman beside me, and I put my arm around her shoulders as the bailiff slipped handcuffs onto Alan's wrists and led him through the metal door to the prisoner holding area beyond it.

Chapter Twenty-one

"Pecan pancakes, please." I handed my menu to the waiter the next morning at the Pancake House, where Wallace, Nadine, and I were celebrating Christmas Eve. We weren't the only ones with the idea, apparently. The restaurant was normally lean on décor, but candy canes hung from rope draped nail to nail in swoops around the walls of the restaurant. It echoed with booming wishes of Merry Christmas, and the whole place smelled like cinnamon rolls and coffee. The only negative was the crowded space felt like a sauna, with too much heater and too many bodies compensating for the weather outside.

The waitress didn't look up from the pad on which she was scribbling my order. "Bacon or sausage?"

"Neither."

Now she looked at me, and her eyebrows descended and pinched together. "What?"

"I'm a——"

Wallace leaned between us, hand out as if to block me. "She'll have fruit on the side, please."

The woman nodded, jiggling her chins, and recited our entire order back to us. Slowly. She had it right, so Nadine, Wallace, and I all made affirmative noises. She walked toward the kitchen, studying the notepad again, and crossing something out.

"Merry Christmas, you guys." I set two small gifts in the center of the table. I had wrapped them myself the night before in shiny gold paper with silver bows and a tiny ornament tied to each. Wallace got bicycle Santa and Nadine motorcycle Santa.

Wallace put two envelopes with them. "Happy Hanukkah."

"You're not Jewish." Nadine frowned. "And breakfast is on me, because nothing says Happy Kwanzaa like the Pancake House."

Wallace's voice sounded droll. "How do you know what they eat for Kwanzaa in Africa?"

"Kiss my ass, Wallace."

"Sorry, honey, but you're not my type."

"So early in the morning . . ." I picked up my envelope. "Can I open it?"

"Sure."

"Me, too?" Nadine asked.

"Of course."

Nadine and I tore into the flaps.

Wallace said, "I got us a pedicure party at Top Ten. All three of us! I have to get my dogs in shape." He winked. "New man in my life."

"Awesome!" I hadn't had a pedicure in months. "When do we get to meet him?"

"Soon, I think."

Nadine stuck her envelope in her purse. "I've never had a pedicure before. I'm kinda picky about who touches my feet, and for what purpose."

Wallace waggled his eyebrows. "Do tell."

"Don't!" I cut in. They laughed. "But I do want to hear all about you and Phil."

"Who's Phil?" Wallace asked.

She held up a hand. "There is no me and Phil. Phil's a regular at the Polo Club. He's been hitting on me for months. I *never* give the douchebags my name." She pointed at me with her raised hand. "Yesterday he got it from her."

"He's a client. You were in the office. How was I to know introductions weren't in order?"

"I didn't say they weren't in order. Now that we've been properly introduced, I wouldn't mind letting him have a go at my feet."

"Stop!"

Wallace laughed. "Emily, you're such a prude."

"I'm not a prude. I just don't want to hear the details."

"So you wouldn't let Jack suck your toes, then, or put them—"

"That's not up for discussion!"

Now they both laughed. Nadine put her hand on my arm. "Since I'm in the holiday spirit, I'll quit terrorizing you." She pulled her hand back and snapped her fingers. "Which reminds me. You filed a complaint on a dirty cop, right?"

"Well, two cops that I think were acting improperly, anyway."

"Potato, Poh-tah-toe. One of the dancers called in sick last night because she's afraid to leave her house. She thinks some cop is after her for something she saw, a murder, she claims. After one of the dancers disappeared last summer, all the girls have been much more skittish. I told her about you, and I gave her your number. In case she needs to talk to someone."

I lifted my shoulders, about to say, "Sure, no problem," when something else popped out instead. "What's her name?" I'd met a dancer the week before at Love's. Irina? Sasha? Something European. Ivanka. That was it.

"Beth."

Our plump waitress appeared with three plates on each arm. She put them down on the table, one by one, all in the wrong places. "Anything else?"

Wallace held up a finger. "More coffee."

I waited for her to turn her back then pushed Nadine's bacon and sausage sides over to her. I tried to convince myself that the flesh on the plate grossed me out, but my stomach growled at the aroma, greedy and animalistic. I grabbed my pancakes and fruit and snatched the butter and syrup before anyone else could get to them. Staving off meat cravings constituted an emergency.

I started slathering butter. "Y'all didn't even open my gifts."

Wallace had ordered biscuits with sausage gravy and a side of hash browns in addition to his pancakes. There was a benefit to maleness and triathlon, for sure. I'd blow up like a whale if I mixed all that fat with all those carbs. I scraped some of the butter off my pancakes, then a little more.

"Shit, honey, I'm sorry. Let's do it when she clears the food." Wallace stuffed a giant bite of biscuit and gravy in his mouth.

I eyed the syrup I'd chosen. Maple. There were a few more in a wooden rack. I read the labels and saw "sugar-free." I sighed and poured a lake of it on my plate.

One of our cell phones rang. I still hadn't reset my ringtone and sounds, and I glanced at mine. Nope.

Wallace pulled his from his pocket and answered in a robotic voice. "You've reached the voice mail of Wallace Gray. I'm celebrating Christmas with my friends and can't come to the phone right now. Don't bother leaving a message, because I won't call you back until—"

He stopped speaking and listened, his face growing dark. "You're absolutely sure of this?"

He looked at me, and it was a look of such incredible pity that I knew immediately something had happened to Betsy. I made a strangled noise. It must have been louder than I'd realized, because heads turned.

"What is it?" Nadine whispered.

"Betsy?" I croaked.

Wallace put his phone down and reached for my hand. "I'm sorry, Emily. Immigration is coming for Betsy."

***

Our breakfast abandoned, Wallace and I huddled in his pristine car and I called Jack. Tiny crystals pelted the windshield and roof of the car. Snow? It looked more like ice. I hated ice storms. I turned the heater to high.

Wallace said, "It won't get any warmer until the engine warms up."

I ignored him.

Jack's voice spoke into my ear. "Jack Holden speaking."

I touched "speaker" on my phone screen. "Jack, you're on speaker with Wallace and me."

"What's up?"

"Wallace got a tip from a friend with Immigration that they're coming for Betsy after Christmas."

"Shit. I was afraid this would happen. She's not a secret to the feds because of the kidnapping and trafficking case against Johnson."

I couldn't hold my anger and fear in, and I shouted. "Don't they have enough criminals here illegally that they can leave one poor little girl alone?"

Wallace hit the steering wheel with one hand. "It's ridiculous. She's not a danger to anyone."

Jack sighed. "They do cast the net pretty wide."

My voice came out shrill. "We have to do something, Jack. We can't let this happen."

Wallace held a finger up. "I can spend the day Monday in the Mexican consulate. We may not know where she was born, but maybe I can find someone who is willing to help me search for birth records for her anyway."

I shook my head. "But you don't have a picture ID for her."

"I'll take her picture and a notarized letter from CPS attesting to her identity."

"Will they accept that?"

"I don't know, but it's better than nothing."

Jack's voice broke in and out. "I'll"—crackle, crackle—"Monday"—kercrackle—"birth"—cracklety-crackle—"enough." Bad cell reception.

Wallace said, "Can you repeat that?"

Jack tried again. "I'll go ahead and file for Special Immigrant Juvenile status on Monday as well. They'll return it to us asking for her birth certificate, but maybe the fact that we've attempted to file will be enough to forestall federal custody."

My voice broke. "But they could still take her, and then she'd be in prison, basically, waiting." I took a deep breath. "I can't let that happen. Maybe she just needs to run away. She might end up with a nice place to stay and then not get found until we've got this all sorted out."

Wallace shot me a killer look. "I'm going to pretend I didn't even hear you make that terrible joke."

I averted my eyes.

"And on the subject of runaways while I have you together, I'm sorry to pass along more bad news, but we still haven't found Greg or Farrah."

I squirmed inwardly, but said, "Oh no."

"Yeah, I wanted you both to know." When neither of us spoke again, Wallace added, "Jack, anything else you need me doing in the meantime?"

"No. I think this is all we can do, Wallace."

"Okay. Well, Merry Christmas, and thanks."

"Yep, you, too. Emily, the weather's supposed to keep getting worse. Dress warm tonight." He ended the call.

Wallace smacked me in the shoulder. "Emily Bernal, what haven't you told me about tonight?"

Worry about Betsy weighed me down, but a flicker of happiness still made it through. "Jack's taking me to Christmas Eve services with him."

"Shut the front door."

"It's not that big a deal."

"The hell it's not. This is a date. A bona fide D-A-T-E."

"Do you think so?"

"I know so."

"Okay, then I need your help."

"I'm glad you've finally realized that."

I punched his arm. "I need an outfit that says 'I'm the one,' but in a Catholic-church-appropriate way. Any ideas?"

Wallace threw his head back and laughed.

"What?"

"Have you ever been to a Catholic church before?"

"Once."

"How did they dress?"

"Normal, I guess."

"There you go. Dress like you would normally, except wear a garter and fishnets underneath."

"Wallace!" He had a point. Everyday lingerie wouldn't do. I had a pair of lavender tap pants and matching bra that would work, just in case.

"You're gorgeous. It will be fine."

My phone rang. Expecting Jack, I hit accept. "Yes?"

"Hi, my name is Beth. Nadine from the Polo Club suggested I call for Emily?"

Beth. Beth who was having a problem with a bad cop. "Yes, this is Emily. I'm with Jack Holden of Williams and Associates. How can I help you?"

"I'm sorry to call over the holidays. I work with Nadine, and I've got a problem. She said you've had a similar one: a bad cop messing with you?"

"Yes, two of them, unfortunately."

"Yeah, well, that's my problem, too."

"Would you like to get together?"

"If it's not too much trouble for you."

"Not at all. But I'm leaving town tomorrow. Can you get together today, say about noon?"

"Yes. Can I text you an address?"

"Sure."

The call ended and seconds later a text came through: *This is Beth. 1000 Shasta, noon today. Thank you for meeting with me. I didn't know where else to turn, and I'm scared to leave my house in case he sees me.*

I replied: *See you then.*

Wallace had unwrapped his present while I talked to Beth. He held up the gift certificate to Sun Adventure Sports, the store he favored for triathlon gear. "You're a peach."

"I feel like I'm contributing to the delinquency of a misogynist."

"A what?"

"A misogynist. You know, a person who enjoys pain."

Wallace groaned, laughing. "Masochist, Emily. Masochist. A misogynist is someone prejudiced against women."

"Oh. Well. Yeah, masochist then. I'm contributing to the delinquency of a masochist."

"Nah. I'm much more into—"

I stuck my fingers in my ears. "La la la la la la."

***

I spent the rest of the morning with Mother decorating sugar cookies for her Sunday school classmates. She was blasting Christmas music through the house and singing along at the top of her lungs. I usually couldn't resist joining her, but I was really preoccupied with worries about Betsy. If I dwelled on it too long, I started to think about the Freeman family, too, so I tried not to dwell. Tonight I had a date with Jack. No matter how grim things seemed, I couldn't lose sight of that, and I certainly couldn't let anything mess it up.

I squirted from a miniature tube of white icing to create snow on a Christmas tree. "You sure you're going to be all right without me tonight and this weekend?"

"Why, of course. I'm so glad you and Jack are spending time together."

I put the top on the tube and licked my fingers. I'd finished my last cookie. "I'm worried you're going to be lonely."

Mother didn't look up from the cookies she was arranging in a red basket. "What, why would you say that?"

"Um, because I won't be here."

"Oh. Yes, well, I'll be fine, dear."

Mother wasn't an unhappy person, per se—although she harbored some bitterness about how hard her life had turned out, especially in comparison to people she felt got more help than she did—but she was especially cheerful today. That was good, I guessed. Better than the alternative: making me feel guilty for deserting her over Christmas. It was the second time in a week, though, that she'd seemed much more jolly than usual.

I scrutinized her more closely. "Is that a new dress?"

"This?" She ran the back of her hand over a black suit-dress with a Peter Pan collar and gorgeous square black buttons. "Oh, well, hmm, I can't remember if you've seen it before." She giggled.

If I didn't know better I'd suspect she'd been into the box wine, or had a boyfriend. Neither was plausible for her, though. I had planned to tell her about Betsy while we did the cookies, but I didn't have the heart to weigh her down with something that heavy when she was in such high spirits. Besides, I needed to be optimistic about Betsy and positive in general. And optimistic meant that I had to plan for Betsy to remain in the U.S., and for me to adopt her. Which meant I needed to tell Mother I was moving out.

I turned on the sink water and rubbed my hands together under it. "You know how I'm applying to adopt Betsy?"

"Yes, dear. How's it coming along?" She started on a new cookie basket.

"Well, fine, except I have to live on my own. And I've found a place." I shook my hands to get the excess water off.

She froze with a cookie in each hand. "Really?"

"Yes." There was a dish towel hanging by the sink, and I used it to blot the last of the water off my hands.

She resumed putting cookies in the basket. "And?"

I turned to her. "It's a duplex off Soncy Road."

"That's close." She smiled at me.

I exhaled. A smile was a good sign. "My lease could start after New Year's. I need to sign it and take the security deposit and first and last month's rent over."

She nodded. "Good for you."

I nearly fainted. That had gone so much easier than I'd expected. Who was this woman, and what had she done with my needy, dependent mother? Battle won—or rather, battle conceded by the opposing side—I didn't linger on the subject.

I leaned back against the counter. "So, what are you going to do this afternoon?"

"My friend Josie is opening her salon for me, and she's doing a complete Christmas makeover on me, including manicure and pedicure."

"That'll set you back a pretty penny." I was a little bit jealous that she hadn't invited me, but I was glad she was doing something fun.

"She's giving me a huge discount as a Christmas present."

"Do you want me to drop you off and pick you up? The roads are getting bad."

"No, that's okay." She finished up Bing Crosby's big number with him, wishing for a white Christmas, which she'd definitely have this year.

I looked at the time on my phone: eleven thirty. "Mother, I've got to go meet a client. I can help you with the dishes later."

She waved her hand at me, and joined in with the next tune. Dionne Warwick: "O Holy Night."

I threw my apron in the dirty clothes, smiling at my mother's off-key voice. I hadn't forgotten about my problems, or Betsy's, but I was keeping them in perspective and looking forward to an evening with Jack. Before I realized what was happening, I heard my own voice belt out, "A thrill of hope, the weary world rejoices."

Mother had broken me down. In a good way, because I was no help to anyone if I didn't stay upbeat. It didn't mean I didn't wish Betsy was here with us so we could teach her all the words to our favorite carols and how to decorate cookies with the perfect swoosh of snow icing. I wiped a tear from my eye, happy mixed with sad, and pulled open the front door, singing, "O ni-ight divine."

Chapter Twenty-two

Siri directed me through the slippery white streets of Amarillo. I took Washington south from I-40, driving slowly and carefully. The pellets earlier had definitely been ice, and they'd stuck. Nothing I hadn't driven on every year since getting my license, but what I'd learned from Dad years ago still applied: heavy sliding objects don't stop or turn well, but they crunch real good. I had stomped my brakes and turned too late one winter day, sliding my car right into one of Tech's new stock trailers, and I still winced as I remembered waiting for the inevitable sound of crumpling metal. Lesson learned: The best way to stop or change direction on ice was to coast.

So I rolled along like a turtle, creeping through intersections, passing other vehicles planted against each other, curbs, and light poles. I saw a tree seller in a parking lot on my right. He had nothing but a few scrubs left, and he was ringing a large handbell. He'd have a heck of a time selling the rest of them in weather like this, but I was impressed that he was trying. I hoped those fuddy-duddy Hodges at least had a Christmas tree at their house.

I made a right on Shasta without losing traction, stopping in front of 1000 without even applying the brakes. The house was at the end of a cul-de-sac, with an oversized square of yard on one side of the front sidewalk and a smaller square of one on the other. It looked like most of the other houses on the street. Small one-story ranch houses circa 1970, brick mostly in shades of tan to match the landscape, what there was of it. The house had no driveway or garage in front, nor any car at the curb. No lights shone from inside, either.

My phone made a random noise. I sighed. I really had to fix the notification sounds. I turned it over. A call, but I'd lost my darn contacts so iPhone couldn't tell me the name of the caller. It was a 340 area-code number, though, and that meant Katie, or someone else from the Virgin Islands.

I accepted. "Hello?"

"Merry Christmas!" Katie's pretty voice sang out.

"And to you, Katie Kovacs! Did you get my card?"

"I did. Ours will be late. But that's not why I called."

"Oh? What's up?"

"You know Ava is in Amarillo?"

"I knew she would be in the area sometime soon, but not when."

"She had a big Christmas Eve shindig there tonight, but it's been weathered out."

How weird to be doing a show on Christmas Eve, in Amarillo no less, I thought. But I said, "Poor Ava."

I got out of the car, slamming the door. The cold and wind and ice pellets attacked my exposed nose. I'd worn a scarf, but now I wound it higher, over my nose, muffling my mouth. I started for the front door.

"Yeah. Her phone battery was on fumes, so I said I'd call you to see if she could crash at your place tonight."

Oh. Oh my. I love Ava, but she is, well, a *handful*. I pressed the button for the doorbell. "Mother and I have a guest room she can stay in, but I'm heading to New Mexico tomorrow with Jack—"

"*With* Jack or 'with Jack'?"

She sounded like Wallace. "I'll let you know when we get back." I rang the bell again and peered through the opaque glass in the front door. I couldn't see any movement inside. I knocked on the glass, hard enough to hurt my gloved knuckles.

"Sounds promising."

I couldn't text Beth while I was on the phone with Katie, so I decided to walk around back and see if I could get her attention from there. I tramped over icy ground cover in the yard. "Anyway, she's welcome, but I won't be here after tonight."

"I'll tell her."

I opened the side gate, leaving it ajar behind me. "And you guys, is everyone doing all right?"

"Oh my gosh, the girls are about to start walking, and Thomas is so hyper. Thank God for my in-laws. And Nick. Nick is a dream."

As I emerged from the narrow strip of brown and white patchy lawn between the six-foot wooden fence and the house, I came around the back corner straight onto a concrete porch, placing my feet carefully so I wouldn't slip on the ice that was thicker there from the gutter downspout. I looked up after I was on the porch and stopped short. One more step and I would have planted my foot in the midsection of a woman, a woman lying facedown and unmoving.

I screamed, once, long and loud, and dropped my phone to my side. Even from that distance I could hear Katie.

"Emily, what's wrong? Are you all right?"

I put the phone back to my ear. "I . . . I, yes, I just found someone who's not. I've got to go. Have Ava contact me."

I hung up and crouched beside the prone woman. She had on gray sweat pants and a matching hoodie with zebra-print house slippers. I rolled her toward me. Her face was ghoulishly pale, but still I recognized her. Ivanka, the woman I'd met at the Love's truck stop. The makeup that had camouflaged her a week ago was absent now, and she looked closer to my mother's age than mine. She was even smaller than I remembered her, almost like a young girl.

I jerked my glove off and tossed it aside, then put two fingers against the cool skin at her carotid. No pulse. I readjusted my fingers to try again. They were already as cold as her neck. I'd never seen a dead person up close, but I'd seen plenty of dead animals closer than I'd liked. Despite my love of target shooting, it didn't translate to hunting. Dad took me one time, and I'll never forget the young pronghorn antelope's eyes as the light faded from them. It had chilled me to the bone. They'd looked like Ivanka's did, and hers were having the same effect on me now.

Suddenly I felt very exposed, and I jumped up, looking around me. The blinds on the back windows were closed. I still didn't see any lights on. I could see in the kitchen through the glass half of the door, but when I pressed my face to the glass for a better look, I couldn't see anyone inside. I tried the back door. Unlocked. I hesitated. I had no business in there, and there was a woman out here I might be able to save. I released the knob. Quickly, I scanned the backyard. It was covered in a blanket of crisp unbroken white. No trees. No shrubs. No furniture. Just weathered boards jutting up to a puffy gray sky. I didn't see anyone, not even any tracks save my own, but that didn't make the vulnerable, watched feeling go away.

I dialed my phone. It went to Jack's voice mail. "Call me. I went to visit a friend of Nadine's, and she's dead in her backyard. Oh, and it's Ivanka from Love's last week, the dancer."

I hung up and dialed 911.

A woman answered in a drawl. "9-1-1, what's your emergency?"

"I've found a woman in her backyard at 1000 Shasta. She's not breathing. Please send help." I dropped the phone and kneeled beside Ivanka. At close range, her cheap perfume nearly knocked me over, and I breathed through my mouth to avoid it. I tilted her head back, listened for the breath I knew wasn't there and started CPR.

***

A bundled-up female police officer arrived five minutes later. I was still doing chest compressions and life breaths with Ivanka, and I didn't catch the woman's name. I didn't even get much of a look at her before she took over the CPR. By the time the ambulance arrived, five minutes after the officer, it was clear nothing would help Ivanka, or Beth, or whatever her real name was. In the meantime, I had slowly but surely nearly frozen to death. I moved as close as I could to the house, out of the howling wind and pelting ice, and wrapped my arms around myself.

A second officer arrived, this one male but equally bundled. He conferred with the female officer for a moment out of my earshot. Her back was to me, but I saw her motion my way.

He walked over to me. "I'm Officer Jones. I'd like to ask you a few questions. We could talk here, or we could sit in my car where it's warmer."

My teeth chattered. "Emily Bernal. C-c-c-car."

As we walked around to the front of the house, my phone rang.

"Do you need to get that?" the officer asked.

Probably. "No." I let it go to voice mail.

We reached the squad car. Officer Jones, who looked roughly my age somewhere peeking out from all the winter clothing on his face, head, neck, hands, and body, opened the rear door for me, giving me an unwelcome surge of déjà vu. I frowned. To think I'd gone my whole life without getting in a cop car and was now being put in the backseat of one for the second time in a week.

He must have understood the look on my face, because he said, "Would you rather sit in front?"

"I would, thank you, if that's all right."

He shut the back door and opened the driver's door, got in, and then opened the passenger door for me from the inside. I slipped in, too. He pulled off all his outerwear except his coat, and underneath I saw that not only was he about my age, but he looked like Channing Tatum. Definitely the hottest police officer I'd seen in Amarillo. Scratch that. That I'd seen, ever, anywhere.

He picked up a clipboard that was between us on the seat and clicked a ballpoint pen. "Just a few questions."

"Absolutely."

"Your full name, address, and birthdate?"

I told him.

"How did you know the deceased?"

"I didn't."

He glanced up from his paper. "How did you come to be in her backyard?"

Lately I'd had far too much need to use the coaching I'd heard Jack give his clients. He always stressed to volunteer as little information as possible to the cops, so I spoke judiciously. "One of her coworkers introduced us virtually, and she asked me to come by."

"You'd never met her?"

My mind flashed to Ivanka's face under the fluorescent lights in the Love's parking lot, snow falling around us, her sashay as she took Wallace's arm. Had she introduced herself to me? She had not. So I answered truthfully, if incompletely. "No."

"Do you know what she wanted with you?"

I'd thought about this question long and hard while I gave Ivanka the breath of life. No way was I telling a random cop that Ivanka and I both held low opinions of some of their brethren. "Um, I work for a criminal attorney. My understanding was that she had run into some trouble and needed advice."

He nodded. "You mentioned her coworker. Where did they work?"

"The Polo Club."

"Ah." He looked up at me, like he was trying to figure out if I was hiding a secret life as a dancer, too.

"I don't work there."

He pinned his eyes back to his clipboard. "Did you see anybody else when you got here?"

"No."

"How'd you end up in the backyard?"

"I knocked on the front door but there was no answer. I knew she expected me, so I went around back in case she hadn't heard me."

He looked at me sideways without turning his head, his eyes narrowed to slits. "Do you always go into people's backyards if they don't answer the front door?"

Truthfully? Usually. "No," I said.

He stopped writing. "And this time you did, because why?"

"It was freezing outside. I didn't want to leave unless I'd tried every way I could think of to keep our appointment, but if she wasn't there, I wanted to get back in the car with the heater on. And not have to come back later."

He twirled the pen through his fingers, appearing to be lost in thought.

My phone rang again. I ignored it.

"Was there anything at all that you saw that led you to form an opinion as to how"—he glanced at and tapped a display screen mounted on his dashboard and facing him—"Beth McIntosh died?"

Other than ice? A hard concrete patio? Again, I stuck to the minimum responsive answer to his question. "No."

"All right, we're nearly done here, Ms. Bernal, if you'll give me a few more minutes."

"Sure."

He began typing into the keypad of the device on his dashboard; I checked my voice mail. Two messages. The first was from Jack. Returning my call. Did I need him to come? Was I okay? I texted my response: *No. Yes. But thanks.*

The second one was Ava. Her phone was dead. She was calling from a pay phone at the bus station for a ride, and, from the sound of her voice, she was extremely cold. If my phone rang again, I would have to answer it. No fair leaving her standing out there dialing me over and over.

Officer Jones said, "So, this isn't the first dead body you've found for us?"

"What?"

"It says here that we responded to a 911 call over the murder of Maria—"

"I didn't make that call, and I never saw a dead body. I was unconscious on the floor. The person that murdered her almost got me, too."

"Hmm. And last week you were brought in—"

"As a form of harassment."

He read some more, and his lips moved.

"Listen, I have a friend who is expecting me to pick her up at the bus station. Hence my ringing phone. She's waiting for me out in the cold. I hadn't really anticipated finding a dead person today. I want to help, I really do, but if we're done, I do need to go."

His eyes moved back and forth as he stared at the display. Acting as if he didn't hear me, he said, almost fearfully, "You filed a complaint against Samson and Burrows?"

"I did, but it doesn't have anything to do with"—I waved my hand in the general direction of Ivanka's backyard—"this."

He pursed his lips, nodding slowly, staring again at the screen. "Yeah, you're probably right." He pressed a button and the slight glow from his screen disappeared. "Someone will call you if we have any more questions, but this case looks like a pretty simple slip and fall. We get those in this kind of weather. Thank you, Ms. Bernal."

"You're welcome."

I opened the door and got out, then leaned back in. "Merry Christmas, Officer Jones."

"Merry Christmas to you, too."

I walked to the Mustang, which was now frigid inside. I turned it on, with heater and defrost on full icy blast, Wallace's comment to me earlier be damned. Only an hour or so had passed, yet a layer of ice covered my windshield. My phone made one of its inexplicable noises. I turned it over.

Laura: *We are ALL looking forward to seeing you tomorrow.* She ended with a smiley face.

I typed one-thumbed, keeping my other hand deep in my pocket as the temperature in the Mustang rose a nanodegree at a time. *Me too!*

I grabbed my ice scraper and hopped out again. I held my hand up and caught some precipitation. It was snow. *Hallelujah.* Winter driving in Amarillo and Lubbock, and some in Dallas, taught me to fear ice and respect snow. The weather forecast on the radio during the drive over here promised snow and freezing temps. Snow would improve the icy roads. Soon, anyway. Right now, I still had to contend with the exposed ice.

When I finished scraping, I did some shoulder shrugs and rolled my neck. The creepiness of finding Ivanka's dead body was slowly dissipating, enough that I remembered my date with Jack and felt a flare of excitement. Then it hit me. I was picking up a houseguest for the evening. A handful of a houseguest. And then I was leaving for New Mexico in the morning. Ava and I would barely even get to talk. She'd think I was an incredibly rude and terrible hostess.

I couldn't—I wouldn't—cancel my first real date with Jack Holden. I supposed I could invite her to go with Jack and me tonight, but hopefully she'd be exhausted from traveling and want nothing but a soft bed and long winter's night sleep. Ava liked men, liked them a whole lot, and they liked her back. I didn't need that kind of pressure on my fledgling relationship. I sighed with a rising note of exasperation. I was being unfair. I'd cast Ava in a role, and she hadn't even stepped onstage yet. I needed to chill. I would chill. Starting right now, I was chill.

I got back in the Mustang and put it in drive.

Chapter Twenty-three

I rolled well below the speed limit down Fourth toward Tyler and the Greyhound Bus Station. The station was only four blocks past the Maxor Building, where Jack and Snowflake would be doing whatever it was they did when the office functioned as their condo instead of workplace. The bus station itself occupied part of a block on the edge of Amarillo's small downtown. It stood about two and a half stories high and had an art deco-ish feel, with rounded corners and square blue tiles three-high around the bottom, sort of in the style of the restored Paramount Theater sign on Polk Street.

I turned right on Tyler. The bus station was just ahead, and I spotted Ava outside the front door but inside the recessed overhang. She wore an electric-blue jumpsuit and black leather coat, and she was stamping her feet in spike-heeled black boots. She didn't exactly blend into the background, even if her outfit did match it. I coasted to a stop, threw the Mustang in park, and popped the trunk.

I climbed out and ran carefully to her. "Ava! What a fun surprise! Get in, you must be freezing." I hugged her and grabbed her two suitcases, practically in the same motion.

"Yah, I freezing my bana, for true," she said, her island lilt an odd sound here, like a scene from *Cool Runnings*. It took me a moment to remember "bana" was the West Indian word for "bottom," too. "Thank you for coming for me." In her accent, "thank" came out as "tank."

"No problem." I threw her bags in and slammed the trunk. I was back in my seat as fast as she was, but, then again, I was wearing retro moon boots I'd appropriated from my mom's closet, not stilettos.

My phone made a weird noise from its perch on the console. A message from Nadine: *How'd it go with Beth?*

Oh God. She didn't know about her friend yet. I typed: *Call me.*

Ava shut her door. "So, how you entertain an island girl in this town on Christmas Eve?"

As I groaned inwardly at Ava asking precisely the wrong question, the phone rang. It was Nadine, way faster than I'd hoped. I didn't know which I dreaded more: telling Nadine about Beth, or telling Ava about my plans that evening. I decided to let Nadine go to voice mail. I'd call her back later.

Ava kept talking, leaving her first question behind us. "The weather here terrible," she said. "How you stand it?"

"Most of the population isn't familiar with the alternatives."

"But you?"

I put the car in gear and coasted into motion on Tyler, then slowed at the corner. There was no traffic. I turned right onto Seventh Avenue. "I have no excuse, other than I'm broke."

"Yah, Katie tell me your husband an anti-man."

I opened my mouth then shut it.

"You got no idea what I talking about, do you?"

I turned right onto Taylor. Suddenly, the connection occurred to me, and the translation of the island slang made perfect sense. Katie had told her Rich was gay. I laughed.

"It took me a minute, but I got it. Yes, Rich likes men, and his guy has expensive taste, so they ran through our cash before I even caught on. But my divorce is final, and I'm pretty much back on my feet."

"You living with your mother?"

"I am." And not wanting to talk about it. "Are you still living with Rashidi?" I referred to the gorgeous UVI professor she sometimes dated who was a mutual friend of Katie's, but not the father of Ava's daughter.

She waffled her hand. "Roommates still. For now."

Rats. I had hoped she was in a serious relationship. "So, your gig got weathered out tonight, huh?"

"Yah, the organizer, Phil, he cool, though. He reschedule me, and he pay me half."

"What kind of group has a Christmas Eve party anyway? Most of Amarillo will be at church."

She laughed. "Phil see me when he visit St. Marcos, and he know everybody. Got me booked for two weeks at parties in three states. He tell me they all private. That they, uh, swingers."

"Swingers?"

"Yah, you know, people who trade partners."

"Yeah, I know, but we have a client named Phil who runs a swingers group."

"Sound like the same guy."

Phil, Phil, Phil. I wondered if Nadine had any idea what she was getting into, or if it would even matter to her. "What I really want to know is how are you, and how is your baby?"

"She good, I good, my mother—she save my life. Don't even think about having a baby without a grandmother near you house, I tell you."

The loss of my baby had left a cold, empty space in my heart, and my fear of losing Betsy tugged the edges wider and wider. I'd love to have a baby anywhere, anytime, now that I knew I couldn't. Or most likely couldn't. But maybe I could have a big girl, maybe I could have Betsy. If I could help Jack and Wallace keep her in the states long enough for it to happen, and keep the whereabouts of Greg and Farrah a secret.

But I kept all of that inside and instead said, "Good advice. I'll remember that. Are you and the father, um—"

I merged onto 287 and quickly veered onto the I-40 entrance ramp, then negotiated another careful merge. These icy flyways were tricky today.

"Lord no. He worthless. So if you know a man need a woman who look good on his arm when he out spending his cash, I the one for the job."

My stomach lurched. That was exactly what I was afraid she'd say. We drove in silence for a few minutes. A dinging noise from my dashboard panel grabbed my attention. I glanced down. Low-gas light. I switched on my right turn signal to exit at Bell for gas.

At the station, Ava ran inside. I huddled in the car for warmth while the gas pumped. A huge army-green panel van backed to the pump station catty-corner in front of my car. It was the kind of van that construction crews use. Them, and serial killers. A man who looked vaguely familiar exited and worked at the pump. Of course, just about everyone in Amarillo looked familiar to me. I either went to elementary school with them or knew them from their kids or I'd seen them at United Supermarket a couple of thousand times or they were Jack's clients or family or, God forbid, victims of Jack's clients.

This guy looked a little older than me. He had a square face with a lot of graying facial hair and wore a cap with wool-lined ear flaps over his head. He took a few drags off a cigarette then crushed it under the toe of his boot. He went to the back of the van and opened one side of the doors—like the batwing gates in Judge Herring's courtroom—and I couldn't help watching, even if it was impolite. His body blocked most of my line of sight, so I leaned to the right for a better view.

"Ho ho ho, Merry Christmas, boys and girls," a deep voice slurred, so loud I could hear him through my car window. A tall Santa lurched in front of my car, toward the back of the van. He was a little on the slim side for Santa, and even more on the drunk side, it appeared. He steadied himself with a hand on the open van door but still managed to knock the driver to the side and, from the looks of it, slosh half a bottle of something all over him, too. The bottle dropped to the ground and rolled away. Santa's eyes tracked it, and he moaned. The driver righted himself and brushed liquid off his body, flicking his hands in exaggerated motions as he did.

"Shorry," Santa shouted, or tried to. "How about shome candy canes for the kiddos?"

The pump clicked and I saw it had shut off. I opened the door to go put the nozzle up and get my receipt. Alcohol fumes hit me as I took the long way around the back of my car to the pump. I pulled the nozzle from my car. As I screwed on my gas cap, I saw the van driver grab Santa by his fuzzy red jacket fronts. I backed into the pump, gaping as he shoved him against the closed side of the rear door to the van. For the first time, I got a good view of the interior. It was filled with kids. *Filled* with them. Long, dark braids and a sweet face caught my attention. I stood frozen, nozzle in midair.

"Betsy?" I called out, but my words were muffled by the roar of the van driver, who I now realized was Trevon Hodges, Betsy's foster father.

"Stay away from those kids with your drunken idolatry."

"But shir, I din mean nothing by—"

"Sinner!" He pushed the man away.

Santa stumbled to his knees, then stood. "Sh'okay." He held up one hand. "I may be a shinner, but Jesus died for my shins, sho I'll be okay." He stumbled toward the van again.

Trevon Hodges reached into the back of the van and pulled out a tire iron, and I heard screams from inside. I shoved the nozzle back in place on the pump. A voice I knew well screamed, "Mama!"

I started to run toward Betsy, but saw she was facing away from me, holding her arms out toward the front of the van. Just barely, I recognized Mary Alice Hodges, a few rows up.

Hodges pointed the tire iron at Santa. He dropped his voice so low I could barely hear him. "That won't save you from the wrath of God, sinner. Now, go, before it catches up with you in the here and now."

Santa turned and staggered away, mumbling. He picked up his bottle and disappeared around the corner of the gas station. I remained inert, my mouth open. Hodges tossed the tire iron back into the rear of the van and seemed to notice me for the first time. He nodded, then slammed the back door, blocking my view of Betsy. A low whimper caught in my throat. Hodges went around the side of the van. I heard the pump click and the sound of the nozzle inserted into its home station. He didn't appear again. I heard his door slam and the engine start, then the van pulled away, dragging my heart along with it.

On wooden legs, I took the three steps back to the door of my car. Somehow, I got it open and lowered myself inside. Betsy. Betsy had called out for her mama and that scary Mary Alice Hodges was the only one there. I was still months away from being able to try to adopt her, and she needed a mama now.

Ava yanked the door open and dove inside, her teeth chattering. She slammed it and looked at me. "Damn, girl, you look like you seen a jumbie." She used the island word for ghost or spirit, which I knew from my time there with Katie.

"Something like that," I said. I bit my lip, holding back tears, and pointed the Mustang toward Heaven.

***

At five twenty-five, I poofed my bangs a little and shellacked them into place. If the sky was still spitting snow, my hair needed the support. Heck, I needed support as much as my hair did. I'd ended an emotional call with Nadine a few minutes before. She was understandably shaken about the death of her coworker/friend. Finding Ivanka and all that came after hadn't been the highlight of my day, either, but it was the sight of Betsy and the sound of her voice calling out to her mama that I couldn't shake. I had to, though. I took a deep breath. Obsessing about it wouldn't do me a bit of good. I turned sideways in front of the bathroom mirror, checking myself from all angles. Peach flocked wallpaper provided the backdrop, and a Phelps family tree cross-stitch sampler framed my head. The lavender lingerie set was hidden, but I smoothed my hand over the waist of my black flowing skirt. No one would have ever guessed I was pregnant less than three months ago from my flat belly now.

The doorbell rang at five thirty, exactly as Jack had promised it would.

Mother's voice chirped, "I'll get it."

"Thanks, Mother."

A few taps sounded on the bathroom door.

I opened it. "All yours," I said.

Ava stepped toward me, her hands splayed at hip level on either side of her. She smacked a kiss in the air five inches from my cheek. "I won't be but a minute."

I couldn't imagine what additional primping she needed for a Christmas Eve service, although it wouldn't hurt my feelings if she changed clothes entirely. The curve-hugging black dress with the peekaboo chest and crisscross back straps might have worked for her canceled gig, but it was bound to raise a few eyebrows at a church. Not to mention her four-inch black pumps with little bows on the heels that accented the back seams in her pantyhose.

We exchanged places in the bathroom. She leaned into the mirror, pursing her plum-colored lips and pushing her breasts farther up and out of her dress. Her perfect, café au lait skin glistened above her neckline, sparkled even, and I suspected she'd dusted her décolletage with something. A lot of something. My mouth went dry watching her, and I wasn't even attracted to women. I cringed to think the impact she could have on Jack. Sure, I was pretty, but Ava was sex on two legs.

I heard my mother greeting him, and the rumble of his hello back to her.

I swallowed and said to Ava, "Meet us in the living room." I turned to go, then added, "The roads are bad, so we need to get moving as quick as we can."

She winked at me. "No problem, mon."

I walked down the dark hallway from the bathroom to the strains of "What Child Is This" playing. My low-heeled riding boots were almost soundless against the carpet. They had seemed a smart, attractive choice half an hour ago but now hopelessly bland. I straightened my red cashmere sweater. The soft wool was luxurious to the touch, but was it too "school marm" beside Ava?

"Enough of this bull hockey," I whispered to myself. "Woman up."

I'd already had a more-than-full day, but this evening was important to me. I wasn't going to let insecurity or anything else spoil it. I pasted on a smile, and walked to the door of the bright living room.

Jack and my mother stood in front of the hearth before a roaring fire. She had pressed a rosy-cheeked Santa mug in his hand, and steam rose from its mouth as the aroma of spiced tea wafted my way.

"I just can't thank you enough, Jack. For everything."

I stayed rooted in the doorway. What did she have to thank Jack for? Hackles rose on my arms. Surely she wasn't talking about him giving me a job?

"Yep." But of course the man of few words—and those usually off topic—wasn't going to expound on her remarks. "Can I entice you to Downtown Methodist with us tonight?"

Mother beamed. "Maybe next year. I helped with the stage set for the children's program this year at Believers, and I can't miss the pageant." She put her hand on his non-mug arm. "I'm thrilled Emily's going with you."

Since the conversation seemed poised to take an embarrassing direction without any further illumination on what my mother had to be thankful to Jack for, I broke in. "Merry Christmas Eve."

Mother clapped her hands together. "There she is."

Jack's improbably topaz eyes met mine. "Merry Christmas Eve to you." His left-sided smile warmed me inside.

I crossed the room to join them. Mother went all out for Christmas, and the living room was overflowing with jolliness. Hand-knitted Christmas stockings hung from the mantel over the fireplace. Mother had made them herself. There were three, of course: mine, hers, and my father's, despite the fact that the last Christmas he'd spent with us was fifteen years before. Her snow globes decorated the coffee table. A nativity scene of embroidered figurines graced an end table. The tree commanded wholly a third of the room from its spot in front of the window, and wrapped gifts spilled over the dark green velvet tree skirt below it. Homemade ornaments—mostly Mother's crafts, but some I recognized from my school days—covered the tree branches. A construction-paper chain in faded red and green. A picture of me glued in a plastic coffee can lid. A Popsicle-stick reindeer with a cotton-ball tail and red puffy nose. I loved it all.

When I reached them, Jack put his hand under my elbow, and butterflies exploded in flight in my tummy.

Fighting to cover my nerves, I asked, "Have you heard anything from Clyde?"

"They kept the old codger overnight, but he's home now, and driving Betty up a tree."

"That's great."

"Unless you're Betty. Are you ready?"

"Well, nearly." The butterflies crash-landed. "I have a favor to ask."

"What's that?"

My mother raised her eyebrows, pulling her thin skin thinner below them.

I put my hand up toward her and shot her a warning glance. To Jack I said, "A friend of mine from the Virgin Islands needed a place to stay tonight, and she wants to join us. Is that okay?"

Jack took one sip of tea, then another. The logs crackled and popped in the fireplace. I looked at Mother and she at me. My chest grew tight and then tighter as Jack remained silent without answering my question.

And then Ava appeared in the doorway. Or shot in like a Roman candle, rather. She had thrown a red shawl over her dress, and I couldn't help but wither as I compared my black skirt and red sweater to her black and red ensemble.

She tossed her thick mane of sun-bronzed black hair behind her shoulder and said as only she could, "Emily, introduce me to this fine boss of yours."

If Ava had an effect on Jack, he hid it well. He raised one brow at me, though.

The frog in my throat made my voice thin. "Jack, this is my friend, Ava Butler, from St. Marcos. Ava, this is Jack Holden."

Ava walked to him and held out one hand.

He took it and bowed his head to her. "Ms. Butler, a pleasure."

Her accent was a musical purr. "Call me Ava. And the pleasure be all mine, meh son." She held on to his hand a little longer than I thought was really necessary, her glistening eyes locked onto his.

"Thank you for letting me crash your party with Emily. Christmas a lonely time for me this year, far from my daughter and the island I call home."

"Okay," I said. My voice, meant to break her spell, came out almost a shriek. But it worked. Ava dropped Jack's hand. "I think we're ready. Mother, please drive carefully."

"You know I will."

Ava hugged my mother. "Thanks for having me. I know Emily come from good people, first time I meet her."

Mother was always a sucker for flattery. She hugged Ava back. "Of course. Stay as long as you'd like." She turned to Jack. "Is the weather going to be good enough for you and Emily to fly out tomorrow?"

I wanted to jump up and down and wave my arms "no," but Ava's phone made a noise, and she pulled it from her handbag to check it.

Jack said, "We'll have to see."

"See what?" Ava asked.

I grabbed Ava's arm. "You're going to fall on your bana in those shoes. Let me help you out to Jack's car."

***

As the service drew to a close, the organist and choir burst into the recessional, "Hark the Herald Angels Sing." I stood up between Jack and Ava and continued singing as the front pews filed out. We had sat near the back, so we had a long time before we would be exiting.

I flipped the program to the back cover. Jack had surprised me again. I had assumed we were going to a Catholic mass, and it turned out he was a member of Downtown Methodist, a church up the street from our offices. I kept singing as I read over it: Announcements. Singles. Ladies Bible Study. Youth Group. Choir practice. A potluck— THE CHURCH WILL HOST AN EVENING OF FINE DINING, SUPER ENTERTAINMENT, AND GRACIOUS HOSTILITY. I smiled. Another gem for my collection.

Our row emptied into the center aisle and we began a slow walk toward the sanctuary exit. Jack led and Ava and I followed, side by side. Inside the nave, the carol sounded exultant, glorious. As we neared the propped-open doors, the sound changed to a happy jangle of music mixed with chattering voices. By the time we exited, the chatter was dominant and the music the background.

Without the aid of the choir, people in the foyer sang out of rhythm and off-key all around me—except for Ava, who sang at full voice and perfectly, which drew as many eyes as did her va-va and her voom. On my left, two openly gay men held hands as they talked to a heterosexual couple with twin boys. Three blue-haired women leaned against each other for support and spoke in slow, tremulous voices to my right. Someone grabbed my arm from behind, stopping me short.

I called out, "Jack," but my voice didn't begin to cut through the din.

Jack kept going, Ava behind him. I turned to my accoster. Officer Samson's towering frame loomed behind me, recognizable even when he wore a sport coat, sweater, and button down over navy pants, instead of a police officer's uniform. He continued pulling me from the crowd, and I considered resisting, but decided that probably wasn't something one did with cops, even when the object of one's affection was walking off with the sexiest woman within a five-hundred-mile radius. I acquiesced, letting Samson lead me to the side of the room, out of the flow of human traffic.

He put his head close to mine without letting go of my arm and shouted, "I heard you reported a murder today."

I scowled, processing his words. Officer Jones told me he thought it was a slip and fall. I had wanted to believe it, but I remembered the eerie feeling I'd had in her backyard, like someone was watching me. I'd shaken it off, but I'd wondered about foul play, especially since she'd been scared to leave her home.

"Murder?"

"Yes, and I'm starting to worry about you."

My fist clenched. Was he trying to intimidate me like that jerk Burrows? "Oh really?"

He released my arm. "You keep showing up where people are dying. That's high risk. You should take up a nonhazardous hobby and spend some time away from crime scenes."

His voice hadn't sounded hostile. In fact, he sounded grandfatherly, even warm. I relaxed. "I'll think about it. What are you doing here?"

"Christmas Eve service with my family."

"Huh." I looked around for a wife giving him the stink eye for talking to me, but I didn't see any likely candidates.

"Anyway, since we're here, about the other day, and your phone." He cleared his throat. "I'm sorry."

His sudden change in subject stalled my brain like the swamped engine of my dad's truck once when he drove through a high-water crossing in Palo Duro Canyon. "Huh?"

He shook his head quickly, in small motions. "There's a lot I can't say. I'm a member of the APD. You've filed a complaint. But I regret that it happened."

I stared at him a moment then shook my head.

"What?"

"You're absolutely sure it was murder today?"

"So they say. I haven't seen the final report."

People streamed past us toward the exits. Cold air blew in from the street, and the arctic gusts blew snow all the way to where we stood. I wrapped my arms around myself. Jack and Ava were probably going steady by now. I couldn't stand here freezing my tail off letting that happen.

As I was about to make my getaway, Samson broke his silence. "How'd you know her? I don't picture you as running in the same circles."

I stuck with the story I'd given Officer Jones earlier. "Friend of a friend."

"And you were there because why?"

"That's all going to be in Officer Jones's report, I'm sure. Listen, my friends have—"

"It said she needed a criminal attorney."

"Yep."

"She dated a cop, you know."

The people around me blurred and their voices squelched like feedback. The crowd seemed to collapse in. All the warm bodies in the overheated space made it humid, close, and claustrophobic. I wanted to rip off my jacket and run but meanwhile my brain slowed to the speed of a slug.

"No, I didn't. Which one?"

Before he could answer, I heard Jack's voice in my ear. "Emily, there you are."

Samson released me, saluting as he disappeared with a few side-steps into the crowd.

I whirled, catching Jack by both arms. "I was just on my way."

He peered more closely at me, then at Samson's retreating figure, but I ignored the question on his face. I'd tell him about Samson. About my whole day, my whole last few days.

Later.

***

Jack parked his Jeep at an angle at Mother's house, with his head-lights illuminating the icy walkway. Ava got out of the backseat on his side and lurched, nearly falling. No shocker. She'd been having trouble on the ice in her heels all night. Jack put his hand under her elbow and guided her around the front of the Jeep, where I joined them and took his other arm. I glanced at the pristine new bumper and silver body-work—yet another shade in the rainbow of colors on the Jeep. He still refused to take my money for the repairs. Slowly, we walked toward the house on the ice-rink walkway and stepped carefully onto the slippery porch.

I said to Jack, "Would you like to come in? Maybe we could talk about whatever it is you wanted to talk about?" I hoped to give him his present tonight, too.

His eyes darted to Ava, then back to me.

Ava eyed him like a Grade A steak. "Yah, Jack, come in. It so cold out here, and there two women inside to warm you up."

Jack's eyes looked as terrified as a calf in the chute before a roping competition. I didn't blame him a bit. Possibly I should have warned him about Ava. Possibly I should have warned Ava I had dibs on Jack. If I had, then maybe I wouldn't be imagining strangling her sparkly throat right now.

He said, "Uh, well, we can talk in New Mexico."

I was disappointed, but I smiled at him.

Ava smiled, too. "New Mexico! When? That where I gig next."

"Tomorrow," Jack replied.

"You two driving?"

"Flying in my plane."

"Sweet! Carry me with you?"

"Uh . . . I guess we could . . ."

"Perfect. I take a bus to Albuquerque from there."

Jack looked at me. "Okay, then?"

Not okay. But what could I say, really? She was my friend, she was stranded, and if Jack didn't object, then how could I?

"Okay, then," I said, and hard as I'd tried to sound enthusiastic, my voice rang a false note to my ear, but neither Jack nor Ava reacted.

"I'll get a report on conditions and text you when I know more in the morning," Jack said to me.

"Sounds good."

I stood my ground in the cold, trying to wait Ava out. I opened the door. "Better get in before you freeze to death, Ava."

She put her arms around Jack and tilted her head back. "I falling in love with Texas, Jack." She kissed him, on the mouth. "See you tomorrow." She walked in the door, then cocked her hip and put a hand on it. "You coming, Emily?"

"I-I-I . . ." I licked my lips, my eyes darting between Ava and Jack. I wanted to give him a chance to kiss me. This was supposed to have been a date. But there was no way the ultra-private Jack would put his lips anywhere near mine with Ava staring at us, if he'd even been considering it at all.

"Ava, give us a moment?" Jack smiled at her and gestured toward the inside of the house.

My breath caught in my throat.

"Ohhhh yah." Ava disappeared from the open doorway, but not before shooting me a lascivious grin.

When she was gone, Jack closed the distance between us. "I thought we'd never get rid of her."

"Me either." My heart pounded harder, and I was afraid he could feel it through his chest.

He took off one glove then slid his hand under my hair at the base of my neck. I closed my eyes and his warm lips covered mine. They were soft and full, and they clung to mine like I realized I was now clinging to him with both my hands. He nudged my lips apart and took my top lip into his, sucking gently. I groaned, and I reached up to grasp the back of his head. Within seconds, we'd drifted away from the porch light and Jack's hands had worked their way inside my wrap, my top, and the silky bra I was suddenly oh-so-glad I'd worn. The man had lightning hands, but mine found his butt just as fast and I squeezed and pulled him close. As cold as it was outside, suddenly, I had an urge to rip a few layers off. Jack turned my back to the wall of the house and leaned into me, harder and harder. His lips broke from mine and he kissed his way down my neck, his lips rough against my cold skin.

"Ooooh," I gasped.

He didn't answer, which was good, because I didn't want him to stop what he was doing. I grasped his hair with both hands and laid my head against the wall.

"Emily, I making hot tea. You want some?" Ava said, her voice shattering the silence only inches from my eardrum.

I yelped, and Jack's face shot back from my chest.

Ava grinned. "Oh, sorry." She turned away. "Um, um, um," she said, shutting the door behind her.

"Awkward," I said to Jack. But she'd probably arrived in the nick of time to save us from a citizen's arrest for public indecency from the nosy neighbor lady across the street who used to bang on the window when I made out with my high school boyfriend in his car. That wouldn't have looked good after my bogus bust by Burrows and Samson last week.

Jack didn't answer. He pushed me back against the wall, and his mouth claimed mine.

To hell with the neighbor lady, I thought, and ripped his shirt hem out of his jeans.

Chapter Twenty-four

Luckily, the runway was clear and the temperature in the thirties the next morning. In the plane it was a nippy forty-five degrees, but as much as I hated the cold, I couldn't have been happier. Jack put Snowflake's kennel in the backseat, and when Ava suggested that she ride up front as a first-timer in a Skyhawk, he told her that he was putting me in shotgun so he could hold my hand. Which he did, off and on, for most of the three-and-a-half-hour flight. My arm actually got tired from holding it up to reach his, but I didn't care. I wouldn't have cared if I had to flap my arms to get us there. I was that happy.

White blanketed the landscape below us most of the way, but the sky was clear and a vivid blue, like the Caribbean Sea around Ava's home island, St. Marcos. It matched my buoyant mood. As we began our descent over the Sierra Blancas toward the tiny strip on Wrong Turn Ranch, however, the clouds grew thicker. Soon we were cruising along above an endless blanket of gray cotton balls. Jack had to let go of my hand, and his face was intense, his eyes locked onto the instrument panel. My head started to ache.

The pitch of the engine changed and we started descending. In seconds, we'd bumped and bounced into the pit of gray cotton balls, and they clung to us, obscuring our vision. The ground could be coming up on us fast, or a mountain peak could be right in front of us. Despite the temperature in the plane, a cold sweat ran down my back. I snuck a look at Jack, and saw he was sweating, too. The gray cottony clouds seemed to go on forever, but finally we slipped out the bottom of them. Then I saw a mountaintop poking through another layer of gray cotton below. These were ominous, darker, more like mounds of ash. I put my head down and started whispering a prayer: "Dear God, if you could help us land safely, I promise to be nicer to my mother."

Before I got to *amen*, a hand tapping my shoulder startled me. I whipped around. It was Ava. I leaned toward her as far as I could, as she leaned toward me. Her dark skin seemed to have a gray-green undertone. I couldn't hear her, but I read her lips.

"Is everything okay?" she asked.

I gave her a thumbs-up sign. Just then, everything around us went dark. The Skyhawk bounced as it hurtled across the sky and toward the earth. I turned back around and clutched the armrests. The turbulence shook us so hard that I lost my sensation of up and down and side-ways, with the only light coming from the instrument panel inside the plane. I could barely see Jack, only enough to know he was keeping his eyes on the dashboard controls. Nausea came over me, and my mouth went dry. The plane bucked violently, and my seatbelt cut into my lap as we dropped straight down. I felt my mouth stretch open and my ears pop. If I was screaming, I couldn't hear myself.

But as suddenly as we'd started shaking and dropping, we stopped falling and floated out of the clouds. The ground was below us, maybe five hundred feet, and I could see the orange windsock that marked the runway at the ranch ahead. I wiped sweat from my forehead and noticed my hands were shaking as hard as the Skyhawk had moments ago. I felt a nervous vibration in my throat.

I studied the ground and took deep, calming breaths. The snow here was only patchy, and it looked like someone had plowed the runway, because it was completely clear. Those were good things. Everything would be all right.

The plane's wheels hit the dirt. Fifteen minutes later, we had loaded an unsteady Ava along with Snowflake and our bags into the Subur-ban—which took twice as long as usual since we'd brought presents for half of Tularosa—had fueled and hangared the plane and were on our way to the ranch house. I turned my phone on and it searched for a signal. When it found it, it made a series of burps and whistles I'd never heard before. Today. Today I was resetting all the dang tones into something recognizable. I read the screen. Three voice mails. Six text messages. Twelve emails. I viewed the list of numbers from which I had voice mails first. All three calls were from an unknown number. I didn't play the unknown-number game. Telemarketers, probably. I put my phone down, then, worried about Betsy being snatched by Immi-gration, I picked it back up and pressed play anyway, then put it to my ear.

A man said, "Emily, Merry Christmas."

I pressed my fist to my mouth, hard. A gravelly voice from the past. A voice I hadn't heard in nearly a decade from a person I hadn't seen in fifteen years. But I would recognize this voice until the day I died, even though it sounded older. It was a voice that turned me into a child who'd been left, again, in a split second. My father, Johnny Phelps.

His message kept playing. "I know you're probably surprised to hear from me. I would really like to talk to you and explain what happened. I've missed you more than I can say, and I love you."

The voice mail ended. Swallowing down bile, I pressed play for the next one.

"Uh, I forgot to tell you how to get hold of me. Please call me as soon as you can. There's some things you need to know, not just for me, but because they're important for you." He recited a phone number.

The voice mail ended. I put my phone in my lap and breathed in and out a few times. I wanted to get the last one over with, so I looked down, and fat teardrops rained on the iPhone screen. I had to wipe them away with my sweater before I could play the last voice mail. I felt Jack's eyes on me, and he reached out and took my left hand.

"Emily, one more thing. If you could please talk to Jack, tell him it wasn't me that took that stuff, I would appreciate it. I've made my mistakes, but I don't take another fellow's things. Thank you, Sweet Pea. I love you."

Sweet Pea? He had the nerve to call me Sweet Pea when I hadn't heard from him in years? And what was this about Jack? My Jack?

I jerked my hand away from My Jack and pressed play again. Listened again. Pressed play again. Listened again. There was no denying what I'd heard. My father knew Jack. Jack knew Dad.

Well, Merry frickin' Christmas to me.

I dropped the phone in my lap then my face in my hands and sobbed.

Chapter Twenty-five

Jack stood on the other side of the door to my bathroom. "I'm sorry. Your dad made me promise to let him tell you. I shouldn't have waited this long."

I was mad enough to kill him, possibly madder than I'd ever been at anyone in my whole life. I sunk into the bubble bath up to my eyeballs, wanting to tune him out, but wanting even more to hear what he had to say. I would have to wait and kill him when he was done.

I eased my ears and mouth out of the water and hollered. "You should have told me the first second you knew!"

Jack's voice grew frustrated. "Looking at a picture of you and your dad in a family album while sitting in the living room with your mother, you want me to say, 'Hey, isn't that Johnny Phelps? I put him in the slammer'?"

"I didn't even know he was alive, much less that he was in prison!"

"How was I supposed to know that?"

"You found out soon enough. You could have told me then."

"I needed to figure some things out first."

"What?"

"Things."

He kept talking, but I sunk beneath the water again where I didn't have to hear him. He could have all the good reasons in the world but the fact remained that I deserved to know my father was alive. I deserved to know where he was. Jack could have found a way to tell me, but he didn't. I came back up for air.

Jack said, "Are you even listening?"

"I'm not sure. What did you say?"

There was a thrump against the door, and when he spoke his voice sounded different, farther away. I pictured him, leaning against the door, arms probably crossed, eyes on the ground twelve inches in front of his boots. My heart tugged a little, and I smacked it away without mercy.

"I said I've been trying to tell you for a week. Things kept getting in the way."

"A week? Seven twenty-four-hour days? And you couldn't find any time in them?"

"It's not like you tell me everything, like who that guy was you were talking to at church last night."

I submerged again. The things I ran out of time to tell him and the things he couldn't find time to tell me were so different they weren't even events in the same rodeo. They were different like bull riding from ballet. The silence of the water thrummed in my ears. I felt my long hair floating, touching my arms. I came up for a breath.

"So tell me now."

"This would be easier if you'd let me in."

"I'm in the bathtub."

"I won't look. I can't talk to you through a closed door."

"In a minute."

"Okay." Something started scratching against the door. "Snow-flake, no," he said in an alpha voice. The scratching stopped. "I met your father ten years ago. In Alamogordo. After he was arrested for murder."

"Murder? My dad is a murderer?" I jumped to my feet, and water sloshed over the sides. I didn't care.

"He's a good guy that got caught up in a bad situation."

"What kind of bad situation?" I sank slowly back into the tub. More water sloshed out.

"He should be the one to tell you." Jack paused, waiting for me to let him off the hook, I assumed, but I didn't. "He got injured and couldn't rodeo, had money trouble, picked up odd jobs. Got crossways with someone he worked with."

Oh no. I squeezed my hands into fists.

"They got in a fight. He killed the guy with a broken beer bottle. Your dad said it was self-defense, but it didn't look good."

I became aware that I was rocking back and forth in the water, arms wrapped around myself, keening softly.

Jack whispered, his voice sounding agonized, too. "Are you okay?"

I made myself stop the noise. I hated that he heard me. I hated being this weak, this vulnerable. I snapped, "Just finish."

Again, I heard a noise like he turned, and then his voice was louder. "I was the prosecutor. He had a shit court-appointed attorney, but no priors, so I took a plea for involuntary manslaughter. He got out in November."

"So where's he been since he got out?"

"Here."

"Here where?"

"Wrong Turn Ranch."

"He was here at Wrong Turn Ranch?"

"Up until two weeks ago, yes. Working for Mickey for a month."

Mickey knew, too. And Laura. Half of Otero County probably knew. My head pounded, boom, boom, boom, like a mallet against a drum. My father, who I hadn't seen in fifteen years, had been working for Mickey. But that meant he worked for Jack, since it was Jack's family that owned Wrong Turn Ranch. *My father worked for Jack. Until two weeks ago.* And now Dad was calling me, wanting me to make peace between Jack and him.

My lips felt numb when I spoke. "Jack, why did he leave?"

The water had grown cold in the tub. I twisted the left spigot. As hot water poured in, I heard Ava's voice. I moved to the end of the tub nearest the door, careful to avoid scalding myself, but trying to catch what she said. She didn't whisper, so it wasn't too hard.

"Good evening, Jack. Emily okay?" Again, her island accent seemed so strange to me, first in Texas, then in New Mexico.

"She's upset with me. She'll be out soon."

"I put dinner on, all right? Take your time. You two taking care of me, let me do something for you."

"We have a big group tonight. It's too much."

"How many?" Ava's voice said.

"Nine."

I added up names in my head. Jack, Ava, Emily, Mickey and Laura, Greg, Farrah, Judith, and me. That was eight.

"Who's number nine?" I blurted.

"Uh, Collin."

I shouted, unable to contain myself, and turned off the water at the same time. "What? Collin is coming to dinner? All the way from Taos, on Christmas? I thought you hated Collin?"

"I got over it. I asked him for help on this smuggling thing."

"Oh. My. God."

"He had to be down to Las Cruces Monday anyway. He's stopping by."

I heard Ava's voice again. "Collin? My girl Katie's brother Collin live in New Mexico. That Collin?"

"The same."

"Nine people then. Can I cook anything I find in your kitchen?"

"Uh, yeah, and there's several very well-stocked freezers in the garage."

"I on it."

This was perfect. Collin, who had messed up my life last time I saw him, coming tonight, when my life had gotten back on track only to tank again. The competing scents of bath products—vanilla soap, coconut shampoo, cinnamon-apple bubble bath, freesia conditioner—suddenly made me feel nauseous. I lifted the tub drain and dried myself off in fast, rough strokes. I donned a robe from a hook on the back of the door. I wrapped the tie around my waist and knotted it. I pulled open the door, and Jack fell into me, pulling my robe open a few inches as he caught himself. Snowflake jumped in the air and put her front paws on my shin.

"Jack!" I jerked it closed.

"Sorry."

"I'm getting dressed now. I'll talk to you later."

He looked at the ground and his posture was so hangdog it was almost comical, except that this wasn't funny, and I wasn't laughing. He turned and left, with a dejected Snowflake behind him.

***

The downside of throwing Jack out of my room, I discovered later, was that he went straight to the kitchen to cook with Ava. Her lilt and flirty laugh rang through the house. I pictured her displaying her assets to their greatest advantage for him, and it raised my hackles. It wasn't like me to be so insecure and jealous, and I hated it in myself, but there it was, green-eyed, shrewlike, and on the rampage, even though Ava was only being kind and thoughtful. Well, I could do penance later. Right now I *hated* that I'd gotten my hair wet and that I had to waste the time drying it when Jack had her fun-loving nature and sexy smile as a contrast to my anger and harsh words. Which didn't change the fact that I was mad at him—very, very mad—and that I wasn't sure if I could ever trust him. He had a disturbing habit of withholding important information, and this time it wasn't his secrets he kept from me, but mine. I jerked a wide-toothed comb through my tangles. It hurt. *Good.*

I went into the bedroom and pulled warm clothes out of my suitcase. More voices had joined Jack and Ava. Young voices. Greg and Farrah? I tried to muster up a smile, but my mouth wouldn't do it yet. Still, it would be great to see them. I slipped into Levi's and a purple mock turtleneck, then shoved my feet into fur-lined Crocs my mother had given me for Christmas. I'd never owned—or wanted—anything like them. But they were mine now, so I was going to give them a try. I grabbed my phone and headed back into the bathroom. I flipped my hair upside down and aimed the blow-dryer at it with one hand and scrolled through my missed texts and emails with the other.

The first few were from a 575 area-code number I didn't recognize.

The first: *Mickey and Laura got us smartphones for Christmas!* I wasn't sure if it came from Greg or Farrah, but the text included a selfie of the two of them in front of the Wrong Turn Ranch sign out by the highway. IF YOU'RE HERE, YOU'VE MADE A WRONG TURN.

HIGHWAY 70 IS BEHIND YOU. I loved that sign. I loved those kids.

And a second text from an unfamiliar 575 number: *Laura said she can teach me how to be a jockey.* Ah, Farrah. So the other number had to be Greg. I had another from Farrah, too: *A colt was born in a manger this morning so we named it Jesus. But pronounced in Spanish, so it's not sacrilegious: Hay-SEUSS.* I couldn't help but smile at that. My mother would be appalled.

I typed one-handed, very slowly. I texted back to Greg: *Looking good. Merry Christmas. C U soon!* To Farrah, I sent: *Amazing, she's great. Cool re colt!* Unfortunately, I knew it was doubtful that Farrah would spend enough time at Wrong Turn Ranch to make the jockey dream happen, but maybe if the seed was planted, she could pursue it some-how, wherever she ended up. It made my heart ache to think about it. I'd never imagined adoption before Betsy, and I'd never considered older kids even since then. These two needed a home, though. I could continue to give Farrah access to this life, and to Laura. I felt disloyal to Betsy even thinking it, but I knew in my heart of hearts that getting her was a long shot. Even if I did, it didn't mean I couldn't adopt other kids, too. It was a lot to take on by myself, though. I chewed on a hangnail and scrolled.

The other four texts were in a group string with Wallace and Na-dine. The topic was Betsy. I chomped harder and lower on the hang-nail.

Boss won't let me take the day to go to the consulate 'for a wild goose chase.' SHIT. Wallace.

Let me see if I can get time off. Nadine.

DOUBLE SHIT. Polo Club short staffed because of holidays. They won't let me go. Nadine again.

And a new text, in the last half hour: *Emily, could you go? I can't prom-ise they'll work with you, but I could get a notarized power of attorney for you to act on my behalf. Or something. Ask Jack what he thinks.* Wallace.

I turned off the blow-dryer and set it on the corner of the counter-top, flipping my head and hair into an upright posture as I doused it with hairspray, the first of my usual two applications—one at half-dry, one at full-dry. I typed fast, and my iPhone autocorrected me into nonsense. I erased the nonsense and tried again, slower, breathing deeply to calm myself: *I'll be back from NM on Sunday and can go to the consulate, no problem. Hate this! Are we absolutely sure they won't come for her sooner?*

I stared at the phone, willing a response from Wallace. Nothing from him, but another from Nadine: *Another one of our dancers is being hassled by some cops.*

That made three: the woman who disappeared last summer, Ivanka, and now this woman. I texted back: *Oh no! Did she say who they are?*

Nadine: *I heard it's that Asian cop Wu and some redheaded guy.*

Some redheaded guy. Burrows. My hands shook, and I clasped them in my lap and stared into my own eyes in the mirror. *Get a grip. Do something, something constructive, something distracting, something positive.* But what? Betsy's face flashed in my mind, as it so often did. I wanted so badly to make it better for her. I couldn't stop the Immigration Customs and Enforcement folks, but I was here in New Mexico, and I could look for her backpack. I had all day tomorrow, and Saturday, too, so that was what I was going to do. That, and ask Jack about my dad's last voice mail, which somehow I had forgotten about in our last conversation. Two sharp raps at my door tore my attention away from the phone and my thoughts.

Expecting Jack, I was terse. "I'll be down when I'm ready."

Farrah's voice answered me, meek and chastened, and I regretted my harpy tone immediately. "Okay, I just wanted to say hi."

"Wait!" I trotted to the door and threw it open.

The girl before me in a green Christmas sweater looked like the midnight version of Cathy Rigby as Peter Pan. She smiled and I opened my arms for a hug. She stepped into them, barely enough to fill them up. The waif couldn't weigh more than ninety pounds. I released her but held on to her upper arms as Snowflake whirled in happy circles at her feet.

"How have things been?"

She lit up like a sparkler. "Awesome."

"I knew they would be." I let go of her and pointed at my hair. "I'm almost done. Tell everyone I'll be down in five?"

"Okay."

I closed the door and went back to the bathroom. The first thing I did was check my phone. Still no answer from Wallace about Immigration. Ugh. I flipped my hair over. I turned the dryer on and tried to turn my brain off.

Chapter Twenty-six

"We having a good, old-fashion St. Marcos Christmas dinner, New Mexico style." Ava lifted a serving dish over her head, which hiked her fitted black top up nearly to the bottom of her breasts. "Johnnycakes."

I watched from where I sat at one of the kitchen table's chairs as Ava slunk toward me, carving a path through the small crowd gathered in the kitchen with the sway of her hips in a short black skirt that matched her top. She set it on the table in front of me. Snowflake put her paws on one of the chairs, trying to get a closer sniff—or a bite—from the serving dish. The fried West Indian bread smelled delicious, but, then again, anything fried smelled good to me.

Collin crossed his arms over his chest, which emphasized that he'd had a lot of time to work out since Tamara had broken off their engagement. "I'll have whatever you're cooking, Ava."

His blue eyes glittered and his serious expression didn't quite hide his trademark grin. I was relieved his eyes were glittering over someone besides me this visit. His short-cropped *Top Gun* hair had grown out some, and for the first time I saw streaks of gray in it. Even Tom Cruise had to grow older some time.

Ava chuptzed him, long and loud, a teeth-sucking act of derision perfected by those in the West Indies. She sauntered back into the kitchen, where Jack was stirring something in a tall pot. Collin, no stranger to the chuptz from his time on St. Marcos, laughed.

"You want some of what I cooking, you best get in the kitchen and help," she said.

Now everyone laughed, and Collin ran the few steps to join her.

She swatted him with a towel, then picked up a knife and pointed it at several chickens, fried whole. "Carve."

He bowed, took the knife, and set to work. I had planned to offer help, but there was no way I was entering that kitchen with Jack and

Collin in it. I'd set the table earlier. That would have to be my contribution.

Judith had arrived after I came downstairs, and she walked to the counter and poured a glass of Pinot Gris from the Wines of the San Juan. From behind her, it struck me how much of her long black hair was shot with steel gray. Today she wore it at the base of her neck in a silver clasp with turquoise, red, and black stones. It was a formal look, in fitting with her old-fashioned straight brown suede skirt and its matching beaded blouse.

She turned to me. "You want some wine?"

"A small one, thank you." I joined her at the counter and took the glass she offered. "How are things at the home office?" I asked, referring to Jack's adobe office in Tularosa, where she had worked since she followed him there from the DA's office in Alamogordo.

She took a sip of wine so small that she appeared to absorb it into her tongue instead of swallowing it. Shades of my mother. "Busy. It's a good thing Jack couldn't represent anyone in the indictments from the Paul Johnson mess, because that tied up all the other local attorneys. Everything else is coming to us."

Although Johnson had—briefly, and under false pretenses—retained Jack, Johnson's men had kidnapped me and assaulted Betsy's father, who died on Jack's land when he was attempting to escape. That made Jack and me both witnesses and conflicted our firm out. The conflict didn't only extend to Johnson, who Jack wouldn't have defended anyway, but to anyone involved in the sordid affairs.

Judith added, "Plus with the work coming out of Amarillo, it's a lot. I told him I might need help if this keeps up."

Without discussing it, Judith and I moved away from the counter and out to the great room. The sky still loomed gray and low, but even dreary it looked spectacular viewed through the east-facing floor-to-high-ceiling windows that stretched across one entire side of the room. I took a sip of the Pinot Gris and savored it. It tasted of pear and some kind of citrus.

"I can't believe you'd let someone else handle anything." I was teasing, sort of. Judith hadn't taken kindly to Jack sharing their load with me, at first.

She nodded, her black eyes grave. "It would be a last resort."

I put a hand over my mouth and cleared my throat to cover a laugh.

Remembering that Judith's brother once worked at Johnson's Ranch as an electrician, I asked, "Say, does your brother still do any work out at Johnson's place?"

She absorbed another few drops of her wine and then shook her head. "It's deserted. They froze all Johnson's assets, you know, and the judge didn't allow bail."

"I was afraid of that. I'm looking for something of Betsy's, and I need to see if it's out there."

"They have big padlocks on everything. At least that's what people say."

It wouldn't hurt to swing by and check. Jarhead would enjoy the exercise. I mentally scheduled it for first thing the next day. But I kept those thoughts to myself. Judith and I chatted some about pending cases until Jack ushered everyone into the kitchen for dinner.

We had all gathered noisily—Judith and me, Mickey and Laura, the kids, Ava, and Collin—but quieted at once when Jack held a finger in the air.

"Thanks everyone for celebrating with us. Mickey, will you bless the food?" Jack said.

Mickey cleared his throat. "Join hands, please." He closed his eyes and bowed his head. As he prayed aloud, I snuck a peek at Jack. His eyes were on me. *Cheater*, I thought, then realized my eyes were as open as his. I closed them. Mickey finished, and together we all said, "Amen."

"And thank you for bringing these two very special young people into our lives," Mickey added.

Laura stood between Greg and Farrah, holding one hand of each. The two kids looked embarrassed, like they couldn't believe Mickey had singled them out. Laura's eyes watered and she laughed and made a show of wiping her eyes. Mickey walked over and hugged her, then patted each teen on the back.

Voices quickly covered the silence following Mickey's blessing, and I heaped my plate with beans and rice, sweet-potato casserole, and johnnycake. I took the plate into the living room and perched on the couch with my plate balanced on my knees. Jack sat down next to me. His knees, boots, and long legs created a higher, more angled tabletop for his plate, and he struggled with it, then gave up and put his plate on the coffee table. I tried not to look at him, but it was hard when he was all my heart could see, and it made me mad at myself and him.

The living room continued to fill. Ava sat on my other side, Collin took a seat catty-cornered from her, and Mickey put his plate on the stone hearth in front of us. The chimney extended to the ceiling behind him, the enormous rocks appearing as if they would tumble onto his head at any moment. The voices of Laura, Judith, and the kids still rang out from the kitchen, but I could barely hear them over the Christmas music someone had turned on. Mariah Carey: "All I Want For Christmas Is You." My very favorite Christmas song. Sadness welled inside me that my dad, Jack, and their big, fat secrets had tarnished this day. I sucked in a deep breath of air through my nose. I didn't need to let it impact anyone else's night, though.

Jack set his silverware on the table. Snowflake eyed him hopefully, then moved on to me. I pinched a small piece of johnnycake and held it out. She took it from my fingers in a lunge, like a trout to a fly, and gulped it down.

Jack said, "Collin, we're hoping to enlist your help with a problem we've been having here."

Collin had just taken a giant bite of rice and beans. He chewed with wide eyes and circled his hand by his mouth to show he was hurrying. Everyone but me laughed. When he'd swallowed, he said, "Of course, buddy. I owe you a big one, for, ahem, taking advantage of your hospitality last time."

"Actually, the problem seems bigger than Wrong Turn Ranch."

Mickey stood and paced. "I feel responsible, and stupid. A few weeks ago, someone made off with a load of our stuff. Someone who had a good idea of what was valuable and enough about us to know when to get to it, where, and how to get it out fast." He looked at Jack, then stopped talking.

Jack nodded. "She knows."

I bristled. *Yes, finally, she knows.*

Mickey took a deep breath. "At first we thought it was an inside job. We'd brought on an ex-con—"

"My father." Everyone's heads whipped around at me, and I realized I'd cut Mickey off. Loudly.

Mickey sighed. "Yes. Johnny Phelps. Emily's dad. I all but accused him, and, later that night, he disappeared."

Jack put his hand on my knee, and I flinched. His warm eyes met my cold ones, and he removed it. "Then Emily and I ran across some of the stolen Wrong Turn Ranch items at ABC Half-Price Resale in Amarillo. Our client is the owner. He admitted he's been selling stolen merchandise."

Collin rubbed his chin. "Somebody's been a bad boy, smuggling stolen goods across state lines."

"Yesterday Phelps called me," Mickey said. "Told me he didn't do it, gave me the license plate number of a blue sedan out here the day of the robbery, and hinted at a connection to some dangerous people. Said he had to figure out a way for it not to come back on him before he'd tell me more."

I shoved my plate onto the coffee table and turned to glare at Jack.

He threw his hands up. "I tried to tell you earlier."

"Define *earlier*." I realized I had something to tell him, too, though, and I changed gears. "Wait a sec. I have the license plate number of a truck that dropped off a shipment at ABC Half-Price Resale." Snowflake slunk to Jack's feet and curled up, trembling. The poor thing hated conflict.

It was Jack's turn to glare at me, left eyebrow arched. "When did you get that?"

My head bobbed sideways a little. "When I bought your Christmas present, Jack Ass," I said, with a tad too much emphasis on the Ass part. The room went so quiet I could hear the ringing in my ears. I didn't dare look around, for fear of what I'd see in people's eyes. I closed my own for a split second to steady my frayed nerves. "Then Burrows showed up and dragged me away."

Jack's olive face turned a crimson hue. He spit out his words like fish bones stuck in his throat. "Do tell."

"Whoa, whoa, whoa, whoa." Collin shook his head. "Slow down here. You've got the license plate of a vehicle being used in the smuggling?"

I opened my mouth, shut it, then opened it again to speak. "I don't know. Maybe." I pulled up the photo and handed it to him.

"New Mexico plates." Collin typed keystrokes on my phone. "I'm texting it to myself."

I felt silly. I hadn't noticed the plates in the dark, and I hadn't even looked at the picture since I'd taken it, what with everything that had been going on, until now.

"Send it to me, Collin." Jack clenched his jaw. "Since Emily didn't." Snowflake huddled closer to her master, her eyes wide and fixed on him.

I put my plate back in my lap. Under its cover, I flexed the fingers of my left hand, then clenched them closed, then did it again, and again, and again.

Collin nodded and typed some more. He handed me back my phone. "Done. Emily, tell us the rest."

Everyone stared at me, rapt. Great. How to tell everything that had happened in the last few days without giving up the moral high ground with Jack? I told myself that it was different. He kept secrets from me that should have been mine. The secrets I kept from him weren't really his. Or were only kinda sorta his. Some of them. Ugh. This wasn't going to go well.

"The night before we entered Alan's plea—"

Jack interrupted. "Monday night."

"Yes. Monday night I went to do some last-minute Christmas shopping at ABC Half-Price Resale, Alan's store. The woman at the register—"

He interrupted again. "Alan's wife?"

"I didn't know that at the time, but yes. Anyway, I asked the woman I later learned was Alan's wife, Janelle, whether Alan was there, and she said he was out back, and she looked upset. So I thought I'd get a picture of the truck's plates for *you*, in case it was the smuggler, and I went around back and took one."

"Just like that."

"There might have been a little more to it than that, but nothing relevant."

"Okay."

"Then, I was hiding behind a dumpster, when—"

"Reckless."

I jumped up. "If you don't stop interrupting me, we're all going to die of old age before I finish telling you the story." I looked around. This time all the eyes on me shifted away from mine. Ava's were gleaming. Collin's were twinkling. Judith's looked uncomfortable. And Mickey's told me he felt guilty. Good. He should.

"Fine." Jack threw his hand out at me in a "go on" sort of way.

"Fine." I huffed a deep breath in and out. "Alan was back there. He was talking to the driver and someone else." I looked around the room. "Alan is our client in Amarillo, who supposedly assaulted a cop but says he didn't. He took a plea bargain, so we aren't sure. Anyway, I couldn't see him, and then the driver walked out in the alley. The driver was short and kind of skinny but I didn't get a good look at him. He drove off. Alan and the other guy disappeared, and Officer Burrows showed up and made me leave."

"Made you leave?"

"Yeah."

"Why?"

"He told me to butt out of police business and that I was going to get myself killed."

Jack snorted.

Collin said, "He sounds like an intelligent guy."

"Ha ha," I said. "Except that he told me to meet him somewhere private. When I got there—"

Jack shouted, "When you *what?*"

"When I got there."

"Why didn't you call me?"

I turned away from him. "As I was trying to say, when I got there, he was weird. He all but admitted he'd been following me."

Jack made another loud noise, but I didn't stop. Snowflake had buried her head under her paws and looked like she needed a Valium.

"Because earlier that day, when I was at the orthodontist's office, he showed up there, too. And of course he showed up to arrest me when Mary Alice Hodges called on the wrath of God."

"Arrested you?" Collin asked. The corners of his lips curved up millimeters short of a grin.

"Long story." One I didn't want to relive. "It was all very mysterious, and then a security guard banged on the car, and Burrows left." I paused to take a drink of water.

Jack crossed his arms. "Is that all?"

"Almost."

Jack threw his hands in the air. He wasn't usually this open and *dramatic*, except around Mickey, but then they went back to childhood as cousins and best friends. Well, I'd asked Jack to communicate better, so I guess I was getting what I asked for. Sort of.

My eyelids fluttered a smidge as I answered him. "On Christmas Eve, Nadine told me a friend of hers was scared of a bad cop. She had the friend call me. The friend said her name was Beth, and we agreed to meet at her place at noon. When I got there, she was on her back patio. Dead."

"That, I knew about."

Ava put her hand over her heart. "Yesterday, when I got there?"

I pursed my lips and nodded. "Right before, actually." I looked at Jack. "Here's the part I haven't talked to you about. When we were leaving church last night, Samson pulled me aside."

"Now you get around to telling me." Jack said.

This time I didn't spar with him. "Yes. He was pretty okay, actually, and apologized about my arrest and the phone, but he did ask me how I ended up at the scene of the murder of a dancer from the Polo Club. That's a strip bar," I explained to the group. "Nadine knew her as Beth, but she'd introduced herself to Jack and me as Ivanka when we met her at a truck stop the night of another murder."

A gasp from the doorway cut me off. It was Greg, looking extremely young with the black knit cap gone, his hair shiny and straight, and clean clothes on his lanky frame. Farrah stood beside him. I wondered how long they'd been standing there, but knew they could have heard us from anywhere in the house.

Farrah whispered, "Oh my God," into the sudden silence, and buried her face in Greg's shoulder.

***

Laura had already reached the kids before I got my first word out.

"What is it?" I asked them. But I was sure I knew. They'd heard me say that someone who'd been at the truck stop was murdered. Whether there was a connection to what they saw or not, it had to be terrifying. I'd be scared if I were them, too.

Laura patted Greg, then went to the other side of Farrah and slipped an arm around the girl's waist. The two were almost exactly the same height, although Farrah was even slighter than Laura. Greg shook his head at me. Laura whispered to him, and the three of them left the room. Snowflake sprinted to catch up to them.

Jack put his hand on my knee again, and this time I didn't object. We looked at each other, and he shook his head, just barely perceptibly. "Anything else, Emily?"

That I love you even if I want to string you up by your heels right now? That I wish I hadn't yelled at you in front of everyone? That I want you to put your arms around me and make this all better? When I opened my mouth, a whisper came out: "No."

Jack squeezed my knee.

"Luckily I've got all weekend with nothing to do," Collin said. He stood up. "But right now, I'm going for seconds."

Jack said, "Me, too." He let go of my knee and followed Collin.

I snapped out of my daze and shifted to go after him, but Ava stopped me by wrapping a hand around my arm, her long fingernails clicking together as she did.

She leaned in. "I so lost. What *up* with this place, these people?"

"It's never like this."

She chuptzed me, and I almost laughed. "You lie, I think. But that okay. I used to the melee from Katie and Nick."

"They're in another league."

"More important question: are you and your boss an item, or not?"

"I wish I knew." Maybe. Sometimes. "Right now I'm having trouble trusting him."

"About your daddy?"

"Yeah. About him."

"Seem like Jack have good intent."

I sighed. "He probably does. But he almost never tells me what's going on."

"He look good though."

Now I laughed and stood. "Yes, he does."

"And it appear from last night you like he tongue down your throat or wherever it was I see it."

I squawked.

Ava laughed. "That better."

Collin came back into the great room and held his hand out to Ava. "Madame, your manservant awaits his next instruction." He bowed.

She fanned herself. "I like the sound of that."

The two of them walked ahead of me into the kitchen. Laura and the kids had disappeared. Judith was placing a giant CorningWare serving dish out on the counter, full of something with a bubbling top that smelled like cinnamon and spice and everything nice. There was a tub of Blue Bell Vanilla Bean ice cream beside it, along with a stack of dessert bowls and a bunch of spoons. I decided to skip seconds and go straight for the good stuff. I dug a serving spoon into the virgin surface of the as-yet-to-be-identified dessert. I ladled out a large chunk. Bread pudding. I put my hand on the side of the serving dish. Still warm. I added two scoops of vanilla ice cream. I looked around the once-again crowded room. No one seemed to be watching me.

As quietly as I could, I walked to the stairs, still keeping one eye on everyone in the kitchen. I tiptoed up each tread unnoticed. When I came to my room, I turned the handle and ducked in the door. I closed it softly, releasing the knob only when the tongue was positioned over the recess in the latch.

Peace. I sat down, taking a moment to breathe. Then I set the bowl on the side table along with my phone. A moment of guilt gave me pause. I'd snuck out before we'd even opened presents. But Laura had left with the kids, so I was off the hook. I flopped backward onto the fluffy white comforter and landed with my head in the mountain of pillows. What a day. What a long and difficult day.

I reached out for my phone. I was relieved to see a text from Wallace, although it wasn't in the group string with Nadine. And I had another from an 806 number I didn't recognize. A sense of dread crept into my chest. Betsy.

I pulled Wallace's text up first: *Please oh please oh please God let Emily not have done something incredibly stupid that will reflect poorly on me and keep her from being approved to adopt.*

It didn't sound like anything had happened to Betsy. More like I'd done something. *What in Hades are you talking about?* I hit send.

Then I opened the other text: *This is Byron from CPS. Wallace gave me your number. He said you communicate best by text. Please call me at your earliest convenience.*

Oh geez. Iciness flowed over my face. Byron was the CPS investigator working on Greg's and Farrah's cases.

Wallace responded: *Tell me you aren't with them. Please.*

If push came to shove, I could answer that one truthfully, but it wasn't time to show my hand yet. *With WHOM? Please give me a little to go on.*

I chewed the ragged edge of my now swollen hangnail. Could Byron have any other reason to call me except about Greg and Farrah? Maybe, but probably not. Could Wallace possibly be referring to anyone other than the two teenagers? Maybe, but probably not. Put the two together, and the answer to the first changed to "not likely."

Wallace: *G & F.*

Just because I expected it didn't mean I didn't throw up a little in my mouth when I read it. I couldn't honestly say I wasn't with them. But I could pretend to misinterpret the question. Then I could be truthful. *No, I don't have them. Has there been news?* Send.

Wallace: *Anonymous phone tip to Byron.*

Oh no, oh God, no, no, no. Who knew the kids contacted me? Jack was the only one who knew everything. I closed my eyes and pictured every move I'd made with the kids in Amarillo. I hadn't seen anyone following us. My mother had never known there were teenagers in our house. So how, how could someone have seen me with them in Amarillo? They couldn't have. They just couldn't have.

That left Jack. What if Jack had told someone? Even one person in passing would have been enough. It had to have been him, even if it was only an accident, it had to have been him. Because it sure wasn't me.

I answered: *Crazy! I'll call him.*

I stared at the phone. I had no idea what to say to Byron. In a text, I could evade his questions. A call was harder. Voice mail would be ideal, but he had to be expecting my call; he'd called on Christmas day. He'd be watching for my number.

My number. Not a random number. *That* was the answer. I'd call from a house phone. I looked around the room. No phone. Jack's bedroom down the hall might have one. There might be one in the kitchen or the office, but I didn't want to go back downstairs.

Spit.

I put my phone's ringer on silent and turned out the light. I slipped out the door and crept down the hall away from the staircase. Jack's door was closed, but his light was out. Holding my breath, I turned the handle even more carefully than I'd turned my own a few minutes before. I eased the door open a generous crack and ducked in, then repeated the silent shutting of the door and latch.

I exhaled. Using the flashlight on my phone, I searched the room. There, on the bedside table on the far side of the room was a phone. Tiptoeing, I reached it in seconds. I lifted it from its base, still using my phone as a light. I pressed the button to turn the house phone on and got a dial tone. I typed in the number from Byron's text and the phone started dialing, then ringing, although I could barely hear it over the pounding in my ears and my labored breaths. I hated lying. I was no good at it. If he answered, I'd hang up.

I heard the tone change in my ear as the two phones connected. I closed my eyes.

"You've reached my voice mail. Leave a message." Byron's voice. Short, uninformative.

I chose my words carefully, with my fingers crossed for good measure. "Um, hi, this is Emily Bernal calling for Byron. Byron, I spoke to Wallace earlier. I wanted to assure you I don't have Greg and Farrah, and I can't imagine who would think I did, or why they'd call anonymously. I guess I have an enemy out there." I was babbling. I hated it when I babbled. It made me sound defensive, and ding-y. "I'm in New Mexico for Christmas. If you find them, please let me know, even through Wallace. I've been so worried about them. Thank you."

I pressed "off." I put the house phone back in the cradle, then I dropped my phone on the bed, where it landed flashlight up, and I lowered my face into my hands.

"That didn't sound good," a man's voice said from across the room.

I screamed and jumped back a good three feet. An eerie face watched me from a doorway across the room. The bathroom doorway,

I realized. The man stepped forward, but I already knew who the voice belonged to. Jack. Which made sense, since I was in his bedroom.

I was in *his* bedroom. I flew over to the bed and snatched up my phone. "I'm sorry, I shouldn't be in here uninvited." I rushed around the bed for the door.

He intercepted me, catching me by the shoulders. "What's the matter?"

"Someone told Byron at CPS that I had Greg and Farrah, and only two people in Amarillo knew. You, and me. And it wasn't me."

"Huh."

That's all he had to say? My brain shorted out, and a blank white screen appeared where logical thought should be. I jerked away from his grasp. "Huh? I could lose my ability to adopt Betsy, and maybe even be charged with a crime. That's more than a 'huh.' At a minimum, it's an 'I'm sorry,' and then maybe you could throw in whether or not you may have caused it, and if you did, it would be nice to hear how it happened, too."

"Uh . . ." He looked at the floor between us.

Tears spilled, and I realized I was losing it, overreacting. Too much. It was all too much. "I'm sorry, I can't talk anymore. I need to be alone." I whirled and fled for my room.

Chapter Twenty-seven

The next morning I was on my way to the stables by six o'clock, sleepy but determined, having left a heartbroken Snowflake in the kitchen instead of bringing her with me. The sun wouldn't rise for quite a while yet, but I doubted that I would be the first person out there. Sure enough, the doors were unlocked, and a light shone into the open space between the stalls on either side, emanating from Mickey's office. It was frigid outside and still really cold in the stable. I'd worn gloves, a wool cap, a scarf, and a heavy jacket, but I knew I'd still be freezing my tushy off for the next few hours. I exhaled, admiring my frosty breath, then knocked on the glass in Mickey's office door. Steam rose from a Purina coffee mug beside him. He looked up, his wide eyes registering surprise, and motioned me in.

"Good morning," I said.

"You're up early."

"And still not as early as you."

He laughed. "It's a holiday. I slept in."

I knew well the demands of rising early to care for animals. I missed a lot about my rodeo days, and sometimes I even missed this part: working alone before dawn, waking the animals, feeding them, being the one they relied on to care for them. I imagined it was a lot like having a baby. My "babies" had just weighed in over a thousand pounds each. A special bond forms in the dark, when you are the only one there, when they need you.

"I was hoping to take Jarhead or one of his friends out for a ride this morning. Would that be all right?"

"Jarhead would love it." He got to his feet. "Is Jack coming?"

"No, just me."

He stopped for a split second, his eyes raking my face, but I didn't let a flicker of emotion cross it. "Let me get you a saddle."

We walked together to the tack room next door. It smelled of leather and saddle soap, and I inhaled it greedily. "If you can point out what you're comfortable with me using, I can take it from there. I don't want to be a bother."

He hefted the saddle I'd ridden on during my last few rides from a wall peg, along with the Navajo blanket underneath it. He added a bridle. "Gives me a chance to talk to you. Grab that brush, will you?"

I picked up the soft-bristled brush he had indicated and followed him out. "So how have the kids done?" I asked.

Mickey set the gear on the ground outside a stall, and Jarhead stuck his nose out, snorting. Mickey put both his hands on the beautiful animal's bobbing face. "They've done well. Laura's the one I'm worried about."

"Laura? Why?"

He opened the stall door and slipped the bridle over Jarhead's ears, then the bit into his mouth. "She's getting attached. The kids need somebody, and she needs to be needed."

"Yeah. Those phones she gave them for Christmas—they seem like a long-term sort of gift." I rubbed the wood-handled brush over Jarhead's back with my right hand and ran my left over his supple flanks. His muscles quivered, and he turned to watch me.

Mickey patted Jarhead's neck. "She's taken Farrah under her wing. The girl loves horses."

I smiled. I could relate. "Anything special about this big fella today?" I kept brushing, working my way around to Jarhead's other side.

"Nah. He's had breakfast, but he's always fine after he eats, as long as you aren't planning on riding him to Alamogordo and back. You know he's a handful, of course."

"That's what I love about him."

Mickey positioned the blanket on Jarhead, swinging the saddle up to land perfectly in place. He pulled the strap through the cinch and tightened it, then pulled the whole rig back a little so it wasn't too close to Jarhead's elbow. Then he tightened the cinch again, a full inch more, and Jarhead snorted and tossed his head.

"He puffs out a little on the first go-round."

"Poor boy. But you don't want me hanging upside down under your belly, do you?" I let him sniff my hand and feel it with the sensitive whiskers on his muzzle. He nodded his head up and down. "Oh, you do? Fine." I laughed.

"Where you thinking about taking him?"

I stuck with mostly true. "Out to the highway and east. I want to expunge the demons from my wild midnight ride on Thunder."

Mickey puckered his lips up and nodded. "All right. Well, the weather is supposed to be fine. The snow cover isn't deep. Everyone is pastured on the west side right now, so I think you'll find most of the gates open and you can leave them that way. If any are closed, they're gonna be hard to manage in this cold, the wires tight. Do you have a phone in case of trouble?"

I patted his shoulder. "Yes, Mom."

"I'm not worried about you, Standing Hair, I'm talking about the moneymaker here."

We both laughed. Jarhead's stud fees were a large part of Wrong Turn Ranch's income. I led the moneymaker from the stall, and he started prancing.

Mickey pointed across the aisle. "You know who that is?"

A black horse stuck his entire neck out the window of his stall. If it was the horse I thought it was, I'd only seen him in the dark before. I walked Jarhead closer to him. The two horses protested at each other's nearness, and Mickey held out his hand. I gave him Jarhead's reins and walked the rest of the way to the black horse on my own.

"Thunder?" I asked.

"Yep."

"Hey, Thunder, remember me?" I rubbed his neck briskly as he sniffed to catch my scent. "Good to see you. You landed in high cotton here, didn't you?" I reached in my jacket pocket for my phone and snapped a selfie with him. For Betsy, later. I stroked his face one last time then moved on. I poked my head through the window of the next stall. A black mare and her knobby-kneed foal. "Is this little Hay-SEUSS?" I asked, pronouncing Jesus in my best Spanish.

The mare moved between the foal and me, blocking my view and pointing her hindquarters in my direction.

Mickey shook his head. "Yeah, and I'm afraid we're going to Hell over that one. But he sure is cute, and it made the kids happy to name him."

He was probably right about the Hell part. Mickey walked Jarhead and me to the door, and I grabbed the horn and reins in my left hand, put my left foot in the stirrup, and swung up and over, settling into the cold, hard saddle. It was a good fit.

"Thanks, Mickey. See you in two hours or so."

He shook his head. "One more thing. Do you have a weapon? The big coyotes get pretty crafty and hungry this time of year."

Under my jacket, I had worn a long purse strap across my chest for exactly this reason. I had money, ID, and my baby Glock tucked inside the little bag at the end of the strap. I even had coffee in the interior pocket of my coat, in a flask I'd found in Jack's kitchen.

I patted my stomach. "My father taught me well."

"About your dad."

I shook my head. "It's okay."

It was, even though *I* wasn't, and I sure didn't want to talk about it. I spent most of the night before tossing and turning, my thoughts back and forth between Dad, Betsy, Jack, Greg, and Farrah, with disturbing memories of Ivanka's bloodless face and the bloodied figure of the truck driver at Love's for good measure. I fretted over good cops and bad and how to know the difference. I obsessed about the potential trouble I was facing with CPS. And I worried about Alan spending Christmas in prison, when I was pretty sure he hadn't done what he was accused of doing. It had been easy to rise early for the ride, because I'd never really gone to sleep.

Jarhead hotfooted in place, eager to be off.

"Your father's a good guy. He talked about you a lot. I hope . . ." Mickey trailed off.

"Really, it's okay."

He nodded and lifted his hand in salute.

I held Jarhead to a walk through the grounds and first gate, then let him warm up in a fretful trot. Patience wasn't his strong suit. By the second gate, he was loping. And by the fourth gate, I gave him his head and let him race his imaginary opponents all the way to the highway.

We crossed over the pavement and onto Johnson's Ranch. As Judith had said, the gate was padlocked. I trotted Jarhead along the front fence line to the east. In about 150 yards, we found a wire loop gate like the ones we'd ridden through on Jack's place. Mickey was right, these things were tight in the cold. But I managed to work the loop up and over the post, and we were in. From there it wasn't that long a ride up to the house and the outbuildings. By the time we reached them, I needed to walk Jarhead for a cool down and find him some water, which I found in an automatic watering tub by the barn. A pump ran continuously, circulating the water, so there was no ice. Jarhead slurped noisily, and water dripped from his muzzle to the cold ground, melting the snow. My phone made a noise so I pulled it out.

There was a text from Nadine to Wallace and me: *The dancer who was being harassed is MISSING. Everyone freaked.*

I replied to my friend: *Oh no, be careful, Nadine. Scary!*

Another dancer, after cops harassed her. Missing. Maybe dead. What was happening to my safe, sleepy hometown? I had worried Ivanka's death was connected to Love's, but was it something else, something worse?

I put the phone away. "Now what?" I asked Jarhead.

"I guess you could start by explaining what the hell you're doing here," a man's voice answered.

***

I slipped my hand into my jacket and into my open purse, closing my fingers around the Glock's grip, then swiveled my head to see who was speaking. A tall, unsmiling man with pock-marked brown skin faced me. He was dressed in jeans with a heavy brown work jacket and cowboy boots. Like Mickey had been wearing that morning. Like practically every man in this part of the world.

His expression changed when he saw my face. "Ma'am." He dipped his head at me. "Nice horse. Sorry if I startled you."

"Thank you. I didn't think anyone was here."

I took my fingers off the gun and slid my hand out. The feel of the baby Glock's grip had grown mighty familiar in the last week. It made me think of my dad, and I didn't want to think about him.

"Only me. Edward Brown, Alamogordo Police. And you are?"

I shook off the thoughts of my father. I'd met this man, although at the time he was dressed in his Sunday best.

"Emily Bernal. Did I meet you at St. Joseph's last weekend? I was there with the Begays and Jack Holden."

He smiled. "Yes, I recognize you now. You look a little different." He pointed at his head.

My head and hair were entirely covered by my cap. My purple scarf obscured my chin. "It's pretty chilly out."

He raised his eyebrows, stretching and flattening the pits in his face. "It is. And early, on the day after Christmas. What brings you out here?"

"Mostly trying to shake demons. I had a bad experience here."

His gaze didn't flicker. "I'm aware of that, of course. I'm sorry about what you went through."

"It's okay. I'm recovering. And a lot of good has come from that night."

"It certainly has. You will be forever revered as a merciful angel by the people Johnson held here."

I swallowed. I hadn't ever really thought of it that way. "I hope you guys find them all. The women and children, I mean." The authorities surmised that Johnson had sold them to the highest bidders, to the kind of people that liked their play things disposable and anonymous. I shivered. Thank God Betsy had avoided that fate.

Brown shook his head. "Me, too."

Brown seemed nice, and helpful, and I decided to take a chance on him with the truth. "The little girl who escaped with me, Betsy—"

"Elizabet Perez."

It warmed me that he knew the case so well. And with so many victims, he remembered Betsy's name. That was good. "Yes. She lost her backpack, and she's been quite upset about it. The last place she saw it was here. I was hoping that I could look in some windows, see if I can find it."

"I'd be happy to take you through the place, but don't get your hopes up."

"Why?"

"Most of the stuff here ended up in evidence or with Johnson's daughter."

"Stella?"

"Yes. And then some of it disappeared."

"What do you mean, disappeared?" I rubbed my arms. Now that neither Jarhead nor I were exerting ourselves, it really *was* getting cold. The horse snorted and stamped, and I knew he felt it, too.

"I mean it looks like the place got picked over. It's been empty for the last six weeks, and sometimes that happens. I like to drop by occasionally for that reason. Keep an eye on things, keep away the thieves, vandals, or squatters."

Like Wrong Turn Ranch across the road. So the thieves had hit more than one ranch in the area. Mickey and Jack hadn't reported it, though, so I kept it to myself. "That's awful."

"It is. So, you want to look around?"

"If you honestly don't mind, I would. And maybe I could let my horse warm up inside while we do it?"

He nodded and pulled out a ring of keys. I followed him into the barn. I'd been inside it once before, unfortunately. We passed the open door to the room where I'd been held against my will, where I first met Betsy. In my memory it was a dark room filled with clutter. Today it was bare except for the swath of dim light across the floor from the high, narrow window. Chill bumps rose on my arms under my layers of clothing.

"You can tie him up here," Brown said, indicating a fat post in the center of the open area that extended all the way to the roof.

All I had on Jarhead was a bridle. Flat leather reins didn't tie well, and they tied short at that. I had on a stylin' web belt though, with a double ring in lieu of a buckle. I looped the belt around the post, then tied the reins to the end of it. That gave Jarhead enough room to move his head.

I patted his flanks. "Back soon, boy."

Brown gestured around the barn. "Do you want to look in here?"

I surveyed the mostly empty space. The only things left in the room were rejects: a flat tire, half a long-handled rake, a pile of mulch, a broken syringe. Whoever had burglarized this place had done a very thorough job. It was disheartening, in light of my search, and more than a little eerie. But I was accompanied by a police officer, one who went way back with Jack and Mickey, and I would be fine. I couldn't give up before I'd even started. I owed it to Betsy.

"Lead the way," I said.

Chapter Twenty-eight

Four hours later, I was showered, safe, warm, and piloting Jack's Suburban toward Alamogordo in sunlight made twice as bright by its reflection off the snow. Jack and Collin had vanished, so I had left Jack a note back at the house.

I borrowed the Suburban. Ava's with me. I'm showing her around and taking her to eat. We'll be back by midafternoon, unless I hear from you that you need us or the vehicle sooner. ~ E

Ava had stayed glued to my side since my return from Johnson's Ranch, pumping me for information on the intrigue going on around her. Over donuts and coffee at Yum-Yum's in Tularosa, I had finally gotten her up-to-date on almost everything: Betsy, Alan, the hush-hush situation with Greg and Farrah, dead people, my arrest, and even my now-ex-husband and Jack. Ava actively participated in stories, so it took a long time, even the short version. I had made it all the way in my narrative to my early morning excursion across the highway, which I was telling her about as I drove and she drank her second cup of coffee.

"Turn left to merge onto US 70 South," Siri's robotic voice commanded.

I obeyed. "Okay, so you know I went for a ride this morning?"

"Yah, mon."

I smiled over at Ava. A wide zebra-print headband held her hair back from her lovely face. She'd tamed her curls into long waves, but it still had the volume of lion's mane, and she hadn't skimped on the eyeliner and lipstick. She dressed in her version of conservative wear for our excursion, which meant fabric covered all her skin, even if it was still fuchsia Lycra. Her spike-heeled, zippered black leather boots were the final detail to an ensemble that guaranteed she would not blend in the crowd today.

"I love hearing that accent," I said.

"Well, we don't want to Yank and sound flat and nasal like every-one else, do we?" she said, in a perfect parody of a Midwestern accent. The Virgin Islanders called stateside accents "Yank" talk, and Ava could switch in and out of her accents in mid-sentence.

"Even my Texas accent sounds foreign in these parts," I drawled.

She switched back to her normal speaking voice. "So, lady, tell me 'bout you ride this morning."

"I took Jarhead across the road to the ranch where Betsy was held hostage. I wanted to see if I could find a backpack that means a lot to her. The place was locked up, but one of the Alamogordo cops that's working the case was out there."

"At god-awful early in the morning? Why?"

"Checking up on the place, I think. Anyway, he took me through all the buildings to search for it."

I set the cruise to seventy-five miles per hour and glanced in the rearview mirror at the lonely road behind me. Almost lonely. A big, dark blue sedan of some type had kept pace a few hundred yards back since we turned onto 70. It was still there. Odd. Would anyone have reason to follow us? And then I remembered Byron's call. It wasn't out of the question.

"You go in a deserted house with a strange man? Girl, you crazy."

"He was a police officer." Which didn't necessarily mean much. "He was nice."

"Nice? He probably looking at your bana then."

"No! He wasn't like that."

She chuptzed. "All men like that. Some just more sneaky."

I laughed.

"Hey, what that thing rolling by the side of the road?" She pointed at a tumbling mass of leafless bush.

"That's a tumbleweed."

"Those things real? And it moving fast. Even in the winter?"

"Year round. The wind out here is fierce."

I hadn't even noticed the tumbleweed until she mentioned it. Some things became part of the landscape after a while. Ava did have a way of making me smile.

She stared out the window, shaking her head. "This a strange place." She looked back at me. "Go on with you story."

"Okay, so where was I? Oh yeah, the cop let me search, but the place—the ranch house and outbuildings—had been picked clean."

"Thieves like rob Jack's place?"

"Just like. Although I'm sure some things went with the daughter and others into evidence first."

Her accent thickened and her voice rose in pitch. "You tell Collin and he 'bout robbers dem across the way?" Dem after a noun was a form of island pluralization, although redundant in some cases, like this one.

"They were gone when I got back."

"You best call."

She was right. "When we stop."

"Where we going, anyway?"

"The police say they don't have Betsy's backpack. I couldn't find it at the ranch. And since I can't ask the robbers, that leaves the daughter, Stella, as the next person to ask about it." I turned to her. "So that's where we're headed. To visit Stella."

"She know we coming?"

"She does. I found her on Facebook and messaged her."

Ava drained her coffee and set the empty cup in the holder in the console. She dug in her purse and came out with a lipstick, then applied fresh fuchsia and pressed her lips together several times.

"I ready," she announced.

Siri directed us the rest of the way to Stella's new abode, with me checking the rearview frequently for a tail. I saw the blue sedan behind me a few more times, but when we made the last turn toward Stella's, it went straight, and I breathed a sigh of relief. It felt safer to be in a residential neighborhood, with people all around. Not that it was the best neighborhood in town. It was mostly inexpensive apartments, although a few complexes were fairly new.

I parked at the curb and texted Jack: *I ran into Edward Brown this morning.* I left out the details. *He said Paul Johnson's ranch got robbed. Thought you should know.*

As if texting him had summoned messages from the heavens, another came in. Byron.

I turned my phone over as if the sight of it would blind me. "Spit."

Ava looked up from her own phone, where her fingers had been flying. "Did you just say 'spit'?"

I ignored the question. "That CPS investigator that thinks I took the teenage kids is texting me again."

She arched her brows. "Well, you did, right?"

I ignored her again and read the text aloud. "Thanks for your voice mail. I would still like to talk. Please call when you can." Well, I couldn't possibly until Monday at the earliest, could I? That would be my story, anyway, and I'd stick to it. "Doesn't sound like they're sending the po-po after me yet. Ready?"

"Born that way."

We got out of the car and headed up the sidewalk. Stella had lived the high life with her father, but her maternal grandmother, it appeared, didn't provide the same standard of living. These apartments were okay—nice for the neighborhood, anyway—but still low rent compared to Stella's old lifestyle. We walked through rock and cactus landscaping to the security panel. I pressed the buzzer for Unit 1222, which Stella had sent me via text. Someone buzzed us in without checking to see who we were. We scurried through the gate. No surprise, stucco covered the walls of the complex for an adobe look, here and on the outside, too. Inside, the apartments ringed an oval pool, which had a winter cover and a layer of snow on it. It looked barren with the large apron of concrete around it empty. Stella's unit faced one of the narrow ends of the pool.

I rang the doorbell.

From inside, a female voice answered. "It's open."

***

Stella was prone on a leather sofa in front of the boob tube and didn't rise to greet us. The length of her body and the way it draped across the couch hinted at her height. The scent of patchouli hinted at weed, but I didn't notice any other evidence of pot. She wore a gray hoodie and drawstring sweat pants that had stains across the front, and her hip bones jutted above the fabric. She'd tucked her hair inside the hoodie, which held it away from her head, but it still poked out the sides of the front, covering some of her blanket of freckles. I remembered that hair, that improbable and amazing afro of hair.

"Sit anywhere," she said.

"Hi, Stella. Is your grandmother here?"

"No. She's addicted to bingo." Her eyes cut to Ava then back to me. "Who's she?"

"This is Ava, my friend from the Virgin Islands."

Stella's eyes narrowed. "For real? The Virgin Islands?"

"Yah, mon. I visiting New Mexico. Albuquerque next week. Hoping to make it up to Santa Fe and Taos after that." Santa Fe and Taos were news to me.

Stella nodded. "That's pretty cool."

My jaw nearly dropped. This was the fourth time I'd been in Stella's presence and she'd never said so much as "boo" to me before, but apparently Ava was pretty cool. Well, maybe I could use her approval of Ava to my advantage in this conversation. I started by upping Ava's coolness quotient even further.

"Ava's a singer. She's here doing shows."

Stella sat up. "That's *really* cool."

"Well, I away from my baby too long gigging, and the money shit, but I guess it cool."

I noticed her accent had thickened. I wanted to hug her. *Go, Ava.*

"Oh, you have a baby, too?" Stella's voice took on a longing tone. How old was she, anyway, that she had baby fever? Seventeen? Far too young.

"Yah, she a beauty. Hard work, though."

"I play guitar. And sing a little. I'm auditioning for a band after New Year's. An all chicks kind of thing."

I jumped in. "Good luck. You'd look amazing on a stage. Exotic."

Another hungry look toward Ava. "You think so?"

Ava, the professional, nodded. "For true."

Stella's features softened. Maybe she was younger than I'd thought. "Thank you."

I smiled at her. "You're welcome. And I'm really sorry about all this with your dad."

A frown pinched her face. "I hate that douchebag. I hope he rots in prison the rest of his life."

I couldn't argue with her about what a horrible person her dad was, but Mother taught me that if you can't say anything nice, you shouldn't say anything at all, so I didn't. "I want you to know that you probably saved my life, and Betsy's, and I appreciate it."

Stella had played guardian angel to the immigrant children in the families her father had trafficked, dressing up like the Clown from the Apache Mountain Spirit Dancers. It had added some magic to their hard lives.

I added, "You make an awesome Mountain Spirit Dancer."

"They're real, you know. The Mountain Spirits." Stella looked at me with narrowed, defensive eyes.

"Oh?"

"Yeah. I've seen them."

I'd seen one myself, on the runway as Jack came for Betsy and me in the Skyhawk. The Apache spirit had saluted me, and I him.

Softly, my back to Ava, I said, "Me, too."

Stella nodded gravely.

"Betsy said to tell you hello."

Stella's face lit up, and she was beautiful, without warning. "Tell her hello for me. She's cute."

"Yes, she is. I hope to adopt her."

Again, the hungry look. "That would be awesome for her."

"She deserves some awesome. Losing her mom and her dad, being alone in a strange place."

Stella's eyes clouded. "Yeah."

I knew she could relate. I didn't know why her mother wasn't in the picture, but she hadn't been as long as I'd known the girl. Stella was one grandmother away from Greg and Farrah's circumstances, from what I could tell.

Out of the corner of my eye, I noticed that Ava was texting and smiling, oblivious to our conversation. That was okay. I knew I could pull her back in if I needed her. Right now, Stella and I were rolling.

"Betsy lost something important to her at the ranch. A pink backpack. She never went anywhere without it," I said to Stella.

"I remember it."

"Do you remember seeing it after everything went down? After you helped me rescue her?"

Ava giggled, and we both looked at her. She noticed and said, "Oh, sorry. Message." She held up her phone then lowered it and started typing again.

Stella raised her brows toward Ava but continued. "Yeah. I saw it in Dad's barn office, you know, when that police guy let me go through and take all the stuff that was mine or special."

My heart leapt. Hope. The backpack had been there after Johnson was arrested. "Do you know what happened to it?"

"Nah. I left it there. I'm sorry. I was getting my stuff."

I allowed myself a moment of intense frustration. Jack and I had made multiple requests for the backpack through the task force, and we'd left messages for individual officers working the case. We'd called and left a voice mail on the phone out at the ranch. The task force said they didn't have it, which I now believed, since Stella had seen it after the evidence collection was finished. But why hadn't the officers called us back? It was there. All they would have had to do was tell us and someone from Wrong Turn Ranch could have run across the street and picked it up. And now? It could be anywhere, with anyone, or nowhere at all. I wouldn't think that it had any value except to Betsy, but who knew what drove some people to take things that weren't theirs? Once my backpack had been stolen when thieves broke into my car at Tech. All they'd gotten was spiral notebooks, loose change, a few pens, and a chicken salad sandwich I'd forgotten to eat that day. I hope they got food poisoning from it, I really do.

I covered my frustration with a smile. "Hey, you didn't know we were looking for it. No problem."

The doorbell rang again. Stella frowned. "Who's there?"

"Manny." The voice from outside the door sounded guttural and demanding, even in only that one word.

"Just a minute." Her eyes flew wide and she whispered, "Oh shit. I look awful."

"Who's Manny?"

"This guy . . ." She jumped up. "I've got to go change."

Ava put a hand on her hip. "Hold up."

"Yes?"

"Did you know that boy coming?"

"Uh, no, uh—"

"Don't you go jumping to please him when he not even man enough to call first. Tell him you got plans. Make him work a little. You worth it."

Stella looked at me. I nodded.

"But, what if he doesn't come back?" she said.

Ava chuptzed. "Then he garbage." The way she said GAHR-bahj and drew out the second syllable made her pronouncement gospel.

Stella went to the door. She looked back at Ava. "That's what you'd do?"

"Yah, mon. For true."

Stella opened the door to the end of the security chain. A guy too old for her with greasy hair and a hooked scar on his cheek pushed at the door. "Let me in, Stell."

She licked her lips. "Sorry, Manny, I have some girls over. Friends of my father. Call me later?"

His face darkened. "What's that shit? I'm busy later."

She sucked in a wavery breath, shot another look at Ava, who threw her hands in the air with an exaggerated roll of her eyes and head shake. I wasn't sure how Ava managed to do everything she did at once, but it worked.

"Sorry, Manny. Another time." Stella closed the door, over his "What the fuck?" protestation.

"Good." Ava marched over to the girl and hugged her. Stella towered over Ava by a good six inches. "Now, Emily and I taking you to lunch. You way too skinny."

Chapter Twenty-nine

After we dropped off a chattering, smiley Stella—whose head was now crammed with advice on men, music, and motherhood from her new idol Ava—I parked to check my phone. I noticed Ava's flying fingers and that telltale grin again.

"Okay, who has you lit up like a firecracker? I asked.

Ava didn't raise her head. "Some guy."

"Does he have a name?"

She stopped and peered at me. "Emily, I your friend, right?"

I caught my breath. "Yes, of course."

"Friends don't let friends wear that hair. We fixing you up once we back at the ranch."

"What?"

Ava pointed at the crown of her forehead. "That. We fixing that, and you can thank me later."

I liked my bangs. I touched them with my fingertips. I hated when they hugged my head like a greasy cap. I wanted them light and fluffy off my forehead. I looked at my friend in her tight, loud outfit.

"The only way you're touching my hair is if you let me make over your wardrobe," I retorted.

Ava snorted and went back to her texting. I realized too late she'd probably been trying to distract me. At least I hoped that was it. A dark blue sedan drove by, and I did a double take. I tried to decide if it was the same one from earlier, but I couldn't tell for sure. I'd completely forgotten to look for it on the way to and from lunch.

Smarting and jumpy, I scrolled my own notifications. Jack, from an hour and a half before: *Interesting. Helpful. Collin working on this today, w/ license plate photo.*

I answered him: *Good. Ava & I took Stella to lunch. She saw Betsy's backpack in barn office after evidence collected!! Gone now though :-(*

Almost as soon as I'd hit send, my phone rang. I jumped. *Please don't be Byron, please don't be Byron, please don't be Byron.* And it wasn't.

"Hello?"

"It's me." Which my phone had already told me.

"Hi, Jack."

"Good news."

"What's that?"

"Collin has tied the license plate from your photo to a driver who lives outside Alamogordo."

"Why am I not surprised?"

"He wants to drop in on the guy."

"Are we invited?"

Collin's voice boomed, and I realized we were on speaker. I hit speaker, too. "Not officially, but I've been told I'm not very observant, so if other people are there when I drop by, I might not even notice them. Besides, Emily, you might be able to help identify him."

Jack said, "We called the guy's house and he's home. We're on our way there now."

"Text me the address and we'll meet you."

"See you there."

I hung up. "Heck yeah!"

"That the best you can cuss?" Ava shook her head. "Girl, you got no game."

"I got plenty of game. We're about to get to watch Collin roust a smuggler, all because of *my* game."

"Forget your game and get back to the rousting part. Actual sexy cop shit like on TV, that kind of rousting?"

"Exactly like that."

She grabbed her lipstick and brandished it like a sword. "Better move this bucket of bolts before I get out and push."

***

I threw the Suburban into park ten minutes later in the bare front yard/parking lot next to the front steps of a glorified mobile home. Almost simultaneously, a vintage green and white Ford Bronco on jacked-up wheels backed in beside us. I recognized the heads in it. Collin was at the wheel, and Jack on the passenger side.

"Whose car that?" Ava breathed.

"It looks like maybe it's Collin's."

"That so fine." She gave her lipstick another swipe and her girls a boost.

I laughed, because the classic SUV was fine, but I'd have never expected Ava to think so. We got out and the guys came around and met us. I hadn't forgotten I was upset with Jack, but he caught my gaze and smiled at me and a little ice in my heart melted. He was trying. It didn't make it any easier to stay mad at him that he had on my favorite blue plaid flannel shirt with his lived-in Wranglers and boots as old as the Bronco in front of us. His hair had gotten a little on the long side— dark, curling at the tips—and his skin had darkened since yesterday. Why did he have to look so good when he'd been so wrong?

Collin grinned. "Yo, ladies, you ready to play good cop?"

Ava wriggled a little and made some funny noise that I tried to block out. I was immune to Collin with his full swagger on.

"What's the plan?" I asked, without rolling my eyes.

"I'll tell him I've received a complaint of a hit-and-run with his license plate number. You three are my witnesses, but you need to wait in the Suburban. Be seen and not heard, unless I ask you a question. Then go with a simple headshake or nod. At most an 'uh-uh' or an 'uh-huh.' Got it?"

The glare off the snow reflected into my eyes, even through my sunglasses. I added a hand shield. "How will we hear?"

"Roll down your window. Hopefully he'll come outside." He winked at Ava. "I can be very persuasive."

Ava purred. "I sure you can."

"All right, enough of that," I said. "I'm feeling like I stumbled into the back booths in an adult video shop."

Collin laughed. He pointed at the Suburban and the three of us went back to it. I deferred to Jack for the driver's seat since it was his vehicle and sat behind him, window down.

The white house in front of us sat on a barren piece of land, three acres or so, with a fenced area behind it. To call it a house upgraded it a little more than it deserved, although someone had added a small wooden front porch and steps and skirted the entire unit with lattice. Whoever it was needed to come back with a hammer and some paint. A corner of the lattice flapped in the wind. Pieces of trash had woven their way into the lattice itself.

Collin walked up the steps. Despite the sun, temperatures still hung below twenty-five degrees, according to the Suburban's display. The wind blew at roughly tornado speed in a straight line instead of a circle. In the lee of the house the Suburban was sheltered from it a little. Still, the lattice vibrated in the wind, and the whole house shuddered. How it hadn't blown away in the wind already was anybody's guess.

Collin knocked on the storm door three times, hard enough to rattle the glass.

Seconds later, the door opened. An Asian-looking woman in a sweater of peacock colors poked her upper body out, her movements jerky. Barely five feet, she looked like a little hummingbird, and I was afraid the wind would grab her if she stepped any farther out the door.

"What do you want?" Her accent made her English hard to understand.

"Hello, ma'am. My name is Collin Connell and I'm here to see Ricky Brewer. Is he your husband?"

She nodded.

"I see his truck is home, Mrs. Brewer." Collin pointed at the tractor rig I hadn't even noticed earlier protruding in front of the far side of the house. "Would you ask him to come out and speak to me, please?"

"Why?"

Collin pulled out his wallet and flipped it open to his New Mexico State Police badge. "State Police business, ma'am, but nothing to worry about. I need to ask him a few questions."

Her eyes drilled over to the Suburban and into each of us in rapid succession, sharp and hostile. "Wait here." She shut the storm door and the inner door behind her. Thirty seconds passed. I heard a car driving by and glanced out at the road. Blue sedan. Too far away to confirm whether it was one I'd seen earlier, but the coincidence was becoming too big to ignore. I prayed Byron hadn't notified the local CPS to have me tailed. It was unlikely they'd follow me onto the private roads on Jack's property, though, so—while nerve-wracking—the kids would remain hidden and safe. I hoped.

The door reopened. My adrenaline surged. A man stepped out. Short. Skinny. Dark-skinned with jet-black hair standing up on one side. He rubbed his swollen eyes.

Collin flipped his wallet open again. "Collin Connell, NMSP. Are you Ricky Brewer?"

The man grunted.

"I'll take that as a yes. We've had a complaint against your tractor for a hit-and-run, and I need to ask to see your logbook, sir."

Brewer crossed his arms. "Not me. I didn't do no hit-and-run."

"Well, the reason I'm here, sir, is that the citizens who reported it gave me your license plate number." Collin's demeanor suddenly shifted. "So, you can show me the log here, or I can arrest you and we can talk about this at the district offices."

"Arrest me? What's my offense when I ain't done nothing?"

Collin crossed his arms. His upper body looked forbidding, and his heavy winter coat added to his bulk. "It's whatever I say it is. Sir."

Brewer stared at him, rotated glances over at us like his wife had, then stared at Collin again. The wind howled around the house. Beside me, Ava shivered.

"All right. Wait here."

Brewer disappeared.

Ava leaned toward the backseat and whispered to me. "I gettin' hot."

"Take off your jacket."

She gave a mini-chuptz. "Not that kind of hot."

I half-groaned. "You're the most overtaxed person I've ever met."

Without turning his head, Jack said, "Don't you mean oversexed?"

"That's what I said," I lied.

Ava shrugged. "Everybody gotta be best at something."

Jack made a choking noise, then coughed. I looked at him in the rearview mirror and saw he was laughing.

The door opened and Ava sucked in her breath.

Brewer had donned a coat, and he carried a ledger. He shut the doors behind him this time. Right in front of us, I saw the blinds part, and the eyes and nose of his wife appear in the gap, like a beak.

"Here," Brewer said, thrusting the ledger at Collin.

Collin took the book from him and flipped pages. "Hmm." He flipped more slowly. "Umm." He stopped, turned the book toward Brewer. "This here says you carried a load to"—he rotated it back to himself, then to Brewer—"Amarillo. Construction materials, I guess, because right here you wrote 'Top Hat Construction.' Who'd you carry it for?"

Brewer grunted, pointing.

"Ah, Allied Distributing. Down in Las Cruces." Collin turned the book around, studied it. "Did you backhaul?"

Brewer grunted again, pointed again.

"Contracted a load from Owens Corning back here. Gotcha."

Brewer cleared his throat. "What's this got to do with a hit-and-run, and them folks there?" This time he gestured with his head instead of his finger.

"I'll ask the questions." Collin slammed the book shut. "Does this book represent all your jobs, all your driving, all your pickups, all your drop-offs?"

"Yup."

"Let me show you something." Collin pulled his phone out of his jeans pocket. He typed in something, scrolled through screens, then turned the phone to face Brewer. "Is that your rig?"

Brewer frowned and leaned toward the phone. Leaned back. "Yup."

"Do you recognize where this picture was taken?"

He leaned in again, his forehead lines scrunched. He licked his lips. "Can't say."

"Do you know when it was taken?"

Brewer's chin jutted out. "If I don't know where, how am I s'posed to know when?"

"So you 'can't say'?"

Brewer nodded. "Can't say."

"I can. That picture was taken in an alley behind ABC Half-Price Resale in Amarillo where the photographer had watched you unload stolen goods, Monday, December twenty-first, at about five thirty in the afternoon. I got the shop owner can testify to that, and the person behind the camera that took this picture. Two witnesses, against you. Does that help you say?"

Brewer didn't answer.

"Your log on the twenty-first doesn't mention ABC Half-Price Resale. That alone is a nice-sized fine, isn't it? Falsifying a log?" Collin handed the book back to Brewer. "But honestly, I don't give a shit about your log. I don't even necessarily give a shit about *you* trafficking stolen goods. I could probably convince the DA not to give a shit either."

Brewer stared at Collin, who remained silent. Ava reached for my hand. I gave it to her, and she squeezed it, hard. As the seconds dragged on, I wiggled my toes, hoping for feeling in them and a quick resolution to Brewer's dilemma.

Finally, Brewer broke. "How?"

"By giving the DA something better than one pissant shipment."

"But that's all I got. I only did that one."

Collin coughed into his hand as he said, "Bullshit. Give me the address where you picked up the stuff you dropped at ABC Half-Price Resale, and the name of your contact, and I'll plead your case to the DA."

Brewer wiped his forehead. "You wouldn't tell who said? Because snitching's likely to get a man killed."

"Nobody that wouldn't need to know."

"When do I have to decide?"

"Five fucking minutes ago, padnuh." Collin pulled out his cuffs. "Time to read you your Miranda rights." He snapped the cuffs onto one of Brewer's wrists. "Ricky Brewer, you are under arrest for smuggling stolen property. You have the right to—"

"Wait." Brewer's eyes were wide and darting toward the window where his wife still took in the whole scene. "Wait."

Collin finished the Miranda warning and pulled Brewer around and pushed his face against his front door, snapping the cuff around the other wrist behind his back as he did. "I'm not feeling it, Mr. Brewer. I'm just not feeling it."

"We can work something out."

Collin gave the cuffs a tug, pulling Brewer upright. "Let's take a ride." As they walked down the steps, he called out, "Jack, can you drive so I can sit in the back and chat with Mr. Brewer?"

Jack exited the Suburban and held his hand out. Collin dropped his keys in them. Texas Rangers key ring. I smiled. You can take the boy out of Texas and all that.

My eyes followed the three men toward the Bronco. From the backseat, I was even with the bumper and for the first time registered the macabre sight at the front end. A scream came out of my mouth before I could clap my gloved hand over it.

Jack turned in a circle, looking for the source of my vocal horror. "What is it?"

I pointed at the Bronco. A large bird was impaled on its front grille, stretched out in full run, beak open, wings out. It was grisly. Ava jumped out to see for herself, and she screamed, too.

Without cracking a smile, Jack said, "Score one for Wile E. Coyote."

Collin kept a straight face and tight grip on Brewer, but he turned his head toward the Suburban. "Anybody hungry?"

Jack and I laughed. Ava didn't.

"What is that horrible thing?" she asked.

Jack answered her. "Roadrunner."

"Fast little fuckers," Collin said. "I don't remember us hitting anything."

"You could've been driving around with a hood ornament for days," I suggested.

Ava laughed as she backed up to the passenger door of the Suburban and climbed back in. Collin pushed Brewer's head down and loaded him in the Bronco, then climbed in the other side. Seconds later, Jack saluted me as he pulled the vehicle away toward Alamogordo.

Chapter Thirty

When I'd finished checking to be sure that I hadn't heard from Byron or Wallace, I put my keys in the ignition. "Well, that was something you don't get to see every day."

Ava gathered her hair in one hand off her neck and fanned with the other. "Wouldn't mind if I did."

She was dramatic. Incorrigible. And she cheered me up, distracting me from all the screwed-up things going on.

I backed out, then put the Suburban in drive. "You're the guest. Do you want to explore, shop, go back to the ranch, or what?"

Before Ava could answer, a dirty Monte Carlo hurtled around us. Mrs. Brewer peered over the steering wheel—barely. She veered onto the shoulder on the left, spewing snow and gravel from her wheels as she did. Ava and I swiveled our heads in tandem to watch her. Mrs. Brewer corrected the vehicle and pulled in front of us, accelerating.

"She in a hurry."

"Like maybe she's going for help?"

"Or to tattle." Ava chuptzed.

We grinned at each other.

"Wanna see which?" I asked.

"Heck yeah," Ava drawled, with a smirk, and I laughed. She impersonated me perfectly.

I pulled within a hundred yards of Mrs. Brewer's car. Its exhaust alone made it easy to follow, even though the white car blended against the snow-covered terrain on either side of the road. Soon, though, we were passing through Alamogordo on the highway. She wove in and out of traffic with no blinker, ten miles faster than the flow. I bit my lip as I changed lanes repeatedly, trying to keep up with her, yet keeping my eye out for a disturbing blue sedan behind me. Our path reminded me of pole bending, a rodeo event I competed in as a kid where you race a horse through a series of six poles in a serpentine pattern, then back again. It was a lot like slalom skiing. And like following Mrs. Brewer.

"She getting away."

I gripped the steering wheel harder. "Not if I can help it."

On the south side of town, the Monte Carlo accelerated. I pressed the gas to pace her. Eighty. Eight-five. Almost ninety. Ava held on to the armrest and the door grip like they were anchors. The Suburban's frame shook. I scanned the dash. We were in four-wheel drive. The snow had disappeared south of town, as if we'd passed a line of demarcation, so I wasn't worried about traction, but I couldn't remember if it was okay to change out of all-wheel on the fly, only that it wasn't recommended for high-speed driving. Hopefully I wouldn't wreck the transmission. I kept my foot pressed down hard. I didn't smell anything burning or see any smoke, and those were good signs.

We passed a highway sign that said LAS CRUCES, 50, EL PASO, 102, CIUDAD JUAREZ, 110.

"We almost to Mexico?" Ava shrieked. "Where she going, anyway?"

"Hopefully not there."

Suddenly, the Monte Carlo turned off the highway into the parking lot of a cluster of flat-roofed warehouse-like buildings. Faded signage out front indicated the property was for sale, although I couldn't tell if it referred to the whole group, or only to one of the buildings. A handful of cars were parked without any regard to linear spacing. We were far enough behind the Monte Carlo to see it pull in at an angle in front of the nearest building. Mrs. Brewer got out, and then we were past her.

Ava's head did a *Fourth Kind* owl move, nearly. "She went in," Ava said. "What now?"

"Let's drive for a few minutes, then we can turn around and see if she's still there when we make it back. Keep doing it until she leaves. Then maybe we can check it out."

Ava nodded. "We make good cops."

"Jack doesn't think so. He hates it when I investigate things on my own."

She chuptzed. "He just jealous of real talent."

I laughed. "And there's no law against it." Well, there were laws against some of the things I'd done in the course of checking things out. Like letting myself into a few homes where I wasn't technically invited. But I only did that when there were extenuating circumstances, like people's lives at risk. Even if that wasn't a defense in court, it sure helped me sleep better at night.

I took the next exit and we reversed course back toward Alamogordo.

When the warehouse was in sight, Ava said, "She still there."

"Yeah, let's make another loop."

As we passed the cluster of warehouses from the south, I noticed a cross in the window of the last one and in plain block letters above the door, CHURCH. A sign in one window read EXORCISE DAILY. RUN FROM THE DEVIL. And in the next window: SEXUAL EXPLOITATION WORKSHOP THIS SUNDAY. My eyes widened.

"That woman need to hurry. I gotta pee."

I shook off the oddly disturbing church signs. "How are you going to be a cop if you can't hold it on a stakeout, or when you're following someone?"

"Where I come from, if you drive as far as we have, you reach the end of the island and stop for rum and Coke."

I mimicked Ava's accent, badly. "For true."

She shook her head and drawled, "Not even close, cowgirl," nailing mine again.

We stopped at a Love's on the outskirts of town, which got me to thinking about Greg and Farrah. Which made me think about Byron. Which made me think of Ivanka. Which made me think of the missing dancer. *Stop it*, I told myself. *Just stop it.*

I decided to take a pit stop, and, afterwards, I bought a sweet tea. While waiting to pay, I stared at my phone. My anger from the night before had nearly gone away. I didn't want to be crossways with Jack. I wanted things to be like they had been on Christmas Eve. I worried my swollen hangnail with my teeth then typed a message to him: *I'm sorry I got so upset last night. Maybe we can talk later and I can give you your Christmas present.*

Ava read over my shoulder. "Ah, you getting soft."

I hit send and handed the clerk my money. "I may have overreacted, but I'm still not completely okay with him hiding my father from me." A father I hadn't called back. I'd decided to block it out until I returned to Amarillo. I'd decide whether to call him then.

We walked out together.

"That ain't gonna keep you warm at night, is it?"

I pointed my drink at a white Monte Carlo at a pump on our far right, ignoring her last question. "That's Mrs. Brewer."

We sprinted the rest of the way to the Suburban—or, rather, trotted as fast as Ava's heels and my sloshing drink allowed—and jumped in.

I craned to see the Monte Carlo. "I don't think she's in it. Maybe she's in the store."

Ava looked, too. "Don't see her."

"Let's get out of here."

I exited the Love's lot on the side farthest from Mrs. Brewer's car and turned back onto the access road, whipping a U-turn under the overpass, then accelerating up an entrance ramp into the southbound lanes. In less than ten minutes we were the sole vehicle parked in front of the warehouse where we'd seen the Monte Carlo earlier. I pulled a scrunchie from my purse and gathered my hair in a high ponytail.

"You want to wait here?" I asked Ava.

"You soft in the head?"

"Come on, then. Follow my lead."

"Why, you got a plan?"

We got out. I always hated that question and found it best not to dignify it with an answer, since the answer was usually no. My footsteps clonked on the pavement and Ava's clicked sharply as we walked up to the glass front door. I grasped the handle and pulled it open, planless.

***

We stepped onto commercial-grade white speckled linoleum in a small lobby area, which was really nothing more than a tall reception desk in front of a closed metal door. No pictures graced the walls, no clock ticked out the time. There weren't even any chairs for visitors to sit on. A powdery odor like dust dried my sinuses while fluorescent lights flickered over our heads, making buzzing and popping noises like a bug zapper, and casting disco lighting onto the water-stained ceiling tiles.

"Hello?" I called. My voice frogged.

Ava put her hand in front of my arm against my wrist. "You scared?"

"Nah."

"Liar."

We both laughed, but our voices sounded hollow.

"Hello?" I called again.

No answer.

I said, "Well, let's poke our heads in that door, take a quick look."

A quick look was like dipping a toe in the water. No commitment. We could always shut the door and leave after our quick look, if the water was too cold. She nodded, and I grasped the knob and tried to turn it. Nothing happened. I pulled, then fell back as the door gave way. Ava had started breathing harder. So had I.

"You first," Ava said.

From a safe distance back from the opening, I called, "Hello?"

No answer. No sound. I leaned all the way in. The lighting in the interior bordered on darkness and seemed to come mostly from high windows near the ceiling. Still, even in the shadows, I got a sense of the inside. Tall racks lined up along the length of the space, leading away from us. It reminded me of the ceiling-high shelves in discount centers and home improvement stores. From where we stood, these looked maybe half-full. What I couldn't tell from this vantage point was what the racks held.

I whispered to Ava. "Can you watch the door? I want to get a closer look."

She peered inside, then looked at me, her eyes dubious. "Maybe old lady Brewer drop something off. Or she work here. What you gonna learn in there you can't tell from out here?"

"Won't know until I look."

But that wasn't true. Seeing a deserted warehouse full of stuff made me wonder where it all came from, and whether I'd find anything from Wrong Turn Ranch.

I put my hand on her upper arm. "I'll be fine. You stand here and hold the door open so I'll have more light, and if someone comes in, shout hello at them loud, like you're hard of hearing. Tell them your friend is looking for a bathroom."

Her brows knitted, but she slid her short frame along the door and backed it all the way open. Fear made her look much younger, like she was a little girl playing dress-up in her mother's clothes and makeup.

"I'm glad you showed up in Amarillo, Ava Butler."

"I let you know if I agree when we outta here."

I held up the five fingers of my right hand. "No more than five minutes."

I backed up. The gloom swallowed me, like I was falling down and backwards into a black, bottomless pit. I fought off the sensation and flipped my phone over to turn on its flashlight and got a bad surprise. Low battery warning: ten percent. I could have had it charging in the Suburban for the last hour, but it hadn't occurred to me it would be on fumes. I'd cried myself to sleep the night before, and now, looking back, I couldn't remember plugging it in. I wanted to groan in frustration, but I kept quiet, thinking. I only needed light for five minutes, and ten percent might be enough. I activated the flashlight, shining it ahead of me, illuminating floating dust particles in its beams. On impulse I turned it back around and turned the ringer off, then resumed scanning ahead of me.

Even though no one had answered our hello, I put each foot down slowly, carefully, and whisper-soft. It was the kind of place that called for it. Plus, someone had left that front door unlocked. They probably hadn't left for the day. Maybe whoever it was had run out for a late lunch, or was in a bathroom, but surely they would be back.

I walked to the far side of the first rack and trained the flashlight beam on its shelves, moving the light and my eyes slowly, methodically across the space, from top to bottom. It was an odd assortment with no discernible organization. Some things were boxed up like new— microwaves, computers, a rifle, mobile phones—and others looked used. A big screen TV on its back. An opened jewelry box. A walkie- talkie set without a box. I came upon bag after bag of feed and fertilizer and bolts of fabric. Some stuff even looked past its useful life. Old shoes. Cracked and stained kitchen appliances. My nerves tightened and twanged like a piano wire. Given the connection of Mrs. Brewer and her husband to trafficking stolen merchandise, this had to be one of the storage facilities.

I scanned both sides of the second aisle as I walked quickly back toward Ava, then the third heading toward the back wall again, practi- cally holding my breath to stay quiet. Halfway down the third, my light flashed across something bright pink. I stopped and pointed the beam back to where I'd seen it, but at that moment, my phone died and the flashlight with it.

"Mother Goose," I whispered.

When I pressed the on button, the phone and light came on like a flashbulb, lasting only long enough for me to see two things. The battery indicator reading one percent and that I had two texts from Jack showing on the lock screen. The first one said: *Collin checked the plate number your dad gave us. It's a cop. Brewer confirmed.* Before I could read the other, the bulb had popped and the screen was dead.

My father was helping catch the Wrong Turn Ranch thieves. Some- thing flickered in my gut, and it wasn't a bad flicker. It was almost a prideful one, vindication on behalf of him. Or maybe I was just happy the case was breaking open. I needed to finish and get out of here, plug my phone in the car charger, and call Jack and tell him what I'd found and get the scoop from him.

I stood rooted in place, giving my eyes time to adjust to the sudden absence of light. Within seconds I could see well enough to make out the shapes on the shelf in front of me, but most of the colors looked like varying shades of gray. I moved to where I thought I'd seen pink. It had been farther back on the shelf, and possibly behind a sander and a Skilsaw I'd seen on the front edge. I reached out to nearest items and ran my hands over them gently. The first one was rounded and smooth. Possibly the cover of the Skilsaw.

I walked my hands farther backward. My eyes continued to adjust and colors slowly seeped back into my field of vision, like the time my ex-husband and I went scuba diving on our honeymoon trip to Aruba. Down at fifty feet everything looked drab. As we ascended, stopping for decompression breaks, the colors returned, more with every passing foot. It was like watching the animation of a black and white movie become colorized.

A brightly colored object caught my eye. I couldn't tell if it was orange, red, or pink, but given its location, I was putting my money on pink. A loud buzz of excitement started ringing in my ears. My fingers walked my hands to it and I put my palms on its surface. Canvas, with slick waterproofing. I inched my hands along the material and came to a long strip of puffy fabric. I followed that to hard plastic with a skinny strap out of its other end. I smiled. A strap. A strap on a pink backpack.

Mindful of the razor-sharp objects between my treasure and me, I hefted the bag high. It was light. I heard noises from the front of the warehouse, but I ignored them as I concentrated, using one arm to anchor the saw, and bumped the backpack over to me. As I got it to the edge of the shelf, it knocked into an item I hadn't seen, sending it crashing to the floor. There was a loud crack, and a shattering of glass. I held myself perfectly still, holding my breath. I strained to hear sounds, any sounds around me.

Nothing. Whatever the noise had been up front, it was silent now.

I exhaled and laughed. Turning toward the door, I raised my voice a little over a conversational tone and a little below a shout. "Ava, I found Betsy's backpack."

A whimper came from behind me, followed by a man's voice. "Ava's indisposed at the moment, but I'm sure she's quite happy for you."

***

Time slowed, seconds seeming to pass between each beat of my heart. Whatever I did next affected Ava more than me, and as much as I wanted to go on the attack, I had to be cautious for her sake. The voice had sounded close. Ten feet? Fifteen? Five? Probably ten, I decided. My hand still held the backpack perched on the edge of the shelf. I released it, hoping it looked like I had only been using the shelf for balance. My baby Glock was nestled in my purse near my stomach. The man didn't have a light on me, so with minimal movement I slipped my hand between the open sides of my jacket and into my purse. I felt the cold, hard grip and wrapped my hand around it. Using mostly my wrist, I tucked it into the front of my pants, just behind one side of my coat.

I turned toward the voice. All I could see of him and Ava was a shadowy outline, large and ominous. Regardless, I curled my lips into the biggest smile I could muster.

"Sorry." I stalled by coughing in my hand. "I was looking for the bathroom in here when I dropped my phone." I held it up. "I found it!"

The shadow advanced on me, and Ava materialized out of the darkness. Blood dripped from her busted lip, and an arm circled her neck. A pistol pressed into her temple. The top of a man's head appeared, his face mostly hidden by Ava's head, as was his body. *Coward.*

I held up a hand. "Wow, hey, there must be a big misunderstanding here. Look, I'm so sorry I trespassed. I've had this really embarrassing stomach problem, and I was desperate, and the front door was un-locked, and—"

"Shut the fuck up."

I raised my other hand. "Okay, okay."

"We're going for a walk."

"Yeah, no problem."

He took the gun off Ava's temple and waved it at me. "Move!"

Just then, Jack's voice shouted, from what sounded like the reception area. "Emily? Ava? Are you guys in here?"

The man jerked his head toward Jack's voice and his arm slipped and loosened. Ava and I made eye contact and I shouted, "Go!" as I grabbed my gun and waved my left arm to the side, hoping she would jump in the direction I was signaling.

Ava donkey-kicked as she wrenched herself down and away from her captor. She dove under his arm and rolled to her right. He grunted and bent forward for a second, firing wildly as he did. I heard the bullet ricochet off shelving to my left. My gun was in front of me in my right hand, and I sighted it just like my daddy had taught me, like I'd practiced for the last fifteen years at shooting ranges in Lubbock, Dallas, and Amarillo. By the time my left hand reached its steadying position, I was crouched and firing.

My first shot missed to the right but the second hit the man's hand. I heard the lovely sound of his gun skittering across the floor. He groaned and staggered to his right. I adjusted my aim, and my third and fourth shots struck their target. He clutched his thigh, screaming as he fell to the floor. Out of my peripheral vision, I saw Ava scoop up his gun as I assessed our situation. My magazine held ten rounds, plus one in the chamber for a total of eleven, so I had seven bullets left. Hopefully I wouldn't have to use them. I kept my gun trained on him and advanced until I was a yard away.

"You're messing with wrong girl," I said.

I resisted the urge to blow pretend smoke from the barrel of my Glock. I'd never shot at a person before—never wanted to have to—but I'd always wanted to say the words my father had inscribed around the barrel for me. The man groaned and writhed, cursing in general and at me in particular. As he rolled I got my first good look at his face.

"Son of a biscuit!" I yelled. It was Edward Brown. Suddenly I knew what Jack's second text would have told me. "Well, Officer Brown, you had me fooled. Checking up on Johnson's place. More like seeing if there was anything else left out there you could steal."

"Fuck you," he spat.

"No, thank you," I said.

Running footsteps approached. "Emily?" The warehouse reverberated with Jack's cry.

"Over here. We're fine," I yelled back.

Looking at Ava, I said, "I don't suppose you have any idea how Jack knew where to find us, do you?"

She stood—holding Brown's gun by its trigger guard with two hooked fingertips—and grinned, blood dripping from her temple like she was the bride of Frankenstein. "Collin and I conversating some via text today." She tossed her hair. "And I might have mentioned what our bad asses up to."

I groaned. "There's probably a lot there I don't want to know, but thank God for whatever it was the two of you were up to last night that saved our bad asses from ending up dead today."

"What the hell, Emily?" It was an angry Jack, closing in on me fast. "Do you have a death wish? What the hell's the matter with you, anyway?"

I shoved my gun into the back of my waistband and raised my hands in the air. "Don't shoot," I said.

He shook his head, and I closed the rest of the distance between us in one giant step, landing with my head against his chest and both his arms around me.

Chapter Thirty-one

I snuck Betsy's backpack out to the Suburban after we called the cops, past Jack, who shook his head and put his hands over his eyes. Yes, I knew I shouldn't tamper with evidence, but there was no way I was letting it get tied up in a multiyear court case. The Alamogordo police had plenty left in the warehouse without this backpack, worthless to anyone except one very special little girl.

When the cops did arrive, things got real in a hurry. It's a sobering time when good cops are forced to process a bad one. Part of me wanted to apologize. Part of me wanted to ask them all politely how the heck the jerkface could get away with this stuff under their noses. I didn't do either, just answered their questions the best I could.

Ava and I drove back toward Wrong Turn Ranch after the police had finished with us, and Jack left in Collin's Bronco at the same time, promising to see us after he'd picked Collin up at the NMSP district offices on the way home. I plugged my phone in to the charger the second we got into the vehicle.

Ava was rubbing her neck. She already had a large fingerprint bruise.

"Do we need to stop and have someone take a look at that?" I asked.

"Nah. It good." She rolled her head. "Things always this exciting round you?"

"No," I said, then realized that wasn't true. "Well, yeah, some-times."

"Still water run deep."

I laughed.

A few minutes later, Ava said, "I feeling a little shaky all of a sud-den. I call my daughter and mom real quick. Say I love dem, hear their voices."

The gravity of the danger we'd escaped was starting to hit me, too, now that the adrenaline had worn off. Brown had shot at me. He'd held a gun to Ava's head. Ava and I had each come a slim whisker from dying. My lips quivered and I pressed them together.

Ava pressed a button on her phone. She spoke to her mother for a moment, then her accent thickened and her voice softened into baby talk. "Mama miss you, baby girl."

I knew her daughter wasn't even a year old. I imagined the tiny girl cooing on the other end of the line, and a lump formed in my throat. I wanted that. I wanted a child of my own—I wanted *Betsy*. Somehow, I had to find a way to keep her in the U.S., to resolve the Greg and Farrah situation, and to prevail on my adoption application.

Beside me, Ava blew kisses into the phone to her daughter, then said good-bye to her mother.

She slipped her mobile back into her purse. "I miss her. Home in two weeks, though."

"I can't imagine. Time will go quickly, though."

I turned on the radio and scanned for stations. Christian pop. Talk radio. 70s rock. Mexican pop. Country. Nothing grabbed me. I switched it back off and we rode in silence. As I drove, I thought ahead to our evening at the ranch.

I said, "Hey, I imagine Jack and I will do a gift exchange with Mickey and Laura and the kids after dinner, since we didn't get to that last night."

Ava readjusted her headband in the mirror. "Sound fun."

"You coming back to Amarillo with us in the morning, or heading on to Albuquerque?"

"Oh, I heading on."

I shot her a look and she avoided eye contact. "Heading on to Albuquerque?"

"Soon. In time for my gig."

"Do you need a ride anywhere?"

"Nope." I caught a smile teasing at the corner of her mouth. I had a pretty good idea how she would be getting to Albuquerque, but if she wanted to be cagey, I could play along.

I stopped for gas in Tularosa. While it pumped, I got back in the Suburban with Ava to stay warm and to call Laura about plans for the evening. I pressed Laura's name in my contacts and my speaker phone connected.

"Hello?" Mickey's deep voice answered instead of his wife's.

"Hi, Mickey. It's Emily. We're all on our way back to the ranch, and, boy, do we have a lot to tell you about today. But first I wanted to see if we could bring gifts over to you guys and the kids tonight."

I heard Laura's voice in the background. It was high-pitched, and she sounded upset. Mickey spoke, but he'd muffled the phone. I caught "It's Emily." Then, louder, unmuffled, he said, "We let the kids go out riding by themselves for the first time this afternoon, and they were supposed to be back by now. We're getting worried. You haven't heard from them, have you?"

Dusk was falling outside, and my stomach started gnawing on itself. "I haven't."

"You don't think they would have run off, do you?" Mickey's voice sounded tight, stressed.

Would they? I knew they didn't want to go back to Amarillo, but the time hadn't come for that yet. "I don't. They love it there. They love you guys. They feel safe."

Anxiety started gnawing at my gut. If the kids hadn't run off, where were they? Sure, they could just be running late, like normal kids. Or a horse could have gone lame. Or one of them was sick or hurt. And there were worse things. Things I didn't want to imagine. I shuddered.

I spoke fast. "Mickey, I need you to know something. Last night I got a call that someone thought I had the kids and reported it anonymously to CPS. I don't want to overreact but—"

Ava gasped and put her hand over her mouth.

He finished my thought. "But we have to find them, now."

"Exactly. I'll be there in ten minutes."

"And Jack?"

"Longer than that, I'm afraid, but he's on his way. Collin, too."

Mickey grunted. "I'll start getting the horses ready."

"Wouldn't four-wheelers be faster?" I knew they had a platoon of them.

"A little, but they're too noisy. We need to be able to hear if they call out, especially since it's dark. They could be injured." *Or worse*, I thought.

"We'll meet you at the stables."

My heart triple-timed as I called Jack.

***

Twenty minutes later, I'd dropped Ava at Jack's and was assembling lights, energy bars, first-aid kits, and canteens of hot chocolate in saddlebags. Packing the bars made me realize it was dinnertime, and I hadn't eaten. Jack and Collin probably hadn't either. Nor would we. Laura and Mickey were saddling up four horses for our search party. They had saved Jarhead for last. The horse was amped up. He could probably sense our own tension.

Mickey threw the blanket and saddle onto Jarhead's back, then said, "Laura's gonna stand by in my office."

Laura said, "You guys can stay in touch with me by walkie-talkie, and if the kids come back, I'll call you off."

I had noticed that they'd placed a walkie-talkie by each bag. "Why walkie-talkies? Why not our phones?"

Laura shifted from saddling horses to helping me with assembly. "Lot of dead zones up there."

Bouncing lights on the stable walls announced the approach of a vehicle. Doors slammed and Jack and Collin came trotting in.

"We're about ready," Mickey said.

"What's your plan?" Jack asked.

"We've saddled horses for each of us, and we put together supplies." He pulled out a map of the ranch and tapped a circled area. "They took off in this direction. They like to go up by the cemetery. I was thinking we'd go in twos for safety—Emily with me, Collin with you, Jack, since you and I both know how to track—and that we'd take these two routes." He traced lines equidistant from the middle of the circled area and its outer edges. One was highlighted in yellow, the other in green. "Emily and I will take the green route. I told the kids the first day that if they heard this call"—he demonstrated the ca-caw of a raven—"to come on back, we were looking for them."

Jack nodded. "Like the parents used to use with us."

"Yeah, it carries a lot better than shouting."

"And just in case of bad guys, doesn't give us away," I said.

"Yes." Mickey looked at Collin and me. "Is everybody dressed warm enough? I've got more gear in the tack room."

"I'm set." I'd already grabbed heavy gloves, a hat, and a scarf to go with my jacket, since most of my things were at Jack's house. Luckily, I had on good cowboy boots that I'd re-waterproofed this winter, with jeans and a sweater.

"Me, too," Collin said. "But I think it's time to call for backup."

Mickey stuffed his map inside his coat and zipped it up.

"I'll call now," Laura said, her face pale and pinched. She walked toward Mickey's office, then ran back and threw her arms around Mickey and kissed him. She turned to all of us. "You guys be safe."

"We will, babe," Mickey said.

Laura disappeared into his office.

Jack walked over to me and touched my shoulder. I turned, and he caught my chin in one hand and kissed me.

"Be careful," he said.

"You, too."

He shook his head. "You're reckless. Please."

I reached for his gloved hand with mine and squeezed it. "I promise."

I led Jarhead out of the stable and mounted up, along with the guys. Jarhead snorted puffs of steam as he trotted in place. All the horses seemed especially eager, actually. Mickey swung a leg over his big roan horse and allowed the animal to take off at the same time. Without another word between us, I squeezed Jarhead with my heels.

He squealed with excitement and I held him to a frothing lope as we followed Mickey into the deepening twilight. Behind me and to our left, I heard the hooves of Collin's and Jack's horses as they peeled off toward their route.

Mickey led the way through the same open series of gates I'd ridden through with Jack and the kids last weekend. The moon was shining so bright that we didn't turn on our tracking lights, not that we'd be able to track them yet anyway. The area we were traversing was too well and recently traveled by many others. Slowly we increased speed, but not enough to satisfy Jarhead, who nodded his head emphatically in rhythm to his lope.

I leaned forward and whispered to him. "It's okay, boy. This isn't a race."

He shook his head, rattling the rings on the edges of the bit in his mouth.

Emotionally, horses and people often operate on the same wavelength. I thought of the way Jarhead and his pals had picked up on our stress back at the stable, and of how Thunder's calm had soothed Betsy when we'd escaped from Johnson's Ranch. Whenever Jib—my college barrel-racing horse—had sensed a race coming up, she'd become so high-strung I was afraid she'd injure herself. I'd learned that singing in her ear and rubbing her neck helped her settle down, sort of like how a snake charmer hypnotizes a cobra with pungi music.

So I tried it with Jarhead, patting his neck and singing "O Holy Night," a little off-key like my mother, my voice cracking on the high notes. After only a few minutes, he had stopped his snorts and head bobs. His ears twitched as he vacillated between his urgent need to sprint and reluctant attention to my song. It distracted me, too, from thinking about why Greg and Farrah hadn't come home.

I stopped singing and spoke aloud. "Maybe one of their horses got hurt."

Jarhead nickered.

"I'm not talking about a permanent injury, here, and I know it's not ideal, but it's better than any of the alternatives."

He snorted softly.

"Okay, how about they were lost but now they've found their way home, and we'll see them any second?"

This time Jarhead blew softly out his nose. I patted him again and resumed singing.

We started up the incline into the treed foothills. The sky grew darker, and the snow less disturbed. I kept Jarhead tight on Mickey's roan. I had only been up here once—to the cemetery with Jack, Greg, and Farrah—and in the dark I had no idea if we were still headed in that direction. We didn't need me getting lost tonight, too. The trees and the wind absorbed the noises around us, and in the relative silence, the hoofbeats of the horses sounded like muted thunder. The air smelled clean, and when I breathed it in and licked my lips, I could taste the earthiness of melting snowflakes, even though I couldn't see the snow falling. The sky looked crystal clear, in fact, and if it hadn't been for the trees and darkness lit only by moonglow, I imagined I would have seen Amarillo in the distance. As it was, I only saw the snowy forest floor, the trunks of aspens and evergreens, and the rump of the horse in front of us.

Mickey slowed his horse and dismounted as it stopped. He held the reins in one hand and switched on his handheld spotlight in the other, pointing it at the ground. He swept his beam across the snowy forest floor, studying the area, then knelt and touched the compressed snow in the imprint of several hooves and brushed powder out of another. It made my heart ache for my father, the one I used to know, the one who had taught me that a real scout gets close to the ground and puts his hands on the earth.

Mickey said, "Looks like two horses came this way today." He pointed ahead of us, but to where I wasn't sure.

I stared at the ground and saw only a mass of hoofprints, despite my dad's coaching. I'd have to take Mickey's word for it. He trained the light on the ground around us in expanding sweeps. He stopped and reswept an area. I clucked to Jarhead. He followed Mickey and his horse, calmly walking instead of bouncing like a pogo stick.

"Four-wheeler." Mickey turned to me. "Also today."

The four-wheeler tracks were obvious, even to me. "Is that good or bad?"

"I'm not sure. Could have been one of the hands. Nobody else has any business up here. The tracks run parallel to the horses. We'll follow the horses and keep an eye on the four-wheeler. I've got enough light without the spot, so I'm going to turn it off for now."

"Okay."

He switched off his light and spoke into the walkie-talkie. "Found two sets of horse tracks and one set of four-wheeler tracks, all recent. We're following them."

Our handsets crackled and I heard Jack's voice. "We've got nothing. Assume you want us to stick to the plan?"

"Roger."

Laura's voice cracked. "Please find them, Mickey."

He whispered something in a language I recognized as Apache from my visits to this area, although I didn't know a word of it, then stuffed the walkie-talkie back into a holster on his saddle. He mounted, leaning back in his saddle, and ca-cawed long and loud. Jarhead snorted. Even I was startled at how realistic Mickey sounded. Wild. Dangerous.

We waited and I listened with every bone in my body but heard no answering ca-caw.

He motioned ahead. "Let's ride, but we need to be extra quiet now."

"Like an Indian scout," I said, then immediately felt like an idiot for saying it aloud. Sure, I had idolized Sacajawea as a kid whose father taught her his white-man version of the ways of Indian scouts. I still channeled her on occasion. But to say it to Mickey, who really was a Native American? My face flamed in the dark.

He nodded, though. "Like that. But tonight we are hunters."

Mickey's horse took off, and I gave Jarhead his cue and he lunged after him.

As we raced silently through the woods, the tracks of horse hooves and a four-wheeler slowly converged until the four-wheeler crushed the hoofprints underneath. A shadow flashed over us, and a screech owl shattered the forest silence with his nerve-wracking cry. My heart slammed into my throat and Mickey pulled his horse up short and whirled to me.

He whispered. "Emily, someone followed them up here, I'm sure of it. Are you armed?"

I shook my head, whispering in return. "Cops have my gun. I shot one today."

"Shot one what?"

I shook my head. "I'll tell you about it later."

Mickey nodded once. "Okay, well, I have a gun, so stay behind me like you've been doing." He shifted like he was going to take off, but instead he said, "Listen, this isn't exactly scientific evidence, but that screech owl—it's a very bad omen. The Owl is evil personified in Apache lore, like an ogre or a bogeyman. It steals souls, especially those of children. Seeing an owl or hearing one, its presence in the woods . . . trust me, this seals the deal for me."

I remembered Mickey telling Greg and Farrah about the Owl. Maybe six months ago I would have dismissed his words as nonsense, but not anymore. I'd seen the powerful magic of the Apaches firsthand. If he told me that the owl meant someone bad had the kids, I believed him.

Mickey ca-cawed again. I held my breath while we waited for a reply, but the only answer was another screech from the owl flying above us.

"The tracks have veered away from the path to the cemetery. I think they're headed toward the old mine." Mickey held a finger over his lips, and we moved on.

But his words lingered in my head, chilling me. The mine? I'd never been there. I'd only seen it in a picture and from a distance. It sounded dangerous. Not a place for kids to hang out in the dark, even teenage kids. Especially not if someone was following them. I tried not to panic, but adrenaline surged through me, the scared kind, and all I wanted to do was get to them, wherever they were, as fast as we could.

We followed the tracks another half mile, the only sound besides the wind was the snow-muffled hooves of the horses and their panting breaths. Suddenly, the forest cleared. Mickey reined his horse in, and I did the same. From the cover of the trees, I saw a black square in the side of the rapidly rising hillside in front of us. It was the entrance to the mine. The snow ended outside its mouth, and the tracks led to its edge, horses and four-wheeler both.

Mickey dismounted and walked his horse away from the mine entrance, along the edge of the clearing. "Oh no." He crouched low. "See this?" He pointed at tracks and gestured back down the hill. "It's the horses. But they're different than before." He looked up at me. "Riderless."

I slipped off Jarhead and bent down beside him.

Mickey pointed back to the entrance. "The tracks come from there. And there's more. Something is blocking the entrance."

I'd never seen the mine before, so I hadn't known what to expect. But I peered closer now, trying to figure out what he saw in the darkness. Slowly, quietly, we moved a little closer, at an angle. Mickey drew his gun and carried it in his right hand. The object in the center of the entrance took shape.

"It's the four-wheeler," I said.

"They're inside," Mickey whispered. "Someone is with them, and they're inside."

The radios squawked. "The horses are back at the barn, Mickey. The kids aren't with them."

Mickey grabbed his radio and keyed his mike. The console light turned red. "It's okay, Laura, we've found them. Jack, Collin—"

A gunshot cracked. Mickey let out an oomph and fell, spinning to the right and down, and purple exploded from his shoulder. His horse bolted, disappearing into the blackness of the woods like a ghost after the horses that had gone before.

Jarhead leapt straight sideways away from the mine entrance before the second shot. The bullet whizzed past us, so close I could hear the zing as the bullet displaced the air against my cheek. I jumped off of Jarhead, holding tight to his reins, and ran with him behind me to a tree. I couldn't risk him running off, too. I needed him for Mickey, at least, and maybe the kids. I repeated my belt trick from that morning to tie his reins to the slim tree trunk. Then I hit the dirt and bear-crawled uphill back to Mickey, praying I was too low to be seen. I crawled past him to his feet, which positioned my body outside of the mine entrance on the opposite side from where I'd tied Jarhead. The horse snorted and pawed, then whinnied and jerked at the reins. If he pulled with any of his strength at all, he'd snap them and be back at the ranch in minutes. *Dear God, please help Jarhead find his zen place without me there to sing him Christmas carols.* A huge gust of wind rustled through the treetops. It whined, the trees moaned, a coyote howled. It was like a chorus, and, surprisingly, Jarhead quit pulling. He still snorted and shifted his hooves, but he stayed in place. God had come through.

I had to hope I'd judged the angle right and that the shooter couldn't get a bead on me anymore. I counted to three for courage, then I stood and rolled Mickey over on his back using torque from his legs. I tried to be gentle, but he groaned. I winced. I hated hurting him. And this would be worse. Grasping hold of one of his ankles in each hand, I dragged him backwards down the slick hill until he was well out of the line of fire. He didn't make a peep.

"Mickey, can you hear me?" I patted his cheeks. "Can you hear me?" My breaths came in quick, quiet pants.

He rolled his head to the right, toward his injured side. "Yeah, I . . . hear you." His voice was low, but he could speak, and that was good enough for me.

"Okay, I'm going to take a look at the bullet wound."

I peeled the edges of his disintegrated clothing away from it. In the moonlit clearing, I could see it was bleeding fast, but not gushing. It was on the right shoulder, so, by definition, that made it less dangerous than if it had been on his left, by his heart. At least I hoped it did. I took off one of my gloves and gathered a handful of snow. I closed my eyes and pushed the snow into the center of the wound, then followed it with the glove.

Mickey grunted.

I grabbed his left hand and put it on the glove, forcing his fingers to grasp it. "Hold this here, tight. You hear me?"

"Yeah, hold it tight. Got it."

I needed his gun. I felt a little squeamish about hunting for it but I didn't have time to pussyfoot around, as my dad would say. I patted Mickey's hips under his jacket. My fingers found the hard metal of the holstered weapon and I pulled it out carefully. It was a full-size Glock 9mm, which was lucky for me. It operated like my baby Glock, only bigger, heavier, and with more bullets.

Mickey lifted his head. "What're ya doin'?"

"I'm borrowing this, so I can go get the kids."

His voice grew stronger. "Wait for Jack and Collin."

I'd forgotten all about the guys. I grabbed my walkie-talkie. I prayed the unit wouldn't feedback and keyed it to life, hoping the wind would cover the sound of my voice. I covered the console with my hand, too, to hide its light. "Don't answer me, just come to the mine. We've found them and we need help. Mickey's been shot. Repeat, do not answer. Use caution and be quiet. They know we're here, but not you. Hurry." I stared at it, afraid it would squawk to life. I added, "Over and out," then turned it off quickly, grabbing Mickey's and switching it off, too.

I checked the glove on his shoulder. He was doing a good job with the pressure. He would be fine. He had to be fine.

"I'm sorry, but I can't sit here with those kids possibly in there with a person who shot you. I have to do something."

He shook his head. "You heard the Owl. He's an omen of death. Don't do something stupid and make it yours."

I checked that I had my spotlight and stuck the gun in the front of my jeans. "That's exactly why I can't wait. If somebody is going to die, I can't let it be one of those kids. And I know you said the owl is an omen, but you also said the coyote can outsmart him, and did you hear what I heard a minute ago, after you were shot?"

Mickey grimaced. "That doesn't mean anything."

"So you heard the coyote, too. And it means every bit as much as hearing an owl. So make some covering noise out here, Mickey, so they can't hear me."

Mickey sucked in a breath then shook his head as he released it. "Gotcha covered, Standing Hair."

I checked his pressure hand on the glove one more time, then crouched down, belly to the ground again. I took the gun from my waistband and held it in my right hand. I began an awkward bear-crawl back up the slope toward the entrance.

Behind me, Mickey screamed like a screech owl. The hairs stood up on the back of my neck as he serenaded the entire forest with his cry. I entered the dark hole in the hill, moving cautiously around the four-wheeler. The stillness was immediate. So was the change in temperature. It was warmer. A stale smell wafted toward me, the opposite of the clean, crisp air of the forest. I went slowly at first, careful not to make a sound, but then I grew in confidence as I mastered the slinking motion. I was ten feet in when I heard approaching hoofbeats. They were louder in here. Good. Backup. I kept going, moving like a salamander through the dark. One of the horses whinnied outside. I crawled faster, their noises and Mickey's continued cries providing the cover I'd hoped for. Fifteen feet. Twenty. Thirty. Fifty.

A male voice spoke, close by, maybe another twenty feet away, but facing away from me. He sounded like he was muttering to himself. "Little bastards. I'm going to go kill your fucking friends first, and then I'm going to come back and kill you, too. Hiding from me won't do you a damn bit of good."

Even at its low volume, the voice echoed off the sides of the tunnel: good, ood, ood, ood, ood. I wanted to shoot at the voice, fire all fifteen shots in the magazine until I heard the man scream in pain, but I couldn't. Not with the kids in there somewhere. Did I recognize him? Was it someone I knew? The tunnel warped the sounds, and I just couldn't tell. At least the kids had gotten away from him. Maybe they'd found a safe hiding place. I hated the thought of them running blind in the darkness, stumbling upon some old mine shaft, and I forced my mind away from it. Action. I needed to act, not let worry cripple me. But first, I had to get a fix on this guy.

My eyes had adjusted some to the darkness, enough that I could see roughly to the end of my nose, where before I had seen only pitch black. I wasn't going to be able to do this by sight. Outside the mine, I heard the mournful howl of the coyote again, and it galvanized me. I could outsmart this guy. It was my only chance.

He had said he was coming this way, and I was running out of time. I reached toward the sides of the tunnel in both directions, but neither hand connected. I had to believe he couldn't see much better in here than I could, so if he was walking out holding a gun, he'd probably be touching the wall with the non-gun hand. Odds were he was right-handed, so that would be his most likely gun hand. He'd be on the left, using his left hand on the wall. So I needed to be to his right, which was my left since I was facing inward.

I rolled to the left, three full revolutions until I hit the side of the tunnel. Footsteps moved toward me, and I realized that as soon as he passed me, he'd be slightly silhouetted by the light from the tunnel entrance. I'd have a shot. Heck, even if he ran into me, I'd have a shot, away from the kids. But if I missed, I could hit Collin. Or Jack. The thought of hurting Jack, of accidentally killing Jack, made my stomach lurch. But if I didn't take the shot, this man was headed out there to shoot them. To kill them. I had to stop him.

I faced my prone body on my side toward the center of the tunnel, the gun in my hands. I held my breath as the footsteps came closer and closer.

A man's foot stepped on my left foot and a huge body toppled forward and on top of me, his feet at my feet, my face under his chest.

"Goddammit," the man's voice growled.

I heard a clatter on the rocky floor of the tunnel, a sound I hoped was his gun. If so, he would gather himself and go after it before I could draw another breath. I closed my eyes against who knows what in the utter darkness, twisted the Glock hard to get the mouth of the barrel aligned toward the body before it moved away from me, and fired up at an angle into it.

"Ugh, pfft . . ." the man said, and his body jerked. Then nothing. He lay completely still on top of me. A warm wetness oozed onto my hands.

"Jack?" I called. I raised my voice to nearly a shriek. "Jack?"

"Emily!" Jack's voice shouted into the mine's opening.

"Emily!" Greg and Farrah screamed my name almost simultaneously from the other direction.

"All clear," I shouted, or tried to under dead weight that felt as heavy as a pony. "I got him."

A light shone from the entrance and footsteps pounded like buffalo toward me from all directions. My head was turned to the side and I saw four feet in boots, and then the body rolled off of me.

Collin aimed the light down on me. "Are you hit?"

Jack fell to his knees at my side. He grabbed my hand in his and smoothed my hair back from my forehead. Lighter footsteps pounded toward us from the interior.

"I'm fine. It's his blood, not mine."

Greg and Farrah careened up to us and both of them threw themselves on top of me, pulling my hand away from Jack.

"I'm so sorry," Farrah sobbed.

I put both arms around her and squeezed. Someone grabbed one of my hands. "I'm just glad you guys are all right."

Greg stood, and by the pull on my arm, I knew it was him that held my hand. He let it go. "I knew he'd come for us."

Collin had crouched by the unmoving figure. I watched him, in a sort of daze as I continued to hug Farrah.

"He's got a pulse," Collin said.

Collin rolled the man to the side, pulling his hands behind his back, and cuffed him. Then he took off his own jacket and shirt and ripped the shirt into strips. He started tying them around the man's abdomen.

I released Farrah and stood. Jack had, meanwhile, pulled out the guy's wallet and pawed through it. He shone a light on its contents. Farrah rose and nestled into Greg's shoulder, clinging to him. Greg rubbed her back in circular motions.

Jack clutched my left hand. "Take a look at this."

He pointed the illuminated wallet at me. A man's Texas driver's license. It was hard to see in the low light, but I read the name.

"Samson." I said it as a statement of fact. He'd tried to pretend he was the good cop, but I was beginning to wonder if there even were any besides Collin.

Greg snorted. "Yeah, Officer Samson. We saw it all. That poor truck driver told him he was done hauling stolen shit for him, and Samson pulled out a gun and blew him away, right in front of us."

Farrah said, "But you got him, Emily. You saved us."

"It pains me to admit that not all my brethren are as principled or as good-looking as I am, but it's actually pretty rare that we find a dirty cop, per se." Collin looked up. "I think he'll live, but we've got to get him out of here. Mickey, too."

I'd almost killed a cop for the second time in a day. Zero for two was something to be thankful for. Jack squeezed my hand, and I smiled weakly.

Chapter Thirty-two

The first thing I insisted on doing when we made it back to Amarillo Sunday afternoon was take Betsy her backpack. The poor girl missed her mama, and she deserved to get this treasure back as soon as possible, before Immigration showed up. I'd texted ahead to Wallace before we left the hospital in Alamogordo. We'd camped out there with Laura until we got a glimpse of a groggy Mickey postsurgery. The bullet missed everything vital, and the doctors dug it out and patched him up. They didn't like his loss of blood, but, other than that, they gave him a good prognosis.

Mickey wasn't the only victim of our escapades who was in the hospital. Brown was recovering down the hall. I'd heard his wounds were really fairly minor. Samson wasn't as lucky. Somehow, I'd shot down through his gut, where the bullet plowed through his abdomen and out his groin. He was still in surgery when we left. Collin said the cops were renaming the surgical ward the "Annie Oakley Police Convalescence Center." Everyone laughed but me. Shooting people was even worse than shooting antelope, it turned out, even when they deserved it.

Wallace was waiting for us when we pulled up to the hangar. He had on a huge black bomber jacket and a plaid scarf wound over and over around his neck, its fringed end fluttering by his shoulder. He looked top heavy on his long slim legs in his get-up, huddling inside the door away from the frigid temperatures and gusting wind. Watching him made me realize what a seasoned flier I had become, because we'd landed in that wind, and I hadn't given it a second thought. I had a lot of other things on my mind, too. As we drew closer to him, I saw another man behind him, a shadow across his face. I craned for a better look but couldn't get one.

We taxied in and Jack hustled out to pull the hangar door closed. I jumped out, too, and the temperature hit me like a sledgehammer. It was even colder than in Tularosa.

Wallace met me as my feet touched the ground. His words were tough, but his face was smiling. "I should kick your ass. I should get your adoption application rejected. I should refuse to do another thing to help you with Betsy."

"I'm sure I have no idea what you're so huffy about." I batted my eyes but kept them averted from his.

"Greg and Farrah. I'm supposed to believe they got to New Mexico on their own, happened upon Jack's ranch, coincidentally hit it off with his cousins, and convinced them to take them in, all without you knowing about it until thirty-five seconds before you contacted me?"

"You left out the part about Samson tracking them there and trying to kill them." I heaved out my purse and suitcase. Snowflake yipped at me from the backseat. "Hold on, girl. You're next." I set my bags beside the plane and launched into the explanation we had agreed upon with Greg and Farrah before we left the hospital. "I was as shocked as you were. It turns out they found Jack's place in New Mexico from the business card I gave them, you know, when I saw them in the field outside Love's?"

"I don't follow."

"The card gives his office address in Tularosa, and his name."

"That's pretty thin."

I pretended he'd bought my answer. "What a blessing that they're safe, and that they've found a family who wants them."

Wallace pulled me to him and hugged me so tight I made a little "woof" noise. "What, are you out to save them all now, too?" He rocked me back and forth.

I pulled my head back. He had tears in his eyes, and so did I. "There's so many of them. But two more are going to be okay." I smiled, and the water in my eyes made him appear glisteny and angelic.

Jack put a hand on each of our shoulders. "Are we all set to go see Betsy?"

Wallace released me, then said, "Oh, my manners. Emily, Jack, this is Ethan. Ethan, Emily and Jack."

The man who had stayed in the shadows stepped out of them now, hand extended to me to shake, then to Jack. I got my first good look at him. He had pitch-black skin, a shaved head, and was nearly Jack's height, but Jack outweighed him by "a sack of feed," in Phelps's household terminology. Ethan was whippet thin.

"Nice to meet you." I shook.

"Likewise." Jack shook, too.

"I've heard a lot about you both. So glad to finally meet you," he replied, his voice like cognac.

"Ethan's a gate agent for Southwest." Wallace turned to me and wagged a finger. "We're dating, don't make a fuss."

"Who, me?" I winked at Ethan.

He laughed. "I met Nadine and Phil last night. Maybe all six of us can go out together soon."

"That would be great," I said. I put my hand up to shield my lips and said loudly, "Wallace, he's so hot."

Ethan laughed again, and Wallace beamed.

Jack let Snowflake out and clipped on her leash. Then he picked up a bag in each hand. I grabbed the kennel and collapsed it.

"Follow me," Jack said.

Half an hour later, Wallace, Jack, and I stood at the dark brown door to the Hodges' tan brick ranch house on the south side of Amarillo, while Snowflake and Ethan waited in the car, engine running, heater at its max. The snow had stopped, but you could hardly tell because the wind still whipped it through the air. The Hodges' home had a shroud of white over its roof, treeless yard, and flower beds. Wallace rang the bell and we waited.

I heard footsteps in the house, and a man's voice, loud and commanding. "Mary Alice. The door."

It opened, and there stood the woman I'd last seen in the front seat of a paneled van on Christmas Eve.

"Hello, Mrs. Hodges," Wallace said.

Her eyes landed briefly on each of us, and her face pinched. "You didn't tell me she was coming."

Wallace smiled. "I'm sure I did. She's the one who found Betsy's belongings in New Mexico. And she works for Jack, the attorney who is handling all of Betsy's legal matters, pro bono. Jack, this is Mary Alice Hodges. Mary Alice, Jack Holden."

Mary Alice gave a brief nod. Jack inclined his head slowly, then raised it. Watching him made me warmer, and proud.

Wallace stepped over the threshold. "May we? It's far too cold to be outside."

Mary Alice stepped aside for him, and Jack followed. I slipped in behind them. Trevon Hodges rose. I recognized the graying facial hair and round face. He was burly but less heavy than I'd imagined when I saw him bundled up outside the Hodges' van.

"What's this?" he asked, his tone like the serrated edge of a hunting knife.

Mary Alice wrung her hands. "Betsy's CPS caseworker has brought some of her belongings. They were recovered in New Mexico, where she came from." She gestured at Wallace, then Jack. "This is Betsy's attorney."

I stepped slightly forward. "And I'm his paralegal." I held up the dirty pink backpack. "Is Betsy here?"

Trevon stared me in the eye. "The children are all busy with chores."

Wallace cleared his throat. "I need to fill out an assessment after our visit. This will only take a minute, if you'd get her for us, please."

Trevon glowered and returned to his seat.

"Betsy," Mary Alice called. "To the living room, please."

Running footsteps moved toward us, and then my little angel appeared, slowing to a walk as she entered the room. Her eyes sought Trevon first, in a way that hurt my heart. Then to Mary Alice, gauging her situation. The woman nodded her head sideways at Wallace.

Betsy turned to him. "Hello, Mr. Wallace."

When she saw him, she caught sight of Jack and me. She gasped, and launched herself in my direction.

"Betsy," Trevon thundered.

She stopped, looked at him. He shook his head, his face dark.

She said, "Yes, sir," and curtsied to me. "Hi, Emily."

I bridged the gap between us, holding out her backpack. "Hello, sweetie. Recognize this?"

"Oh," she squealed and reached both hands out.

"What do you say?" Mary Alice asked.

Betsy grasped the backpack and hugged it to her body. "Thank you."

She unzipped it, and when she saw what was inside, she looked up at me. I glanced quickly at Trevon and Mary Alice. The woman had moved over beside her husband's chair and was looking down at him. His attention was on the silent TV, which flickered a news show. I put one finger to my lips, briefly, and Betsy gave a tiny nod. She set the pack on the floor and reached in with both hands, pulling out the picture of me with Thunder and the beautiful horse from Alan's store. She swallowed and ran her hand over the horse's mane. "Thunder. I missed him."

"Yes." We smiled at each other.

She dug her hands in again, and came out with worn brushes for her hair and her teeth, some scrunchies, and a tattered set of Barbie pj's. Then she pulled hard on something from the bottom of the inside, and I heard a tearing sound.

My mouth fell open a little, and I looked at Jack. He shrugged his shoulders.

Betsy tossed aside a dirty pink panel rimmed with Velcro. Then she fished a plastic baggy from her backpack and handed it to me. "Mama said I could never lose my backpack, because of the paper inside."

Paper? I took the gallon ziplock baggy from her. "What kind of paper?"

Betsy lifted her shoulders. "Something important, she said."

I examined the ziplock. There was one sheet of paper inside. I pulled the edges of the bag apart and turned it upside down. The single piece of paper fell out. My Spanish minor at Texas Tech came in handy in moments like these.

I read the words aloud. *"Certificado de Nacimiento."*

Wallace came to stand beside me. "What is it?"

I smiled so hard I thought my face would split. "It's Betsy's birth certificate."

Chapter Thirty-three

An hour later, I sat at my desk in the Williams & Associates offices and sealed the FedEx envelope containing Betsy's filing packet for Special Immigrant Juvenile status and adjustment to permanent residency. Jack felt sure that once we had proof of filing, DHS would let her stay in foster care pending a decision. And USCIS would owe that decision to Betsy within six months, not much longer than it should take for me to get a yay or nay on my own status as a prospective adoptive parent. That was a long time, but it wasn't forever. The wheels were turning now, and there was every reason to be hopeful.

"You'll drop it in the morning?" Jack asked.

"I'll be waiting when they open."

He smiled at me, one side only, and retreated back down the hall to his office, Snowflake trotting behind him. I wiggled my mouse, and my screen woke up to the picture of Betsy. I was back on track to becoming her mother. Adoption. Parenthood. Heavy stuff. A lifetime commitment. Or it was supposed to be, anyway. I wondered for the umpteenth time why my father had chosen not to keep his commitment to me for the last decade. I still couldn't make up my mind whether to call him back and find out. I picked up my phone and held it in my hand, staring at it, not dialing his number. Instead, I called Laura for an update on Mickey. He was resting well, and she said he had more nursemaids than he knew what to do with, in her and the teenagers formerly known to her as George and Frannie and now going by their real names of Greg and Farrah.

I ended the call and picked up a page I'd printed from the USCIS website on the Special Immigrant Juvenile status decision process. Almost instantaneously, I heard a knock at the door to the offices. Snowflake tore down the hall, yapping and spinning. Thinking it couldn't be anyone other than Wallace coming to check on Betsy's application, I kept reading my printout as I walked across the room. At the last second, I looked up and through the window.

Officer Burrows waved at me through the glass. I unlocked the door and opened it, but didn't move aside. Snowflake lunged at his ankles, dodging, feinting, and sniffing.

"I hope I'm not bothering you." His tone was one I'd never heard from him before. Friendly. Conciliatory.

"What are you doing here? My boss, Jack, is just down the hall."

"Good. I came to thank the two of you."

"Really?"

"Really. I have some things to tell you that I think will help you understand what's going on."

I stood aside to let him in and put my desk between us. He shifted back and forth beside the couch.

Jack's heavy boots on tile gave away his approach before he appeared beside me. Snowflake ran a few laps around Jack then went back to inspecting Burrows.

"John Burrows." The officer stuck out his hand.

Jack shook it. "Jack Holden. Thank us for what?"

"I moved from the Plainview PD here to work undercover for the last few months, trying to bust the smuggling operation. I couldn't have wrapped it up so quickly without all that you guys did."

My mouth dropped. "But I thought you were a rookie. That you were training with Samson."

Snowflake jumped onto the couch and put her head on her paws.

He smiled. "So did he."

"So you were investigating *him*?"

"Pretty much. Samson managed to do most of his dirty work when I wasn't with him, but we've suspected he was involved for some time now. I was certain of it when he hacked and monitored your phone—"

"He *hacked* it?"

"Yeah."

Jack folded his arms across his chest and rocked back on his heels, a smug grin teasing up the left corner of his mouth.

No wonder Samson figured out I had the kids. And he had to have been the one who called Byron. Found the kids in New Mexico. The blood drained from my face. Got to Ivanka before I did. I put a hand to each cheek and shook my head. It hurt me to think that talking to me had led to a woman's death.

"Wait—do you know anything about the missing dancer?"

He rubbed his lips together like they were chapped. "Yeah, someone reported it Friday. She turned up at a wedding chapel in Vegas." He shook his head. "I met her a few days before that. Busted her for drug possession. She seemed like she was heading down a bad path. I hope the nuptials are a good sign, but somehow I don't think so."

"But at least she's alive, that's good. Better than Ivanka, or the dancer still missing from last summer." I was relieved, especially for Nadine, who had been understandably concerned about the average life span of employees of the Polo Club, such as herself. I lowered my hands and made a rolling motion with one.

"Oh, she's not missing."

"What?"

"She's dead. Wu killed her."

"Who, whoa, whoa, back up. None of this is making sense."

Burrows grinned. "Wu was Samson's enforcer. Samson had Wu in his pocket because he knew Wu had 'accidentally' killed his dancer girlfriend, supposedly a rough-sex thing. He's still working for Samson, or he was until we busted him this morning. Anyway, when Freeman threatened to rat Samson and Wu out, Wu tried to strong-arm him, and Freeman fought back. Wu and Samson slapped assault charges on him to discredit him."

"Oh my God."

"I'll bet you'll never guess who Samson's little sister is, either."

"I have no clue."

"Mary Alice Hodges."

"Oh my God," I shouted. "That's how she sicced you guys on me so fast."

"Yep. And I had to go along with it, with all of it. Samson was always wary of me. The big stuff, like running the smuggling operation in Amarillo, murdering the guy at Love's and then 'Ivanka,' framing your client to get his cooperation—those he did when I wasn't around. I did my best to shadow him, but it was hard to do without tipping him off, especially once Emily started poking around."

"Hey, I think I did some good."

Burrows clapped me on the shoulder. "Without even getting yourself killed. You guys managed to bust this whole thing open from the other end."

Jack put his arm around my shoulders. "That was all Emily."

I looked at him, locking eyes at close range. This was the guy who hadn't called the cops on my father, even when he suspected him of the robbery at Wrong Turn Ranch. He'd given him a first chance, and a second. Like he'd given me. The knot of tension inside me eased further.

"No, it took all of us to figure it out," I said. My father, Alan, Greg, and Farrah. And Ivanka, may she rest in peace. Stella, Ava, Mickey, Collin. "And barely soon enough for Greg and Farrah."

Jack tightened his grip on me, and I relaxed into him.

"So anyway, Samson will be charged when he's coherent. When he's well enough, he's looking at the rest of his life in prison, where things aren't very pleasant for cops."

"Good. He deserves it."

"I hope you don't think all cops are like him and that guy in New Mexico, Brown, who's already been charged, I understand. You've seen the bad side of things, but by and large, we're good people."

Jack added, "Doing a hard job."

"You could have fooled me the last few times I've run into you," I said, but I smiled.

"I was trying to keep you safe and protect the operation without blowing my cover. You'll see the real John Burrows from here on out."

"That's good to hear." I smiled, then frowned again quickly. "We've got to talk to Alan, Jack. This may change everything. Wu is dirty. He has no credibility."

Jack said, "Yep. Might not happen overnight, but we'll fix it."

"I hope so." To Burrows, I said, "So, are you going back to Plainview now?"

"Nope. I'm a full-fledged member of the APD."

"Good. I feel a lot better with you around."

Jack returned to his office while I chatted a little longer with Burrows. After he left, I stomped around the office, making as much noise as I could. Jack and I had gone straight from the airport to see Betsy and back to the office. I didn't have my car, and I was counting on Jack for a ride home. He didn't seem to notice my hints. After another fifteen minutes of waiting around, my stomach growled.

I leaned against Jack's doorframe. "Are you planning on taking me home any time soon? If not, I can call my mother."

He jumped to his feet. "Sorry. Clyde emailed me for a status report. He saw the news."

"Clyde emails?"

Jack's dimple did its thing. "He dictates them to Betty."

I shook my head. "That woman is a saint."

Jack grabbed his coat off the back of one of his conference table chairs. He stuck his hand in one of his pockets and rooted around. He nodded, then shrugged on the jacket. "Let's go."

The drive out to Heaven was a quiet one except for the wind whistling as it buffeted the Jeep back and forth. White powder blew in almost a straight line across the road, except during the deep gasps between gusts. The heater struggled to keep up with the cold outside. The interior was warmish, but the pockets of air near the windows stayed below freezing, and the side windows frosted over.

We pulled up to my mother's house.

"Thanks. I'll see you tomorrow, I guess. If the weather doesn't get worse."

Jack turned off the Jeep. "I want to pay my respects to Agatha."

"It's freezing. You don't have to do that. I'll pass the message."

He grinned at me, and the left side of his face came alive, jumpstarting me with it. "I'll race you inside," he said.

I shook my head, but when he bolted out the door, I scrambled after him, laughing. I slipped and slid up the walkway in my ancient moon boots. I reached the porch first, but only because Jack stopped to grab my suitcase from the backseat before taking off for the house.

I knocked the snow off my feet. "I win."

The door opened before I could turn the knob, revealing the figure behind it.

Johnny Phelps. My father.

***

I still couldn't believe the couple sitting on the couch holding hands was my parents. They looked much the same as my child's eye remembered them from last time they'd sat with me, although Dad had aged far more in fifteen years than my mother. His strong, broad frame had withered to half its size. He'd kept his hair, but it was nearly white. Deep furrows creased his face and age spots covered the backs of his hands. Still, he held his head high and his shoulders squared. His light blue eyes sparkled as he looked from Mother to where I sat on the hearth with Jack and back again, like he was surrounded by Cracker Jack prizes and couldn't believe his luck.

Mother was trying to explain it all to me. "Your dad called me a few weeks ago. When he got out."

"You knew he was 'in'?"

"Yes." She smiled at the man beside her. "About a year after he, um, took up residence there, he wrote to me. And to you."

I jumped to my feet. "He wrote to me?"

"He did."

My dad nodded. "Once a week ever since the second year."

Mother smiled, but it was a shaky one. "I kept them for you, dear."

My voice came out as a screech. "Why didn't you give them to me before?"

She frowned. "Your father left us, he humiliated us, and his being in jail only made it worse. He was in jail because he *killed* someone. What would Rich have thought? His family? Your friends? Your employers? I didn't want you hurt. I didn't want anyone to know."

"More like your friends. Your church. Your employer." I turned to my father. "And you were okay with that?"

He shook his head. "I didn't know. I thought you weren't answering. I didn't blame you."

I paced back and forth in front of them. I whirled on my mother. "I was a grown woman. You deciding for me? That's not okay. Not okay!"

She hung her head. "I understand that now. I'm sorry."

Dad put his other hand over their clasped ones. He looked at me. "Sweet Pea, I was pretty angry at your mother, too. But I've thrown away a lot of my life, spent it apart from the ones I love. I don't have time to be angry anymore. I forgave her, and she forgave me."

I sank back to the hearth and put my head in my hands. Jack slipped an arm around my waist. I couldn't wrap my head around this. The father who had deserted me really hadn't. The mother who didn't leave me had kept him from me, out of supposed misguided intentions, or, more likely, bitterness. And now they'd kissed and made up like the last decade didn't matter? Maybe it didn't to them, but it did to me.

I lifted my head, glaring at both of them. "So this"—I pointed at their clasped hands—"came about how and when?"

Dad lifted their hands. "Well, she started writing me back a few years ago. Then, when I got out, I called her. Asked if I could come see her."

Mother beamed. "He got here Christmas."

I made a growling noise. "And, just like that, you forgave him, after all these years angry at him, all those years keeping me angry at him, too?"

She cocked her head at me. "He's my husband. Your father. I love him."

They looked at each other like two teenagers. Mother giggled. She *giggled*.

My father touched their hands to his chest, one, two, three times. "And we won't waste another second."

"Amen." She put her head on his shoulder.

I scraped my teeth over my bottom lip. "So I'm supposed to forget how you struggled, Mother? Or that I couldn't understand why my father didn't want to see me win Southwest Region Champs my senior year at Tech? Or give me away at my wedding?"

"Well, that didn't work out so well, dear."

I glared at my mother. "That's not the point. The point is how do you propose we forget all of this?"

Her blue eyes made big **O**s. "We don't. We just move forward."

Dad stared at his knees or his feet or something on the floor away from my face. He cleared his throat. "I'm sorry, Emily. For everything. I've got so many regrets."

"Well, at least you're sorry."

"Emily—" Jack said.

I turned on him, reclaiming a bit of my earlier anger. "What about you, Jack? Are you sorry? Sorry for hiding things from me and lying to me?"

His face lost color. "Uh—"

I jumped to my feet again. "How come you all think I'm so fragile, that I can't handle the truth?"

Dad's wrinkles deepened and sagged. Jack stood beside me, but it was Mother who spoke. "Oh, honey, it's not about you being fragile. It's about you being loved."

I looked at the three of them, wanting to pounce, but it stopped me mid-leap. Love. Love stopped me. All that love, imperfect and painful and real and waiting. I didn't want to waste any more time either. I took three big steps toward my father, and he stood in time to catch me in his arms as my tears fell.

I saw Jack motion to my mother and the two of them slipped from of the room. Dad patted my back and rocked me until I quieted and my tears dried up.

Dad held me away from him. "Once your mom came around, she started sending me pictures, keeping me up-to-date on you. I'm so proud of you."

I wiped my eyes, shaking my head. "I've made such a mess of everything."

"Oh, Sweet Pea, I'm an expert at making a mess, and I can promise you, you are a minor-league mess."

I laughed.

"About the time I found out about you being back here with your mother, Jack got in touch with me. I'm sorry if the way I decided to handle things upset you. I wanted to come home and talk to you face-to-face myself."

"I understand. I don't like it, but you're the dad I've known and loved all my life, and I understand."

His big hands squeezed my shoulder. "I hear you're the big hero once again. I swear, Emily, after hearing what you did to save that little girl and all those people in New Mexico in the fall, and now how you saved those kids and Mickey, I'm two inches taller again."

I fell back into his chest, unable to stop the tears again. "Oh, Daddy, it was all you. Everything I did, it was all what you taught me."

He laughed against my hair. "They just didn't know they were messing with the wrong girl."

***

Half an hour later, Jack sat at the kitchen table talking with my dad, while Mother chopped vegetables for a salad and I stuck the steaks in the oven on broil.

"I'm having a glass of wine. Anyone else want one?" I opened the refrigerator door.

Jack stopped. "Not me. But I need to talk to you before dinner."

"Oh my gosh, I'm so talked out." I groaned as I unscrewed the cap from the white zin. "What do we have left to talk about?" I pulled a glass down from the cabinet and began to fill it.

"Betsy."

I stopped mid-pour. "Did we forget to do something for her?"

"It's not that. But maybe we could step out back for a moment?"

"Are you crazy? It's"—I looked the thermometer in the window—"seventeen degrees outside. Colder with wind chill."

"So wrap up. It's important, and last time I told you we needed to talk and then we didn't, you got pretty darn mad at me."

"Honey, don't be difficult with Jack." Mother, taking Jack's side, his biggest fan as always.

"Okay." I capped the wine box. "Where's my ski suit?"

Twelve layers later, Jack and I stepped onto the back patio. It was a hair past seven thirty and dark outside. The porch lights shed enough illumination that I could see the shadowy outline of our dilapidated little barn at the back end of our property, looking abandoned. Well, now that Dad was back, that would change. A lot of things would change.

I realized Jack was speaking. "What?"

"The state of Texas isn't going to move you to the front of the line to adopt, not with the way things stand now."

"What do you mean?"

"Well, you live with your mom for one thing. And dad now, too, I guess."

"I'm putting my money down on a duplex this week."

He shook his head. "That won't get you past the unmarried issue."

The skin prickled on the back of my neck. "That's not as big a deal as it used to be."

"Why give them any more red flags than you have to?"

"You're depressing me. I'm trying my best, Jack. This is me, try-ing."

"I know it is. And you're doing good."

I shivered. "It's freezing. If you're done busting my chops, can we go back inside?"

He crouched on one knee on the snowy concrete. He pulled a small box out of his jacket pocket. "I'm trying, too. Here."

"What the heck are you trying to do?"

"Just open it, please."

"Why are you down on the ground?"

"I'm beginning to wonder that, myself."

I pulled the wrapping paper off the box. Inside was a jeweler's box. A small one. My heart and breath froze, and time stood still. I opened the lid. In it was a piece of paper folded over and over and over.

"Cute. I almost fell for it." I snapped the box shut.

"Open it. And please be very careful when you do."

I reopened the box and unfolded the edges of paper. Inside it was another piece of paper, folded up like the other.

"You know, some people think the whole psych-out gift thing is funny."

"This was supposed to be easier." He stood up, brushed snow from his knees, and straightened the paper out in front of me. "Look at it." He shifted the partially shadowed real-estate flyer. "Gorgeous new 4 BR/3 BA family home on 5 acres w/fencing/stables in Bushland, TX." There was a cross-out mark through Bushland. Above it HEAVEN was written in block capitals. Jack's handwriting.

"You're buying a new house?"

He sighed and kneeled again. "Open the other paper."

Out of the corner of my eye, I saw movement in the kitchen window. Two heads together, watching us. I examined the white paper and felt something hard sliding around inside it. My irritation gave way to confusion. I unfolded it, and poured its contents into my hand.

A ring. A gold band with a big fat shiny teardrop diamond.

Jack took it from me, grasped my left hand, and held the ring toward it. "Emily, will you please marry me and move into this house with me and let me adopt Betsy with you?"

A million thoughts flashed through my mind. The first time I'd seen Jack's face. My palms sweating when he offered me a job. Jack at the emergency room with me when I lost the baby. Our first kiss. Jack, angry and hurt and remote. Learning about his wife and kids. Jack at their graves. That I hadn't told him about my own pitiful reproductive situation and needed to, soon. Realizing I was in love with him, that of all the men on Earth, he was the man who did it for me.

I opened my mouth to answer, but nothing came out. Instead I gave his shoulders a shove. He toppled off the patio, and I followed him. Down, down, down to a drift of snow, where I landed on him with a windblown, icy-nosed kiss.

The End

Now that you've finished *Earth to Emily*, won't you please consider writing an honest review and leaving it on the online sales site of your choice and/or Goodreads? Reviews are the best way readers discover great new books. I would truly appreciate it. Be sure to watch for *Hell to Pay*, the third book in the *Emily* series, coming soon. — Pamela

Acknowledgments

As I was writing the *Emily* books, I couldn't help but be impacted by the events going on in the world around me: the shooting in Ferguson, Missouri, religious hate groups, and immigration reform, to name a few. Hopefully their influence on this book was a positive one.

Thanks to my husband, Eric, for brainstorming the *Emily* books with me over many miles hiked in Pedernales FallsState Park and on our property in Nowheresville, and during 11,000+ miles logged in the Bookmobile. Eric gets an extra helping of thanks for plotting, critiquing, editing, listening, holding, encouraging, supporting, browbeating, and playing miscellaneous other roles, some of which aren't appropriate for publication.

To each and every blessed one of you who have read, reviewed, rated, and emailed/Facebooked/Tweeted/commented about the *Katie & Annalise*, *Emily*, and *Michele* books, I appreciate you more than I can say. It is the readers who move mountains for me, and for other authors, and I humbly ask for the honor of your honest reviews and recommendations.

Blessings and hugs to my friends Stephanie, Betsy, and Walt, who inspired me to write about my own hometown.

Editing credits go to Rhonda Erb and Sara Kocek. The beta readers and critique partners who enthusiastically devote their time—gratis—to help us rid my books of flaws blow me away. The special love this time goes to Patty, Gay, Melissa, Nandita, David, Carla, Dina, Ginger, Ridgely, Melissa, Terry, Rebecca, Susie, and Betsy. Thanks to Walt for expert assistance, as well.

Kisses to princess of the universe, Heidi Dorey, for fantastic cover art. Thanks for evolving with us as we evolve with the world of publishing.

Finally, my eternal gratitude to Eric and our kids for teaching me the ways of blended household love.

About the Author

Pamela Fagan Hutchins holds nothing back and writes award-winning and best-selling mysteries and hilarious nonfiction from Nowheresville, Texas, where she lives with her household hunks—husband, Eric, and their one-eyed Boston terrier, Petey—plus three rescue dogs, a herd of goats, a coupla cows, a flock of turkeys, and a peacock. She is the author of many books, including *Saving Grace*, *Leaving Annalise*, *Finding Harmony*, *Going for Kona*, *Heaven to Betsy*, *Earth to Emily*, *How To Screw Up Your Kids*, *Hot Flashes and Half Ironmans*, and *What Kind of Loser Indie Publishes?* to name just a few. In 2014, just two years after publication of her first book, the *Houston Press* named her as one of the Top 10 Houston Authors.

Pamela spends her non-writing time as the Chair of the Board of the Houston Writers Guild, a writing coach, a workplace investigator, and as an employment attorney and human resources professional, and she is the co-founder of a human resources consulting company. You can often find her with her husband—and a few grown kids from their blended brood of five—hiking, running, bicycling, and enjoying the great outdoors.

If you'd like Pamela to speak to your book club, women's club, or writers group, by Skype or in person, shoot her an email. She's very likely to say yes.

You can buy Pamela's e-books, audiobooks, and paperbacks at most online retailers. You can also get her paperbacks from "brick and mortar" stores. If you want a signed copy, contact SkipJack Publishing: http://SkipJackPublishing.com. If your bookstore or library doesn't carry a book you want, by Pamela or any other author, ask them to order it for you.

You can connect with Pamela all over creation, and you should:
Website http://pamelahutchins.com
Email pamela@pamelahutchins.com
New releases newsletter http://eepurl.com/iTR
Facebook http://facebook.com/pamela.fagan.hutchins.author
Twitter http://twitter.com/pameloth
Goodreads http://goodreads.com/pamelafaganhutchins
LinkedIn http://linkedin.com/in/pamelahutchins

Books by the Author

Fiction from SkipJack Publishing:

Saving Grace (Katie & Annalis, #1)

Leaving Annalise (Katie & Annalise #2)

Finding Harmony (Katie & Annalise #3)

The Jumbie House (Katie & Annalise Outtake)

Going for Kona (Michele #1)

Heaven to Betsy (Emily #1)

Earth to Emily (Emily #2)

Hell to Pay (Emily #3), coming 2016

Nonfiction from SkipJack Publishing:

*The Clark Kent Chronicles: A Mother's Tale Of Life
With Her ADHD/Asperger's Son*

*Hot Flashes and Half Ironmans: Middle-Aged Endurance
Athletics Meets the Hormonally Challenged*

How to Screw Up Your Kids: Blended Families, Blendered Style

How to Screw Up Your Marriage: Do-Over Tips for First-Time Failures

Puppalicious and Beyond: Life Outside The Center Of The Universe

What Kind of Loser Indie Publishes, and How Can I Be One, Too?

Other Books by the Author:

Eve's Requiem (anthology), Spider Road Press

OMG - That Woman! (anthology), Aakenbaaken & Kent

Ghosts (anthology), Aakenbaaken & Kent

Easy to Love, But Hard to Raise (2012) and *Easy to Love, But Hard to
Teach* (coming soon) (anthologies), DRT Press, edited by Kay Marner &
Adrienne Ehlert Bashista

Audiobook versions of the author's books are available online from
Amazon, Apple, and Audible.

Other Books from SkipJack Publishing

The Closing, by Ken Oder
Old Wounds to the Heart, by Ken Oder
Deadly Thyme, by R. L. Nolen
The Dry, by Rebecca Nolen
Tides of Possibility, edited by K.J. Russell
Tides of Impossibility,
edited by K.J. Russell and C. Stuart Hardwick
My Dream of Freedom: From Holocaust to My Beloved America,
by Helen Colin

CPSIA information can be obtained
at www.ICGtesting.com
Printed in the USA
FSOW02n0145270815
10172FS